NO PLACE LIKE HOME

Mischievous Malamute Mystery Series Book 7

HARLEY CHRISTENSEN

For Max

PROLOGUE

Leah Campbell

Leah cursed herself for all the times she'd committed—and then failed—to clean out her vehicle's trunk, now that she had been forced to battle the car jack (a.k.a. CJ), a nuisance that had issues respecting one's personal space, particularly where her ribs were concerned.

That being said, whoever had conked her on the head and dumped her in here with all this crap was going to suffer.

Badly.

She decided that the second they'd messed with her hair.

Wrong move, dudes.

Gritting her teeth as she attempted to shift her body weight, she vowed there would be no tears. The pain from CJ was just the latest in a string of injuries she'd sustained. And she would handle it.

Instead, she used what energy she had left to assess the situation. Time had gotten away from her upon meeting with the wrong side of a fist after she'd backhanded her attacker when he'd grabbed a fistful of pointy locks.

Best guess? Several hours had passed. She smelled less ripe than she would have had those hours transitioned into days.

At least she had that going for her.

As her head bounced against the wheel well, no thanks to the driver, she pieced together the events leading up to her current predicament. Most of which she wasn't all that proud of.

Days earlier, she had lied to the only person she could count on. She'd seen the hurt in her best friend's eyes when she'd packed her belongings, claiming she was heading to Los Angeles to work on a long-term project.

That was before she'd turned her back on their friendship and walked out the door.

She knew it was cowardly but couldn't bear

to continue looking in the rear-view mirror as she pulled away, even though she had seen AJ lingering on the sidewalk, her hand held high in the air in a feeble attempt to wave, just before she had collapsed onto the pavement and folded into herself, her shaking frame visible.

Only when Leah had safely exited the neighborhood did she allow the tears to fall. She'd never lied to her best friend before. Not in twenty-plus years.

But making AJ believe a lie had been safer than telling her the truth.

Hadn't it?

Leah chuckled just thinking about what AJ would have done had she revealed her plan, wincing again in pain at the movement—her nose was probably cracked, if not broken. Yet it felt good to laugh.

Still, she'd hated how they'd left things, and now that it was likely she'd never get the chance to make it right, she wished she'd never broken her best friend's heart.

Her intentions had been genuine—Shelby had gone missing, after all—and AJ would have respected and understood that.

Thinking of Shelby brought forth another type of anxiety…and pain.

Was the girl still alive?

After weeks of searching, she'd finally caught a glimpse of her former co-worker, followed by that desperate call. Shelby had reached out to warn her, only to have the connection broken.

Moments later, she'd been accosted. She hadn't seen it coming, nor had she seen her attackers, other than to note that they were swift and strong—and seriously lacking a sense of humor.

Just then, her body slammed into the front of the trunk as the vehicle came to an abrupt halt.

Grimacing as she rolled on her back and shook off stars that did not look like any member of Duran Duran, her heart stopped short as she heard heavy boots collide with the ground. Panic infused every nerve as she contemplated her options. Even her feet were useless as weapons as they were not only bound but also tangled in the crap that surrounded her.

Chalk it up to lessons learned the hard way.

Her hands were no better of a match, even if her shoulder hadn't been dislocated and one of her arms possibly fractured. As it turned out, zip ties were effective, though they really sucked if one was on the opposite side of 'em.

The trunk opened and a familiar face stared down, smirking at the pathetic scene, despite her previous bravado.

Leah hacked out a harsh laugh that betrayed the resignation she felt deep in her gut.

"Let's agree not to insult one another by beating around the proverbial bush, shall we? Why don't you just tell me—how does this end?"

The smirk of her adversary transitioned into a sneer, followed by a wicked laugh that made her stomach churn.

"You tell us, Campbell."

CHAPTER ONE

Arianna Jackson (AJ)

"She never got on the flight and her possessions—luggage, laptop, notebooks, purse, identification, etc.—were left behind."

Abe's words cycled through my head in slow motion as I tried to make sense of the fact that my best friend's car had been located at the airport.

True, she had been leaving town, or so I thought, but she had intended to drive to L.A. Not fly there.

Then again, she had also told me she was going to Los Angeles to work on a long-term project for Abe, which he'd just confirmed was false.

I couldn't remember the last time Leah had lied to me and even when she had, it was over something stupid, like eating two cookies when she'd really eaten a dozen. Or pretending she liked my silver spandex when we were going through a 1980s reboot phase.

But packing her belongings for an extended research job with Abe and his brother, Elijah, at Stanton Investigations in Los Angeles?

So not Leah Campbell.

I could have shrugged it off had her vehicle not been abandoned.

With blood dripping from the trunk.

And no Leah in sight.

That was disturbing enough, but why was Ramirez involved?

Speaking of the devil.

Easing into the roundabout that fronted the home I'd inherited when my parents unexpectedly passed, a familiar truck had taken up some prime real estate. Also known as my parking spot. Nicoh and I had company awaiting us, but my guard dog was apparently on sabbatical as he leisurely chewed his paw, his massive frame spanning the backseat.

I sighed. I'd known I was going to have this chat eventually and guessed that it was better to have my former beau deliver the news about my best friend than a member of law enforcement who hadn't frequented my doorstep.

Believe me, as of late, it would have been hard to drum one up. If the rumors had made their way around, other officers would have drawn straws and given a fist-pump to the universe when they lucked out on not having to perform that task.

Dark circles lined the underside of his eyes. His usual swagger was stiff and slow, as though the movement intensified the pain with each step. His hair was longer than I'd seen it, grazing the top of his ears and tickling the back of his neck. But road-worn or not, the hummingbirds flitting about in my stomach suggested he still knew how to show up on the scene.

Taking a deep breath, I not so gracefully stumbled out of my vehicle and strode toward the detective, who surveyed me with the intensity of a hawk; his hands tucked into the pockets of his jeans, tugging them down ever so slightly. I frowned. He'd lost weight, too.

He noticed me staring and started to speak, but I beat him to the punchline. Or rather, I shifted from his current state to Leah's.

"Just lay it on me, Ramirez. How bad is it?"

"Bad," he replied, his eyes never straying from mine.

I scowled, almost having forgotten his affinity for single-word responses.

"Are you sure you want to do this out here?" He nodded over my shoulder. I twisted my head, noting that one of the neighbors was peering at us from behind their splayed blinds. If they didn't want us seeing them, they'd have to do a better job. Or maybe that was the point—they wanted us to know they were watching. Probably even had their itchy little fingers on speed-dial, ready to call the cops.

Little did they know, he had already arrived.

"Fine. Nicoh! Get your lazy butt out here."

My well-trained canine ignored the passenger door I had opened for him and hopped on the driver's seat before jumping out of the driver's side door and ambling over to Ramirez's outstretched hand.

"Traitor," I mumbled as I slammed the doors before stomping toward the house.

The luggage would have to wait.

Everything would have to wait.

Until Ramirez answered my questions.

To my satisfaction.

I unlocked the door and hustled in to turn the alarm off. After a cursory glance around, I ushered Ramirez and Nicoh in before turning the air conditioning on to cycle out the air that had been bottled up since I left for L.A.

"So, I'm afraid to ask. If homicide is involved…where's the body?"

"No body," he replied, his gaze searching mine.

"Ramirez," I ground out between clenched teeth. "I hate to remind you, but *you* sought me out. This is *my* house. And if I have to continue drawing every word from you like a cartoon bubble, I guarantee there will be. A body." I added that last bit in case he wasn't clear.

He was.

Shaking his head as he leaned back onto the arm of the couch, he absently scratched Nicoh's ears.

"Fine. But what I'm about to tell you—"

I raised a hand. "I know. I know. Is classified. Top secret. *For-your-eyes-only*." I added finger quotes for effect.

He waited me out, though his frown deepened. "You know this is a two-way street."

"What? I don't know squat."

"I wasn't talking about Leah," he murmured.

"Excuse me?"

"AJ. If you'd shut up for two seconds, I'd tell you what I know."

"Be. My. Guest," I huffed.

"Got that out of your system?"

"Waiting." I tapped my foot.

"Have you always been this frustrating?"

"You know what they say about absence," I quipped.

"Whatever," he grumbled. "As I was saying, what I'm about to tell you stays between us."

"And your department."

He shook his head. "This info came straight from the bedhead's mouth."

I blinked. Ramirez was the only person I knew who could get away with referencing my best friend's choice of hairstyle in that manner without losing his teeth and a few other necessary body parts.

He nodded. "Yup. Leah."

I collapsed onto the chair opposite him.

"I thought that would shut you up. But I had no idea it would be so effective."

"Ramirez," I growled.

"I almost wish I didn't have this information. And I don't think I can withhold it for much longer." He glanced at me before continuing. "I know what Leah was up to before she went missing."

"Please *elaborate*." I enunciated each syllable.

One-word answers would no longer suffice.

"Just don't kill the messenger," he replied, holding his hands up. "You won't be happy with what I'm about to tell you."

"If it helps us figure out what happened to her, then I'll just have to suffer through it."

Ramirez nodded, grinding his jaw for a moment. "I knew about her plan—even tried talking her out of it—but you know how Leah is."

I nodded. "When was this?"

He looked away and my stomach dropped. "Shortly before she moved out of your house."

"So she told you about that. I assume that

she also told you she was heading to L.A. to work for the Stantons?"

"I know that's what she told you."

I squinted at him. "What do you mean?"

Ramirez blew out a long breath. "That's the *story* she told you. Her rationale for moving out was fabricated, too. And while she felt awful about it—part of the reason she confessed to me —I couldn't change her mind."

"Story? Packing up, heading to L.A.—was a lie?" My voice ratcheted up to a level that made Nicoh howl from his perch in the corner.

"She wanted to protect you—keep you safe."

"Keep *me* safe?" I realized I was starting to sound like a parrot and tried to keep my frustration at bay. It was time to unmask this charade. "Tell me about this *plan* of hers. And please, start from the beginning."

Ramirez nodded, though the crease between his brows intensified as he laid things out. "Leah called me out of the blue a few weeks ago and asked if she could run something by me. I thought she wanted to talk about Jonah, or perhaps even try to rekindle their relationship. But when we met, she said she may have made the biggest mistake of her life—one she knew she would forever regret. She then told me how she'd lied to you."

I looked away, feeling the color rising in my cheeks.

"As I mentioned, she thought it was the only way to keep you safe. If we kept you out of the loop, you wouldn't be in harm's way."

My eyes returned to his. "But safe from what, Ramirez?"

"A journalist friend of hers went missing while doing some investigative work on a piece she'd been writing. Leah, being Leah, decided that since no one was taking the girl's disappearance seriously, or as seriously as she thought they should, she'd track the girl's movements herself. In order to do so, she had to get off the grid."

"And?"

"I never heard from her again. And now she's missing, too."

I'd forced Ramirez into divulging what he knew but had failed to prepare myself for the ramifications.

And now I wasn't sure I wanted to know what had become of my best friend or what this "plan" of hers fully entailed.

If it was similar to any of the others I had been privy to over the years, it wasn't looking good.

Still, I had to find my friend and bring her home. It was time to channel my inner-Powerpuff Girl and suck it up, Buttercup.

"What do you mean by 'off the grid'? And, who's this 'friend'?"

"The friend's name was Shelby Harris." I squinted. The name did sound vaguely familiar. Thankfully, Ramirez noted my confusion. "She was an intern when Leah worked at the paper. Leah liked the girl's spirit, took her under her wing and showed her the ropes. She said Shelby had talent but was a bit of a challenge when it came to following the rules. Tended to get herself into all sorts of trouble—kind of like someone else I know." He gave me a pointed stare, which I ignored.

"Moving on."

"She didn't make it long on her own after Leah left and tried her hand at freelance gigs, though she hoped—according to Leah—her big break would come in the form of one of her investigative pieces."

I felt a pang of regret mixed with shame. Leah had barely mentioned Shelby and yet she'd been instrumental in her mentoring. Instead, I'd been wrapped up in my own drama, oblivious to my best friend's challenges and struggles—and attempts to use them to help someone else.

I shook my head, proud of my best friend but frustrated by my oversight in acknowledging it sooner.

Ramirez's voice snapped me out of my reverie and back to the present and the matter at hand. "Leah said that Shelby's latest story du jour was a scam she happened upon in the vacation home rental industry."

"Vacation rentals? As in homes or condos that people rent on a short-term basis to out-of-town baseball fans during spring training?"

He nodded. "Shelby told Leah that she'd uncovered some strange things going on in some of the older neighborhoods near Old Town Scottsdale. Many of the homes had recently been sold, then flipped and repurchased by a property management company. Leah also said that she had alluded to some hinky connection—Leah's words, not mine—between the people doing the flipping and those taking on the managing, but that wasn't what caught Shelby's attention."

I shifted back, realizing that I had been sitting on the edge of my chair, hands clutched on my lap to the point of numbness.

"While at a club in Old Town with friends, Shelby noticed a group of girls enter the club, immediately spreading out and mingling with other club-goers."

"I hate to tell you, old man, but it sounds like a pretty typical Saturday night in Old Town."

"I'm not too old to forget," he replied, without a hint of snarkasm. "What struck Shelby as odd was that while all the girls arrived together and were dressed and made-up similarly, they weren't really together…as in, they didn't even seem to know one another."

"That's definitely odd." Sometimes groups congregated out of obligation and were indifferent toward one another, but unfamiliar?

"'Odd' does not begin to cover it." For the first time since we'd started this conversation, Ramirez broke out of character as his lips curled into an unflattering scowl and his eyes became slits as he recalled what Leah had told him.

"Shelby watched as they worked the crowd and made themselves comfortable with several of the patrons who rewarded them with cocktails and attention. When the conversation dwindled, or the drinks stopped readily flowing, they would move on to the next target."

"'Target'? Don't tell me all those club-hopping days of yours left you jaded. Surely, even you realize that's typically how the game is played. Present company excluded, of course."

Ramirez rolled his eyes. "Can I finish?" I returned the eye roll.

He grunted. "As I was saying, the girls made the rounds, chatting up other club-goers but never interacting with one another. Occasionally, she would see a girl slip a guy a card before moving on. Finally, around one thirty a.m., the girls began peeling themselves away from the crowd and exiting one by one. When Shelby followed, she noticed that the guys who had been given the cards were also making their way out. One of them unknowingly dropped his card so she grabbed it.

"All it said was 'After-party? Meet me in the parking lot at one thirty-five to board the party bus in the northeast corner of the lot—you can't miss it. Present this card. Entry not permitted without it. No exceptions.' She caught up with them in the parking lot just in time to see them boarding the party bus."

"Was it actually a bus?"

He hacked out a laugh. "No. One of those limo-style Humvees."

"Typical cliché in Old Town. So what happened to the guy who dropped his card?"

"They denied him entry, so he had some

choice words for the driver. Shelby wanted to chat with him but had to decide between him and following the party bus to its destination.”

“She chose the latter,” I responded, causing Ramirez to grumble something I didn't quite catch. “Yeah, yeah. I know because I would have done the same. Shoot me.”

“Right. Shelby followed the van. She didn't have to travel far. The party destination was a few short blocks away, tucked into one of the older but recently revitalized South Scottsdale neighborhoods. Or, as some would put it, being taken over by the vacation rental industry.”

“So, let me get this straight. The party was being held at one of these vacation rentals?”

“Several of the homes were recently converted into rental properties after the original owners sold them—it's been a popular area for buying and selling. Since most were built in the 1950s and 1960s, they were taken down to bare bones after the purchase and rebuilt with a more modern look and feel.”

“Curb appeal.” I nodded. “It's been going on in my neighborhood, too. Unfortunately, it often results in a monstrosity with zero charm that quickly loses that appeal after the new owner defaults on their equally monstrous loan. The bank usually takes over, and the home is repurchased at a fraction of the cost by individuals interested in flipping it to make a quick buck. I don't condemn the entrepreneurial spirit, being an entrepreneur myself, but when you destroy a neighborhood's uniqueness in favor of fast money, I have serious qualms."

"Pretty much the same thing going on in these neighborhoods, too. You'll hit some streets where there's a one-in-ten ratio of homeowners actually living in their homes to those that are occupied solely by short-term renters."

"And in this situation, short-term constitutes a day or two, as opposed to weeks?"

"Usage-wise, yes. Whoever is running this game books it for the minimum, though they could request a day-term, which can be granted on a case-by-case basis."

"That option seems risky," I replied. "It's better for them to fly under the radar, not put themselves *on* it."

"Exactly what Shelby said to Leah. Anyway, once she got to the drop-off location, she watched as the driver deposited his passengers and then took off."

"Did she happen to catch a—"

"License plate—yes. It led nowhere."

"It was stolen?"

Ramirez shook his head. "More like it never existed. It was a well-crafted fake, belonging to a company that no longer existed."

"Forget what I said about risky," I murmured. "What did Shelby do next?"

"Probably the same thing you and your cohort would have done—she waited them out." I smirked at his remark and gestured for him to continue. "At four forty-eight in the morning, a different white van returned—plates were also fakes—and collected the guys."

"Odd time, don't you think?" Before Ramirez could respond, I added, "Wait…collected the guys? What about the girls?"

"If you'd stop interrupting, I would have gotten to it," he replied. "But to answer your first question, sunrise was at four fifty-two, so perhaps, not so odd. You don't want the residents who actually live in the neighborhood observing your comings and goings when you're doing something shady, do you?"

"As if they didn't already notice," I muttered. In some communities, like mine, people noticed what everyone was doing, no matter the hour.

"Perhaps not, but to answer your second question, Shelby let the bus go so that she could continue watching the house," Ramirez replied, absently scratching Nicoh's head.

"Let me guess. Another white van showed up."

"Yes, but not until around noon." When I shot him a look of confusion, he added, "Shelby watched as the women, who had changed into regular clothes—shorts and t-shirts—hauled garbage bags to the dumpster. When the van driver showed up, they all filed out, each boarding with a partially filled garbage bag in hand."

"What was in them?"

Ramirez shrugged. "Shelby figured it was their party clothes, makeup…stuff like that."

"So there were spare clothes already waiting for them at the house?"

"Sounds that way. No way they were getting paid a garbage bag's worth just to party and pick up some random dudes."

"You'd be surprised," I replied with a snort, causing Ramirez to roll his eyes.

"I have no place to go with that, so I'm just going to move on. Shelby followed the van. Most of the girls were dropped back at the club."

"Interesting."

"Indeed. But despite her best efforts, she lost track of it on the freeway."

"I take this is not the end of the story?" I asked.

"Not by a long shot. Later, she returned to the house. Nothing happened for six days, so she returned to the club the following weekend and again, nothing. She went to another club and another and a week later hit pay dirt at yet another club."

"Same girls?"

"Not one of them. Not even the van or driver. Same setup, though. Different house."

I blew out a long breath. "Wow."

Ramirez nodded. "She did this for several weeks—even added in a few extra days to her club-going—and finally, patterns emerged, a few of the same girls, drivers, houses. Even ended up back at the original house and watched the same process play out. And because it was the house where it all started, at least from her perspective, she went as far as staking out the house, watching days on end where nothing happened. Until it did.

"On a random, middle of the week day, a luxury SUV showed up, and the driver opened the door for his passenger—a woman in her late twenties to early thirties, dressed to the nines. Rather than escort her to the door, the driver promptly got back in and drove away, leaving his passenger as she entered the house.

"Minutes later, a van appeared, filled with eight to ten girls of various ethnicities, ages, etc. All were dressed in casual clothing—jeans, shorts, tank tops and t-shirts. The other woman emerged from the house, and they had a quick pow-wow on the front lawn before she ushered them in. Shelby had her window rolled down, hoping to catch something, a bit of a conversation, etc. But the woman spoke in hushed tones, and it seemed clear that the others knew better than to question her authority. Anyway, several minutes later, she swore she could hear a vacuum running."

"They were cleaning the house?"

Ramirez nodded slowly. "It would seem so. After a while, one of the girls rolled a mop bucket out and drained its contents into the street, followed by a couple of others hauling rugs out so that they could beat them with a broom."

"Odd," I murmured.

"Not as odd as the moving truck that showed up to swap out furniture."

"What? Like stagers?" I had known real estate agents who did that and had shot more than a few pics of homes with furniture that was rented by the hour so that the home had more star power in magazines, on their company's website or in online promotions.

"I guess?" Ramirez shrugged. "Couches, carpets and the beds were all new, for sure." He chuckled when I scrunched my nose. "But yeah, everything else seemed new-ish, probably from some furniture or staging warehouse."

"This is starting to play out like a soap opera. I'm almost afraid to ask what happened next. But please, go on."

"After the furniture movers left, another truck showed up."

"Don't tell me it was the stripper pole installers."

Ramirez raised a brow. "You think they need an entire moving truck for that?"

"Well, I doubt you can order them on Amazon and then expect the driver to set it up for you."

"Hmm…I wouldn't be so sure about that." I shot him a dark look, realizing he was having some fun at my expense.

"Seriously, what was it?"

"Clothes. Racks and racks of clothes."

"I was closer to the mark with the soap opera analogy than I thought," I murmured. "Let me guess—party clothes."

Ramirez nodded. "Shortly after that, an SUV arrived—different SUV from the one that dropped off the first gal—and Shelby thought this group of individuals comprised something she called a glam squad." He shrugged and raised his hands. The sincerity behind his befuddlement caused me to chuckle.

"Makeup and hair, Ramirez."

I was rewarded with a healthy frown.

"Right. Whatever *that* entails." When I started to respond, he raised a hand. "Please. No. I do not need you to elaborate. Let's just say the girls came out several hours later dressed rather…provocatively. I'm still not sure what takes women so long."

"Well, if you would have allowed me to expound." I shrugged, opening my hands in a "what can you do?" gesture. He opened his mouth. Shut it again. Frowned. Though limited in his facial expressions, the man amused me to no end. "Come on, Detective. The 'glam' in 'glam squad' didn't tune you in?"

Confusion turned to a tightened jaw that worked itself hard enough to cramp. "I don't appreciate your amusement or your tone. And for the record, the lack of clothing didn't help clear up matters. Nor did the pound cake worth of makeup or the massive amounts of hair that sprouted out of their heads that wasn't there before. According to what Shelby told Leah, of course."

"Of course." I strained to withhold a snicker. "Those were probably extensions. As in hair extensions," I clarified in an attempt to throw the man a bone. A "pound cake worth of makeup"? The man needed to seriously amp up his game.

"Laugh it up, AJ," he ground out. "Need I remind you why we are having this conversation?"

The helium sufficiently released from the balloon, we returned to our somber discussion.

"Point taken. I assume Shelby followed them to one of the clubs in Old Town?"

"She did. Same setup. Only this time around, she zeroed in on one of the girls in an effort to get more details."

"Okay…" I replied, guessing this is where things got sketchy.

"The girl was not only willing to chat with Shelby, she also gave her a card—one designated for potential girls only—"

"Potential girls?" I interjected. "As in for recruitment purposes?" When Ramirez nodded, I pressed my eyes shut. This was getting worse by the minute.

When I opened them, I found him studying me. His own features had softened as he revealed a look I'd seen before—concern. I nodded to let him know I was okay. I wasn't, but the sick feeling in my gut was far worse when I started thinking about what could have happened to Shelby and Leah.

"Any idea why Shelby zoned in on that girl?"

He nodded. "Shelby recognized her. Her name was Tamryn. Tamryn Mayer."

I held up a hand. "Wait. Why does that name sound familiar?"

"She's the daughter of that billionaire electric car rental guy. You know, the one who's been buying up all the real estate around the valley—who reneged on the sports complex?"

Recognition dawned. "Craig Mayer? Also known as Cro-Magnon?"

"Nailed it." Ramirez released a harsh chuckle.

I shook my head. "That makes no sense. Why would a girl like Tamryn, coming from an affluent family like the Mayers, need to resort to…that?" Perhaps I shouldn't have been so quick to pass judgment but was feeling scritchy because, like Alice, Leah had chased the white rabbit down the rabbit hole. And Tamryn, by way of Shelby, was at the bottom of it.

Ramirez shrugged. "Why does anyone do anything?"

"Don't go getting all philosophical on me now."

"Fine. I honestly can't say for sure. Maybe because Tamryn's a rich twenty-something with a chip on her shoulder, which was brought on by her father when he publicly disowned her after flunking out of Arizona State University.

Something clicked in my memory bank. "Um, I'm pretty sure the whole fall from grace stemmed from something far more…scandalous than flunking out of A.S.U."

He tilted his head. "Go on."

"According to Leah's intel back when it happened, Tamryn posted several provocative videos on social media of her…consorting with various athletes—both college and pro—as well as a few coaches, some of who were married. It was a video diary of her exploits, but in a very public arena. In fact, I wouldn't be surprised if her dad backed out of the sports complex *because* of it."

Ramirez frowned. "Backing out of a business deal is one thing. Disowning your child is taking it to another level. Seems a bit harsh, no matter what she'd done."

"Yeah, you might think that, but after he received several angry calls from his business partners, as well as members of the school's administration, he took away her allowance—and I use that term loosely—she retaliated by posting pictures of him in a few compromising positions with his own co-ed."

"Cold."

"You know what they say about revenge."

"Almost makes you feel sorry for the guy."

"Don't. There's a reason Tamryn's the way she is," I replied.

"Karma, then."

"Why Ramirez, I didn't think you bought into that kind of thing." I mock-punched him in the arm, causing him to fake a wince.

"I think you just made me a believer. Anyway…why don't we get back to Shelby."

"Right. You were telling me that Shelby started chatting with Tamryn and that Tamryn offered her a card." When he nodded, I added, "Let me guess. Shelby feigned interested and used the offering to get on the inside track, which means she went undercover as one of these girls to get details for her investigative story. And when she went missing, Leah followed her lead and did the same. And now she's missing, too."

Rather than answering, he worked his jaw, refusing to make eye contact.

"What is it you're *not* telling me?"

Ramirez met my eyes and my stomach dropped, even before his voice cracked as he said the words.

"About Leah. I was the last person she contacted before she disappeared."

CHAPTER THREE

I opened my mouth and then shut it, not wanting the shock, frustration, and perhaps judgment to creep into my response. The downturn of Ramirez's mouth and the hunch of his shoulders suggested he may have been feeling guilty enough without me tossing my two cents in—which he confirmed when he hung his head, cradling it with his palms as his elbows dug into his knees as they bounced with untapped energy.

I took a couple of moments before speaking—one to compose myself and my thoughts; the other to offer Ramirez the same.

"We've talked about Shelby, but not how Leah inserted herself into the situation. Why not start with Leah's plan and work our way toward the discovery of her car." He lifted his head and nodded, shifting back on the couch. "So, this plan of hers…did she come to you to verify the logistics of her plan…to make sure it would work?" I felt a pang of jealousy, even as I asked the question.

I was typically the one Leah ran her schemes by. When had we gotten so far off-course that we couldn't share something like that?

Ramirez shook his head. "She shared her plan with me, but it had nothing to do with confirming whether it would work. I think she knew that I'd tell her it wouldn't, that it was a matter for law enforcement, but you know how *that* would have gone."

I shrugged. There was no denying it. Leah would have ignored him and gone ahead with her plan. It's what I would have done.

"And this reason?"

"It was two-fold. First, Leah wanted someone to know if something went sideways, that she hadn't just disappeared."

"And the second?" I prompted, as my heart did the Cha-Cha in my chest.

"She wanted me to let you know she was

sorry for hurting you," he replied, still refusing to make eye contact.

"There's still something else, isn't there?"

He pulled in a deep breath, then faced me, his brows pressing together as he spoke. "She asked—no, told—me that if something happened and she was no longer around, that I was to watch out for you."

I bowed my head. "Oh."

I could feel his gaze as he sat silently and emotions swarmed, threatening to overtake the last bit of strength I had. I shoved them aside, knowing I'd have to address them eventually.

For now, I would not…could not entertain the possibility that my best friend was no longer walking this earth.

Finally, I nodded. "Thank you. I appreciate you telling me." He nodded in return. I blew out a breath and pressed forward. "And her plan— was it feasible?"

Ramirez raised a brow. "Plan? Come on, AJ. Leah's been your best friend for what—twenty years? Have you ever known her to 'plan' anything?"

His overt use of finger quotes—a gesture that I'd used more than twice and typically an-

noyed the heck out of him—was not appreciated. The colorful selection of language I shot
back was not lost on him, either.

He sighed. "To answer your question, her
fuzzy-headed *scheme* was not feasible, and I told
her as much." I scoffed and prompted him to
continue. "Regardless, she felt she had enough
information, based on what Shelby had told her,
to follow her down the rabbit hole. The same
rabbit hole."

When my mouth formed an "o," but no
words found their way out, he nodded. "Yeah. I
tried to convince her she was better off taking
what she had to the proper authorities and even
suggested a few contacts to help her. But she
wouldn't have it. Even threatened me, quite creatively, if I took it upon myself to get any of
them involved."

"Threatened?" I frowned, convinced he was
exaggerating. Leah rarely made threats and even
then, they were in jest.

Ramirez gave me a single shake of the head,
but said nothing more. I studied him for a moment. He'd been forthcoming about his conversation with Leah, but there was something about

the way he'd claimed she'd contacted him that just didn't ring true.

Meaning he was still holding something back.

Question was…should I call him on it and risk having him shutting down? Or give him a pass and miss out on whatever "it" was he had yet to divulge.

For now, I chose the latter. I would not waste any more precious time waiting for him to dole out scraps of information.

If anyone was going to track down Leah, I was the most qualified.

I just needed to figure out a way to convince Ramirez that I'd leave the matter to his pals in law enforcement so I could tackle it on my own.

CHAPTER FOUR

Fortunately, that conversation became moot when Ramirez received a call that required his immediate attention. He agreed to keep me posted but left after reiterating a directive I'd heard more times than I could count—to trust law enforcement to do their job. He added a stern warning. Something along the lines of my failure to comply would not only impede their efforts, but could also get Leah and Shelby hurt. Or worse.

Roughly translated: "Stay out of it, AJ."

Yeah. Like that directive had *ever* been heeded in the past.

I listened to the rumble of his truck as it pulled away and fired up my laptop, jotting down what I knew to date and what I'd learned from our conversation. Something told me it was best to capture these thoughts now. I had a feeling that once the shock of Leah's disappearance settled in, another set of emotions would arise.

Ones that could affect my already cloudy judgment.

As Ramirez had intimated, I didn't want to do something out of anger, fear or guilt that would make things worse.

Without access to Leah's phone, computer, or any of the items that had been left in her vehicle, I had no way of backtracking anything she'd done up to the point she'd disappeared. However, if she hadn't been found, Ramirez's law enforcement contact must not have made any headway, either.

I considered contacting her former coworkers but doubted that there would be anything helpful to glean from them. Besides, asking a group of reporters about my best friend's actions would certainly perk up more than a handful of feelers, if not incite a few of them to start an investigation of their own. I wasn't prepared for them to have this information…yet.

Not to mention Shelby could have shared it with them, but had chosen Leah to confide in. Leah, in turn, had confided in Ramirez. Meaning both had felt it was safer to only share the information with one person.

And look where that had gotten them.

I wasn't about to follow them down the same path, though I wondered if I would have a choice.

One thing I was sure of—I had to find Tamryn.

A quick Internet search brought up her social media profile. I was surprised to find that her posts were more toned down than what they'd once been. There were definitely no gratuitous images of her or anyone else in compromising positions. Just pics with friends, heading to a movie, eating out or random quotes—typically hers—rounded out by an occasional cat or dog video that she'd reshared.

Compared to the previous iteration, Tamryn

version 2.0 appeared pretty tame and a bit more polished.

Heavy emphasis on *appeared*.

Perhaps it was the price she'd paid to separate her personal but still very social life from the one in which she indulged in a variety of party-going festivities. Something told me she had a second, more private profile for that.

And to gain access to that secondary lifestyle, I'd have to crack the first.

Meaning, I had to focus on what I had in front of me—a profile that literally screamed:

Friend me and I'll be your forever friend right back!

No wonder she had over a million loyal followers, I snorted.

After liking a few of her posts, I sent her a friend request. With any luck, she'd respond. Then I could direct message her rather than posing my query for the masses to view.

Within seconds, she friended me back with a quick:

Welcome to my world!

Now that we were forever friends, I carefully crafted my direct message. Too little and it would get lost in the circus; too much and I would probably get myself blocked or reported.

Finally, I settled on the following, grimacing as I sent it into the social media black hole:

Hey! Noticed we have some friends in common... Have you talked to Shelby lately? Am hoping to catch up. DM me...

Several hours went by without a response. I nibbled at my nails, scrolling her feed for activity. Had I been too aggressive and scared her away?

If she was knee-deep into whatever Shelby and Leah had gotten themselves into, or knew what had happened to either of them, perhaps she was in just as much danger. Then again, if she was involved, had I put them at greater risk?

I rose and paced the kitchen, only to kick Nicoh's water bowl, dousing my shoes and pant legs while creating a lake on the tile. He lifted his head and huffed before tightening himself into a ball that defied the laws of Malamute physics and returning to his doggie dreams.

At least one of us was getting some rest, I mused.

After checking the non-existent messages on my social media account one final time, I closed the laptop and shoved it to the side, placing my chin on my hands as I contemplated my next move.

I could always reach out to my mysterious, often missing in action, biological father, Martin Singer. Or Bio-Pop, as Leah had aptly named him. It hadn't been a term of endearment, though he'd defrosted a few icicles as we'd gotten to know him.

Then he disappeared on us. Again.

The last time I'd seen him, it was just before he'd packed up his meager belongings and moved out of the house he'd been leasing a street over from one of my friends who was in Dallas doing lawyerly things on a long-term contract. I hadn't heard from Martin since and wasn't even sure he was still in Arizona.

I still had the cell phone number he'd given me, though, and knew I could reach out whenever I needed to. Perhaps he could use his network—I still wasn't entirely sure what *that* entailed—to help me get some information on the rental property scene and see if there were any rumblings from their end of anything hinky going on.

Question was—could I do it without mentioning Leah's disappearance? I wasn't convinced I wanted Bio-Pop that far into my business. Truth be told, I still didn't trust him. And I was nowhere near figuring out his intentions, though my feeling was that they would always linger in the grayer realm.

True, he was my father, but he wasn't the man who had raised me as his own. No, Martin had always been…something else, even longer than I had known him or of his role in my life. I could spend a lifetime getting to know him and still not uncover all of his secrets or the things that made him tick. It was a threshold I wasn't sure I was willing to cross, even if presented.

It didn't help that he rang all of Ramirez's warning bells. I'd been warded off him and every time there had been an argument followed by a period of separation, Martin had been at the core of it.

If I plunged ahead and contacted Martin, Ramirez would eventually find out and I'd risk losing a lifeline in my efforts to locate Leah. He would simply cut off contact. For good this time.

Then again, if I contacted Ramirez instead and pressed him into being more forthcoming about what Leah had shared, I still could end up empty-handed.

I wasn't a fan of either option.

In the end, I stabbed my finger at a name in the Contacts list on my cell phone and hit "Call," grudgingly selecting the path of least resistance.

It wouldn't be the first time I'd chosen the wrong path.

CHAPTER FIVE

"No," was his response when Martin's name was mentioned.

It was firm, but without the intensity I had expected.

"Alright. Have you found out anything about Leah's disappearance we can use?"

"What's with this 'we' bit?" When his question was met with silence, Ramirez released something between a huff and a sigh. "It's only been a few hours, AJ. These things take time."

"Tell that to Shelby. Or Leah," I growled before disconnecting.

Yeah, I'd been snappish with the detective, but I was sick and tired of being spoon-fed details while he withheld the ones that could actually help me get a foothold onto something tangible. After all, I was her best friend and maybe able to connect some of the dots that law enforcement would not.

At this point, I felt I had no choice other than to call Martin, figuring it couldn't hurt to leave a message about needing his assistance. As our relationship was still tenuous, his interest would at least be piqued by a call from his only living family member.

He startled me when he answered on the first ring.

"Arianna, my dear. What a pleasant surprise." There wasn't a hint of caution in his voice, only a sense of calm mixed with a bit of curiosity. And was that…joy?

He was a hard man to read.

"Hey, Martin." We hadn't gotten to the place where I'd felt comfortable calling him "Dad" or "Father." That was reserved for the man who had raised me. "I haven't heard from you in a while. Are you still in Phoenix?"

"Do you need me to be in Phoenix?" I rolled my eyes. That was Martin for you—evasive and always answering a question with a question.

Sometimes it was eerie how similar he and Ramirez could be in some respects, even though each would adamantly deny it.

"That's not what I asked," I replied.

He chuckled. "I did it again, didn't I?" When I made some verbal sounds to suggest the affirmative, the chuckling transitioned to a laugh. "Sorry. No, I'm not currently in the Phoenix area. But I can be if you need me."

It wasn't a question. Martin was observant enough to let me rummage through my thoughts, remaining silent as I weighed Ramirez's warning —make that plural—against what my gut was screaming.

I went with my gut—hoping it wasn't actually growing hunger pangs—and filled him in on what had transpired when I had returned to Phoenix.

When I finished, he was quiet for a moment before responding.

"I'm truly sorry about Leah. I know how much she means to you. I've also grown accustomed to her…antics and have developed a bit of fondness for her despite them."

"But…" I prompted.

"Why do you always assume the negative,

daughter?"

I flinched at the familial reference. "I just thought…" I murmured, my skin flushing though he couldn't see me.

"Patience, my dear. You forget, I was a scientist and my analytical mind is no match for your creative spontaneity."

"Gee, thanks. As if talking to you hadn't already given me enough of an inferiority complex," I muttered.

He sighed. "Arianna, do we really have to do this every time? I wasn't judging your approach. It was merely a distinction in our viewpoints. I admire your insights differ vastly from my own. It provides balance in the universe. And makes for better solutions when challenges arise."

I immediately regretted my reaction. Why did Martin always seem to bring out my childish, bratty side?

"You want to find Leah and this other girl, Shelby, don't you?"

"Yes," I replied meekly, sounding like a reprimanded child.

"Stop that." Startled by his brisk tone, I inadvertently gasped, causing him to quickly add, "I'm so sorry to have snapped at you. I'm obviously terrible at this—communicating with an adult child. I'm sure it goes both ways—"

"I know you're trying. And I am too," I interjected.

"Good. Good," he replied, his voice returning to its usual calm. "What I want you to understand, above all else, is this: if it's important to you, it's important to me."

After a moment, he cleared his throat. "I'm happy you felt comfortable coming to me. I know it caused you a good amount of inner turmoil. And I know the cost may be high…" His voice trailed off, perhaps allowing me time to respond, but I wasn't prepared to dwell on something that could be irrelevant down the road when I need to be focused on the present.

Whether he took my silence as confirmation I wasn't sure, but he moved on. "I believe I can be of some assistance. Would you be able to pull the items together that you've collected on Tamryn so far?" When I said that I could, he gave me a cloud location to drop them to, which I did.

"And now what?" I asked.

"Now we work on getting Leah and her friend back."

When I didn't immediately respond—frankly, I was shocked—he added, "What? Is that not what you wanted?"

"No, Martin." I was still digesting that my request had produced the desired response with such little effort. "It's *precisely* what I wanted."

"Then what?" he urged.

"It's just not what I'd expected."

Martin chuckled lightly. "Is it ever?"

I wore a pattern on the carpet as I paced back and forth, nibbling at the nubs that had once been nails.

Had I made the right decision involving Martin?

How would Ramirez react? Actually, I knew the answer to that. "Badly" would be an understatement.

The better question was—*what* would he do once he found out?

Was Leah hurt? And Shelby?

Was Tamryn involved? If she made contact and was willing to discuss the situation with me, could I trust her? What if she reported back and it made matters worse?

What if I ended up getting Leah killed?

Too many "ifs." And far too many questions to which I had no answers.

I considered calling Martin back and telling him to pull the plug—that I had been overreacting—but despite my restlessness, I couldn't justify doing so. Not when I had the ability to do something. And Martin, with the help of his band of cohorts, was as good of a bet as any.

I couldn't waste time banking on Tamryn anyway. Just because I'd sent her a direct message didn't guarantee she would ever reach out. She hadn't so far, and I couldn't risk spooking her by sending her a follow-up message, especially if she was on the fence. My pushiness could make her jump off of it and un-friend me, leaving me no branch to communicate with her privately. I would not resort to stalking her in public. And wouldn't even know where to start if I tried.

I resigned myself to the couch, watching infomercials trying to sell me air fryers, hot pots, hair removal systems and creams for baggy eyes and dark circles—I actually contemplated that last one after walking by a mirror and scaring myself—and was just nodding off when my cell phone rang.

Popping up in surprise, I mumbled a salutation without checking the caller id.

"Did I catch you at a bad time, dear?"

I was immediately awake. "No, no, Martin. I was just catching up on some channel-surfing. You got something?"

"I almost wish I didn't."

"Almost?"

"I know how important it is to you to find Leah."

"I sense a 'but' coming," I replied, resuming my nail-biting and coming up short. No pun intended. My ragged cuticles would have screamed had they been afforded lungs.

"But I'm worried about the cost, and I don't mean financially."

"That bad?"

"That bad." Martin's tone was somber.

"Is this something you can tell me over the phone?"

"I won't have to. Look out your window." When I squinted toward the front door, he added, "The slider window *behind* you, Arianna."

I swiveled my head in that direction, finding Martin standing as he'd indicated at the slider door. In my backyard. Meaning he had bypassed my locked gates.

I'd given up trying to figure out how or why Martin did things. Instead, I ushered him in and we muddled our way through awkward hugs before settling back into the living room.

"Where's Nicoh?" he asked, peering around.

"Probably napping. On my bed." When Martin raised a brow. "He had a hard day." I shrugged. "So…Leah."

"Right. It appears her friend Shelby's instincts were on the mark. What she witnessed is not only more widespread in Phoenix than we'd initially thought—and I'm using 'we' to reference the associates in my network—it's been an ongoing issue in other cities where vacation rentals are prevalent. Typically, the larger the area, the harder it is to track, and therefore the longer it takes to find the root of the problem."

"But there is a root?" I replied, my energy surging. "One that can be plucked and destroyed."

Martin shook his head. "It's not that simple."

"It never is, is it?"

"I suppose not." He tilted his head, seeming to reflect on that before continuing. "According to my sources, the bigger the vacation rental market is in each metro area, the easier it is for activity like this to fly under the radar. Orlando, Las Vegas, San Diego are just among a few of the top destinations to fall prey to it."

"And now Scottsdale," I murmured.

"The Phoenix area is not immune," he replied. "But yes, Scottsdale is among the more desirable locations for operations like this to branch out and take hold."

"You mentioned it is harder to track. But these other areas, they are aware this is going on in their backyards? Literally?"

He nodded. "There were rumblings in these cities about 'alternate uses' for vacation rentals, but not much in the way of solid or even usable evidence." When I cocked my head, he added, "In some locations, small task forces were formed to assess the situation, but none of them could get the inside track—nothing to the level of what Shelby could, anyway.

"Even when they did net a lead, the operations were always one step ahead and were disbanded, shuffled, or moved before the task force could get anything concrete from it. So, other than being a nuisance to residents in those communities, there just wasn't enough manpower or the threat of law-breaking to warrant going any further with it."

"Until now," I replied.

"It's still hearsay, Arianna." He held up a hand when I started to interrupt. "Yes, you, Ramirez and I know that Shelby and Leah are legitimately missing, but when you look at things from law enforcement's perspective? Two adult females may be missing under suspicious circumstances where friends and family are concerned—especially when you factor in the evidence left behind in Leah's car—but with nothing concrete and zero ties to these vacation rental operators, our word as to what happened isn't all that helpful.

"To make matters worse, it could just as easily be construed as two separate, isolated events. And the only one who claims that Shelby was missing was Leah. And now that she's gone…" His voice trailed off as he offered me a shrug.

I wasn't happy about it, but he had a point.

I blew out a long breath. "Okay. We know they're out there. The task forces know they're out there. The people using the vacation rentals for 'alternate uses' know when law enforcement has been alerted to their activities and are obviously smart enough to get the heck out before they get caught. So how do we track them? And please, don't say 'follow the money,' because we've got zilch going on there."

Martin raised a brow. "I wasn't about to. Where would you get that idea, anyway?"

"TV. Movies. The usual places."

"Hmm… Well, I'm afraid it isn't always as easy as trimming it down into a bite-sized two-hour segment and tossing a 'follow the money' solution at it. Though I'm sure if we keep digging into these operations, we'll be able to root out the money angle. They've got to have some form of cash-flow in place, though we are nowhere near identifying that part of their business yet."

"If not the money, then how?"

"We follow the evidence," he replied.

"*What* evidence?"

"Leah left some behind, did she not?"

I bobbed my head. "Her laptop, personal belongings and pretty much everything she left with. But the cops have those. So what else could there be?" As the words exited my mouth, I knew. "Blood."

"Not just blood." Martin's voice grew quiet.

A shudder rippled through my body. He wouldn't lead me down this path unless he'd learned something significant. For as much as I feared the confirmation, I *needed* it.

"It was Leah's, wasn't it?"

A look passed between us before Martin moved toward me and embraced me in an awkward one-armed hug.

"I know it doesn't help, but there wasn't enough of Leah's blood present to conclude that the injury had been life-threatening."

I pulled away. "What do you mean by 'enough of Leah's blood'? Is there something you're not telling me?"

"A second blood type was found in the trunk. Considerably more than the first."

"How much more?"

"Enough that would suggest that without immediate medical attention, the person would have expired."

CHAPTER SEVEN

I had nowhere to go with that, but the lump in my throat prevented me from uttering a syllable anyway.

Martin took my silence as a sign to continue. "Unlike Leah, this person was not in the system, so identification will be more difficult."

"The blood belonged to a female, though, didn't it?"

He nodded. "But that doesn't necessarily mean it was Shelby's."

"You didn't have to say that." When he squinted, I added, "You know, to make me feel better."

Martin blinked. "The thought wouldn't have occurred to me."

"How reassuring," I murmured.

Martin either ignored my quip or hadn't caught it. "On a more…promising note, I learned that one of the last people—other than Detective Ramirez—Leah talked to was a freelance forensic accountant who Shelby was acquainted with and had contacted before her disappearance."

"Do I want to know how you came by this information?"

"Probably not." He pursed his lips before adding, "Let's just say I know some people who are well connected that can…acquire such information and leave it at that. The good news is that he's agreed to meet with us."

"I hear the 'bad news' portion coming around the bend."

Martin cast me a curious glance. "I wouldn't necessarily label it as 'bad,' though he will only agree to talk to us if we don't involve the police or mention his name."

"Which means telling Ramircz is out of the question."

He nodded. "The forensic accountant did

admit to being a tad skittish where law enforcement is concerned."

"Can we trust him? I mean, if he's a criminal—"

Martin put up a hand. "My people checked him out. It's nothing like that. He unknowingly got caught up helping the wrong people and when they were taken down, he was caught in the crossfire. Not literally, of course. Anyway, he was put through the wringer, but a sympathetic district attorney cut him loose after he agreed to divulge some key details about the organization."

"Great. So he's a snitch," I grumbled.

Martin shrugged. "Do you want to find out what he has to say or not?"

"I don't think we have much choice. When are we meeting him?"

"Tonight. I'm just waiting for him to call with a location. It was the only way he'd agree to meet. Once he does, we'll have an hour at most to reach the destination, or he'll bail."

"Just what we need…more intrigue." In case Martin had missed my sarcasm, I added, "We should probably coordinate our outfits. What do you think—black jumpsuits? Crepe-soled shoes? Knit caps with face paint?"

He caught it and lofted his own hardball. "Well, if you prefer, our alternative is to track down people in other cities. Either that, or we can find someone in the Scottsdale area that knows what's going on—one that will talk to us."

I raised a hand. "Alright, alright. So this forensic accountant is our best bet at the moment. I also think I've got a track on Tamryn, the girl Shelby contacted at the club in Old Town." He listened as I told him about sending her a message on social media after she'd friended me.

"How do things stand with her at the moment?"

"I'm waiting for a response to my direct message. I don't want to push her."

"You may need to."

He was right. "Suggestions?"

"Tell her that two people's lives rely on it," he replied.

"Okay, but to be honest, this is a crappy Plan B if things don't work out with the forensic accountant."

His mouth formed a tight line, but he said nothing.

Sighing, I crafted another direct message and sent it off into the unknown.

"Done."

"And now we wait."

"As if we needed any more of that," I grumbled.

"Patience, Arianna. And please, have a little faith."

I gave him a sideways glance. "Sorry. Both are on the light side these days."

We waited in silence. Martin did whatever Martin does on his tablet while I puttered around, attempting to look busy while trying not to be obvious about peering over his shoulder.

"Coffee?" I asked after I could stand the void no longer.

Without looking away from the tablet, he replied, "Please. I'll take a decaf if you have it."

"I do. But are you sure? Could be a long one."

He glanced up, offering me a tiny smile. "I want to be sharp. Not jittery."

After preparing and serving up his request, I checked my social media account for the umpteenth time. Biting my lip, I crafted a follow-up to the message I'd previously sent, hoping to elicit a more immediate response from Tamryn. I was getting ready to send it when my phone buzzed.

Ramirez.

Guiltily, I picked it up before it went to voicemail. After the niceties were out of the way, and Martin imparted several curious glances, Ramirez relayed the purpose for his call, which turned out to be nothing more than what Martin had already told me, with one glaring omission.

While he confirmed the blood in the trunk was Leah's—known—and that it wasn't an amount that could be construed as life-threatening—also known—he failed to mention the presence of a second blood type.

I ground my teeth to prevent my brain and mouth from taking control and snarkily asking him how it could be possible that blood was leaking from the trunk and not be considered life-threatening. Not to mention, he'd left me to assume it was all Leah's blood. After I had sufficiently calmed myself, I framed an appropriate response. One that belied what I already knew.

"I'm relieved that Leah's injuries weren't life-threatening. At that time, anyway. Was there anything else of relevance in the trunk?"

Martin's brow raised as he'd been intently listening to every word on my end of the conversation, even though there hadn't been many.

"Nope," Ramirez replied. "I know you wanted more. And I'll be sure to share anything new that comes up, no matter how small."

"Um, hmm," I mumbled, rolling my eyes at Martin, who simply shook his head as a frown grew. "I appreciate that."

"You do the same, AJ. You hear?" Ramirez sounded genuine and I'm sure he was, as long as it benefited him and his agenda.

"Will do, Detective," I replied, forcing every ounce of enthusiasm into my response.

We signed off. Martin and I looked at one another and said nothing.

Now that we had Ramirez's number, we had confirmed the score.

We'd been right to assume we needed to proceed on our own.

At least with Martin, I knew where he stood. For now.

CHAPTER EIGHT

Martin gave me the courtesy of not mentioning the conversation.

Either that or he'd heard enough.

Still, I caught him studying me as I stood at the counter, pretending to organize sugar packets. Fortunately, his perusal was cut short when his cell's ringtone broke the silence, causing me to jump.

Wait! Was that Jefferson Starship's "We Built This City"?

Huh, I'd figured him for a *Dark Side of the Moon* kind of guy.

As the sugar packets were sufficiently faced, I moved on to scrubbing the counters, purposely trying to look like I wasn't listening in. Then again, Martin's side of the conversation comprised nothing more than a few "Uh hums" and "Okays." Not really interesting or that useful.

I had just started searching for errant crumbs—a task that's harder than it sounds when you're feigning busyness—when the call ended. I gave up my feeble attempt and waited with anticipation.

"He's ready to go," Martin replied, sounding less than enthused.

"And?"

"He wants us to meet him at a salvage yard in Phoenix. We've got one hour. Otherwise, he'll assume we're not coming." When he relayed the specifics of the location, I shuddered, causing him to frown. "What?"

"Nothing good happens in the avenues at night."

"Is that from some movie, or are you being literal?" he asked, cocking his head to one side.

"Does it matter?" I grumbled.

"Well, it would be helpful to know if we were simply dealing with a flashlight type of situation or one that required a bit more…oomph."

I cast him a withering glance. "Oomph doesn't even begin to cover it."

"Oh?" He furrowed his brow.

"We could bring the Batmobile and still come out looking like Swiss cheese."

"Arianna, I have no idea what that means."

I sighed. "If you've got any firepower or a Molotov cocktail or two handy, bring 'em."

"Would a rocket launcher suffice?" He didn't even crack a smile when he laid that one on me.

"Um, sure. But just in case it's overkill—you know, once we survey the situation—an AK-47 might be the route to go."

Martin nodded, his tone appreciative. "Old school. I like it."

I waited until I turned back to the counter to roll my eyes. Only in Martin Land.

After ensuring Nicoh's needs were tended to and he was nestled into *his* pet bed, we hustled to Martin's vehicle, a non-descript blue Toyota Camry. It was clean but worn. And definitely not something that I'd expected him to drive.

"Bought it off a guy, for purposes of this very nature," he said, after noticing me giving it a once-over.

I raised my hands. "Hey, no judgment. Just observing."

He nodded, but kept casting glances at me as we jetted to our meeting location. Of course, by 'jetted,' I mean Martin remained *precisely* at the noted speed limit, with hands adequately spaced on the steering wheel.

No, it was my mind that raced. Unfortunately, thinking it would not incentivize Martin to do so.

"What?" I asked after several additional side-eyes.

"Um, I just wanted to know *what* you were thinking?"

I swiveled to face him. "Are we having 'girl time' now, Martin?" I chuckled when he turned red, but gave him a pass. This time. "To answer your question, I was just thinking that we're placing a lot of faith in this forensic accountant guy."

"There's that f-word again," Martin quipped, his mouth cracking a tiny smile as he glanced at me.

"Good one!" I stuttered out between laughs, which caused him to shake his head and chuckle.

It felt good to engage in a bit of shared

laughter, but the endorphins were short-lived as we neared the salvage lot.

"How do you want to play this?" I asked, trying unsuccessfully to keep my nerves at bay, as Martin pressed a firm hand on my bouncing knee.

"He knows what we want. Let him do the talking."

"What about physical proof? We need something tangible to nail these guys."

"We'll see."

Well, that was ominous. Thanks, Martin. "I have no idea what that means," I murmured, tossing his words back at him as he pulled into the parking lot. Or rather, the gravel path outside the foreboding barbed wire gates leading to the yard. Which was secured with a camera and keypad for which we had no code to gain entry. "Well, that bites."

Martin turned to me. "I assume that phrase means it is a bad thing. But if you're referring to the keypad, don't worry."

He got out of the vehicle, opened the trunk and pulled out a seriously heinous-looking piece of artillery I swore I'd seen Jason Statham one-arming in a recent movie.

"Is that—"

Martin put a finger to his lips as he reached into the trunk again, shoving an industrial-sized flashlight at me before striding to the keypad and punching in a number. When he pushed the gate open, he looked over his shoulder.

"Are you coming?" he deadpanned.

Um, okay, Rambo, I thought, not realizing that the former scientist had a skill-set that neared Jason Bourne's, Jack Reacher's or even Jack Bauer's as I hustled to catch up with him.

"I was just waiting for my own firepower. This flashlight seems so…girly." As it turned out, it wasn't.

My arm started to cramp as I hefted it high so that we could see, but I wasn't about to let Martin know that. Especially not after he shook his head and his Father-knows-best voice made an appearance.

"Best if only one of us has to answer for this if anything goes south." It was awkward, to say the least. When I tilted my head, he added, "One of us has to have plausible deniability in the event the other needs to be bailed out of jail."

"Thanks for clearing that up." The remainder

of my commentary was precluded by something that caught my eye.

"What…is *that*?" The flashlight's beam did little more than illuminate the odd shape, and though Martin tugged my arm, I strode toward the object of my curiosity.

Wrong move.

"Gah!" I uttered before reeling back as I took in the scene before me.

A jagged iron spire surged upward from the ground. I had no idea what purpose it had served before, but now it was an instrument of death. A man's body was impaled on it, his frame arcing where it pierced through the lower part of his back and exited through his chest as though he was being prepared for roasting on a barbecue spit. His eyes were wide and his mouth opened in a silent, endless scream. This man had seen death coming.

I'd seen all the *Halloween* and *Friday the Thirteenth* movies, which did nothing to prepare me for the horror before me. Mind you, I'd seen death before, but this? This was beyond gruesome. It was utterly…grotesque.

And the blood—oh man, all the blood—heavily tainted with that metallic tang, still dripped from his corpse, saturating his clothing in a crimson blanket as it traveled to its destination and wove its way into the crevices of the gravel beneath his frame.

Had he released that final scream? Was he forced to endure every excruciating moment of the pain as it raged through his body before he expelled that final breath?

I shuddered, covering my mouth as I fought the urge to vomit. I hoped it was all over before he realized what had happened.

"I don't suppose he tripped and fell," I choked out as Martin caught up, casting a worried glance in my direction.

"I highly doubt it," he replied as he took in the scene before us and frowned. "You should leave. No one knows you were here. I can handle it."

"Someone knows." I nodded at the camera.

He shook his head. "They were disabled."

"How do you know?"

"He told me he would."

Ah, so this was our forensic friend. How convenient. "And you believed him?" I raised a brow.

Martin scoffed. "Give me some credit, Arianna. I think I can tell whether the cameras are on.”

“Still…”

He gave me an exasperated sigh. “Fine. He was the owner.”

My eyes widened. “Of this place?” When he nodded, I added, “Why in the world would a forensic accountant own a salvage yard?” I doubt it was to cover a hoarding addiction.

“I can think of a reason.”

So could I. “Let me guess—he was hiding.”

Martin shrugged. “More or less. We should probably call the proper authorities before someone else does.”

“In this neighborhood?” I mustered a weak laugh. “Do what you gotta do. I’m going back to the vehicle.”

He looked from me to the car, as though contemplating something. Realization dawned.

“Come on! Are you seriously concerned I’m gonna barf in your car?”

“The thought did occur to me,” he murmured.

“Whatever.” I stomped to the Camry, muttering under my breath. “Thank you for your concern, Mr. Sensitive.”

"I heard that," he replied to my back.

"Just calling it like I see it, Martin."

"You could at least leave the flashlight."

"You're handy. I'm sure you'll make do."

How's *that* for sensitive?

Once I got back to the vehicle, I decided to keep an eye on Martin, but realized he was no longer standing near the body.

In fact, he was nowhere in sight.

Cursing under my breath, I threw the car door open, fully prepared to storm back to see what he was up to when the flash of blue and red caught my attention. I was both relieved and trepidatious as an onslaught of police cruisers arrived, followed by a fire truck and an ambulance. All were in stealth mode, so other than the lights, there was not an audible alert to their arrival, which made for an ominous entrance to an already horrific scene.

Why couldn't they "go silent" like that in my neighborhood, rather than blasting the sirens at all hours of the night? Apparently, they didn't have to heed the noise ordinance like the rest of us.

As they exited their vehicles, I pointed in the direction of the body and as one officer approached me, noticed Martin had materialized by my side.

He shook his head when I started to speak and took the reins when the officer's questions began. I was impressed. The story Martin told didn't stray too far from the truth, if you overlooked the fact he had to leave out the real reason we were in a salvage yard at this hour.

In fact, he did a fantastic job of sidestepping, creating a plausible alternative story—we were here to purchase scrap sheet metal for a home renovation project. I assumed Martin meant my home as he had no permanent residence locally that I knew of. Still, I was having a hard time conjuring a practical use for repurposed sheet metal.

When the officer asked about the late hour, Martin simply said, "The nature of my work prevents me from getting out during normal business hours. Nicolas—Mr. Oliveri—was kind enough to meet us after hours so that we could make our purchase."

I frowned, realizing I hadn't even known the man's name. How sad was that?

"Was the victim, Mr. Oliveri, accustomed to

fulfilling these late-night requests?" the officer asked.

"Yes," Martin replied, grasping my hand as I involuntarily twitched at the fabrication.

The officer nodded and noted Martin's response in his notebook before turning to me. When I had nothing more to add, he gave us the cursory reminder to contact them if we remembered anything else, just as another officer strode toward us and leaned in to whisper something into his ear.

Martin tugged my arm and tilted his head back and down. Glancing at the officer, who was frowning as the other spoke in hushed tones, I looked to the place where Martin had nodded, my eyes widening as he wiggled his opposite hand behind his back. In it was a tanned leather Moleskin journal, no bigger than an index card.

Movement behind us caused the officers to stop their conversation, their forms rigid and faces stony as the sound of crunching gravel drew closer.

Before I could turn to see what had captured their attention, a familiar voice echoed through the air, sending shivers up my spine.

"Why am I not surprised to find the two of you here."

It was not a question.

I also didn't need to witness his expression for confirmation.

Detective Ramirez was clearly not amused.

I gave Martin the side-eye, hoping he could sell his pile of fiction to Ramirez as convincingly as he had to the officer. Unfortunately, the detective was already well versed in Martin's game.

"Did I not warn you, Ajax?" I quivered as he called me by my nickname, which was typically reserved for friendlier situations. When I remained silent, he opted for sarcasm. "Well, this is a first. You've got nothing to say?"

"We've already given our statements." Martin stepped in, nodding at the officer, who shifted uncomfortably from one foot to the other while looking from Martin to Ramirez.

Noting that the two appeared to be in some

sort of Old West standoff, I muttered under my breath, "Not helping."

"I'll take things from here," Ramirez told the officer, who didn't attempt to mask his relief as he skedaddled toward the scene. Once the man was far enough away that the conversation could not be overheard, Ramirez tilted his head toward his cruiser. "Let's take a ride."

"Should we call representation?" Martin asked, crossing his arms.

I noted the logbook was conspicuously missing from his hand this time around.

"Up to you," Ramirez replied, "but if you come quietly, I won't insist on handcuffs."

I noted he hadn't read us our rights, though I wondered how we would collect Martin's car later. I assumed Ramirez wouldn't be making a round trip. At least not with us.

Martin lifted his chin. "Lead the way, Detective. Arianna and I have nothing to hide." Then, as if sensing my hesitation added, "Don't worry about the vehicle. I'll fetch it once the detective is finished with us. Surely, he'll have better things to do than chauffeur two law-abiding citizens around."

Ramirez rolled his eyes while I nodded absently, thinking that there had to be many open homicide cases in Phoenix. How was it that Ramirez, one of several detectives, was assigned to this one? And why had he not stayed at the scene to investigate?

Sensing my scrutiny, he avoided eye contact as he ushered us to his cruiser. When he opened the back door, Martin walked around, opened the front passenger side door, and hopped in.

I caught a hint of a smirk as he pulled the door shut. Ramirez's frown was not so inconspicuous, causing a snicker to escape.

"What's that?" he asked as I climbed into the back.

"Nothing," I replied, withholding a smile. "Nothing at all."

"Hmpf," he grumbled as he retreated to the driver's side and fired up the engine.

It was going to be a long ride to the station.

Or was it?

Ramirez pulled into a parking lot that was slightly less sketchy than the one at the salvage yard and shut off the engine before turning toward us.

"Okay, you two. Left to right. Top to bottom. What's going on?"

"Which is it? Left to right or top to bottom?" I sniped.

"I see handcuffs in your future, AJ. How about you, Singer? You want this one for a cellmate?" He nodded his head in my direction, a smirk playing on his lips.

Martin frowned before relaying the events that had transpired leading up to our arrival at the salvage yard. He left out a few carefully selected bits here and there, including my request for his assistance. And, of course, the journal.

Ramirez was silent for a moment, perhaps mulling it over. Finally, he turned to me.

"I thought I told you not to involve him."

"Are you seriously chastising me?" I scoffed. "I'd think a dead body would take precedence over your 'I told you so,' which Martin obviously had no part of."

Ramirez held up a hand as Martin opened his mouth. "It takes priority, as does your blatant obstruction of justice. You should know better." He looked at Martin before turning back to me. "You, I expect it from, but without your *usual* partner in crime—"

"You wait just a minute, *Detective*," I growled. "That's a low blow and you know it."

"Got your attention now, don't I?"

I conjured several fitting comebacks, but Martin gave me a single head shake.

"Arianna's not entirely responsible. I insisted on inserting myself into this…situation upon learning of Leah's disappearance." When Ramirez narrowed his eyes, Martin added, "Despite her shenanigans and sometimes annoying colloquialisms, I've grown fond of her. And if she's important to Arianna, then she's important to me."

Ramirez shook his head. "You expect me to believe—"

It was Martin's turn to interject. "It doesn't really matter *what* you believe, Detective. As Arianna often says, 'It is what it is.' Period."

"Martin's right," I replied, giving him an appreciative nod—the man actually paid attention once in a while. "Besides, we've come clean with what we know. Can you say the same?"

Ramirez narrowed his eyes, forming creases at the corners that highlighted the growing dark patches beneath. "Are you suggesting that I've been less than forthcoming?"

"Your response, as well as your other, non-verbal cues, suggest you have been." Martin shrugged as Ramirez's gaze shifted to him. "Look at your body language. One typically wouldn't respond with such combativeness if he was telling the truth."

Caught. Ramirez shifted his stony gaze to me. But I wasn't about to go easy on him either. There was no "good" cop in this scenario.

"We know you were holding back on the second blood type."

"Hmm. And did this information come about in the same way that you learned about Oliveri, that he was among the last people that either Leah or Shelby spoke to before they disappeared?" When neither of us spoke, he responded, "Pot, meet Kettle. I divulged more than I should have because of your connection to the case." He glanced at me. "Despite my better judgment. As for the second blood type. No one was to know. Not even the two of you. We needed it, in case…" His voice drifted off, as did his gaze.

"You think they're dead, don't you?" Martin asked, causing me to suck in a breath, wishing he hadn't put it out there.

Leah wasn't dead. Couldn't be dead.

Ramirez puffed out a long breath. "Before Oliveri, I would have said no. But someone's cleaning up loose ends. Which means Shelby and Leah are both fair game."

"Perhaps there are other plans for them," Martin replied.

"What do you mean?" I definitely didn't care for the way this conversation was going.

Ramirez nodded. "Martin's right. They were snatched for a reason. And Oliveri was killed."

"But you aren't sure, are you?"

Ramirez worked his jaw. "I wouldn't have left an active crime scene for this little sidebar if that's what you're asking."

"So you're just using your position to pick our brains," I replied. "Without offering any form of reciprocation."

"I *am* still the one with the handcuffs."

"You may have the implements, but you have zero control." Ramirez raised a brow at Martin's apt comeback.

He surveyed Martin for a moment. "Fine. You and your 'network' have certainly gotten a leg-up on this. And I need leads. Fast."

I winced. Martin wasn't a fan of overt finger

quotes and only used them sparingly, typically when he wanted to get a rise out of me. But for Ramirez to shove a reference to Martin's network in his face in that manner?

I wanted no part of that.

"Are you suggesting we work together?" I asked, not bothering to assess Martin's demeanor. "Because you agreed to quid pro quo earlier, then reneged. How can we trust that you'll stay true to your word this time around?"

"Because this time, we really *are* running out of time," Ramirez huffed.

"As if we weren't before," I growled.

"Like I said, Oliveri's death takes this to another level. If he had inside information—the kind that could be obtained and used before…" Ramirez glanced away as his words faded.

I thought again of the journal Martin had pilfered from the salvage yard, but he responded before I could say anything.

"We'll assist you in any way we can, Detective, as long as you are forthcoming as you can possibly be, given your…limitations." Without waiting for Ramirez's reply, he added, "Keep in mind, we'll know when you've elected to withhold pertinent details."

"Is that a threat, Singer?" Ramirez tilted his head as Martin shook his.

"Just a reminder to keep the playing field level and the threats at bay. They serve no one—especially not Leah or Shelby."

CHAPTER TEN

Sufficiently schooled, Ramirez set us free. And while he didn't end up hauling us off to jail in handcuffs, he didn't drive us back to Martin's vehicle, either. Instead, he dropped us at the nearest convenience store without so much as a word. I swore I saw a smirk slip when Ramirez noted the downturn of Martin's mouth as he surveyed our surroundings, but it vanished just as quickly as Martin thanked him and reached out to shake his hand.

"Perfect. Arianna and I can take it from here. We appreciate your…generosity, Detective Ramirez."

Ramirez muttered something inaudible before slamming the door of his cruiser and pulling away.

"Mmm, quaint," Martin murmured before tapping on a contact from his phone.

"Let me guess, one of your network peeps is gonna swoop in and collect us in a dark, windowless panel van so that we can get debriefed," I quipped.

"If you haven't already gotten your fill of being probed for one night, it could certainly be arranged." When I raised a brow, he chuckled. "I thought an Uber would be more suitable, given the circumstances."

"What about your car?"

"We can't exactly head straight back after the detective…so insistently removed us from the scene."

"True. But aren't you worried about leaving it in *that* neighborhood?"

"With a full investigation underway? It's the safest place it could be at the moment." Martin chuckled. "I'll have the driver drop you at your house and then take me to the nearest hotel and deal with the vehicle later."

I'm not sure what came over me, but I shook my head. "Nope. Not necessary. I've got plenty of room." When his eyes widened and his mouth twitched, I quickly added, "Don't worry, I won't make you stay in Leah's room."

"I wasn't worried…about that." He looked down and seemed to struggle for words. "Are you sure…that it wouldn't be awkward?"

I patted his leg. "I'm giving you a place to sleep for the night—err, make it the morning—not an invitation to move in so that we can drink cocoa, braid each other's hair and sing sappy songs from the good ol' days."

His eyes widened. "So *that's* what people your age do."

I suppressed a chuckle. Either he had no idea or was revolted by the possibility. Regardless, he looked uncomfortable.

"Just kidding, Martin." He only looked partially relieved, his brows still furrowed as his shoulders sagged. "Seriously, I'd feel better having someone else around."

To be honest, between my nosy neighbors and a sometimes menacing-looking canine companion, the loneliness was starting to get to me. The house, even with Nicoh snuffing around, was just too quiet.

Martin studied me for a moment. If he could

see beyond my ruse, he said nothing and instead nodded over my shoulder.

"That's our driver. Probably shouldn't make him wait."

I glanced behind me as Martin waved a hand at the bright blue Toyota Prius that edged toward us.

Neither of us spoke on the ride to my house and even though Martin had been there before, he squirmed in his seat like an uncomfortable child. I patted his hand, causing him to flinch. At least the squiggling had stopped. When his eyes met mine, a look passed between us, only to be broken moments later by an exuberant Uber driver, announcing that we had arrived at our destination.

We shuffled into the house, where Nicoh waited expectantly at the door, his tail curled high as he wagged his tail side to side, murmuring a series of whoo-woos, which increased in intensity when Martin leaned in to offer head scratches.

"Don't encourage him," I warned, laughing.

Martin chuckled. "He is rather…demanding."

"Indicative of the breed," I replied, shocked

as Martin engaged Nicoh in a round of doggie-baby talk, which was met with appreciative howls.

"Also tells you a lot about his human," he teased, noting my expression.

"Ha ha," I replied, pretending to be offended. Nicoh's bright eyes and tongue-hanging smile gave me away as I chuckled and joined in on the scratches.

"Mommy's not demanding, is she." It wasn't a question, and of course, Nicoh betrayed me, resuming his full-blown howls.

Martin did his best to hold back, but when my laughter turned to piggy-snorts, his own chuckles only egged Nicoh on all the more and after another round, we were lucky to catch our breaths.

"I should probably let him out," I said after the mild-mannered hysterics had, for the most part, subsided. "I can make us something to eat if you're hungry." It had been a weird night that had transitioned into morning and I couldn't re-member the last real meal I'd had.

"Why don't I pull something together while you tend to Nicoh," Martin replied. When I shot him a dubious look, he added, "I think I can find my way around the kitchen."

"The kitchen, I'm not worried about," I retorted. "The supplies, on the other hand? Not so much. Sorry to say I haven't had much time to do any shopping since I returned from L.A. And anything that I do have—I'd check it closely for mold or other…oddities."

Martin chuckled. "Considering I've dealt with worse, I think I can make do."

I waved a hand. "Alright, be my guest. But know…you were warned. Any trip to the emergency room is totally on you." I gave him a cryptic laugh, followed by a wink as I ushered Nicoh into the backyard.

As expected, Nicoh made the rounds, sniffing every nook and cranny while I check the gates to ensure they were locked. I'd learned the hard way that you can never be too sure.

By the time we moved back into the house, the kitchen was filled with the delicious scent of something homey and warm.

"Grilled cheese?" Martin beamed as he plated two gooey and perfectly crusted portions of cheesy goodness before winking. "With Hatch green chilies that I found stashed in your freezer. Thankfully, you had the foresight to vacuum-seal them."

"Ooooh," I sputtered before the drool trailed out of the corner of my mouth.

"And…" He reached across the counter and pulled a napkin off a second plate, revealing another scrumptious-looking sandwich.

"Peanut butter and pickle!" I rasped as the salivation surged into overdrive. "How did you know?"

Martin offered a broad smile. "Because it was your mother—err, Alison's—favorite. She could put away a couple when she was pregnant with you and Victoria."

I fought a shudder the mention of my biological mother and twin sister—both of whom had been murdered. Thankfully, Martin didn't notice as he busied himself cutting the sandwiches into fours.

"Anyway, I wasn't sure which you'd prefer, so I made both."

"Thank you," I breathed. "I might be able to 'make do', as you said. And possibly even manage to share."

He chuckled as I seated myself at the kitchen

island and slid a piece—okay, two—of each sandwich onto my plate.

As I took a bite of the peanut butter and pickle and moaned, his eyes widened. "Should I worry about my fingers?"

"Nah, though you may want to grab a piece or two yourself while I'm distracted," I teased, moaning even louder after I took a bite of the grilled cheese.

Martin placed a glass of milk in front of me, careful not to stray too close to the beasty's plate while she was eating.

"Thank you," I murmured after polishing off a piece of each sandwich.

"My pleasure," he replied, nodding as he finally bit into his own. "Not bad."

"'Not bad'? You could open a food truck and sell out within the hour. Or a little bistro in Scottsdale and sell these puppies for big money. You'd have a line around the block."

"Probably need to add a sizable liquor license into that equation," he murmured. When he caught me snickering, he blushed. "Oh, did I say that out loud?"

"You slay me," I replied, nearly spitting out the milk I'd just slogged down. "Pretty much on the mark for these parts. We do tend to like our libations."

"That would be a form of highway robbery, wouldn't it?" he replied, somewhat thoughtful, as though he was actually contemplating the idea.

I almost burst out laughing at the sincerity of his response, though a snort might have escaped. *"Please*, it wouldn't even be that difficult. You'd just slap some fancy name to it and you'd be an overnight sensation. Now that I think about it, you wouldn't even need a food truck. You could probably sell the goods out of the back of that car of yours."

"You know, that's not a bad idea. Maybe we could even hock our treats outside the clubs, in the wee hours of the morning." I chuckled, knowing that he was right. It would be a big hit after all the club-goers were done partying. A serious munchie-fest was likely to ensue.

We fell into a comfortable silence, each munching on Martin's simple but divinely delicious concoctions.

I was the one who disrupted the quiet. "Do you ever wonder…" my voice trailed off as I struggled to decide how to pose what had been weighing on my mind.

"How things might have turned out had I not made the choices I did," Martin completed my sentence, picking at the crust of his remaining section of grilled cheese.

My brows hiked at the preciseness of his deduction. When his eyes met mine, I nodded, causing him to release a sad chuckle.

"Of course it plagues me…haunts my every waking moment." He stopped, gauging my expression. "What? Did you not think I was capable of such emotional depth?" When I shrugged, he winced. "I'm sure my…demeanor…often gives one that impression, but it is far from the truth."

"Why?" I asked.

He tilted his head. "Why what?"

"Why do you mask your feelings?"

He shrugged. "Self-protection. Fear."

"Fear?" I hadn't considered that he was no less immune than the rest of us. He certainly had never alluded to it.

As though reading my mind, he blew out a breath before responding, "Same as a lot of people, I would suppose. Judgment. Betrayal. Plus, depending on the day, a combo of any number of anxiety-inducing concerns, doubts, worries."

I nodded. He had been a party to all of the above.

"We might be the same in that way," I murmured. "Only I may have a biggie that hasn't made its way to your highlight reel."

"Oh?" Martin leaned back, assessing me.

"Abandonment." I cast my eyes down. Shame coloring my cheeks like a blossoming poppy.

"Don't."

He reached across and gripped my hand. "Don't consume your soul with an emotion that was not your doing. You feel embarrassed. Shameful. Unworthy even. Am I right?"

Still looking down, I nodded. "Among other things."

"Look at me." After a moment, I did and found his eyes searching mine as he now clasped both hands in his. "*None* of it is your fault, Arianna."

"But people…leave me," my voice cracked as the sting of tears threatened to escape. "I create circumstances that force them to make choices. Terrible choices."

"Bollocks."

"What the heck does that even mean?" I chuckled, still barely managing to keep my sniffling and waterworks under wraps.

I wasn't sure what had come over me, but something about Martin always seemed to draw out the thoughts, fears and emotions I tried to hide from others. Perhaps we were more similar than I liked to admit.

I still struggled, however, to put all of my faith or trust in him. There were too many questions, not to mention the things he wanted I could not…would not give him, including the chips embedded with his research that he'd entrusted to Victoria and me before everything went south and our worlds were divided.

"I think you know what it means." Martin pulled me out of my reverie. "We're responsible for our own choices. No one else's."

Even though he was right, I wasn't willing to admit it yet. I shifted the conversation.

"So, the item you stole…err, borrowed from the salvage yard."

"Ah, yes." Martin moved to his jacket and extracted the worn leather journal, carefully placing it on the counter between us.

I picked it up and thumbed through it. Dates, times, initials.

"A logbook of sorts," I commented.

"It is," Martin replied, quirking a brow at my lackluster response.

"It's the forensic accountant's?" When he nodded, I added, "And you just happened to stumble upon it after we found his body?"

Martin frowned. "No, he told me where to find it along with his cell phone from which I extracted the SIM card."

"Um… What?"

"He was afraid—to the point of paranoia—that something would happen to him and told me where he'd hidden them, should anything go wrong."

"Turns out he was right to be paranoid. But I still don't get why this journal is so important now that he's dead. It's not like we have the magic decoder ring that will help us decipher it."

"That may be true, but it also might be the only shot we have at finding Leah and Shelby alive."

CHAPTER ELEVEN

I groaned. Of course it was.

But it didn't make the person who'd created the coded entry system any less dead.

Martin absorbed my facial expressions. "Don't worry, I have people who can tackle this."

I shook my head. This was so much bigger than that. "Yeah, well, so do I."

Martin cocked his head. Okay, perhaps I'd been a bit snarky.

Sighing, I reframed my approach. "Listen, I brought this situation to your attention and you agreed to help me out, which I am truly grateful for. Having said that, I don't need to fight with you, too—you know, in addition to Ramirez." When he nodded, I moved on. "Why don't we scan the pages and send them to both groups of 'people'?"

Martin frowned. "We both know that you don't have people. You have *one* guy."

"Figure of speech, Martin. I'm not here to argue semantics with you," I growled. "Besides, *my* guy can probably do more with his little pinky inside of ten seconds than your entire network can in a week."

Martin's overt scoffing was not lost on me. "Gotta scanner?"

I had a few choice words to share, but ground my teeth instead before directing him to my office. I connected the scanner in silence. When done, Martin got down to business, immortalizing the journal pages in a digital format.

I turned to him as I exited. "We'll do it your way, but I want a copy, just in case. And, no fair sending it to your people until I say so."

Martin stopped mid-scan, frowning. "I wouldn't dream of it."

Staring him down until I was satisfied that he was telling the truth, I left him to it and went about cleaning up. Absently, I glanced at my laptop and spotted a notification.

Tamryn had left a message.

Sucking in a breath, I read it.

"She wants to meet but that I have to come alone," I told Martin when he returned to the kitchen several minutes later.

When he quirked a brow, I turned my laptop around and stabbed at the screen.

He was quiet as he absorbed the message, his emotions revealing nothing.

"Well?" I could stand the silence no more.

"Respond," he shrugged, "but insist on bringing a friend."

"What? No." I shook my head. "She won't go for that."

"I won't have you walking into a trap, either." Martin's voice was firm, which forced me to meet his gaze.

I nodded. "I get that but…"

"But I'm an old fuddy-duddy and I may scare her off." Martin polished off my sentence.

"I didn't say that." I fought the urge to agree on the latter as he studied me.

Apparently, my body language betrayed me.

"Mmm…you didn't need to. Your face said

it all." He chuckled when I gave him a curious look. "Come on, the way your mouth twisted as you scrunched your nose? You don't need to be a genius to figure that one out."

"Maybe just a mad scientist," I muttered, causing him to hack out a chuckle. "All I meant was that you may represent the type of person—say, a father figure—that Tamryn is trying to escape."

"I still say no."

"You don't have a say in the matter. Tamryn was *my* idea." I thrust a hand on my hip, but Martin just shook his head from side to side.

"And you can't keep me from following you. So you might as well invite me to the party." His tone was adamant and combined with his own rigid body language, was not-so-fatherly after all.

Truth be told, it was downright belligerent.

I threw up my hands. "Gah! First the journal and now this."

When Martin shrugged, I growled but directed my frustration into crafting a response to Tamryn, asking her to name the date, time and place.

She replied within seconds.

Soon.

Exasperated, first by Martin, then by Tamryn, my tone turned snappish. "Nothing is happening tonight. Let's get some sleep and then we'll discuss this further while retrieving your car tomorrow…err, later today."

Martin checked his watch, took in Nicoh's snoozing form and finally conceded. Once I set him up in the guest room, I checked my notifications but Tamryn hadn't followed up. I hoped that her interpretation of "soon" was on the same end of the spectrum as mine. Otherwise, if I hadn't heard from her by the time we collected Martin's car, I would have to craft another plan.

Truth be told, I wasn't all that great with anything that went beyond Plan "B."

Plus, Leah and Shelby's lives depended on it.

I hoped I wouldn't have to go that route, especially if Tamryn felt like I was backing her into a corner. It wouldn't serve anyone's best interest if we got off on the wrong foot.

I closed the lid on my laptop and placed my head in my hands. My frustration and anxiety were only outweighed by the exhaustion that had been plotting a mutiny. Catching me in a moment of weakness, it charged into battle and despite the rising sun, I quickly surrendered, letting the darkness take over, transforming my dreams into nightmares.

I shuddered awake, my heart slamming against my chest in an erratic rhythm, threatening to bully its way out. Shaky, I squinted at my surroundings from behind bleary eyes, groaning as I realized the repercussions of falling asleep facedown, partially on a granite countertop, partially on the lid of a laptop. The imprint of the laptop's logo on my right cheek did nothing to brighten my spirits as I rubbed it with my fingers until it was no longer numb.

The drool that had trailed out during my slumber would just have to wait.

Suddenly, I remembered I had company just as a voice resounded behind me.

"Sleep well?"

I grumbled something in response before remembering my manners. Martin may have been, well, Martin, but he *was* a guest in my home.

"You?"

Martin nodded, carefully avoiding my gaze once he'd taken in my appearance. "Very comfortable. Thank you."

I was thankful he didn't make any commentary or add any words of wisdom about quality over quantity. Because I had gotten neither and it would have struck a nerve.

Speaking of nerves.

"You change your mind about tagging along?"

Martin shook his head once. "Certainly not." After surveying me for a moment, he added, "And if you try to sidestep me, I'll have no choice but to involve Detective Ramirez. We both know what he'll do next."

That would only hinder our efforts and risk precious time for both Leah and Shelby.

I knew he wouldn't hesitate, but I wasn't tossing in the white flag just yet.

"Two-way street, Martin. You abscond with the journal and the scanned pages, along with the SIM card and I'll reward you with the same kindness," I retorted. "And don't forget, I've got Ramirez on speed dial."

Martin's brows pinched together. "Ah yes, the Dirty Harry image that pops up when he calls, along with some sort of whistling ringtone that one typically associates with what people in my day called spaghetti Westerns. An odd combination where the detective is concerned, though taking your perspective into consideration, perhaps not that far off the beaten path."

I tilted my head. "You're familiar with what that means, then?" He offered a curt nod, to which I replied, "Good. Just so we're clear."

Martin twisted his mouth. It landed somewhere between a frown and smelling something offensive before he responded. "Crystal."

"Let's retrieve your vehicle then, shall we?" It wasn't necessarily a win, but I lightened my tone. Martin didn't need to know that I was still on the fence about including him in my plans for meeting Tamryn.

I'd need to make that decision soon enough, without further commentary from the peanut gallery.

After letting Nicoh out, I shoved a cup of coffee in Martin's hands, grabbed my keys, and headed out the door, only to find him scrunching his nose as he sipped from the steaming mug.

"What's the matter, not *gourmet* enough for you?" I sniped.

"Gourmet is one thing. Drinkable is quite another," he replied, rubbing the tip of his tongue with his free hand. "It was better when Leah was in charge of selecting the brew."

"Noted." I pulled an ice cube from the freezer, plopped it into his container and watched him gasp as liquid sashayed particularly close to his hand. "How's that for hospitality?" I suppressed a chuckle when Martin froze in place, open-mouthed and blinking as he watched the cube bobble and sink.

It took him a moment to collect himself before following me to my vehicle. Though, to his credit, he was still clutching the mug.

The return trip to the salvage yard was uneventful and pleasantly void of chitchat. I wasn't sure what I'd expected upon arrival—crime scene tape, barricades and the usual hubbub—but instead, we were met with silence. And except for evidence of a few burned-out flares, there was no sign anything out of the ordinary had occurred in the last several hours.

Certainly not a homicide.

I grumbled upon seeing that the gates to the yard had been secured with chains.

"Let's not sit around pondering this for too long," he replied, though no question had been posed.

Out loud, anyway.

For once, we were in agreement.

"Meet me back at the house?" I mumbled absently, squinting at the yard, trying to get past that niggling feeling I'd missed something.

Something important.

I tore my eyes away, only to find Martin nodding. "I have a couple of errands to run, but I'm sure you'll text me if you hear from the girl."

Inwardly groaning, I realized in a moment of distraction that I'd essentially invited him along. I nodded, but gritted my teeth. I still wasn't excited about his insistence on participating in this venture, primarily because I didn't want to risk scaring Tamryn off.

Then again, at least Martin would be there to either mitigate any damage or pull my butt off the battlefield before things went sideways or I got caught up in something that I couldn't talk my way out of. My thoughts drifted to Leah.

If she hadn't been able to manage it alone, how could I?

I sighed. What I wanted to do and what I needed to do were seldom in concert. This time was no different.

I hoped Tamryn would agree, just as I received her message, designating a time and place.

I slipped the phone into my pocket and waved to Martin as he reached the Camry.

What happened in the avenues stayed in the avenues…and now, safely out of sight, Martin didn't need to be privy to any of it.

CHAPTER TWELVE

Staring at Tamryn's choice of location and time for the meet, I realized I had one opportunity left to evade Martin.

Until he walked into my kitchen via the side door.

Wait—wasn't he supposed to be running some errands?

"Hope you don't mind that I didn't knock first?" he asked hesitantly.

I shook my head, then squinted at my phone again.

Wrong move.

"You heard from Tamryn."

I waved Opportunity goodbye.

"I did."

"And?" He stepped closer, not enough to invade my space, though I did subconsciously pull the laptop toward me. Martin caught the gesture and studied me for a moment. "I thought we already discussed this."

"Gimme a second, would you? I just got the message and am trying to digest it," I ground out while giving him the stink-eye. "And for the record, there really wasn't a discussion. You sort of inserted yourself using the power of veiled threats."

Martin scoffed, but said nothing.

I gnawed the inside of my cheek and after a few moments of deliberation forced out a response. "She wants to meet at the Arizona State University Research Park. At a quarter past twelve. And I'm not talking in the afternoon."

"You can't be serious." I turned the computer around so that he could read the message. Once he'd confirmed it for himself, he glanced up. "It's the weekend, so it will be a ghost town."

I hiked a shoulder. "Likely the reason Tamryn chose it."

"I don't like it. All the more reason you

should give up the idea of getting rid of me and going it alone."

"What? I never said that."

"You didn't need to."

"Right. My facial expressions revealed all. Thank you, Obi Wan, Jedi Master and gifted one in all ways of The Force."

Martin's brow furrowed. "I'm no Jedi Master, but I'd probably stay away from the poker tables if I were you."

"Sage advice," I mumbled, though somewhat amused by his lack of knowledge related to anything associated with popular culture. "It's just what I need at a time like this."

Martin shrugged. "You're welcome?"

I rolled my eyes and as if on cue, Nicoh entered the kitchen, gave us both a once-over, followed by a huff as he shuffled back to wherever he'd been napping.

"That's right, folks—nothing to see here," I replied, chuckling when that, too, was lost on my Bio-Pop.

"Come on, Martin. Let's talk strategy over some tacos. I'm starving and I'm betting you are, too. We've gotta keep our strength up— then, we've gotta girl to see."

Martin opened his mouth, shut it.

"What?"

His face flushed as he worked to formulate an appropriate response. "You're not cooking, are you?"

I raised a brow. "You don't think I can manage tacos?" When his blush deepened, I hacked out a laugh. "Don't worry. I have a place in mind."

"Okay," he replied slowly, though it came off sounding way too relieved.

"I'll remember this, you know."

Martin pressed his lips together, then pooched them out before responding, "Oh yes, I *know*."

I withheld commentary as I grabbed my keys and headed toward the door.

Noticing Martin's hesitation, I raised my hands. "What?"

"We're not taking Nicoh?"

"You've seen his table manners. What do you think?" I rolled my eyes, tossed my bag over my shoulder and walked out.

As I headed toward my vehicle, Martin piped up. "Why don't we take my vehicle?"

"First the cooking, now my driving?" I

mumbled under my breath.

Had I not been so distracted about everything that had transpired in the last several days, I would have given his request some consideration. Instead, I shrugged and gestured for him to take the lead.

Thankfully, he wasn't one to gloat—Martin was way too efficient for that—as he opened the door for me before striding to the driver's side, noting his surroundings before he slipped into the seat beside me.

"Everything okay?"

He nodded once and turned on the ignition. Considering he hadn't asked me for directions, it amused me to no end when he pulled out of the driveway and into the neighborhood.

I inwardly smirked and kept my mouth buttoned, waiting for him to speak—almost delighting in anticipation of the ask.

But as we turned onto a familiar street, I frowned.

"You knew?"

"Give me some credit, Arianna. Though I pride myself on being observant, I also managed to dissect the lingo that you and Leah tossed about so freely. So yes, I happened to know where the best tacos in town are located. In fact, to quote Leah, it's the place where you two 'get your taco fix on.'" He offered his own smirk, to which I rolled my eyes.

"Whatever. It's true, though."

"Yes, I know." When I raised a brow, he added, "After a while, I had to venture out by myself to see what the fuss was all about."

"And we were right," my tone was smug as he pulled into the lot.

"Yes, the two of you were right—they're the best," Martin replied, casting a look over his shoulder as he climbed out of the vehicle, "in *this* town."

I squinted and was prepared to launch into a retort, but heard him chuckling as he closed the door and began moving toward the establishment's entrance.

Nah, I would not to give him the satisfaction of getting my goat. Not this time, anyway.

It was an order at the counter type of joint, so at least Martin had the common courtesy to wait until I'd caught up with him+. When I stepped to the counter and made my selection, I moved aside so that he could make his, only to find him shrugging. "I'll have the same."

Considering I liked my sauce on the hot side, I was tempted to warn him but figured this wasn't his first time at the rodeo and let the chips—or in this case, hot lips—fall, however, they were intended to.

I offered to pay, and though I could tell Martin wanted to object, he nodded, then elected to secure a table while I handled the tab.

"Nice choice," I said when I found him sitting at a table on the patio that overlooked the plaza. It did not escape my notice that he had positioned himself so that he could see people both coming and going, as well as vehicles entering or exiting the street.

"Figured it was a nice evening, might as well make the best of it." He watched me watching him but said nothing.

"Indeed. So few days that we can do so during the hot months. Gotta make the best of the good ones while we can. Plus, there's the view." The sarcasm was not lost on him.

"Just getting a lay of the land, so speak."

"Um…hmm." When he quirked a brow, I added, "You sure you're not worried about something?"

Martin frowned. "Worried? No. Overly cautious? Perhaps." He shrugged, glancing back toward the street. "Old habits die hard, I suppose."

"You ever think you'll feel you'll be able to drop your guard? That you'll feel completely…"

"Safe," he finished before shifting to meet my gaze. "I honestly don't know. But if I ever do, I'll let you know."

I nodded and thankfully, our number was called, saving me from having to respond. As it was, a lump had formed in my throat, reflecting on the similarity of the conversation I had recently shared with my best friend and how she, too, just wanted to feel safe again.

If Martin had spent a lifetime side-stepping land mines, even after giving up everything to escape his past, where did that leave the rest of us?

I collected our order, harnessed my emotions, and headed back to the table. Once the food was doled out, tested, and given the double thumbs-up, the conversation shifted to strategy—how we would approach Tamryn while explaining Martin's presence, how the questions should be framed to elicit the information we needed without scaring her off and of course, contingencies should anything go astray.

As Martin pointed out, just because he'd insinuated himself didn't mean Tamryn wasn't above bringing someone along as well. And while I knew Martin's intentions for being on site were mostly legit, neither of us could say the same if Tamryn brought her own backup.

After eating, we strolled along a nearby canal, lit only by the occasional overhead lampposts. Had I been alone, I might have been nervous, but Martin's confident stride and demeanor made any hesitation fall away and before long, he was checking his watch. "Best get a move-on. We've got a girl to see."

On the way, I bit my nails down to the nub as we neared the research park. The area was relatively expansive and anything and everything could go sideways since it was vacant. No one would be the wiser until it was too late.

"Nervous?"

"Just too quiet," I murmured.

"All the better to identify possible threats," he replied, and when I gave him the side-eye, he added, "If we use all of our senses."

"Well, I'm not tasting anything, if that's what you're suggesting," I groused. "Already fell into that trap once, when my Geology 101 professor insisted we get a sense of the rocks by licking them, and all I received for my efforts was a mouth full of salty grit."

"I was merely suggesting that we keep our ears and eyes open."

"You could've just said that instead of this 'all of our senses' buffoonery," I muttered under my breath, shifting subjects when his head jerked toward me. "What do you suppose made her select *this* location?"

"Avid bird-watcher?" he offered, chuckling when I rolled my eyes. "Your guess is as good as mine."

"Well, she obviously has some familiarity with the area; otherwise, she wouldn't have chosen it. Hey, why are you parking here?" I asked when Martin pulled into a lot that was nowhere near the location Tamryn had indicated.

"Precautionary. We're hoofing it the rest of the way in."

"So much for a quick getaway."

"If we end up in an ambush, this will at least give us a chance to get away," he replied, his tone matter-of-fact.

"Well, if that doesn't put a glass half-empty spin on things."

He raised a brow. "I assumed you wanted me to be honest. Would you prefer a version with four-leaf clovers and a dancing leprechaun?"

"That's just plain mean, Martin," I sniped.

He blinked. "Come again?"

"Everyone knows the leprechaun steals all the marshmallows out of the Lucky Charms."

Martin frowned. "As usual, I have no idea what that means."

"As usual, precisely my point." When I received a bland stare, I muttered, "Never mind," before getting out of the car and making my way to our meeting location, which I guesstimated was about a quarter of a mile.

We'd have to hustle to make it in time, so I wished Martin would have shared his 'precautionary' measures with me. I could hear him tromping behind me and was about to say as much when a beacon of light blasted me in the face, preventing me from seeing who had wielded it, as I lifted my arm to shade my eyes from the blinding glare.

I didn't have to wait long.

"Strike one, Arianna Jackson. I told you to come alone."

CHAPTER THIRTEEN

Before I could utter a syllable, Martin stepped in, donning his own flashlight, but when he panned it in the direction Tamryn's voice had come from, she was nowhere to be found.

I squinted into the darkness, cursing. Considering the sheer number of trees, paths and random hidey-holes, there were too many ways she could have made her escape.

I peered around again, but Tamryn was long gone. I had defied her request and gotten slapped upside the head for my blatant disregard of her terms. I'd known this might happen and still, I'd allowed Martin to worm his way into my brain, using his analytical rationalization mumbo-jumbo. And look where that had gotten me.

I could hear Leah now—even envision her particular facial expression—as she chastised me. And yup, she would have been right. I had no one to blame but myself for once again allowing this silver-tongued fatherly type to use his power of persuasion to get me to do what he wanted.

It was time to pull up the big girl panties and face facts. I had gambled with time that Leah and Shelby did not have. And lost. My only thread had effectively been cut. More time, ticking away.

And now I had to make it right.

First, however, I had to deal with the problem loitering in front of me.

"Well, I hope you have a backup plan, because this one certainly fell way short of the mark."

He nodded, though he didn't bother taking ownership for his part in the epic failure. "Certainly disappointing."

"And predictable." He cast a sideways glance when he caught my tone. "Come on, Martin, you didn't see this coming?"

"I just—"

I raised a hand. "I need some fresh air."

We were already outside, so that spoke volumes.

"Arianna—"

"Go home, Martin, I'll text for an Uber," I interjected, with a terse wave of a hand. "You've done enough for one day."

If he called after me, the blood boiling in my ears blocked the sound as I hastened my pace.

It wasn't until I walked out of the research park that I realized I'd forgotten to call for that Uber. I'd only just touched the app when a lemon-lime shoebox-sized Fiat pulled up, missing my toes by inches.

Before I could hop back, much less squeal, the passenger window rolled down.

"Get in," Tamryn snapped, rapping her fingers on the steering wheel. "Come on! Let's get a move on before the old man catches up."

I glanced over my shoulder before hunkering down so that I could fit in the car. I'd barely gotten one cheek on the seat when she pulled away, leaving me to quickly tuck in while grabbing the tiny flailing passenger door, partially for support and partially because I worried if it ripped free, I'd soon be tumbling on asphalt along with it.

"He's a little old for you, don't you think?"

"What? He's not my—"

"Mep." She cut me off with a zipping motion across her lips. "Sorry, not for me to judge. I've seen way worse, believe me."

I shook my head. "I'm sure you have, but Martin is not my boyfriend. He's my…biological father." Nothing like facing down a minor threat of road rash to kick the truth engine into full gear. Apparently, that little burst of honesty surprised Tamryn as much as it did me.

Her mouth formed a sizable "O" right before she scrunched her pert little nose. "Eeew."

This time, I rolled my eyes. "Get real, Tamryn."

"Yeah, well, he almost cost you. Big time." She glanced at me. "Honestly, I thought you were smarter than that."

"Hmm…you're not alone…"

I shrunk into my seat—as much as one can in a car that was barely designed to fit one person, let alone two. I watched the landscape flitter by as she punched the gas and zipped in and out of neighborhoods. Neither of us spoke, though I was biting my lip to prevent myself from spouting every question I'd conjured over the past few days. I could have been wrong, but it almost seemed like a competition to see who would break the silence first.

I took the opportunity to peruse Tamryn in the flesh. Her chestnut-colored locks fell to her midsection, a hint of a wave danced at the ends. Her makeup was minimal, setting off the paleness of her skin as she flashed me a curious gaze, the greenness of her eyes illuminated by a passing car. Aside from the multi-colored talons insisted on rapping on the steering wheel, she appeared to be more girl-next-door than her former overly made-up, puckered-up social media persona.

"I'm hungry," she abruptly announced before pulling into the parking lot of a 24-hour restaurant boasting "Breakfast served hot and fresh all day!" in neon letters.

Perhaps it was exhaustion, but I snickered as I wondered if that meant everything *not* breakfast-related was served cold, coagulated or burgeoning with mold spores. Take your pick—a diner's demise!

I caught her frowning and realized my inner

thoughts had morphed into outer dialogue. "Sorry. It's been a long couple of days."

She surveyed me but said nothing before she focused on whipping the little contraption into a parking space designated for "Ultra Compact."

As we extricated ourselves from said compact, a flat steel-colored Mustang rumbled into an adjacent spot and two guys who dwarfed The Rock emerged.

I'm not sure what my facial expression projected, but Tamryn didn't seem to care what I thought.

"Roman and the dude I like to call Beefalo are with me." She nodded in their direction as though there had been some confusion.

I cocked my head. "Interesting." But what I really wanted to say was, "Gee, Tamryn, it's okay for you to pack two thuggies along to deal with the likes of little ol' me, but one older dude, the size of one of these guy's biceps backing me up raises your hackles?"

Apparently, this time, my inner commentary translated to my face.

Tamryn snorted. "My rules. You want something from me you play by 'em. Otherwise, it's a long walk home for you, Arianna Jackson.

Never know what may happen to a sweet little thing like you in this part of town."

She may have intended it as a threat, but I took it as an annoying quirk and accepted it as a challenge, nodding for her to take the lead.

The thugs did not follow. Perhaps they had already surpassed their quota of carbs—or "sweet little things" like me—for the day.

We nestled ourselves into a corner booth, as instructed by the sandwich board at the entrance. Glancing about the establishment, a handful of people were seated at the counter drinking coffee—regulars, most likely—plus a table with a couple playing kissy-face over a plate of fries.

"Shame. Those things are gonna get cold if they keep that up," I murmured.

Tamryn glanced over. "Sinful. They're already cold. You think we should report them?"

Just then, the waitress slogged over with a mumbled greeting, exhaustion extending to her half-lidded eyes as she slid us each a menu before padding away.

Tamryn shoved it to the side, lacing her hands together. "So. How do you know Shelby?"

I shrugged. "To be honest, I don't know her—"

"Then why are we meeting?" Tamryn leaned in. "Listen. You said that her life depended on it. What, exactly, are you playing at?"

I raised a hand. "Hold up. There's no 'playing' going on here. Shelby's life and the life of my best friend are at stake. And you may have information that could save them. So spare me the entitled prima donna act, would you? It might work on your followers and for your paid thugs, but for those of us who *see* you for who you are? Please, just stop."

I huffed out a breath for effect, not bothering to look at her before I continued. "If I thought there was another way to obtain what I need and bring my friend home, believe me, I wouldn't have bothered knocking on your proverbial door." Finished with my soapbox, I stared her in the eye.

To her credit, and my surprise, she raised a brow but gestured for me to continue. I told her what little I knew, from the call I'd received from a "friend" while in L.A. to finding Leah's car and learning that she had followed Shelby's last known path after confirming she'd gone missing.

Her gaze didn't waver when I mentioned her

missing acquaintance or that another person was M.I.A. as a result, which either suggested she already knew was involved. Or both.

Before I could rule out any of those options, the waitress materialized at our table, clutching her pad and pen and nodding in my direction.

"I'll have coffee, please." The meal I'd shared with Martin was still sloshing about, likely plotting a mutiny in my stomach.

Tamryn shook her head. "*She'll* also have the Ultimate Scramble with pancakes, loaded with butter—the real stuff—and I'll have the same." Before I could object, our waitress jotted it down, then shuffled to the kitchen. "Believe me, you're gonna need your strength for this conversation. Besides, you look like dog crap, and you're thinner than single-ply toilet paper. If you're not careful, people will start to talk."

I grimaced, for the first time taking in the girl across from me. Not to cast stones back at her, but she could have done with a good dose of her own advice. Unless she'd been using some sort of filter on her social media posts, she'd lost a significant amount of weight. But despite her rail-thin frame and the hollowness of her cheeks, she was still a very pretty girl.

"What I'm about to tell you stays between us —not a word to your 'friend,' your pops, no one —got it?"

I shrugged. Until I heard what she had to offer, I wasn't committing to anything.

Her eyes narrowed. "You don't trust me. Got it. But seeing how you reached out to me, and we share a common interest, I'll let that slide. Besides, by the time I'm done, you'll want to be my new best friend."

I seriously doubted it but then again didn't have a lot to lose, other than time, so I settled in and gestured for her to proceed.

CHAPTER FOURTEEN

"You have to understand that when I got into this, I had no idea what *it* was."

"It?" I prompted.

"Let's just say it's a form of curated courtesy."

"Is that a catch-phrase? Or a type of business?"

Tamryn hesitated before responding. "Never had to put it into context, but I guess I'd say it's a type of…service-oriented business of sorts."

"So, how did you get into it?"

"Was out clubbing in Old Town with a few friends one night and at some point, we all split off—some went to another club—some left with the hottie du jour, whatever." Her lip curled as she chuckled and waved a hand in the air.

"Shortly after they bailed, this chick approached me, said I looked familiar and we started chatting. Before long, a couple of her friends joined us and asked I wanted to tag along to a party. *Sure, why not?* I thought and then commented about following them in my ride, but they just looked at one another and laughed.

"One of them linked arms with me and whispered in my ear, 'Why drive when you can start the party early?' while pulling me out of the club in my Louboutin's. I figured they had called for an Uber or something, but when we exited the club, a Hummer limo was waiting, complete with a driver with slicked-back hair, wearing a snazzy pinstriped suit with penguin shoes—total old-school gangster look. For a minute, I thought we'd gotten our wires crossed and were heading to a speakeasy or maybe some new burlesque show, but the original chick sidled up, giggling. 'Don't worry, no one here bites. At least not yet.' And with a quick wink, she hopped into the limo, gesturing for me to follow suit."

"Quite an undertaking in Louboutin's," I murmured.

Tamryn huffed, rolling her eyes. "Tell me about it. Turns out, the limo itself was plush, decked out in leather—seats, throw pillows, the works—and was stocked with a full bar and a crap-ton of snacks. Most of the girls went straight for the red licorice and gummy bears, forgoing the spirits altogether as the driver secured the door and returned to his own seat, where he maneuvered around the valets and other club-goers mingling outside the club. I passed on both when offered and instead checked out my surroundings, noting that there were no guys with us other than the driver, which struck me as odd.

"The same girl must've noticed my reaction because she told me not to worry, that the 'fresh meat' would join us there—which was not really a concern nor a consideration, but further piqued my interest. As you probably gathered from my social media persona, I'm always up for something new, so I rolled with it as she encouraged me to 'fly with it and make the most of our time to bond and let our hair down before the market opened for business'. She seemed particularly amused when she said it but then flitted on to an entirely different topic with another girl. Whatever…I would have tired of her soon anyway and was glad to be done with idle chitchat.

"I thought we'd be heading to some tricked-out mansion or end up at some old rocker's love shack—believe me, it happens more than you think around here—but no sooner than we'd gone south a few blocks, the driver turned into one of the nearby residential neighborhoods. I had a bad feeling about it and was tempted to feign sickness so that the driver would be forced to pull over to let me out to heave, giving me the chance to make my move. Before I could produce my first retching sound, we pulled up in front of a normal-looking rambler on a quiet, family-friendly street. The driver got out then assisted each of us to the sidewalk. No monkey business, no nothing.

"The girl who appeared to be leading the pack invited us inside. It was not particularly upscale but modern and clean. And except for the usual appliances, a couple of couches, chairs and a framed landscape or two on the wall, there wasn't really anything…personal about the home.

"I asked the chick what was up—had the owners gone on vacation and left her to house-sit? She snickered and made some vague comment about them being snowbirds from somewhere back in Michigan or Wisconsin or one of those types of places people escape to avoid freezing their butts off.

"I must have looked unconvinced because she told me that the home was a vacation property, typically rented to out-of-towners but when the season was in a lull—or the temps in the Phoenix-metro area were too insane to reel even the deal-seekers in—the management company was allowed to use their discretion to option it as a stay-cation, of sorts. Her phrasing, not mine.

"Our conversation was interrupted by the arrival of another Hummer, only this time a herd of dudes in a variety of ages and if their behaviors were any indication, backgrounds. Some were already pretty wasted; others were just pretentious and obnoxious jerks. And some were downright…creepy. I asked her if fraternity-type cattle calls fell into the 'of sorts' category, nodding towards a group of the guys ogling some of the girls while the more boisterous ones made obscene gestures.

"She rolled her eyes and laughed, winking as she replied, 'Don't think those out-of-towners from the Midwest are any less prone to the *What happens in Scottsdale* mentality. These guys don't even register on that scale.'

"A couple of the girls caught her attention before I could ferret out the rest of the plan for the evening, but not before one of the creepier dudes zoned in on me like a piece of tenderloin —he was literally drooling all over himself. Yuck. It was enough to convince me it was time to make my exit before the bad juju hit the fan. Or I did something I regretted.

"Once again, however, I got waylaid—it was almost like the girls sensed I was about to cut and run—only this time, I found myself linked arm-in-arm with the girl who'd originally approached me at the club. 'Come on,' she said, winking at me. 'Stop looking so… judgy. At least the drinks are free.' I refrained from pointing out that I didn't need free drinks, figuring it would've been lost on her. For a little thing, she had me hooked good as she pulled me back on one of the couches with her. I had wanted to avoid that at all cost, but at least it didn't smell like a pine tree car freshener. Or bleach from cleaning away signs of activity."

Tamryn laughed when she caught me scrunching my nose.

"Now you know how I felt. Anyway, there really wasn't anything I could do but sit and watch the scene unfold. I'll admit, I was curious."

I raised a brow. "The consummate party girl…curious?" I hadn't meant it as judgment and was glad when she took it in stride, tossing her head back and getting a round of piggy-snorts out of it.

"Yeah, even a party girl can get curious. There was something too calculated about it. Too staged. So yeah, I was *curious*." She offered me a wry smirk.

"As expected, once the guys showed up and the liquor started flowing, things turned into the usual party house shenanigans. The guys got drunk to the point they were running amok like wild beasts, pawing at the girls, diving into the pool, singing 'bro' songs while slinging their arms over one another's shoulders—dudes they'd just met—all while sloshing expensive liquor all over the place. I was glad it wasn't my house.

"The girls were just as involved and either

served up more booze, engaged in the partying or played coy while dodging the creepier dudes. The hostess, however, stood off to the side and watched. And by watched, I mean secretly videotaped the whole debacle with her phone while pretending to send text messages. Having been on the receiving end of that myself in the past, I was careful to avoid her.

"This went on for a while, but as things started to wind down—and just before anyone could pass out—a couple of drivers arrived and assisted the hostess in collecting everyone and escorting us out. Instead of the Hummers, there were two massive SUVs waiting to shuttle us away. From there, we were separated from the guys."

Tamryn stopped and looked at me expectantly. For what, I had no idea. Surely, this wasn't the end of the story?

"And?" I prompted, a hint of annoyance tinting my voice.

She winked. "Thought I was gonna leave you hanging there for a second, didn't ya? Not to worry, I didn't put forth all this effort just to tell you something that routinely occurs every weekend in every city in the country. Nah, I'm not cruel either. At least, not to people I'm still trying to decide if I like or not." She chuckled when I shifted uncomfortably.

"Okay, on to the good stuff. Throughout the evening, some girls slipped a card to a dude of her choosing—in his pants pocket or wherever, none of them seemed to mind by that point. Not all the guys were 'chosen,' so to speak, and I have no idea why some were selected as card recipients over others. It certainly wasn't based on their charming behavior, though I did notice the hostess giving each girl a head-nod before the card was handed out, so she definitely had some control over how the show was being run."

"Once the guys stumbled into their vehicle and it was safely out of sight, a handful of girls were we were directed to enter the other. It wasn't full, but the driver shut the door and, like the first vehicle, disappeared.

"Nobody in the remaining group seemed too concerned. Perhaps it wasn't their first rodeo, so I kept my piehole shut. Didn't matter. Before I could ask, a different Hummer than the earlier one pulled up—this driver even lowered a little step for us after he got out. It was at this point the hostess handed us a card."

"I could tell from the vibe that it was to be discretely tucked away and not examined until later, so I followed suit, slipping it into my bag. The rest was uneventful. We were taken back to the parking lot outside the club and deposited. It was only then I realized the girl who had invited me was nowhere to be seen."

"She wasn't in your Hummer?"

Tamryn shook her head. "And not the first one either."

"Interesting," I murmured. "What about the hostess?"

"She didn't join us."

"She stayed behind?"

Tamryn shrugged. "She was there when we got to the house. Don't know any more than that."

I could tell she wasn't entirely truthful about the last bit but let it slide for the time being. There were a lot bigger things that weren't adding up. Like, how did this tie into Shelby's disappearance? It appeared to be nothing more than an after-club meet-up.

Tamryn noticed me mulling things over and offered me a wry smile.

"Curious, isn't it?"

I regretted making the party girl comment, but our food arrived before I could respond. Tamryn squinted over my shoulder as the waitress sat our plates in front of us.

I turned to see what had caught her eye but she swiftly pulled me back in. "As I mentioned, I'd gotten the distinct impression that we were not to look at the cards when we received them, and as there had really been no opportunity, I waited until I was in my car to see what all the fuss was about."

"What did it say?" I prompted, hoping we were finally getting somewhere.

Tamryn's attention strayed again. This time, the squint was accompanied by a frown.

"You gonna eat that?" she asked suddenly, stabbing a finger at my plate. I shook my head and she snapped her fingers at the waitress, rolling her eyes as the woman slogged her way over.

"Something the matter, Miss?"

"We need our check, *now*," Tamryn demanded.

The waitress glanced at our uneaten food but said nothing as she pulled a small stack of tabs from her pocket and shuffled through them until she located ours. Placing it closer to Tamryn, she mumbled her thanks, collected our plates and returned to the kitchen.

Tamryn slid the check over to me. "Take care of that."

"What? What's going on?" I stammered.

"As if you don't know," she growled, nodding over my shoulder.

This time I cast a quick glance in the direction of her scowl, noting a woman sitting alone in a corner booth, surreptitiously drinking a cup of coffee while reading a newspaper, her hands gloved and her body covered from head to toe in clothing that was much too warm given the current weather.

I turned back to Tamryn and found her studying my reaction behind the poorly disguised glare.

"I don't understand."

"For your friend Leah's sake, I hope you're being straight with me." She shoved the check closer, gritting her teeth. "As I said, take care of that."

And with that, she slid out of the booth and walked out of the restaurant.

Frowning, I placed enough cash on the table

to cover the tab, plus a sizable tip for the poor waitress and scooted my way off the rubber seat, somewhat annoyed. If Tamryn hadn't wanted to pay the check, she could have just said as much, rather than concocting some drama about the woman in the corner booth, I thought to myself.

That was, until I casually glanced in her direction, noting the coffee cup and newspaper were still present, but the booth's occupant was not.

Cursing, I hustled out of the restaurant, though the woman was nowhere in sight.

Neither was Tamryn.

Or her car.

CHAPTER FIFTEEN

Her thuggy sidekicks were in the wind as well. But they were the least of my concerns at the moment.

Tamryn had stranded me in the witching hours in a neighborhood where nobody wants to be caught alive. Or found dead.

Especially when their cellphone battery just went kaput.

Grinding my teeth in frustration, I would have to rely on the generosity of the waitress with the nonexistent personality, hoping she would allow me to use the restaurant's phone.

Sighing, I pulled the door of the restaurant open as a car screeched into the parking lot.

Turning to see how many wheels it actually had on the ground, I recognized a familiar smirk from behind the driver's seat of a faded blue Toyota whose tires had seen better days but were in better shape than the rest of the rusted-out body.

"Get in," she called through the passenger-side window.

Apparently, this was becoming a theme between the two of us.

"This wasn't the car you were driving before," I replied as I eased into the front seat, carefully avoiding any sharp metal objects that might warrant a tetanus shot. "Did you steal this?"

Tamryn rolled her eyes. "Pahleese. Do I look like a Corolla kind of gal to you?"

I shrugged. Perhaps not. It still didn't explain how she'd come into possession of the vehicle and disposed of another so quickly.

Chuckling as she exited the parking lot in the same manner she'd arrived, she added, "I can hear those gears cranking, Arianna. You'd be better off giving them a break before they burn out. Besides, you didn't seek me out for inconsequential details—like how I got this car—did you?"

I shook my head despite the fact I was still curious.

Tamryn snickered. "Relax. The car belongs to a friend."

"Those thugs—guys in the parking lot?" When I didn't quite catch myself in time, she shot me an icy glare.

"Hey! Those 'guys' work for me."

"Work…as in hired muscle?"

"What are you, stuck in a 1970s TV show?" Tamryn shook her head. "Yes, you could say they are…bodyguards, of sorts. That's what my dad had them around for before they came to work for me, anyway." The latter came out paired with a sneer.

Apparently, things were still not-so-rosy between her and her pops. Still, I wondered what she needed bodyguards for. Or better yet, who she needed to be protected from. I knew she wasn't about to tell me, so I left it alone and shifted the conversation to something that had been bothering me.

"Who was that woman in the diner?"

Tamryn raised a brow. "You tell me."

I turned to face her, looking her straight in the eyes. "I honestly have no idea. What would make you think I would?"

She focused on the road, her fingers tapping against the steering wheel. "Well, for starters, she was at the research park, though she arrived ahead of you and your cohort. Once we were at the diner, she was tracking our every movement in a not-so-sneaky way. Not very pro, if you ask me."

My scoff didn't amuse her, given the stink-eye I received in return.

"Come on, Tamryn. That's hardly proof. Maybe she thought she recognized you…from social media?"

She snorted. "Seriously not part of my follower demographic, Arianna." When I shot her a bland stare, she added, "She was more in line with your old man's age."

I waved a hand. "Whatever, Tamryn, believe what you want to."

She perused me for a moment, and I let her. Finally, she graced me with a response.

"Well, truth be told, I knew she wasn't with you. Or more importantly, you didn't intentionally bring her along for the ride."

I opened my mouth. Closed it.

All that rigmarole was leading up to this?

She chuckled before divulging how she'd drawn this conclusion. "Your reaction when I kept glancing over your shoulder was the first tell. Though I wasn't one-hundred percent sure then, your body language suggested you were curious about what I was looking at, then showed nothing when you saw what…or rather, who, it was. At no point did you seem tense or anxious about being found out. If anything, your emotions mirrored mine."

"So you studied psychology and body language in college," I retorted. "Not that I'm saying your conclusion was off the mark, but I wouldn't recommend drawing them based solely on what you learned in your Psych 101 class."

"As if," Tamryn huffed. "You didn't let me finish. My dudes suspected she was with the old man. And I trust them. Can you say the same thing about Pops?" I started to reiterate that Martin's actions did not reflect my own but was cut off with a snap of the fingers. "Chill, would you? We know it was his doing and not yours. You know you could have saved yourself the aggravation by leaving him at home." It was not a question.

"Pops is going to earn you an untimely toe tag if you're not more careful in the future. So, for your benefit, I suggest next time you do as I ask. Chain him to the tailgate. Lock him in the bathroom. Dump some extra fiber in his prune juice…whatever. Just don't bring him along."

"Oh, so *now* you trust me?" I countered, though her suggestions actually didn't sound half bad.

Still, they wouldn't have stopped Martin. I may not know all-things-Martin-Singer-related, but of this, I was sure.

Tamryn didn't respond, though her mouth turned up as she stared ahead, surging onto the freeway heading north. The traffic was light given the hour, so the road and the glimpse of dawn on the horizon were ours for the taking.

I was the first to break the silence that had grown between us. "Where are we going?"

"Ahead," came the response.

I tried another angle. "You never did say— what was on the card?"

"What card?" I'm sure my annoyance at her response translated loud and clear to the body language expert. Pursing her lips, she responded after a moment. What that was all about, I had no idea, as she'd already cleared me of colluding with Martin. "A number."

"What *kind* of number?" I asked through gritted teeth. "Lottery? Shoe size? I.Q.?"

Tamryn rolled her eyes. "A text message number, of course."

"And?"

"It belonged to a person."

"Wow, we are *really* getting somewhere now," I muttered. "Good thing, because I could have easily assumed it belonged to someone's cat."

"Do you want to know, or not?" she snapped.

I tapped my fingers on my thigh, matching her drumming beat. "Just waiting on you, Tamryn."

She shot me a look, her hands crushing the steering wheel as she looked back to the road.

"It belonged to a woman who wouldn't tell me her name. Said she was in charge."

In charge of what? I thought but instead asked, "So it wasn't the girl who gave you the card?"

"I thought so at first, but it wasn't."

"How do you know?"

"I just do, okay?" I raised my hands in surrender. "The thing is, you never *really* know who's in charge because there are too many layers."

"Like a pyramid scheme?" I asked.

"A what?" She raised a brow.

"Never mind. Tell me about this woman."

"She said that I had made an impression. Of course, I was amused as I had done nothing that would have made me stand out. Not on *that* night, anyway." Tamryn chuckled. "So I asked her 'On who?' and what I'd done that was so memorable. 'People who matter', she said. Later, I found out that these 'people' had been watching us via hidden cameras. The live feed was distributed to God knows who, but apparently, these people have some sort of clout."

"What about your second question?"

Tamryn's lips pressed together in a firm line and a slight shudder erupted from her shoulders as though a sudden chill had passed through the vehicle.

"She said that these people were pleased to have found such a 'promising asset'."

"What the heck does *that* mean? Because they recognized you from social media?"

"Probably." She shrugged and frowned. I wondered if it was the first time she'd considered it. "Anyway, I let the whole 'asset' part float and asked her what the deal was with the card and all the intrigue crap. I mean, you don't need to devise some complicated ruse to convince a bunch of dudes to come to party, meet chicks, drink free booze and act like idiots. It's like drawing mice to a big old piece of stinky cheese."

Typically, that was part of the trap but refrained from interjecting.

"She indicated that she served as a liaison to affluent parties who were looking to add to their collections."

This time, I couldn't help myself as I inadvertently croaked out, "Collections?"

Tamryn frowned. "I know. Creepy, right? I said as much and she quickly clarified. Honestly, though, it didn't make me feel any less disgusted."

"And?" I prompted, growing impatient.

"*And*, there's this group of people—I can't say dudes, because my gut tells me that there's a good mix of both—that like to procure…other people of a certain persuasion to help them fill these collections."

"I assume by 'collections' you're referring to people." She nodded. "For the purpose of sex?"

"Not necessarily—no matter what you think of me, that's not something I would invest my time in." When I snorted, she scoffed before adding, "What you read isn't always the truth, you know."

"I wasn't thinking about your memoir but more about your documentaries."

She laughed. "Oh, the videos. Things aren't always what they seem, Arianna."

I thought, if anything, they *seemed* like a childish display of selfishness, manipulation, if not a cry for attention, but bit my tongue. This wasn't about her.

"I think it was my social media presence, coupled with my father's far-reaching influence that drew them to me."

"So they had their eyes on you for a while, then." It was not a question.

"Definitely. The girl who first approached me in the club was assigned to 'collect' me. And she did. Even got a hefty bonus for it."

"You know this for a fact?" She nodded. "Did you see her again?"

"I did. But we need to talk basics first. I assume you want to know what all of this is about and how it impacts your friend?" She glanced at me and I offered her a single head nod.

"Good. Then let's talk about the collection process, for lack of a better phrase. The call turned out to be sort of an interview, though I saw it as more of an opportunity to assess them. Besides, the interview was just a formality. I was already in if I wanted it. And, because my ability to influence others had previously been established, although a bit too public at times, I wasn't required to start at the ground level."

"What? You got profit-sharing from day one? Bypass probationary period and collect one-hundred dollars?"

"You jest, but you're actually not that far off. Basically, it was broke down by layers. If I wasn't driving, I'd draw you a flowchart. And even if I did, it would only scratch the surface."

"Because you can't tell me?"

She frowned and shook her head. "Because I don't know. And it isn't for the lack of trying. And believe me, I've tapped into what I thought was the source of that well, only to find out that I was nowhere near it by a long shot. Honestly, I think it's meant to work that way."

"Plausible deniability."

She hacked out a caustic laugh. "Something like that. Anyway, from my limited scope, it was broken down into layers—which is just my name for them based on what I witnessed—and included clubs, parties, hosts, participants, deliveries, and incentives.

"The club setup, I've mostly explained how that works. Girls hand out cards to prospects, letting them know about an exclusive after-party. They're to look for girls and guys who meet a specific set of criteria and then grant them access via the cards they've been given. A limited number of cards are given to each girl, depending on how they fared on prior outings, so they must choose wisely, or they may end up receiving less on the next go-around."

"So, it's like a sliding scale…they have to work their way up and if they screw up, they have to work back up to where they were before?"

"Yeah, or they are opted out of the system altogether."

"What does that mean?"

"Dunno." Tamryn was quiet for a moment, staring intently at the road ahead. "They just don't receive any more opportunities."

Something in her tone, and the fact she'd hesitated, suggested that those who were "opted out" didn't just return to their normal, everyday lives.

"You ever see any of those people again?"

Her brow furrowed. "Why would I? I didn't know them to begin with. If they are going to repeatedly screw up their chances, then that's on them. I want no part of that."

Her face softened, but her words were still laden with stone. "It's not like this is brain surgery, Arianna. And if people get too hasty or greedy…they don't deserve the opportunity they were given."

She was holding something back, but I didn't want to throw a wrench into the progress we'd made. "Sure, I get that. So you receive your cards, then what?"

"You get a text the day of the party. Miss it or decide to ignore it, and you forfeit one of your cards. Second time, you lose what you had and if you were on your last one, you're out.

There's always someone ready to take your spot."

"Okay, let's say you never miss an opportunity."

"You show up at the designated club when you're supposed to, appropriately dressed. Sexy, but not slutty. No drugs. No over-drinking. And no side-hustles. *That* one will get you in hot water." She gave me a side-eye and a curt nod. "After the cards get handed out to the prospects, you are to meet your driver in the parking lot no later than one thirty-five a.m. Though the drivers and the vehicles are never the same, you're given a signal as to which is yours."

"What, like a secret handshake?"

Tamryn scrunched her nose. "Gross. No. There's typically a theme to the party, which is included in the text. The driver, or his vehicle, will have that theme going on."

"Seems kinda random."

"Not if you see the themes. They're borderline crazy without being too distracting for people who shouldn't be looking."

"Care to indulge me?" I expected full snark in response and was surprised when she tilted her head and actually appeared to be giving it some consideration.

"I honestly can't recall all of them, but just to give you a broad sense, one night, it was the color purple woven into a sock hop theme." When I raised a brow, she added, "I know, right? I had to look it up on the Internet. Turns out, it's some sort of dance-type thingy from the 1950s."

Her lip curled into a sneer as she shook her head, as though it was the most ludicrous thing she'd ever heard. "Anyway, on that occasion, the driver played his part to perfection and was outside the club leaning against his ride, decked out in a leather jacket and jeans—in this heat, no less—with his hair all slicked back and oozing with some kind of petroleum-based product. To top it off, he'd hiked one of his pant legs up so that you could see his purple socks. Then again, maybe they were rolled up. Dunno. Either way, the right people definitely would not miss him. Oh, and there was also music from that era coming from the vehicle's speakers and other stuff like that."

"Hmm. Still pretty random."

She shrugged. "Hey, I never got in the wrong

vehicle, and the people I handed cards out to made it to their vehicles."

I nodded. It was hard to argue the point, though it still wasn't all that substantial. Interesting, perhaps, but not helpful. "How are the locations chosen?"

Tamryn paused a moment, but it was short enough that I realized it was solely for effect than backed by any actual processing of thoughts. "Not sure who's in charge of doing the research and making the arrangements, but from what I've gathered, they are all rental properties, typically used for people visiting from out-of-state."

"Vacation rentals by property owners," I clarified, trying to keep the frustration from smacking her in the face as I ground my teeth and worked to sustain a calm, engaged tone.

Tamryn clearly knew more than she pretended, and it was getting old. Fast.

Focus on the goal, AJ. Leah and Shelby—their lives were at stake, I reminded myself.

They were *all* that mattered.

I hoped my patience would be worth the price.

"Yeah. You know how the resort season has

ebbs and flows based on the weather, and what's going on in the metro area at that time of year… like spring training baseball or all the car auctions?" I nodded, though I couldn't quite bring myself to look at her. She hadn't presented anything that anyone who'd lived in Arizona for any amount of time didn't already know.

"Well, people with vacation properties are affected in the same way during the summer months and into the monsoon season. Nobody in their right mind would plan a vacation to come here, even if they were on a limited budget or looking for a major deal.

"Anyway, like the resorts, the property owners—many of whom don't live in-state—are desperate to get some income flowing. So they allow the management companies overseeing the properties to rent their houses out on a daily or weekly basis at a reduced rate. Ultimately, the hope is that locals will get so fed up with their own lives, their kids being home for the summer, the general nastiness that occurs after one-hundred-plus days of excessive heat, whatever…that they'll opt for a stay-cation. You know, just so that they can pretend they are getting away from their own crappy lives and in doing so, get a chance to use someone else's pool, amenities, air conditioning…basically someone else's life." She shrugged when she caught my frown.

"Okay," I replied slowly. Was she missing the big picture? "But I don't think the club-going crowd falls into that camp, do you?"

Tamryn tilted her head back and got a good laugh out of that one. "If the cash is green, who cares?"

"What about the cities? There must be rules in place to regulate this?" I pressed.

"So far, many of them haven't caught up with the changing trends in the vacation rental industry. Not saying everyone is trying to pull a fast one in the interim, but there are certainly people and organizations out there that are taking full advantage of this lapse. Besides, in the end, when has commerce ever been a bad thing? It's adding big bucks to the economy during periods when businesses come to almost a standstill, right?"

I could see her point where homeowners were concerned, but the mention of "organiza-tions"—not the property management firms as she'd previously referenced—piqued my inter-est. That suggested a much larger operation was in play and that the money was lining someone's pocket, *not* filtering back into the economy.

"But this can't be a new thing. I mean, it has to be going on in other places, and not just here in Phoenix."

"Yeah, but those other places don't have what we do," she replied with a smugness that made me want to tug on the steering wheel while smushing her face into the driver's side window.

Instead, I tucked that fleeting notion away and responded in kind. "A motivated client base."

The knowing smile she offered was of no comfort to me. "Now you're getting the picture."

"Am I?"

"Well, for such a judgy type, you've certainly drawn some pretty fast conclusions and didn't end up having a complete freak out in the process."

I had nowhere to go with that and let the silence sit for a moment.

"Tell me about these prospects you mentioned. What decides who makes the cut versus who is in charge of defining and enforcing the rules?"

Tamryn raised a brow but nodded. "There's a

certain level of motivation required to start. You either have it, or you don't. The way I was selected…well, I already kind of explained how that went down, from the girls' side of things.

"From there, the girls are kind of given general guidelines. You know, things like dudes who take good care of themselves, are relatively well-mannered, and who pay their bar tabs in cash. Cash is important. Credit cards could belong to daddy and debit cards, well, those are a crapshoot."

"And later, the guidelines become…more strict?" I prompted. It couldn't be that simple, could it?

She gave a so-so gesture with her right hand. "Strict? Maybe. More specific, for sure. The girls were instructed to look for a variety of age ranges and socio-economic classes. And, if you were someone of notable mention or had connections to someone who was, it earned you double bonus points."

I noted how she spoke of "the girls" as though she'd been merely an onlooker and not an active participant. Interesting.

"Kind of like you, only from the other side of the equation."

Tamryn raised a brow as she glanced at me, nodding at the conclusion I'd drawn, though her lips pursed as she responded. "Exactly like that."

"Okay, so is this some sort of point-based system?"

"More like incentives, but we'll talk about that in a bit."

"I'd rather talk about it now," I replied through gritted teeth.

Her smile was forced, but the sharpness of her tone spoke volumes. "I think that's enough for now, Arianna."

Frustrated that I was running out of time, I pushed. "Oh? I thought you wanted to talk about Shelby."

"I do. But nothing is going to happen tonight that's going to make a difference."

Considering my best friend's life was at stake, I wasn't having it.

"Really, Tamryn?" I started to argue until I noticed she'd pulled to a stop.

Her retort was more resigned than snappish. "Really. And, as your chauffeur for the night, I must inform you that you've reached your destination."

I looked out the window, realizing we were about half a block from my house.

She chuckled. "Sorry, you're gonna need to hoof it the rest of the way." As I hesitantly exited the vehicle, she gripped my arm. "Don't sweat it. We *will* talk again later."

"When?"

"Soon." She released my arm and locked the door just as I shut it, pulling away in a manner that suggested she wasn't concerned about waking the neighbors.

Tired and confused, I walked the short distance to my house, wondering if sleep would be on my side, even for a few hours.

I turned the key in the lock, noting that Nicoh wasn't all that interested in securing the house as his giant form had yet to present itself, which typically meant he was using my absence as an opportunity to sleep *on* my bed, rather than next to it.

Some guard dog, I mused, tossing my stuff on the counter. As I passed through the living room on the way to my much-needed slumber, a voice emerged from the cover of darkness.

"Where have you *been*?"

I couldn't help but smirk. The pronunciation of "been" came out sounding more like "bean," reminding me of a line in *Trading Places* when Dan Aykroyd's character, Louis Winthorpe III, pleads with his girlfriend as she expresses her distaste with his current state of dress and odoriferousness.

Still, he had no right to ask.

I swiveled on my heel and found Martin sitting in the darkness. A wisp of light from the street lamp slipped through the edge of the blinds on the picture window behind me, just enough so that I could see him as he sat on the couch absently scratching *my* guard dog, whose tongue lolled to one side as he lapped up every bit of attention.

Apparently, the two had been bonding in my absence.

Traitor.

"*Been* a long time since someone's waited up for me past curfew, in my own house. Oh, right…that would have been a parent's J-O-B." I gave him a pointed look, though he remained infuriatingly expressionless. "Missed out on those days, didn't you, *Martin*?" I would not. Call. Him. Father.

Instead, I flipped on the nearest light switch, causing him to blink as Nicoh panted beneath the absent-minded scratches that Martin was still plying him with.

I stared down at my traitorous canine and was rewarded with another insult as he leaned into his new bestie, nuzzling Martin's hand with the side of his muzzle.

But the hits didn't stop there.

"I'm assuming that's more of a rhetorical question or an attempt to garner some form of an apology," Martin replied. "And you still haven't answered my question."

"Touché," I replied, crossing my arms as I

leaned against the wall. "Out, with Tamryn." His brows furrowed, causing a slight crease between his eyes that I hadn't noticed before. "*That's* the answer to your question."

"Oh?" He went back to scratching Nicoh, but he did so half-heartedly.

I knew that wouldn't last long. If there was one thing I knew for sure, my canine companion wasn't much for halfway doing anything, whether it was a sandwich off the counter that didn't belong to him, hogging the entire span of the bed he wasn't allowed on or accepting a mediocre effort where scratches were concerned.

As expected, and much to my delight, no matter how childish it was, Nicoh released a heavy sigh before he lumbered toward his favorite blanket.

"Don't toy with me. You know darn well that she picked me up after we went our separate ways at the research park."

"I don't know what you mean." Once again, that crinkle deepened, his quiet sincerity almost making him believable.

But this was Martin.

"Your…associates, from the network. You had them following us every step of the way.

They were probably even lurking in the bushes when we got there."

Martin scoffed. "People in the network do not lurk."

"Oh, so you admit that there were people following us." Not a question.

"Arianna, dear—"

"Don't patronize me, Martin," I snapped, causing him to shift. "Tamryn was onto us— them, even before she picked me up on my way out." I huffed when he gave me nothing more than a bland stare. "The woman in the diner? Ring a bell? You probably know more about what's going on than I do, yet I got saddled with Tamryn all night."

"Morning," he clarified. "It *was* after midnight."

I gave him the stink-eye.

Martin wisely attempted an alternate route. "So she didn't have any information, after all."

I shrugged. "Oh, she had information, which she doled out in breadcrumbs. Most of the time was either spent trying to justify your appearance at the meet-up or convincing her I was not in cahoots with the woman in the diner." That last part wasn't entirely true, but I needed Martin to come clean, if not for me, then for Leah's sake.

"I don't know who that is."

"This is seriously how you're gonna play this?" I ground out.

He shrugged. "I don't know what you want me to say, Arianna."

"The truth would be nice, for a change, Martin."

I didn't wait for his response. Instead, I did the last thing either of us probably expected. I spun on my heel, collected my phone and stomped…out of my own house.

The basis for my destination had no rhyme or reason. I just needed to get away from Martin before I said or did something I regretted. Probably both.

I was equally frustrated with myself for allowing him to get involved. It had been against my better judgment and yet I had accepted his assistance. No, make that his *insistence* on butting his nose in where it didn't belong. And where had it gotten me?

Days had passed since Leah had gone missing and here I was, flapping about like a chicken with its head cut off. She would be sorely disappointed in my efforts and my decisions.

I kicked a rock, only to have my toe connect with the edge of the curb. Cursing to myself, I ran through everything I had learned so far, which amounted to a lot of pieces that may or may not have fit the puzzle I was trying to solve.

Why had Tamryn agreed to meet if she wasn't all-in on finding Shelby? Was she simply sizing me up, tossing some stale pizza crusts at me to get me worked up while she drilled me for what I knew?

Too much of her story didn't add up, starting with her rationale for why she was chosen to be part of this whole setup. Wouldn't her notoriety have acted as a deterrent rather than deeming her an immediate asset? She was way too high profile to take such a risk, especially if underhanded shenanigans were happening at these parties—as in people disappearing. Was she in cahoots with whoever had a hand in Shelby's, and likely Leah's, disappearance?

Whatever had drawn her to me, she knew far more than she was letting on. Just how much remained to be seen.

It felt like I had only been walking—okay,

storming—for a few minutes, yet when I stopped and looked down at the plaque on the bench before me, I realized that while I had not been intentional about my destination, something had drawn me to this location.

Sighing, I sat as I ran my hand over the inscription.

In loving memory of Alison & Victoria…you will never be forgotten. And for Arianna…may you continue to live your life with purpose… knowing that you have been and will always be…loved.

"It's lovely," a feminine voice whispered as if not to startle me.

I turned, looking up into steel-gray eyes that did not quite meet mine as they shifted to the plaque. A glimmer of something—sadness, maybe regret—passed over her face but was gone as quickly. She pulled her coat tighter around her thin frame—a calf-length raincoat, to be exact, and an odd choice for an early morning in the desert. Her hands were covered with leather gloves that were too thick for the driving variety but not warm enough to withstand a chill. Again, overkill.

Catching my gaze, she subconsciously

touched her hair, the auburn locks falling forward just over her shoulders and partially covering her face, but not before the rising sun caught the mottled patch of skin that ran from her temple to her chin and trailed down to her neck until it disappeared behind the collar of her coat.

I averted my gaze, trying not to stare and nodded at the inscription. "My—biological father had it made for my mother and sister."

"He must have loved them very much."

Her response gave me pause. Some part of Martin did love them, or the *idea* of them and of a family—perhaps he still did—but so much water had passed under that bridge that the plaque seemed almost as though it was an afterthought. Or an atonement.

One that would only ever be seen by yours truly.

Bypassing her comment, I returned her gaze and found it oddly familiar. "Don't I know you from somewhere?" Before she could respond, I added, "Other than the diner earlier this morning, that is."

She pressed her lips together in a firm line, grimacing as though the effort caused her pain. "May I?" She gestured toward the bench.

I slid to one side, far enough to put distance between the stranger and me, should I need to defend myself. Or bolt. Again, she winced as she lowered herself to a seated position.

"Are you alright?" I lifted a hand to steady her, but she waved me off.

"Thank you, I'll be fine. Things tend to get stiff the older one gets." She chuckled, but the humor did not quite reach her eyes.

Considering she couldn't have been much more than fifty, give or take, I suspected there was more going on than a few creaky bones but let it slide.

"Why are you here?"

"It is a public park." She shrugged, though the slight curve on the right corner of her mouth rejected the nonchalance she was attempting to pass off. If anything, she seemed amused.

I squinted at her ever so slightly. Was any of this…amusing?

When she caught the expression, her smile—what there had been of it—faded.

"So, did Martin put you up to this?"

She tilted her head. "Martin?"

I clucked my tongue. "The man who asked you to follow me."

"I don't know what you—"

I put a hand up. "Listen. I don't know who you are or what you are up to, but I have had it up to here with half-truths and being given the runaround. I came here for some solitude. So if you don't mind—" I started to rise.

"Wait." A gloved hand touched my arm. "I honestly don't know Martin." Her face softened and her voice, but a whisper, was earnest. "Please stay."

I lowered myself, waiting for her to continue.

I expected an explanation, but when she finally spoke, it was in the form of a question. "Why were you with Tamryn Mayer?"

"How do *you* know Tamryn?" It wasn't my first question, but it was the first one that popped out.

"Doesn't everyone?" I met her chuckle, as light as it was, with a bland stare. "Sorry. It seems as though you've had your fill of game-playing today. From Tamryn, I assume?" When I offered no response, she nodded and blew out a breath. "Let's just say I've had my eye on her for a while."

"On Tamryn, specifically? Or on this vacation property scheme she's gotten herself wrapped up in?" Her eyes widened at the mention of it.

"So you know about that?"

I shrugged. "I know enough."

"Care to expand?" I raised my brow and she nodded. "Right. To answer your question, I've been keeping a close eye on both since I came to Arizona. But I've known about them a lot longer."

"Since you came to Arizona? Where exactly did you come from? And how are you involved in all of this?" My onslaught of questions did not appear to faze her, though she did not respond as I had hoped.

"I know that I'm asking you to take a huge leap of faith, but I can't tell you any of that… yet. I will, however, answer anything you ask me—in due to time. For now, all I can say is that from what I can tell, you and I are working toward a common goal."

"And what 'common goal' might that be?" I

asked, crossing my arms as I leaned against the bench.

The steely coolness of those eyes surveyed me and her lips pursed as she appeared to be taking a measure of something.

Finally, she spoke.

"To make things right with the people we love. And to bring them home."

CHAPTER SEVENTEEN

"What could you possibly know about that?"

"I've been keeping an eye on you, too, since your flubbed meet-up with Tamryn and her hoods at the research park." She nodded when I opened my mouth and shut it. "I gathered she was not pleased you brought reinforcements. You ignored her terms and when the opportunity presented itself—meaning you separated yourself from the deal-breaker—she swooped in and whisked you off."

The heat rose in my cheeks at the accuracy of my faux pas. "To the diner."

She nodded. "I assume the man you were

with at the park was the Martin you mentioned. If so, I don't know what your plan was, but he'd lost you by the time he'd returned to his vehicle. As far as I could tell, no one followed you after that point."

"Other than you." My tone was a bit crispier than I'd intended, causing her brow to arch.

"And Tamryn's thugs," she clarified.

"Right. How could one forget?" I mumbled.

"Is this Martin someone you can trust?"

"It's complicated."

She hacked out a chuckle so rough you could have sanded barnacles off the underside of a boat. "I understand complicated. For now, I'm hoping that we can keep this discussion just between the two of us."

I waved a hand around, acknowledging that we were indeed alone, receiving a cryptic curve of the lip in response, followed by a succinct nod.

"I realize I'm going out on a limb here—it's not like you have any reason to trust me—but I'm guessing whatever your intent, it goes beyond getting to know Tamryn Mayer or her involvement in what's going on in this town with regards to the after-parties." I offered her a single nod. "Okay. Then why don't you start at the beginning?"

As she had said, I had no reason to trust this woman, much less had any misconceived notion she could actually assist me. Yet, there was something about her—whether it was her earnest demeanor or perhaps my desperation—that compelled me to take her at her word. At least for now.

And so she sat and listened as I laid out what I knew—from the moment I received word that Leah was missing, to learning of the possible connection to Shelby's disappearance and later, to Tamryn and how I'd gone about drawing her out.

After running through what Tamryn had piecemealed together before dumping me for the final time—both befuddled and frustrated—at my front door, I expelled a long breath, mentally cursing Tamryn for the valuable time I'd lost.

I grimaced when I realized that colorful twist on the English language had escaped the inner confines of my brain and spewed out of my mouth.

The woman smiled but nodded. "It appears as though Tamryn left out some of the juicier details."

"What do you know?" I pressed. "Can you tell me where Leah is? Shelby—"

She raised a hand. "I'm sorry. I didn't mean to get your hopes up. I don't know anything about your friend or the girl she was looking for." My heart collapsed, though I knew the answers I sought wouldn't come that easily. "But, I can fill in some of the gaping holes in Tamryn's story."

Sighing, I gestured for her to continue.

"Tamryn outlined the system to you up to a point, but that's just a small piece of a bigger pie."

"Maybe that's all she knew."

"You know better than that, and so do I." She chuckled. "Don't let her aloofness fool you. Tamryn is in it as deep as one can go. And is smart enough to hold her own, while setting her own rules and ensuring their outcome."

"Sounds like you know her pretty well."

She shrugged. "I know the type." I wasn't buying it—she had crossed paths with Tamryn at some point. Or, more accurately, crossed Tamryn and her rules. "People like Tamryn don't do anything that doesn't benefit them or get them what they want."

"And what does Tamryn want?"

"What does anyone truly want?" When I struggled for a response, she smirked. "Exactly. It's not a question that we can answer for others. Only Tamryn knows."

I nodded, wondering why Tamryn, specifically, was of such interest to her and a subject she seemed so well-versed on? Tucking that away, I shifted back to the topic du jour.

"So, getting back to those plot holes Tamryn failed to fill?"

"Smooth transition." The woman shook her head as a chuckle escaped. "But you are right, I offered to expand on the breadcrumbs she elected to dole out—where to begin is the question." She tapped a gloved hand to her lips, eyes squinting as she took in our surroundings. On the lookout for what, perhaps? Or who?

Before I could ask, she moved on. "Alright, Tamryn's detailing of the clubs— how the girls and prospects are selected and transported to and from the after-party, the general role of the hostess and vaguely, how follow-up contact is made via the cards handed out at the evening—though she didn't say as much, the guys who also receive cards are further vetted in much the same way, once they text the number on the card, etc. Anyway, all of that is good and fine when it comes to outlining the low-level tier stuff, but—"

"Wait." I hated to interject but had a feeling she had just touched on a critical component of the system. "Can you tell me more about these tiers?"

"Sure. First up, you've got your party boys with wealthy parents and cash to burn. They are usually younger—somewhere in the twenty to thirty crowd and are not yet established. But thanks to mommy and daddy and often a juicy trust account, they have a steady stream of cash and more where that comes from. That's your first or lower-level tier.

"Next are the bachelors, who are more estab-lished—whether they were born with it or cre-ated their own path makes no difference—like the younger guns, they have cash to burn. Some may be looking for a longer commitment than the first tier is getting with the party girls, but we'll get to that later. Finally, in the upper echelon are the professionals—businessmen, politicians, sports figures…you name it."

"Okay, but what differentiates the second and the third tiers?"

She gave me a tight-lipped smile. "Leverage."

I tilted my head. "Come again?"

"The third tier is comprised of established individuals who need privacy where their extracurricular activities are involved—they could be married, in a position that places them in the public eye. Essentially, the top two tiers are where the meat of the operation lies."

I was curious to delve more into the meat but needed some filler to tie me over. "How are these…people acquired?"

She nodded. "An excellent question. Several of the means are the same regardless of the tier. Some tiers just prove more fruitful when luring new prospects to a particular setting or forum. But it can be a combination of social media, where the specific platform utilized is often dictated by the tier. Or web ads, clubs, college boards, conferences, trade shows, sporting events, car auction or other live events, high-end shopping and grocery establishments, political rallies, charity events…the list goes on and on." She paused to allow me to digest.

To be honest, I was floored. "Really. That is quite something. This is certainly not the type of system that could have been rolled out overnight."

"Oh, no." She laughed. "While this may be a new concept to you, operations like this have been in the works for a very long time. The boom in the vacation rental business just provided another avenue to capitalize on, and resort markets are well-suited."

I nodded. "Tamryn mentioned that each person in the system played a role and that typically no two players, so to speak, crossed paths more than once, if at all possible."

She gave me a so-so gesture with her gloved hand. "Yes and no. The girls and maybe some of the lower-level tier guys end up at the same after-parties, but everything else is carefully choreographed so that prospects never see one another."

This was interesting. "Ever?"

"It's part of the attraction. Everything is basically handled by a minimum of contact. It's very lucrative and with less involvement, there are fewer eyes to *see*."

"By involvement, you are referring to the hostesses and van drivers," I prompted.

"Yes, and the people who clean and stage the house, and those hired for other purposes—vehicle rentals, clothing suppliers, stylists, makeup artists—you name it, everything is meticulously orchestrated so that things go off without a hitch."

"Interesting," I murmured. "And what about the hosts—how are they acquired?"

She blew out a breath, the creases around her eyes crinkling at the effort. "Oh, sometimes girls who present themselves well, have proven reliable and compliant are promoted internally. Other times, girls are recruited from outside— usually the go-getter types who are interested in diverse experiences, as well as an opportunity to make some decent money from a side-hustle."

"Always female?"

She nodded. "It tends to make the other girls

more…comfortable on the front-side and the prospects prefer it."

"What about Tamryn—you think she would be considered good hostess material?" I was only partially serious. Thankfully, she found it equally humorous.

"Ha! I highly doubt it. Not only is she too high profile, Tamryn is best-suited right where she is. Right now, she's in a position to bend things to her every whim and ensure she maintains adequate control."

"Control? Of who?"

"That *is* the real question, isn't it?"

Once again, I got the impression that she knew more about Tamryn than she was letting on, and as I caught her eyes, she knew I knew it, too.

Too hastily to avoid notice, she continued. "The compensation and bonuses can be quite lucrative if you are someone who has no other alternatives."

And, apparently, a low threshold where moral standards are concerned, I thought as the woman prattled on, perhaps still eager to sidestep the topic of Tamryn.

"Same goes for others who supply or do

things for the operation. Secrecy and reliability are paramount. And are generously rewarded. Some have been able to expand their businesses solely on the bonuses."

"How does everything get paid out? I doubt there's any tax documentation involved."

She shook her head. "Cash, under the table."

"To other cities? States?"

"Yes, that too." She pressed her lips together as though that was all she was willing to say on the subject.

It was.

I let that settle for a moment before shifting gears. "What happens to the people who don't make the cut, for whatever reason?"

She raised a brow. "Such as?"

"For starters, what really happens *after* the after-party? Or to those who fail to follow the rules of this system?"

"There are…penalties for those who do not comply…at any level, whether it's the girls, prospects, continuing prospects, etc."

"Care to elaborate?"

"I do not." To confirm she had my full attention, her stare was direct and the message was clear—I was not to push the subject.

"Gotcha. Perhaps you can tell me what happens when people—regardless of who they are, what tier they're in, whether they're fully invested or whatever—simply want out? What then?"

Her gaze shifted from mine and this time and though she was looking into the depths of the vacant park, appeared to be focused on nothing. "You'll have to ask your friends Leah and Shelby about that." She returned her attention to me, and upon capturing my expression, added, "I'm sorry. I'm not intentionally trying to be harsh. It's just the reality of the situation. As sad as that is."

"Right. Just a sad reality," I murmured, wincing as my stomach continued to twist. "Unfortunately, it's the one I've…we've been dealt."

"Meaning?"

"We may not like the situation we've found ourselves in, but we also don't need to sit around bemoaning it either."

"What are you suggesting?"

"We proceed with what we know and we take action. Actively, deliberately and rigorously going after what we want."

Both brows arched. "And just how do you propose *we* do that?"

"Well, based on what you and Tamryn have said, the system relies on secrecy, confidentiality and discretion. But if one of those pieces is missing, the system fails, which puts the operation and all parties at risk, at least at a local level.

"Correct me if I'm wrong, but I'm guessing this is the reason behind the need for strict adherence to the structure; otherwise everything would go south pretty quick and you'd have a lot of unhappy campers. Probably the reason behind the penalties, too?"

She nodded. "And the rewards, which ensures the system continues to operate smoothly."

Her choice of words made me curious. "So each micro-operation, for the lack of a better word, basically self-monitors?"

"In some ways, yes, but they're always bigger players, watching."

"While maintaining a low profile, I would assume?"

"Yes, for obvious reasons." When I gestured for her to continue, she sighed but indulged me. "The higher one is, the steeper the fall."

I quirked a brow. I wasn't looking for fortune cookie wisdom here. "Are you talking tiers again?"

She nodded. "As you can probably imagine, many of the prospects in the top two tiers have far more to lose than just money. While they are rewarded for their 'support' of the organization, certain protocols must also be stringently followed. Meaning, that if one of these individuals places themselves or the system in a position of risk, there are penalties that must be paid to atone for the potential damage to the whole operation, in its entirety."

"Penalties?" Were we talking like knee-breaking kind of stuff here? "And wait—bonuses? I thought those were reserved for the people working for the operation, not the ones receiving benefits from it."

She chuckled, though the emotion didn't translate to her face. At least not from my vantage point. "So many questions."

"Like you said, Tamryn left some key points out. Just covering my bases."

"Right. Can't fault you for that. Those in the upper tiers are offered a wider variety of options, so rather than your after-parties, there are private parties and/or online viewings, where the prospects are given a first-hand look at some of the more…prime offerings. I'm sure you're able to conjure your own imagery without needing me to fill in the blanks."

I gave her a curt nod, carefully holding the contents of my innards at bay while trying to breathe in enough air to allow the anger to pass.

"There are those, however, who require something a bit more…curated than what can be accommodated locally. In those circumstances, the bonuses include opportunities to sample off a more cultural menu. One that is…fresher."

I couldn't help myself from blurting out, "Are you suggesting that they are buying girls, children even, from overseas for these freaks—err, prospects to *play* with?"

She pursed her lips. "I'm not *suggesting* any-thing. It's a fact."

"I realize that, but these people don't need a 'curated courtesy' operation to do any of this, not when they can easily procure it themselves."

"The difference is that it's the *operation* putting its neck out there, rather than the client. Sure, they could do it themselves, but why would they when they can pay for someone to curate the perfect girl based on their preferences?

"It's much easier to make a mess when someone else is cleaning it up. This goes back to the leverage I mentioned earlier. If one of *these* types slips up, it doesn't just put them in danger —the entire operation could be at risk. That's why the clients are researched and vetted before they are even invited into those tiers."

It still didn't explain the leverage component. "I don't follow."

"*Everyone* has something to hide. More vetting ensures the operation knows precisely where each potential client's weak spot resides."

"So they can be leveraged, if needed," I replied. "So getting back the penalty portion of this leveraging—are we talking blackmail?"

"They would consider the term crass—it's more like reparation."

"Sound like an opportunity to refill the coffers to me."

"I'm sure the operation likes to think of it more as a necessity, especially if the faux pas was severe enough that they were forced to write off that location."

"Or pull up stake and move to a new one."

"That too," she replied, her tone weary as she pulled a handkerchief from her coat pocket and patted her lips. Her skin had taken on a more grayish cast since we started chatting and a small bead of sweat lined her lip. Once again, I started to ask her if she needed assistance, but she waved me off, changing the subject in the same movement. "You talked of talking action earlier."

I nodded, pleased that she'd circled the conversation back. "We continue what Shelby and Leah started and peck away until we find someone who will break that trust."

"Okay, I'll bite…but *how*?"

"By getting inside." She raised a brow but I pressed on. "I mean, you already seem to know how a lot of this works, right?"

She nodded slowly. "Let me give it some thought."

I wasn't sure if she meant today, tomorrow, or next week and though I didn't have time for any of it, she'd at least heard me out.

"I'd appreciate that. It's more than Leah, and likely, Shelby, had."

She looked down, clasping her gloved hands

together as though she was attempting to rub away a chill.

"You know, there's one thing I never asked you."

She tilted her head, hands still clasped. "What's that?"

"How is it that you know so much about all of this?" *And why do you care?* I desperately wanted to ask but didn't. There had to be a reason she'd sought me out, other than to learn what I knew about Tamryn. "Were you involved in the operation at some point?"

The cryptic smile returned but she offered no response.

A moment of silence passed before I turned to her. "Why did you even tell me all of this? What is it you want from me?"

She laughed and this time, though tired, it sounded genuine, like little bells clinking together on a breezy day. "Does there always have to be an ulterior motive for what people do?"

I shrugged. Perhaps I'd become jaded in the last few months, but in my recent experience, strangers just didn't show up offering the promise of rainbows and sunshine—unless they wanted something in return.

The laughter fell away and she matched my silence. "Fine. You've got an 'in' that I don't. Tamryn. Plus, you've got youth on your side and you're motivated. You just need a bit of…direction."

I shot her a withering look. "And that's what you are offering—'direction'?"

She offered me nothing more than a shrug.

"Fine. Then answer me this—what do *you* get in return?"

The response came quickly.

"Salvation."

With that, she smiled, patted me on the knee and rose to leave. I wasn't sure whose she was hoping to attain but didn't have the heart to tell her that at the end of this, salvation may be thin.

"One more thing—you never told me your name."

"Dina."

"Dina what?"

"Just Dina."

"What…like Cher? Madonna? Beyonce?"

She smiled but said nothing.

"Wait—don't you want to know who *I* am?"

She glanced over her shoulder, once again giving me that pained but cryptic smile. "Somehow, I think I've always known, Arianna Jackson."

She turned back and before I could utter a syllable, she disappeared into the depths of the park.

No sooner than I had turned around and nestled back against the bench after watching Dina's trench-coated frame disappear into the backdrop, I heard a familiar snuffing, followed by a wet nose in the ear.

"Would you believe me if I told you that Nicoh wanted to stretch his legs?" Martin came around the bench but stopped short of sitting down. Taking measure of my twisted mouth and squinted eyes, he raised a hand.

I absently scratched Nicoh, more to encourage him to cease his investigation into my inner ear canal, but still using the distraction as an opportunity to allow the silence to linger.

Martin shifted from leg to leg and began whistling—a pet peeve of mine. Finally, unable to take it any longer, I rolled my eyes, stood, and gestured for him to speak.

He stopped whistling, seemingly unaware he'd been doing it in the first place. "Oh, right. Ramirez called."

"Ramirez. Called *you*?" I crossed my arms and tapped a foot on the ground.

Martin's face pulled as he frowned. "He *did* try to get ahold of you first."

Not wanting to give him the satisfaction of having to check it, I was thankful when I remembered that I'd turned it off when I'd stormed out of the house.

"I didn't realize the two of you had gotten so tight that you'd actually exchanged numbers. Better watch out, Martin. Next, you'll be sharing selfies."

"Comes with the territory when trying to keep track of you," he muttered under his breath, only realizing that I'd caught every last incriminating syllable when I singed him with a withering glare. Nicoh tugged on his lead, raring to run the park as Martin sighed. "Do you want to hear what he had to say or not?"

It was my turn to return the exasperation. "Honestly, it depends."

Truth be told, it did.

"On what?" He cocked his head and appeared genuinely interested.

"On whether he's just going to feed me more puzzle pieces that don't fit and loose ends that go nowhere while getting us to do his legwork," I huffed.

Martin nodded, though I wasn't sure whether it was simply an attempt to make nice. "Who's your friend?"

"No one." I stared him down until he looked away.

"She seemed…familiar," he murmured, glancing in the direction that Dina had disappeared into the trees.

"Did she?" If he wanted to play that game, he would need to show his cards first.

Martin's eyes cut back to me and for a moment, I thought he might continue down that path, but he didn't.

"So…Ramirez."

"Yes," I replied.

"Yes, you want to involve him, or yes, it's open for discussion?"

"Aren't those one and the same?"

Martin rubbed his free hands through his neatly trimmed salt and pepper hair. "I told him this would be difficult."

I choked out a laugh. "'This' would be difficult? Or *I* would be?"

"One and the same," he deadpanned.

I waved a hand. "Fine, do whatever you gotta do."

"About that." His cheeks turned an unnatural shade of crimson.

"What?" I growled. "Geez! Just spit it out."

"He said he'd meet us back at the house." He glanced at his watch. "Now."

My mouth opened. Closed. Finally, I drummed up a PG-13 response, though I thrust a hand on my hip, for effect. "Well, then. Good thing you just *happened* along, isn't it?"

"I wasn't following you. If that's what you're suggesting."

"But…" I prompted.

"But…what?"

"I suppose it didn't hurt that you found me, having a private conversation with someone who 'seemed familiar'."

"If you want to know if I overheard your

conversation with the woman, Arianna, just say so."

"So."

Martin shook his head. "I'm heading back to the house. I drove. Come along if you want. Or not." He avoided looking at me as he shoved his hands in his pockets as he ambled past, back in the direction he'd come.

I withheld the snaky quip about being invited to my own house, choosing to collect my canine, who was happily chasing some guinea fowl into the bushes and none too happy about being forced to retreat.

Ramirez's truck was already parked in the driveway alongside Martin's vehicle when we returned.

I lingered outside the door, hoping to catch some banter or random chitchat, and was surprised when I heard none. I walked in to find Martin leaning his back against the far kitchen counter, lips pressed together as Ramirez leaned on the island, checking text messages on his phone. He glanced up at my arrival, or more accurately, to Nicoh's invasive nose-in-the-crotch welcome.

He nodded hello as I chose the space the farthest distance from Martin without physically leaving the city. Ramirez finished scrolling and crudely crafted a short text using some ancient hunt and peck method. After deleting more words than he'd typed and starting over, he pushed "Send" and tucked the phone into his pocket. Suddenly aware of the silence, he glanced first at me, then at Martin and back again.

"Did I interrupt something?"

Martin opened his mouth to speak, but I beat him to it.

"Martin said you had something to tell us." My tone sounded alien and flat, even to my own ears.

Ramirez squinted, his eyes searching mine as he gauged my current demeanor. "Yeah. Hmm. Guess I'll get right to it, then."

I offered him a curt nod, ignoring Martin's attempt to catch my eyes. Ramirez looked at us one more time before shaking his head.

"I think I got you a lead."

*Don't you mean to say that **you** got a lead and that you are choosing to share it with us?* I wanted to snipe, but Ramirez had done nothing to deserve that retort. Honestly, I was kind of over being gravelly with Martin, too. It was just too exhausting.

Though it wasn't in his nature to specifically say so, I wouldn't have been the least bit surprised if the feeling wasn't mutual.

"This isn't an official lead, by any means. It was more of a right time, right place type of situation," Ramirez added.

"Thought you didn't believe in those."

"I didn't say coincidences." He winked, causing me to blush.

I did not venture a glance in Martin's direction. Oh, heck, no.

"I was getting my morning cup of Joe—I'm a regular, so the barista called me 'Detective' when my drink was up. A gal, who I assumed had been in line, caught up to me as I was heading back to the truck and asked if she could have a quick word. I had a few minutes to spare, so I agreed. Though she was obviously nervous and seemed to have second thoughts, she finally told me she had a hypothetical situation she wanted to get my 'expert opinion' on. Her phrasing, not mine." Ramirez chuckled.

"Does this sort of thing happen often in your

line of work?" Martin asked after an awkward moment of fidgeting and silence.

"Not really." Ramirez waved a hand. "People tend to either ask straight up, or they avoid us altogether—like we've got the black plague or something."

"Blue. Blue plague." When he quirked a brow, I added, "People see law enforcement and even though they've done nothing wrong, once they think they might be on the cop's radar, it makes 'em all jittery and they act out of character, almost to the point where they inadvertently do something stupid that ends up attracting attention."

Ramirez was somewhere between aghast and contemplative, as though nothing so foreign had ever crossed his mind. "Experienced this much?"

I nodded. "All the time."

He glanced at Martin, who shrugged. "I guess it seems somewhat logical. Where Arianna is concerned."

"Okay, Spock, like you've *never* looked over your shoulder, worried the fuzz was onto you." I hacked out a laugh, and even Ramirez chuckled.

Martin looked…perplexed. "Fuzz?"

"Never mind." I rolled my eyes at Ramirez, who shook his head, still flummoxed by the left-turn this convo, amid a bit of a cold war, had taken. "So, this hypothetical situation."

"Right. I'm going to paraphrase what she told me, for brevity's sake, but I think you'll still get the gist. Basically, her scenario is centered around two sisters. The younger one moved from their home state to stay with her sister while looking for work."

"Where's this hypothetical home state?" Martin asked.

"Kansas," Ramirez replied. "And yes, this was the younger sister's first solo trip without her parents. So, to celebrate this new freedom, while helping her lil' sis get acclimated, the older sister decided to take her out on the town and show her the sites on her first Saturday night in town. Enter the club scene in Old Town Scottsdale."

Martin and I released a collective groan. "Let me guess…while at the club, they were approached by another girl and invited to an after-party."

Ramirez cocked his head at me, likely realizing he was a couple of skips behind and that he had no idea what the two of us had been up to since the last time we spoke. "Yes, they were approached, but while they were at the party, the two got separated."

I shrugged. "It happens." Garnering sideglances from both of them, I quickly added, "Or so I've heard."

Martin stare turned frosty, his frown clearly pasted across his face, which was not only making me uncomfortable, it was not his place to judge or admonish my behavior. I was a grown adult. Ramirez cleared his throat, and for a moment, I thought I'd accidentally spewed that last bit out loud, but thankfully, it was solely to move on with this hypothetical story he'd been told.

"Anyway, the younger sister caught a ride back to the club with the other girls, where her sister's car was parked. She repeatedly called and texted her sister's cell but received no response and without keys, left her sister a final message, caught a taxi and went home."

"This story doesn't seem to have a point, *Detective*," Martin commented. "Are you sure the girl just didn't have some sort of crush on you and so she devised a way to talk to you alone?"

"Seriously?" I muttered under my breath, which Ramirez caught, but his face was solemn.

"Unfortunately, there *was* a point, *Martin*," he replied, shifting his gaze to the older man. "In this scenario, the older sister had gone to a few of these after-parties and occasionally had such a good time, she went on to another, or two. Only this time, she never made it home."

I gasped. "'Never made it home' as in she's still missing?"

Ramirez nodded. "Sound familiar?"

I sucked in a breath. Now he had my attention. "Horrifyingly so. What else did she say?"

He ran his hand through his hair again as he shook his head. "That was about the extent of it. She then asked what I would tell someone if that hypothetical situation were true, after adding in that I should assume that all the girl's friends had been contacted but that none of them had seen or heard from her and that her workplace called, saying she hadn't shown up.

"Anyway, I told her I would tell the younger sister in this scenario to give law enforcement the benefit of the doubt and report her sister missing. She freaked a little at that, and that's when the 'story' became a reality. She did an excellent job of keeping it together until that point when she broke down and came clean.

"Turns out, this girl's parents had warned her against leaving home—and had put a lot of pressure on her older sister as a result—and with her now missing, she was afraid to tell them. First, because she didn't want to let her sister down, and second, she didn't want her parents demanding that one or both of them come home."

His brows cinching as he appeared to be thinking about something. "What she added to that made the hairs on the back of my neck bristle. Before they had gotten separated, her sister told her that whatever happened at the after-party, stayed at the after-party."

"That's just something that people say, Ramirez."

"I get that." His eyes met mine. "But her sister also said that if either of them 'talked' to anyone—and yes, I am using finger quotes here —*both* of them would be at risk."

"Wow." I shook my head, wishing I could forget what I'd heard. "Unfortunate just how quickly that came true." Martin and Ramirez nodded solemnly. "So, what did you tell her?"

Ramirez pressed his lips together, working his mouth while rubbing his chin as creases etched the corners of his eyes. "She still refused, so I did the next best thing I could think of in a pinch—I convinced her to meet you." He hesitated, clearly studying my expression. I'm sure it fully conveyed the surprise I felt and quickly shut my mouth to prevent any flying insects from taking up residence. 'Cause that's just nasty.

Surprised by the lack of words that typically followed, he took the rare opportunity for silence and pressed on. "Without going into all the details, I said I knew someone who had experienced something similar with her best friend. Didn't want to frighten her any more than she already was. Poor thing was shaking so badly by the end, I had to coax her to sit down and drink some water and have a bit of a muffin. Anyway, I'm hoping you can talk to her and convince her to talk to me."

I gave him a noncommittal shrug. I wasn't opposed to talking with the girl but wasn't comfortable swaying her into doing something I wasn't likely to do myself.

Ramirez surveyed me for a moment before adding, "If nothing else, maybe the two of you could just do your girl-bonding thing. She may be more at ease with you to the point she'll open up and fill you in on some of the details that she wouldn't tell me—specifics that could help her sister, and maybe even Leah. Anything will help at this point."

I nodded. "Good thinking. When does she want to meet?"

Ramirez glanced at his watch and winced. "Right about now."

"What? Here?" While I had no problem chatting with the girl, I wasn't comfortable inviting a complete stranger into my house, kindred spirit or not.

He held up both hands. "Relax. Not here. That wouldn't be wise for anyone. As it turns out, she works at the coffee shop and will have a break soon. Otherwise…"

"I get it." I waved him off. "Sorry, you just caught me off-guard. I should have known you would opt for safety first."

"I was hoping that would have been a forgone conclusion by now," he murmured, garnering a raised brow from Martin, who had been noticeably quiet. And diligently observing, as always.

I ignored both of their man-moods and returned to the matter at hand. "What's her name?"

"Sea breeze."

"Excuse me?"

"Sorry, just a little exercise that I've been using to jog the brain cells. Her name is Misty."

I fought the urge to roll my eyes—it was something I'd have expected from Martin. But not Ramirez. Besides, "Play Misty for Me" would have killed two birds with one stone. "Right. I take it you aren't coming?"

He shook his head as he checked an incoming slew of text messages. "Wasn't invited. Besides, I need to get back to work. Just wanted to deliver the news in person."

"I appreciate that." And I did. I hoped the sincerity of my tone aptly conveyed that, though I doubted it made up for my little outburst. "What about him?" I nodded at Martin, who ignored my gaze.

"Best if you go alone," Ramirez replied, his eyes still focused on his messages.

"My thoughts exactly. I just wanted *him* to hear it."

Ramirez raised his head and quirked a brow. "You could have just as easily told him yourself."

"He's standing right here and can speak for himself, in case anyone cared," Martin grumbled.

"Now you see why I wanted to go alone."

Ramirez shrugged. "Sounds like a family matter. I'm strictly here in an—"

"Just stop right there, Detective. You can't use the old 'official capacity' bit. Otherwise, you wouldn't have shown up at all." I'll admit, I laid the snark on a bit thick.

"What's that supposed to mean? Of course, if it was a law enforcement matter, I would have shown up."

"Do I need to point out that you are a *homicide* detective?" I crossed my arms and leaned back, thoroughly enjoying the open-mouthed, befuddled, and possibly aghast expressions that were running across the detective's face.

"She's right. No bodies here, Detective." I gave Martin an approving nod. It was one of his better comebacks.

"Not yet, anyway." Ramirez caught on and pointed a finger at each of us.

"Careful, Ramirez, your colors are showing," I chuckled.

"Before you say 'blue' again, I'm making my exit." He shoved his phone into his pocket, nodded at Martin, and started for the door, pausing as he pulled it open. "Later, you will fill me in, on all of it."

I noted it was a demand and not a request.

"Likewise," I replied, causing him to pause as something…unreadable crossed his face. I would have asked him, but under Martin's watchful eyes, let it pass as he grunted and tugged the door shut behind him.

"Guess that's my cue to be on my way to meet Ms. Sea Breeze," I commented loudly enough to ensure I had Martin's full attention. Though I said nothing more, I cast him a look that would have curled his toenails if he insisted on following me.

I'm not sure it had the desired effect, but it sure felt good to get that piece of business out of the way.

I had to hustle to get to the coffee shop in a reasonable amount of time. Of course, it didn't help that I elected to take Nicoh. He was more belligerent than usual about leaving the house during his nap time but given his recent behavior, decided that he and Martin had engaged in more than enough bonding time.

Translation: I didn't want Nicoh taking liberties when it came to who the boss in this household was. Or Martin either, for that matter.

Canine finally coaxed into venturing outside his strict schedule—we departed.

I had expected to receive at least *some* pushback from Martin and was surprised when he had quietly busied himself, repairing a wobbly leg on one of the kitchen stools. I hadn't asked him to do so and wondered if it had been a peace offering after our recent bout of spats.

I still wasn't convinced that he wouldn't attempt to follow, but I was so late in meeting Misty that I couldn't bother worrying about what he might or might not do. I could only hope that if he ignored Ramirez's recommendation, he'd make himself scarce.

Misty was waiting for us in the outdoor patio area when we arrived. Though Ramirez hadn't given me a description, the area was empty, aside from a sole female occupant, making it easy to identify her. That, and she was craning her neck from side to side as she surveyed the parking lot and short line of walk-up customers. Spotting me, she rose and offered a timid wave, tucking her strawberry-blond braid over her shoulder as she self-consciously smoothed invisible wrinkles from her work t-shirt and shorts.

"Arianna?" her voice was childlike, and combined with her petite stature, I would have pegged her for much younger.

"AJ, please. And this is Nicoh." I tilted my head at my companion, who murmured a low round of his own form of greeting as he leaned in for a proper introduction.

"Hi, AJ. Nicoh," she chuckled. "I'm Misty." Her eyes widened as Nicoh went in nose-first to her hand, nudging it insistently.

"Nicoh. Behave." I ignored the grumbling that ensued as I ushered him back and apologized. "He's friendly, but if you prefer not—"

"Oh, no…he's fine. He's just…really…big!" Misty laughed as Nicoh shifted so that he was within optimum scratching distance.

Some people might have considered it an invasion of their private space, but she took it in stride and giggled as she complied with his demands, which had escalated to the audible variety.

"My dad has hunting dogs, though I'll admit, we use that term loosely. He actually rescues older dogs—many of them are retired working or hunting dogs—that serve as his companions while he works out on the farm, on his hunting trips…well, pretty much anywhere. We like to tease him about preferring canines to most people. And, funnily enough, he doesn't deny it."

Our laughter fell away as the topic turned to the matter at hand and we got situated at a patio table in the corner. Nicoh lapped water from a nearby doggie dish. I inwardly groaned as he downed it in a few short intakes—most of which trailed down the sides of his mouth in a jowl-like formation.

Misty either didn't notice or was too polite to comment. "So you're friends with Detective Ramirez?"

I bobbed my head, keeping watch on Nicoh as I did. Last thing I wanted was for him to do was douse the poor girl with slobber before I could rein him in.

"Yeah, Ramirez—err, the detective and I have known each other for a while. So yeah, I guess you could say we're friends. Or at least friendly…that is, as friendly as one can get without it actually meaning something more." A nice, succinct answer would have sufficed, AJ, I thought to myself.

Fortunately, Misty hadn't noticed my bumbling about for a response, murmuring, "Sounds nice," as she absently scratched Nicoh.

Where had he come from? I bristled, realizing he'd effectively proved my point about taking my eyes off him for even a second.

"He told me about your hypothetical situation."

She opened her mouth to speak but closed it as her face reddened. Belatedly, I realized my delivery could have been finessed a bit had I not been so distracted by my canine's antics.

"I'm so sorry, Misty. I didn't mean to embarrass you—especially when things are probably so hard right now."

She waved me off, the embarrassment fading from her cheeks but perhaps not from within.

Her voice was shaky as she replied, "It was stupid, I know. I didn't know what else to do. He comes in every day—but it took me a week to muster the nerve to approach him. I was sure he would—" she shook her head. "Honestly, I don't know what I thought he'd do. Or could do. I'm sure he told you he encouraged me to file a missing persons' report."

I nodded. "Have you given that any further consideration?"

"Every waking moment. I just…" she shrugged, staring off into the parking lot.

"You worry about what your parents will think."

"Yeah, if I told them, only to have her show

up…well, they'll blame Jilli for leaving me alone out here. I know they'll make me go back home, and she'll lose their trust. I guess I just don't want to be responsible for that."

Despite my desire to do so, I didn't need to rehash the ground Ramirez had already covered. She had done enough ruminating and worrying on her own, based on the dark patches beneath her eyes. "Your sister, Jilli, was it?

Misty nodded. "Short for Jillian, but only close friends and family call her that."

A tiny smile escaped as she extracted her cellphone from her pocket and opened it to the home screen, which displayed a smiling picture of her with her sister in happier times. There was no mistaking the family resemblance—the hair, the ocean blue eyes and the pale, freckled skin. Like her sister, Jillian appeared younger than her years. A wave of sadness rushed over me.

"Detective Ramirez said your best friend is missing, too?"

"Yes, Leah. We've been friends…well, longer than we haven't." Leah and I were not sisters by blood, but she had been part of my family for almost as long as we'd been alive.

I explained that I'd been out of town, assumed that Leah had been in L.A., and had only recently learned that she had been in Phoenix prior to my return.

Misty nodded. I wasn't sure whether she could tell that I was withholding details, but pressed on. "Would you like to tell me what happened with Jillian? Only if you're comfortable doing so, that is."

I assumed she knew I meant the real version and not the one she'd initially offered Ramirez. Thankfully, she did not disappoint, relaying the event in first-person rather than as an onlooker in some hypothetical scenario.

At first, much of what she outlined meshed with Tamryn's regarding the clubs, vans, parties —adding in that they were encouraged to freshen up their wardrobes, accessories, hair and makeup, compliments of the host, upon arrival —which coincided with what Dina had said.

"It was amazing. There were racks and racks of these really high-end clothes, plus cases of jewelry—which was not real, but sure looked like it. And the hair and makeup girls were so nice. Each commented that I had that 'it' factor. Jilli had told me she was glad we never had brothers because they would have turned out to be total pigs." She scrunched her nose and offering me a knowing look and was about to continue down that path until I interjected.

"Wait a minute. I thought you and your sister got separated?"

Misty started wringing her hands as that cherry tomato tint resurfaced to highlight her cheeks. "Um, that's just what I told Detective Ramirez."

"The hypothetical one."

The redness deepened. "Well, he never asked me to clarify. I didn't think he'd take me seriously if I told him everything…you know, about the parties."

"So there's actually been more than one?" She gave me a single nod. "Okay, how many?" When she stared at her hands, I patted them and quickly added, "I'm not judging you, Misty, just trying to get a sense so that we can figure a few things out."

Her response came out in a whisper, still focusing on her clasped fingers. "A handful, I guess."

I raised a brow. "So your sister *didn't* disappear on that first night?"

"I never actually said that. Detective Ramirez just drew that conclusion."

And she had let him.

I withheld a sigh. From Ramirez's telling, I had already gotten the impression that Misty had been selective in the details she's elected to tell him as well as those she'd left out. Though I could assume it had to do with the cop factor, I had to wonder why she was still playing it that way with me?

Ramirez had assumed that she would be more forthcoming with a kindred spirit of sorts but had he unintentionally forced her hand? Had she gone along willingly to avoid him pursuing the missing persons' report further? There was nothing I could do about that now but press forward…gently. The guilt and anxiety were clearly weighing on her and pushing her too hard may send her running for cover. And possibly into the hands of danger.

"Okay, so what was different about that night? Anything seem off? Or anyone giving off a bad vibe that you recall?"

Misty squinted. "Not really. My sister got a text a couple of hours beforehand that she said had the name of the club."

"So you didn't see it? The text, that is?"

"No," she replied. "And actually, now that I think of it, I never saw any of them."

That was curious—why had Jillian chosen to keep them from her sister, and how had she gotten on this notification list in the first place?

"What about the cards?"

Misty cocked her head. "What cards?" She shook her head as I quickly explained what I'd previously learned. "No, I don't think I saw anything like that going on, and if Jilli ever received one, she didn't mention it."

"So, how did you end up at the party the night your sister disappeared?"

"I didn't."

"Excuse me?"

"I never actually went to a party that night."

I bit my lip. Hard.

Had I missed something along the way? Or was Misty intentionally keeping me in the dark?

"But your sister got an invite at some point while you were at the club and went to one?" I found it hard to believe she'd leave her younger sister, a newcomer to town and barely legal, just so that she could attend some swank after-party alone. Then again, I only had Misty's view of her sister's character to go on. Not exactly unbiased.

"She must have." Misty frowned. Perhaps it was starting to make less and less sense to her, too. "I mean…I waited in the club and then in the parking lot later, but she just never came back." She bit her lip and refused to meet my gaze.

What was causing this sudden reluctance? Realization dawned. "You and your sister didn't always end up going to after-parties together, did you? Sometimes she went and you waited."

Misty replied, her voice quiet as she resumed wringing her hands. "Actually, I only went to the one. My sister said it worked out like that sometimes and asked me if that was okay. I said it was. I truly didn't mind staying at the club. And she always showed up, sooner or later. That was, until the night she didn't come back."

"And you did a thorough search of the club and asked everyone—bartenders, waitresses, bouncers, other patrons?"

She nodded, tears welling. "Everyone. I was pretty much the last one to leave, besides the staff, and no one had seen her since earlier in the evening. Most didn't remember her at all."

"What about the girls who returned from the after-party?"

She shook her head and sniffled. "None of them remembered seeing her either."

I chewed my lip, trying to make sense of what had happened between the time the two girls had arrived until Jillian vanished. "Let me ask you this—did you see your sister talking to anyone in particular that night—someone perhaps that you had seen on a prior occasion?"

Misty wiped her eyes with the back of her hand. "I don't think so. I don't know that many people, though. What are you thinking?"

I didn't want to tell her I was starting to wonder if her sister had made it to a party that night at all and had instead disappeared from the club before the pickup. Perhaps she was tricked into a diversion by an acquaintance she'd met on a previous occasion that had nothing to do with the after-party angle—but why? And for what purpose? It was all too coincidental.

Regardless of the scenarios running through my mind, none of them served Misty without something more to go on than my wild conjectures. I released a long breath, using it as an opportunity to redirect.

"I just find it curious that no one remembered seeing her, especially considering she's been to the club on more than one occasion."

Misty nodded. "And I honesty asked everyone, too."

For now, I moved forward based on the assumption Jillian had left the club of her free will.

"Well, one of those girls would've likely invited her to the after-party, so there is at least one person who should have remembered her, but didn't." Convenient.

"Do you think she—whoever 'she' is—lied to me?" Her facial features contorted as she considered this.

"*If* your sister was invited to the party and you spoke to everyone on the girl's transport when it returned, then most definitely. Besides, if she made it to this party, the driver should have recognized the photo you showed him, too, yet he didn't."

Her eyes widened. "You're absolutely right! Darn it—I was so stupid. And weak. I should have pressed people harder. If the situation had been reversed, Jilli would have." She wrung her hands, then pressed them to her eyes. "If anything happens to her…"

Reaching over, I gently pulled her hands down. "Don't beat yourself up. From what I've gathered, secrecy is highly sought-after and rewarded where these after-parties are concerned. So I doubt they would have told you anything—at least not without putting themselves at risk."

I quickly realized I should have chosen my words a bit more carefully, as Misty released an audible gasp.

"Oh…no…no…no. You don't think I put Jilli in more danger, do you?"

I shook my head but, in reality, wasn't sure. Regardless, the girl had enough on her plate without heaping another serving of guilt and worry on top.

"I'm sorry I was less than truthful with the detective," she commented after a moment. "At the time, I had drummed up all kinds of excuses to justify it. Honestly, I was just scared."

"Misty, look at me. Anyone would have been scared in that situation."

She gave a half-shrug but nodded. "What happened with Jilli…is that what happened to your friend Leah?"

I sucked in a breath. I knew this moment would come—it wasn't a matter of if—but when. Did I come clean about Shelby and Leah and potentially cause Misty more worry and anxiety? Or did I protect her feelings by simply agreeing and risk her finding out later?

In the end, I selected with option one, figuring it was better if she knew how my best friend had gotten involved, but stopped just short of relaying the condition of Leah's car when it was in long-term parking at the airport. No one facing a missing loved one would be served from learning that the only reason it had been found so quickly.

Misty nodded as I relayed the details, often covering her mouth to rein in the shock over something. When I finished, she expelled a breath and sat for a moment. I allowed her time to digest what I told her—it was a lot—even for me.

Finally, she spoke. "Thank you for telling me. I know that can't have been easy for you, either. I don't know how you're managing to keep it together so well. It's not like you're used to having someone you love disappear on you any more than I am."

I could have told her otherwise. But knowing my past would not help her in the present or bring her sister, Shelby, or Leah home in the future.

My phone vibrated in my pocket. I extracted it, noting I had a message from Ramirez—that would have to wait—and about to shove it back in my pocket when Misty gasped and grabbed my wrist, nearly causing me to release my grasp on the cell as she stabbed the home screen with a bubblegum-colored nail that had been chewed beyond repair.

"Why do you have *her* picture on your cell?"

I didn't need to follow her wide-eyed gaze.

The memory of that day was embedded in my mind as my best friend had snatched my phone to catch one last selfie. The two of us. In a happier moment. Laughing.

It was the day my best friend had all but disappeared from my life.

CHAPTER TWENTY

Misty jabbed her finger at the screen as she swiveled her head, her eyes more white than pupil as they met mine.

"You *know* her. Who…who is she?"

I wasn't sure what she saw when she looked at me, but a sinking sensation riveted through my body as I responded, "It's Leah. My best friend."

"The one who is missing," she murmured, staring at the picture again. "I've *seen* her."

I still didn't believe in coincidences and I didn't like where this was headed.

"Where?" My voice sounded calmer than I

felt. Overwhelmed and nauseated didn't even begin to cover it.

"At the club. I recognize that hair. Jilli said she looked just like Meg Ryan in some 1990s movie where her character stalks her ex-boyfriend or something or other. I'd never heard of it, but Jilli said there's a song about it and everything."

"*Addicted to Love*," I replied, referencing both the title of the movie and the song by the late Robert Palmer. I'd heard my best friend likened to that character—her hair, not her demeanor—on more than a few occasions, though it had never been her intention. Leah was one-of-a-kind. "Did you talk to her?"

Misty shook her head. "She was talking to another girl—one that Jilli said looked familiar. That's what made us notice your friend."

"Can you describe her—the other girl, that is?"

She did, and I withheld an urge to groan. Either Tamryn had a doppelganger out hitting the same clubs she frequented, or Leah had gotten herself up close and personal with my new and not-so-reliable-source-of-information.

"Then what happened?"

"The other girl's attitude changed—she looked mad enough to kill someone. It was like she had been putting on a show or something before your friend left. Once she was gone, she confronted this other girl who had this crazy colored hair pulled up high. Which made it look even crazier. I think she had some sort of tattoo on her neck. Anyway, it seemed like they were really getting into it."

"About Leah?"

Misty frowned. "I'm not sure. We weren't close enough, though it might have been something your friend said to the first girl that set her off. The two had moved to the bar and when Jilli went to get us a couple of waters, heard her say something to the other girl along the lines of 'asking about Shelly' or something like that." She squinted, then shook her head. "I just don't know."

Yet another coincidence. Not.

"Could it have been Shelby?"

"Maybe." she shrugged. "Jilli said it was super loud, but whatever the other one said in response made the one with the crazy hair pull her cell out and start texting so fast her cell should have caught fire. Whoever she was sending them to called her back, too."

"How can you be sure?"

"She was in such a hurry to get out of there to answer it, she ran into Jilli. Said some pretty rude things, even though she knocked Jilli's drink into both of us. It was like we were in her way and should have known to clear a path." Misty rolled her eyes.

"When was this?"

"Um…well, at least a couple of weeks ago. Before Jilli went missing, of course."

And around the time Leah was supposed to have left town.

Had her car been stashed in long-term parking all that time? Merely as a diversion? If so, by Leah, or the person/people who had absconded with her?

Either way, Tamryn has some serious explaining to do once I was finished with Misty.

At that moment, my cell chirped, startling both of us.

Extracting the phone from my pocket—I knew who the caller was from the ringtone and excused myself to take the call.

"What's up?"

"Are you still with the girl…Misty?" I could tell Ramirez was still using his memory-conjuring exercise as I glanced over my shoulder to find Nicoh in Misty's capable hands, playing his version of "shake," which was more like an awkward game of patty-cake.

It was nice to see the girl smile for a bit, even if my canine's unabashed buffoonery was the cause.

"Yes, why?"

"Okay. Act like you're schmoozing a client."

"Excuse me? I don't—"

"Just do it, AJ," he snapped.

I gritted my teeth. This had better be good. "Absolutely. That's no problem. We can shift the photo shoot back to accommodate—if you just let me know your *plans*."

"There's been a development. And before you get excited and blow your cover, it's not about Leah."

My heart sank a little, but I sucked it up and played along. "Okay…I'm listening."

"Did Misty happen to show you a picture of her sister, Jillian?"

I wasn't sure how he knew that. I'd been under the impression that Misty hadn't gotten that far in her story. "Yes, that's correct. Can you just confirm those details again?"

"Strawberry blond with fair skin and freckles. Looks no more than sixteen but is in her early twenties, at most."

"Perfect. I couldn't agree more."

"We may have located her."

"That sounds great. Do you know when they'll have that ready? I can pick it up and go from there."

"You're doing real good. But that's not going to be possible. A girl has been found, matching that description. Dead."

I pressed my eyes together and released a breath before responding, thankful my back was still to Misty. "Would you mind clarifying the specifics, just to ensure we are on the same page?"

"AJ…I'm not sure—"

"I'm ready to take down the details whenever you've got 'em handy."

Ramirez sighed. "Fine. I can't tell you much. A buddy over in Scottsdale caught the case while we were catching up over a game of hoops. Asked him to keep me posted. Anyway, from the initial call, a bartender who works at the club found her and then identified her as a regular. He had gone in early to do some bar prep, and as he was entering through the back entrance, he saw a person slumped against some pallets. At first, he thought she was a homeless person and tried to roust her without success. After confirming there was no pulse, he called 9-1-1.”

I huffed out another breath and tried to maintain the facade, even though my composure was failing miserably. I popped a quick look at Misty and found her still occupied, which offered me a momentary reprieve.

“Keep it together, AJ, for just a bit longer.” I appreciated the boost of faith, and from his earnest tone, knew he meant it. “Turns out, she dropped her license in the club—issued to one Jillian Rochester. The bartender fished it from the lost and found box. Wasn’t sure who found it in the first place but remembered it being in there when someone came looking for a pair of sunglasses the day before. Anyway, he’ll be checking with the rest of the staff once they arrive. He’s motivated, both he and his boss want this off their plates, so my buddy thought he’d be hearing from them soon.”

"Any idea what 'it' was?" I struggled to find the words I wanted to ask without alerting Misty.

Ramirez blew out a long breath. "The medical examiner needs to confirm, but it was either the blunt force trauma-related injuries she sustained or an overdose. He just needs to figure out which came first. Did one induce the other? Or is someone trying to mask the trauma under the guise of an overdose-related injury?"

"Oh!" I put a hand to my mouth, whispering, "Poor Misty."

"Poor Jillian."

I noted something simmering behind his calm delivery. "Are you not finding that a plausible explanation?"

"Are you?"

"Not in the least." True, Misty had been less than forthcoming with him, though I believed whatever happened to her sister had been put into motion that night at the club. Jillian had put herself on someone's radar and whatever transgression she'd made would have to have been made right on a later date. Which would explain why she had never made it to the after-party she'd been invited to. Something told me that

Tamryn knew it, too. "But I'll have to fill you in later."

"Before you go, there is one thing I wasn't sure I should mention. Without confirmation, that is."

His hesitation gave me pause but before he could retract it, I pressed on. "Whatever it is, I think it would be good to know."

"I asked my buddy to check." He blew out a breath before delving the next blow. "Jillian's blood was a match to the second type found in the trunk of Leah's car."

I had no words and was thankful when I received a reprieve when two events coincided: 1) Ramirez got called away on cop stuff and 2) Misty's break was ending and she, too, needed to return to work.

After letting Ramirez know I'd touch base with him later, Misty and I swapped numbers and she sent me a picture of Jillian. I gave her one of Leah, just in case. When I thanked her, she surprised me by pulling me in for a quick hug before kissing Nicoh on the top of the head and rushing back to her barista duties, apron in hand. I was glad she hadn't made me promise to call her with any information, because the next time she received news about her sister, it wouldn't be good. And it wouldn't be coming from me.

If there had been any shred of hope that Jillian would turn up on her own, regaling her sister in some crazy *"What happens in...stays in..."* tale, Ramirez had effectively squashed that with his call.

What made matters worse was that Leah and Shelby had been gone longer, and Jillian's death had brought forth a reality that I wasn't prepared to accept, for either of them.

Not by a long shot.

It gave me no pleasure knowing that the blood in the trunk matched Jillian's. It had been an inevitable truth, which had been made more difficult now that we had a person, with a sister, a family and what had once been a life, to attach to that. And though Ramirez had provided a best-guess on the causes of death, it still didn't account for how Jillian had ended up in Leah's trunk or why her body had been dumped in the alley behind the club.

The similarities of that last detail in both Jillian's and my twin sister Victoria's deaths—the careless way in which their bodies had been tossed aside like their lives had meant nothing—sent a shiver through my body.

It both infuriated and motivated me.

It also made me feel somewhat protective of Misty, who not only appeared youthful despite her years, but was innocent and naïve to the cruelties of this world. I vowed I would not allow her to endure as much pain as I had. Such cruelty had not only cost me a sister, it had caused damage in ways that would never be repaired.

As I headed home, I mulled over Misty's recollection of her outings with her sister and how Tamryn—if it had in fact been Tamryn that Misty and Jillian had seen—had reacted to whatever she and Leah had been discussing.

Two things piqued my spidey senses. The first was that Tamryn seemed to have more pull in this operation than she'd initially alluded to and second, she'd flat out lied about it.

Why?

There was more going on than after-parties, hookups and special favors for those who could pay, and I knew she was holding back on whatever "it" was. I gritted my teeth. I would get what I needed out of her, one way or another.

I just had to track her down first.

I was pondering that as I walked into my house, haphazardly tossing my keys and phone onto the counter before belting out an obscenity, just as Martin's head popped up from behind the stove that he had pulled out to do God knows what.

"Oh, you're finally back. We need to talk."

"*Now* is not a good time," I growled, noting he was cleaning behind my appliances. *Cleaning?*

"It's imperative," he replied, taking no note of my pained expression, having just seen the evidence of what he'd found in the dustpan and murky mop bucket liquid, which I could only assume had once been water.

I, too, was undeterred. Sort of. "For you? Or me?"

Martin frowned. "It's about…Leah."

That got my attention. "What do you know?"

Before I could sputter another syllable, Ramirez's frame filled the doorway as he knocked and walked. Apparently, my home had become the Cheers bar of Phoenix, 'cause… good, bad, or otherwise, everybody seems to know my name.

"Hey, the gang's all here."

I wanted to make a snarky comment, but somehow it translated to, "I thought you were called away. Important coply stuff."

"I did my 'coply stuff' and now I'm here."

I mumbled an incoherent but blatantly negative response that made Martin flush.

Hey—my house. My rules.

"You didn't tell Misty about her sister." Ramirez's tone turned serious. I noted he hadn't framed it in a question.

"I said I wouldn't."

Martin's head swiveled as though watching a tennis match. "Wait. What's this about the girl's sister?"

I rolled my eyes at Ramirez, knowing full and well that Martin could see me.

"I take Martin's a bit behind in the game." Again, Ramirez posed no question, though I shrugged, which further aggravated Martin as he stepped closer, wiping his muck-covered hands one of my hand towels he must have deemed a rag, that actually had been a tee towel Leah had proudly cajoled Michael Jordan into signing when she'd spotted him out on a golf course in North Scottsdale several years earlier. Yeah, *that* Michael Jordan.

My eyes slid from the tragedy to his face when he closed the distance yet another step, tossing the towel into the trash. "What is Detective Ramirez referencing, Arianna? What did the girl, Misty, tell you?"

"Before I do that, you both need to hear what *Tamryn* told me."

I sighed as dust particles floated into the air, placing my inefficiencies as a domestic goddess on full display.

"Might as well find yourself a comfortable seat…preferably not one Martin has to inspect first. This may take a while." I moved into the living room and flopped on a chair.

The dust bunnies didn't care.

I filled them in on Tamryn—everything from the research park, where Martin and I had our first encounter, to where she dropped me off at the house. Without pausing to assess their demeanors or invite commentary, I progressed onto my encounter with Dina in the park, followed by the conversation at the coffee shop with Misty—which included the description of the girl she and her sister had seen conversing with Leah and the seemingly agitated follow-up with another girl who had yet to be identified, who collided with her sister.

"And then you called and told me of Jillian's death." Again, I elaborated on the details for Martin's benefit before tilting my head at Ramirez. "I don't suppose there is much you can do, officially?"

"I wish there was." He shook his head, more to himself than Martin or me. "Misty's sister is out of my jurisdiction. I shouldn't have gotten you involved in the first place. As for Tamryn, regardless of what you think about her actions—which I agree are suspicious—she's not broken any laws. Or at least, there is no evidence of it."

I allowed that statement to settle. I didn't like it, but he was right.

If I wanted someone to finally take notice, then I'd have to be the one to amp up the pressure.

I glanced at Martin, who'd been particularly quiet, even for Martin. He wasn't about to venture into that "We have to talk" conversation in Ramirez's presence, so I turned my attention elsewhere.

"So, that's all I have. Do you have anything to share, Detective? Or were you just popping by to pick my brain?" This earned me a healthy frown. "What? No quid pro quo?" The frown morphed into a scowl. I clucked my tongue. "Seems hardly fair."

"I did tell you about Misty's sister."

I tossed him my best eye roll. "Which I helped you confirm." He must have figured there was nothing to be had by arguing the point and wisely shrugged his agreement. At least that was the way I was taking it. Satisfied, I moved on. "You got that picture I sent you from Misty, didn't you?

"I did."

"And, no news." The slackening of his jaw told me all I needed to know, but still felt he needed to expound.

"These things take time, AJ. And it's not in my juris—"

I waved a hand. "I know, I know…the cop buddy was doing you a favor. I got it." He shrugged, a wise move, knowing he had nowhere to go but toward fire and brimstone. "But surely, regardless of jurisdiction, your coply intuition can tell me a little more about Jillian's cause of death."

"AJ…" he growled.

I shook my head. Holding back info wasn't gonna work. Not this time.

Ramirez sighed as he looked from me to Martin and then back.

"Well, for one thing, someone moved her after the head trauma was inflicted."

"Think I could have figured that one out for myself, Detective, considering her blood was found in Leah's car," I snarked. "Any idea what caused the injury?"

Ramirez shrugged. "They're still working that out, but what is odd is that when she was dumped outside the club, her clothes were relatively clean."

"Seems like there should have been a significant amount of blood."

"Yeah, and grime from the trunk. Another thing—the clothes didn't fit quite right, and Misty confirmed they weren't the ones her sister was wearing when they went to the club."

I nodded. "Hmm… So someone changed her clothes after they did the deed. Then tried to make it look like—"

Ramirez whistled to get my attention. "Hold up. It's still not been ruled a homicide."

"Well, I doubt she hauled herself out of that

trunk while bleeding and thought, 'Wow, I think this is the perfect spot to catch up on some zzz's behind the club.'"

"Still doesn't mean she was murdered. She could have just as easily gotten caught up in the party vibe, decided to try out some pharmaceuticals, had a bad reaction or an accident as a result, and whoever was with her was worried about getting in trouble."

"Then why change her? Why not call 9-1-1? You wouldn't think about dumping her off without attempting to get her some help if you weren't trying to hide something."

"You're running in circles to create a scenario that fits."

I opened my hands. "Then give me a path to follow. Please."

Ramirez's grimace softened at my pleading.

Martin cleared his throat as though we'd forgotten he was present. "She could have also been placed there to put someone on notice."

I raised a brow. "Like a warning?"

He shrugged. "If you consider what this Dina woman said about the penalties, it could make sense."

Ramirez nodded, turning to me. "What do you make of her story?"

I blew out a breath. Honestly, so much had occurred, I hadn't given it much thought. "She confirmed some things that both Tamryn and Misty said about the parties. She had no reason to approach me, and yet she did."

"But that's the question, isn't it? Why did she approach you?"

I wiggled a finger. "Careful, Ramirez, it's not good to look a gift horse in the mouth."

He hacked out a coarse laugh. "Are we talking about you? Or the woman?"

"Funny guy. Seriously, though, what's your hang-up?"

"No hang-up. I just think it's convenient this woman pops out of the woodwork just as you've concluded your conversation with Tamryn."

"Are you suggesting that Tamryn sent her? Why?" I puffed out a breath when Ramirez shrugged. "I'm not discounting your concern, but she expressed a certain amount of disdain for Tamryn's…type. Not to mention she seemed to have intimate knowledge of the operation. Perhaps not all the local specifics but how it functions as a whole. I definitely got the feeling she knew more than she alluded to for someone who hadn't somehow been on the inside herself."

Ramirez shook his head. "All the more reason to call everything she says into question. There has to be an ulterior motive and I don't like where it's headed."

"You can't be serious. Martin…tell him."

"Sorry, dear, but I agree with the detective on this one." I didn't dare glance in Ramirez's direction, though at least Martin had the decency to look somewhat abashed. "Not until we know more about her. She may not be working with Tamryn, but she certainly seems to have her own agenda. I don't like the notion that she may be using you to further that."

Ramirez nodded. "I think it would put all of our minds at ease if she offered up a bit more. Surely she gave you her number?"

I gritted my teeth. Like Tamryn, who was on my list to track down and throttle, Dina had exited stage left with nothing more than a cryptic smile and snappy one-liner. Tracking either of them down before my head exploded seemed an overly optimistic possibility.

I was about to admit defeat at the hands of the pair, patiently waiting for a response, when

Ramirez's cell buzzed. He looked at it and frowned. "Gotta jet."

"News?" I asked, hopefully.

"Not unless you were looking for a crispy corpse in a burned-out car in South Central Phoenix."

"Not so much." I grimaced. "I don't suppose there's some piece of wisdom in there about smoking and driving."

Ramirez took that comment, along with our facial expressions, as a cue to make his exit.

"Well, that was…interesting," Martin murmured, turning his attention back to the task I had interrupted upon my arrival.

"Not so fast."

The crispness of my tone caused his brows to rise in a cartoonish manner, and had I been in a better mood, I might have chuckled.

But this was not the day, nor was I in a jovial mood.

"You were awfully quiet while the detective was here, Martin."

He casually reached for the broom and dustpan. "No more so than usual."

"Come on, before Ramirez showed up, you were adamant that we needed to talk, so spill it,"

I replied, using the moment to survey him. His face remained an expressionless mask. "Unless you were just trying to get my hopes up…'cause you sure as heck wouldn't want to bait me right now."

Martin sighed as he placed the dustpan back on the ground. "You aren't going to be happy."

"Happy? I think any positive emotion went out the window the minute I learned Leah was missing. So what's the deal?"

"It's about the journal."

"The one you found at the salvage yard?"

Martin nodded. "My people have been making some headway, and it's not looking good." He paused, whether it was for effect or to ensure I'd caught the impact of what he was saying, I wasn't sure, but I didn't have the patience either way and gestured for him to continue. "Okay, but please understand, they've only begun cracking the codes, but from what they've extracted so far, everything is leading toward a dangerous and extremely criminal path."

"Meaning?"

Something passed over his face but quickly fell away as he noted me studying him, though there was a level of concern in his voice that I hadn't heard in some time.

"Whatever Shelby and Leah have stepped into is much larger than the club and vacation rental setup in Scottsdale."

"But we knew that. They branch out as soon as they see a profitable market or need to move quickly to an alternate location."

"It also allows them to validate the receptiveness and sheer volume of prospects."

"So the clubs essentially serve as a barrier to entry?"

"Yes, they are going after the affluent, but they are doing so cautiously."

"Which means prospects and players with moral flexibility, and a low pain threshold when it comes to being exposed or leveraged in some manner."

"Exactly. So they may start with the clubs, but the endgame is to entice these prospects into other, more lucrative areas where the waters are easier to navigate and officials are more willing to look the other way. That's where the bread and butter, so to speak, is for operations like this."

"You're talking about outside the United

States, then?" When Martin nodded, I added, "How far?"

"As far as they can reach and as deep as they can dig their heels in without incurring any blow-back should things go south."

"Which is why they need to be able to leverage the prospects."

"Yes. Once they've acquired just the right combination of pliable prospects primed and ready, and in a position where they can be leveraged? They've gotten their hooks into them for good. All while creating a nice little failsafe to ensure their own anonymity in the event anything goes awry, either with the product or the authorities. And thanks to the help of the 'motivated prospects,' these operations have been able to dodge and shift before they are caught and anyone is the wiser."

I noted he had also been careful not to look me in the eye as he'd been talking—why was that? What wasn't he telling me?

"Caught what? And products? What, specifically, are we talking about here, *Martin*?"

His eyes met mine and I saw the emotion I knew had always been there, but that he fought to keep below the surface.

Fear.

"Tell me, please."

He reached out, perhaps intending to grasp my hand and though it lingered in the air for a mere second, he settled for placing it on the counter in front of him, still holding my gaze as he spoke plainly, without hesitation.

"We're talking about humans, Arianna. And if the forensic accountant's journal is correct, Shelby and Leah have just stumbled into the largest human trafficking operation in history."

After recovering from that whammy, I blew out a breath. "I don't suppose you've been able to extract anything positive?"

"If there was, I doubt the forensic accountant would have gone to the lengths he did to keep the details he collected in the journal safe."

No arguing there. It had cost the man his life.

"What else? I can tell there's more." I caught his eyes and held them, noting that they had a softness that wasn't always present.

"Are you sure you want to know?"

I didn't, but I had to know, so I mustered my best stiff upper lip and offered him a single nod.

He absently dusted nonexistent crumbs off

the counter. One might have thought he was about to divulge Martha Stewart's Top 10 Housecleaning Tips. Though domestic goddess I was not, I almost wished it were the case.

"What we're talking about spans every viable country, socioeconomic region, demographic, cultural base…you name it. And while the United States has tempestuous relationships with some of the most favorable and profitable locales, the operation has its tentacles in almost every major market worldwide. It goes without saying, but your coyotes and low-level human smugglers don't even make it onto their radar. We're talking large money. Big players."

"And massive risks." Martin nodded at my assessment. "So, what are we talking about? Girls for cash?"

"Not as simple as that. Bidding wars would be more accurate."

"Bidding wars?" The first thing that came to mind was that show where people would stab their mother in the back for a shot at the contents of some abandoned storage unit.

"Online auctions where players not only get a visual sampling of the goods but a substantial buy-in is required to bid on those goods."

"Gawd, Martin! We're talking about human beings here—flesh and blood—not commodities."

"Arianna, what you have to understand is that in this world, they are one and the same."

I knew he wasn't saying it for shock value, but it sent ice through my veins. What about Leah? And Shelby? What did this mean for them?

"Then why bother with the club-vacation rental property setups? Seems like they'd be more trouble than they're worth."

Martin shrugged. "As I alluded to earlier—to test out the area. To serve as a decoy for the real operation. To test the prospect's interest level or how far they can be leveraged if the need arises. It could also extend to the people working for the operation—their loyalty, reliability and again, the leverage angle. Any combination of these could be considered a factor.

"Plus, getting set up in a new location would take a significant amount of time. There's a lot to contend with, both legal and otherwise. You'd need reliable individuals to vet the area before the decision to open up shop is made and then ensure the market has the appropriate individuals in place so that the operation functions smoothly out of the gate. It takes time and patience to get those roots firmly planted, the right palms greased, etc."

The more he relayed, the more intense the repulsion became. I desperately wanted to get the vile taste out of my mouth, but something told me it had already wormed its way into my skin and would stay there until Leah was home safe.

"Are you suggesting politicians, law enforcement and people in power, willing to look the other way?"

"I'm sure the incentive is to ensure they are more than willing. Many are likely getting rich because of their connections and the fact that they know who is ripe for leveraging or potential manipulation in their own backyard."

"I understand what you're saying, but aren't those really still one and the same?"

"Not always—in these types of games—you need both. Leverage comes with its own risks: greed, self-indulgence, arrogance. The list goes on and on. In the end, you also need people who are free and clear of blemishes or proclivities from the start. Either way, I agree—it's a vicious and honestly, a nasty cycle."

"Surely these others that can be leveraged are already on *someone's* radar or watch list?"

He sighed, shaking his head. "Unfortunately, that's both the brilliance—albeit abhorrently so —as well as the exasperating part of players like this. The ones who are the most successful are patient. They spend the time necessary to research the landscape and study its resources. This allows them to zone in on resources not already leveraged. Or provide just the right incentive to push said resources in a direction that they may not have previously given any consideration to."

I'm sure it appeared as though my brows were hitting the ceiling. "Are we talking about giving basically decent humans the right incentive to cross their own lines between black and white?"

Martin nodded. "And once they've stepped over, who do you think steps in to point out the error of their ways?"

"And so the manipulation begins." I spat out the words like the poison they were.

Martin's blanched expression mirrored my

own. "The leverage component has gone into effect, yes."

"That is just vile."

"True. But it's the way the world works."

I knew he was right, but the reality of it was daunting.

And so were the ramifications.

"How far-reaching are these operations?" I knew there was no way I could expect Martin to fully quantify something he didn't have all the supporting data for but hoped whatever answer he offered would help me wrap my mind around it.

He raised a brow. "Are you sure you want to know?"

Though it gave me pause, I said that I did

He nodded and was silent for a moment before responding, "About as far and deep as you could ever imagine. Times a million."

"And Leah and Shelby?"

He shook his head and fussed with the lid of the trash bin, which had been lopsided. Funny how I'd never noticed that before, and yet Martin, the fastidious one, selected this moment to right it. If there was ever an analogy for our relationship, perhaps that would have been it.

What he uttered next knocked me out of musings and into a reality I'd known all along was lurking from the darkest corners of my mind.

"When they opened that can of worms, they became a threat. And like any other liability, whatever happens to them will be viewed the same."

"Which is?" It was a question I didn't need to ask but needed to hear him say the words.

"Collateral damage."

"Meaning?" I couldn't leave well enough alone.

"If you had spent countless hours, money and resources, making the Scottsdale area a viable component of your overall business, how would you react if an outside variable suddenly threatened to destroy it all?" He watched the shock emerge on my face like a fast-moving poison. "Right. So, adding the questionable morals component in, what conclusion would you draw about eliminating the source of that threat? And, what would you think the outcome of that would mean?"

Eliminating the source of the threat. The

phrase "swims with the fishes" popped into my head, and I desperately wished it hadn't.

"Exactly." I shot a look at Martin. Either he'd become a mind-reader in the last five minutes, or I'd inadvertently shared that bit out loud. I wasn't sure which would have been worse, though that thought was cut short. "And doing so by any means necessary. It's possible they would put out a bounty to elicit results with least amount of blow-back."

"So they wouldn't care if the source was…" I couldn't bring myself to use the word, though the slicing motion I made across my neck probably wasn't much better.

Martin shook his head. "They wouldn't give it a second thought. Nor would they lose any sleep over it, though they may toss in a bonus if it didn't contaminate domestic soil."

I gasped as I processed this. "You mean Leah and Shelby could…"

"Easily be handled elsewhere," Martin finished my thought, squinting and frowning as he absorbed my reaction. I'm sure it wasn't my best look, especially when he felt the need to add, "Don't worry. We'll get to them before that happens."

"I can't believe that a little poking around led them to…this." I put my elbows on the counter and buried my face in my hands.

Martin sighed. "Even a 'little poking around' is too much of a risk. I know I sound like a broken record, but sometimes you girls tend to go off half-cocked without understanding the consequences of what you are doing." I lifted my head and gave him a frosty gaze. He held up a hand. "Hear me out."

I gestured for him to continue but gave him a look that suggested whatever he had to say had better be good.

After a bit of throat-clearing, he continued. "Think about it. If you were trying to pull something off that fell into a gray area—illegal or not—in a well-established residential area of a highly desirable market. And if some unknown walked in and suddenly decided to pull back the curtain to expose who and what you really were…would you let them?" I frowned but shook my head. "Right, you wouldn't. So, how would you go about ensuring you got what you wanted, when you wanted it, and that nobody stood in your way while you were doing it?"

"*If* I was that sort of person, charged with

ensuring the viability of a flourishing 'business' of that nature, I'd probably make sure I was keeping some local players in my back pocket to handle such challenges when they arose and then I would reward them generously for their efficiency and discretion."

"Yes, politicians in favor of what the vacation rental business brings to the local economy —tourists, jobs, etc.—who would be looked upon favorably by their constituents."

"And law enforcement." Martin nodded, offering a grim smile at my assessment. "People higher on the food chain who could tell their subordinates to 'go easy' on the neighborhoods where the parties were happening. Of course, they'd still be expected to maintain their due diligence, especially where neighborhood watches and community groups are in full effect. You don't want those people riled up. Nor do you want to make an enemy of them." I rolled my eyes and gave him a knowing look.

Let's just say I'd been on the receiving end of that wrath when Nicoh was younger, less well-trained and prone to bouts of howling when I let him out in the middle of the night. His old gal pal, Pandora, may have helped incite that, but it was tough on the humans.

"Exactly. So you've got the gist of why this operation would not want people poking around." Martin reined the conversation back to his original point. "It could lead to serious problems elsewhere in the business."

"Right. The higher you are, the greater the risks. I get that. But surely Shelby and Leah… they couldn't have…" I shook my head and focused on my now clasped hands, unable to finish my thought or withstand Martin's searching gaze.

He was silent for a moment, and though I wasn't sure whether he was allowing me a moment or simply trying to figure out how to conclude his point without aggravating me, as often tended to be the case. Either way, I appreciated the reprieve and tucked the negative thoughts away for the time being. I still held out hope, believing that we could do things to prevent the worst-case from reaching fruition.

Wasn't there?

Martin cleared his throat and slowly, I lifted my eyes to meet his. "There are some things I've needed to say. For a long time." He raised a hand when I started to respond. "Hear me out. I know you don't always trust me, but I *am* trying. I hope you can bring yourself to give me…give us a chance.

"I know you're mulling over your next steps. Won't you please at least let me try to help you? You may not believe this, but I do have your—and Leah's—best interests at heart. And if we can pool our resources, and learn to trust one another, perhaps we can make up for lost time."

"And all of the above—the disses on Leah and Shelby's actions—was endearing me how?" My tone was more snappish than I had intended, as Martin jolted as though I'd forced him to jam a fork into the light socket. Well, maybe not to that extreme, but he was taken aback, based on the frown he was having trouble concealing.

I held up a hand. "Sorry, that didn't come out right. Let me start over." I blew out a breath and collected my thoughts.

And while I wasn't sure whether he had been referring to the current situation or our relationship, I also knew he was not simply offering another olive branch.

He was asking me to make a choice.

And this time, it was about him.

I let that settle for a bit longer and though he searched my face, I doubt he knew what I was thinking. I sure as heck didn't. Yeah, I needed him more than I cared to admit. In life and in this situation.

For now, I decided to focus on the latter, though I can't say it was the simpler choice. The fact of the matter was, I was getting nowhere on my own. And if I planned on tracking Tamryn or Dina down again, I needed his resources, as well as his experience.

"Okay," I said finally.

He offered me a quick nod, his expression ever passive and stoic, despite the fact I had taken my sweet time in deliberating and then delivering such an abbreviated response. "I take you have a plan?"

I forced a smile. "Funny you should ask…"

CHAPTER TWENTY-THREE

"Not only do I dislike it…intensely. It won't work."

Wow. *Intense dislike*? Way to use your words, Martin.

I'd barely outlined the bones of my plan and hadn't even had an opportunity to dig into the meaty goodness.

Then again, I hadn't actually formulated that part yet—so technically, there wasn't one—but he hadn't even given me a chance. I wasn't quite sure what there was to dislike, intensely or otherwise, anyway.

My plan was simply to extract the information I needed to track down Shelby and Leah's current whereabouts from Tamryn and Dina—pitting the two of them against each other to see what fell out. As long as it gave me the desired results, I didn't care.

"It's just not a sound plan, Arianna," he said when I'd gotten to the part where I'd coerced Tamryn into introducing me to some of her peeps and getting me on the fast track to the upper echelon. Like extreme fast-track. Pronto.

And that was just for starters. Who knew what else I could drum up. Let's just say I was highly motivated. Off the charts. And, this time, no one would stand in my way. Big girl grunders were on.

Leah and Shelby's lives depended on it.

First, though, I had to get past the Martinator.

I realized he was still talking while I'd mentally stepped out, and was currently going on about the ways the plan would fail…blah, blah, blah… Then he said something that snapped me back to giving him my full attention.

"I hate to say it, Arianna, but if you insist on continuing down this path, I'll have no choice but to get Ramirez involved." If he was working to keep that self-satisfied tone out of his voice, his eyes betrayed him.

"Do it," I replied, effectively stopping him mid-rant, mouth opened, waiting for something to fly in and take up residence. "Here. Use my phone. It'll get you a faster response."

Rather than taking the phone I'd extended, he tucked his hands into his pockets. At least he'd closed his mouth.

"No?" Still no response. Had the circumstances been less dire, I would have smirked, made some smart-aleck remark, or checked for a pulse. "Let me get that for you."

I stabbed a finger on Ramirez's name and placed the call on speaker mode, humming the Jeopardy theme song as it rang.

I was almost thankful that it went to the count of three before Ramirez answered, just as Martin's lemon-sucking expression started to look as though it might stick that way.

"This is becoming a habit, AJ." His tone was low and sultry, causing the heat to rise in my cheeks.

"*This* is an official call, Detective. *Martin* and I have you on speakerphone. And, we need your assistance."

Ramirez hacked out something that was short of a laugh. "Well, admitting you need help *is* the first step."

I mouthed something less than lady-like before outlining my plan a second time, while Martin made several exaggerated attempts to point out what he deemed as faulty logic. He even tried snagging the phone away until I threatened to press "Mute" the next time he interrupted me.

"You two seem to be getting along nicely," Ramirez chuckled. He was clearly enjoying the convo from the safety of his side of the connection.

"Are we amusing you?" I snapped. "Wait, the better question is—are you going to help us, or what?"

Notice I had the smarts not to ask whether he was going to help *me*.

Of course, Martin piped up and attempted to land a final strike.

"Detective. If I may impose on you. Please, talk some sense into her before she proceeds with this cockamamie scheme. You know full and well from past experience, it's bound to happen. And she'll not only end up endangering herself, she could also place Leah and Shelby in even greater danger."

I ground my teeth. I couldn't say for sure that he was incorrect on that latter point. And Ramirez would be remiss to ignore it.

But apparently, even he could pull a surprise out of his hat on occasion.

"Actually, Martin, I have to go with AJ on this—I'm inclined to help. If I can."

Well, color me purple with sparkles and an alicorn—also known as the horn of a unicorn. I barely contained a delighted gasp while Martin's coloring shifted into the over-ripened tomato category as he blustered. I'll admit I felt for him.

But just a smidgen.

"Hold up, Martin. I didn't say I wholeheartedly *agreed* with AJ, just that I would assist. Mind you, you've made some very valid points." It was hard not to fist-pump into the air as Ramirez spoke. It was all I could do not to look too victorious. "Problem is, where's *your* solution? You've given several reasons *not* to proceed with AJ's plan, though you haven't supplied an alternative. Truth be told, I don't like it much better than you do, but there aren't all that many viable solutions."

I put a hash on my mental scoreboard as Martin grumbled a rare obscenity, thumping the palm of his hand on the counter. I clucked my tongue—loudly—and received a snort from Ramirez's end.

"Anyway, I can't play referee to you two all day. Can we meet up at the house a bit later?"

I cast a glance at Martin, who refused to look at me. Always with the cleaning. What was up with that? "How much later?" I asked.

Ramirez blew out a breath. "Whew—the day has gotten away from me. Give me a couple of hours."

Both Martin and I gave him our verbal thumbs-up, though it seemed like he was just going through the motions so that we could move past this conversation.

"Shall I bring some adult beverages, provided we can all agree to be adults?"

I shot a glance at Martin, who still preferred his domestic goddess tasks over engaging in eye contact with the likes of me.

"Working meeting—best to keep clear heads," I replied, though I appreciated Ramirez's gesture. "We can celebrate once we get our girl home."

"Indeed. Okay, make coffee, then. A lot of it. I'll bring some pizzas."

Martin muttered something about making sure I had decaf. I made a raspberry noise in response that Ramirez mistakenly thought I'd directed at him.

"It hasn't been *that* long, AJ. I remember what you like. Extra green chiles coming up."

More faces and random grumbling noises came from Martin's direction, including, "Your stomach isn't going to like you very much."

"Well, then I guess it's a good thing *you* won't have to deal with it."

Ramirez chuckled, though he sounded tired. "That's my cue to exit. Domestic disputes are outside my purview. I'll leave you two to… whatever. See you in a bit." And with that, the detective left us to contend with one another.

"Chicken," I murmured, staring at the "Call ended" message. Though it didn't top my list of fave things, I knew the next thing I needed to tackle had to be done. "I'm sorry, Martin. That…didn't go quite the way I meant for it to, and I know you came up short, despite your best efforts. Nice play with pulling the Ramirez card, though. I was seriously impressed."

He temporarily stopped puttering to offer me an awkward shrug. As he bent down to pick up the dustpan, however, I couldn't help but notice the wisp of a smile escaping the corner of his mouth.

"You're not mad." It wasn't a question, though I was a tad taken aback by his casual demeanor.

"I never said I disagreed with you. I merely wanted you to understand the ramifications of what you were proposing."

"*Ramifications?* I'm living them, Martin. Every. Single. Minute. What would you have me do? Leah is all the family I've got left." I realized my slip the minute it left my lips, and though he tried to conceal it, his brow furrowed ever so slightly as he absently began moving the stove back into place.

"Martin….I'm sorry." I realized it was the second time I was apologizing to him in the span of a few minutes.

He said nothing as his focus remained on the stove, hitching it a little one way or the other until it was perfect and annoyingly centered.

The silence was maddening.

"Please. Look at me."

He did and the man who stood before me seemed weary—older even—than he had just moments earlier. "What would you have me do, Arianna? I'm your fath—" he stopped short of saying the word, sighing before amending it to, "I'm concerned."

I nodded and touched his arm. "So am I. But concern doesn't help them. Or bring them home. Taking action is the only way. And unless you can drum up a better idea in two hours—we're proceeding with the plan I just outlined to Ramirez. I know it isn't a great plan—but it's the best bad plan we have on short notice."

He puffed out his cheeks and offered me a begrudging nod before gripping my hand in his.

It wasn't much. And maybe it wasn't even an agreement or a concession.

But it was…progress.

Ever the punctual one, Ramirez arrived just shy of two hours, bearing gifts in the form of more pizzas than three people could—or should be able to—consume.

Most people are not me.

I had done my due diligence as well and after helping Martin tidy up the rest of the kitchen, I brewed enough coffee—both leaded and unleaded—to last us well until dawn, if needed.

Nicoh, who had been quietly watching from his perch in the living room, inched his way toward the aroma wafting from the kitchen island and was nearly successful in snagging an entire box nestled near Martin's elbow—until I busted him.

"Mep. No way are you getting a piece of this pie, buddy. Try that again and you'll be drooling from outside the slider." Ramirez and Martin chuckled when Nicoh bemoaned his poor treatment and slowly and loudly tromped all the way to my room, where his sad story echoed.

I'd pay for my stinginess later when I found dog slobber on my pillow.

I pointed at each of them. "Keep laughing it up and I'll send you on a time-out with the big guy."

"Hey! I brought the pizza," Ramirez teased.

"And I…I folded the napkins," Martin chimed in.

"Yeah? Well, you're in *my* world now." I laughed as I shoved a piece in my mouth, not caring when the cheese trailed down my chin.

"Use a napkin, Arianna, for goodness sakes!" Martin's eyes were like saucers as he watched me inhale the cheesy goodness in a minimum of bites.

"Just watch your fingers and toes, Martin." Ramirez gave him a knowing look and chuckled at Martin's exasperated, pink-cheeked expression.

"Good thing you're here, Detective. He may need help finding them if he keeps it up." Ramirez rolled his eyes. "And for the record, Martin, you 'folded' a paper towel."

Martin glanced down at his handiwork as if truly seeing it for the first time. He lifted his head, an amused smile playing across his lips before he burst out in an uncommon round of laughter, which turned out to be contagious.

After the chuckles fell away, we ate in comfortable silence, perhaps savoring that last bit of peace before we prepared for war.

It was Ramirez who broke the silence as he loaded his plate into the dishwasher.

"Before I got here, my cop buddy over in Scottsdale called me. Misty identified her sister's body."

"Oh, no! How is she doing?" I'd only just met the girl but had immediately liked her and my heart went out to her. No one should have to witness something like that.

Take it from someone who'd been there.

Ramirez blew out a long breath. "He said she was pretty shaken up but that she kept it together. He confirmed later that she'd contacted her parents and they were on their way."

"That's good—I'd hate for her to be alone. But still, do you think I should reach out or possibly offer to hang out with her while she waits?"

Ramirez shook his head. "I think you need to stay out of it, AJ. I know you want to help but with Leah's disappearance. Things could get messy."

"I agree with the Detective. It could make things more difficult for all parties," Martin added.

I nodded, knowing they were both right. It didn't make it any easier, though—I understood what Misty would be going through and wished there was something I could do—but if it caused her more grief or unintentionally put her in harm's way, I couldn't live with that.

I shifted gears. "Have they gotten any closer to a ruling on the cause of death?"

Ramirez shook his head. "Too soon."

"But they suspect something, though, right?"

He wouldn't bite, shrugging noncommittally, before shifting the conversation. "So, about this plan. Shall we get our ducks in a row?"

Or prepare for the worst, I thought to myself.

I'll admit, the more I ran through the plan, the more I saw Martin's point. It was skeletal at best. And what it boiled down—and ultimately would rely on—was sheer luck, synchronicity in the universe, and a whole lot of smoke and mirrors that I hoped wouldn't come crashing down on top of me. Sure, you may think a touch of desperation should be added to the mix, and I wouldn't argue.

But just don't add too much.

To my surprise and amazement, Martin and Ramirez listened, offered commentary—some helpful and often insightful, while others were stern words of warning.

I would be pretty much on my own—I had planned it that way—and wanted to do a feasibility assessment just to ensure it would hold water, at least for a while. Martin didn't attempt to dissuade me this time around and neither did Ramirez. There were a couple of moments they were so amenable that I thought perhaps they had teamed up behind my back and formulated their own plan. The more I thought about it, though, the more ridiculous that notion became.

In the end, I thought if I could just get the

first two parts right, the third might just fall into place.

Ramirez couldn't involve himself officially, as it was outside his jurisdiction.

So once I got his official stamp of approval—okay, it was more of a shrug coupled with a casual head nod—he grabbed some coffee and hit the road. Though he didn't say as much, I think he preferred whatever grim and unconscionable acts that he witnessed as part of his job day in and day out over having to worry about me walking into a potential pit of quicksand.

Martin, too, was suspiciously quiet, busying himself with the cleanup of the remnants of our dinner. Collecting the pizza boxes and other items, he headed out back to the alley to dispose of them, pausing to pluck some errant weeds from the backyard as he went. It was almost as though we'd never had the conversation and that nothing was about to be set in motion that couldn't be undone.

I sent Tamryn a direct message on the same social media channel as I had before. We hadn't spoken in a while and my guess was she was probably more than a bit curious about what I had been up to since we'd last chatted, so I kept the message ominous and straightforward, hoping it would further pique her curiosity.

Need to talk. Meet me in the park near my house. Bench on the south side near the pond. 7:45 am tomorrow. Come alone.

I didn't have to wait long for a response. For as simple as my message had been, she had me beat as the reigning champion for simplicity.

k.

Martin re-entered the house just as I was closing the laptop.

"It's on."

He nodded and leaned against the counter while I finished cleaning up. I glanced at him after a moment of silence, noting that his brow was furrowed as he scratched the scruff on his chin. It wasn't like him to let it grow for so long. Then again, he hadn't planned on becoming a guest in my home either and had little time to prepare for more than an overnight stay.

"Something on your mind?"

His hand dropped as the look of consternation evaporated into its former emotionless mask. "Not particularly. You?"

"All good."

Again he nodded, this time a bit more absently.

"Come on, Martin, spill. You're way too quiet, even for you."

"It's nothing really." His gaze met mine and I held firm, silently waiting for him to continue. "Are you sure—"

"Yes," I replied. "I am."

Another nod before he added, "At least consider taking Nicoh."

I laughed. "What's that big lug gonna do, drool on her?" Apparently, Martin did not appreciate the humor, his face remaining impassive at my retort. I rolled my eyes and sighed. "Fine, I'll take him. I think you've been feeding him too many snacks on the side, though. He's getting a bit lumpy, if you know what I mean."

"I do know what you mean but I assure you, I would never—"

I held up a hand. "It was a joke, Martin. Lighten up. Everything is gonna work out fine. Trust me."

He offered me a curt nod and only a hint of a smile, but it did not reach his eyes. "I think I'll turn in early, if that's alright?"

"Sure. As long as you're okay. Are you…okay?"

"I am," he replied, his eyes widening ever so slightly, as though my show of concern had surprised him, before patting me on the shoulder and heading down the hall.

"Martin…"

When he turned, I caught a glimpse of sadness pass as he met my eyes. "Yes, Arianna?"

"Thank you."

A small smile escaped—this one more genuine than the last but still offset by the lingering sorrow—but he said nothing as he turned back and plodded down the hall.

"I mean it," I whispered.

It might have been my ears playing tricks on me or indulging me in what I wanted to—perhaps even need it to—hear, but I could have sworn I heard him whisper back, "I know you do."

CHAPTER TWENTY-FIVE

Nothing like spilling coffee down a brand new pair of jeans out of the gate—especially when they're white.

Nope, my day hadn't gotten off to the best of starts. I'd slept fitfully and somehow, I recalled dreams filled with cartoon characters, where the callout bubbles that surrounded their heads were filled with quirky sayings that reaffirmed Martin's warning about drinking coffee after such and such time.

Uh-huh.

I'm sure you can see the irony—after not heeding his warnings the previous night—I'd knocked over the overfilled to-go mug, which had conveniently launched itself directly in the path of the largest white space it could find, a.k.a. the aforementioned jeans. Coffee often has a funny sense of humor that way.

Suffice it to say, I'd also gotten up late and was cursing myself for my poor choice of meeting times.

Yeah, not a morning person—what had I been thinking?

Thankfully, Martin wasn't around to offer his thoughts on that. Where was he, anyway?

I glanced around as I wrangled my hair into a messy ponytail but could see no evidence that he'd emerged from his room yet, which was odd. Shrugging, I dabbed the stain from my jeans the best I could and hustled Nicoh out the door.

Fortunately, he was game to jog to the park and we made it to the bench I'd designated with a few minutes to spare. The park was empty, so scoping the surroundings was easy work, barring anyone lurking behind trees or bushes.

Then again, some weren't so quiet about it.

"Of all the places you could have picked, you could have at least made sure there was caffeine nearby. Seriously? At this hour, whatever you have to 'chat' about had better be good." Tamryn rattled that off so fast, I couldn't get a word in edge-wise, much less offer her the extra coffee I'd brought along before she added, "Morning people suck!"

"Wow. Okay." I wasn't sure how to respond to all of that. So I took it bit by bit. "Hello, Tamryn. Thanks for agreeing to meet. I brought coffee, in case you are interested, sweetener and creamer included. I'm not much for mornings either, but I figured you'd want to ensure necessary safety and privacy precautions could be taken, so I picked a remote section of the park where I knew we wouldn't be interrupted." I looked around. "Where are your thugs…urm, guys, anyway?"

Tamryn took the coffee from my extended hand and huffed. "Probably sleeping. Like I should be doing."

I ignored the fact that she didn't thank me as she gulped down the contents. At least she hadn't made a face—I'd added enough sweetener to make Willy Wonka cringe.

"Late night?"

She scoffed as she wiped her mouth with the

back of her hand. "Early morning is more like it."

That explained the telltale bags under her eyes and the smudged remnants of too much mascara and eyeliner. Her hair was tucked into a designer ball cap with rhinestones, but wisps escaped at all angles, suggesting she had dressed in a hurry.

"Are you judging me?" Her eyes narrowed as she pulled a large pair of fuchsia sunglasses from her matching mammoth Hermès Birkin bag and shoved them on, concealing the better part of her face.

"Not at all," I chuckled. "As you can see, I have plenty of morning challenges of my own." I pointed at my stained jeans.

She glanced and waved a hand with black cherry-colored talons. "I didn't say anything about challenges. I'm not a klutz." She let that linger in the air. "Why am I here?"

"Shall we sit?" I gestured toward the bench, and while I wanted nothing more than to snap those ridiculously oversized shades from her face, figured I'd let my words inflict the punishment.

Tamryn shrugged and followed me to the

bench, noting Nicoh for the first time. "I hope he's had his shots."

"Yup, everything but ticks and fleas," I replied jovially, causing her to flinch. "Relax," I laughed. "I was only joking, wasn't I, buddy?" I scruffed Nicoh behind the ears, noting that he was less than impressed with our new arrival once he realized there would be no snacks or scratches. He nestled against my leg and gave her the death-glare.

What a good boy.

"So, what's this all about?" Tamryn snapped, brushing the bench with the edge of her sweatshirt before sitting down.

"I'd like to tell you a little story." I told her everything I'd learned since our last encounter. And while I was careful to keep Dina's name out of it, I gave a play-by-play of what Misty had told me she and her sister had witnessed and pretty much everything I knew up to date.

"You've been busy," Tamryn drawled, smirking as she leaned into the bench and slung an arm over the back. "I'm impressed."

"So you don't deny it. Any of it?"

"With some minor qualifications. But no."

She shrugged and leveled an amused gaze at me. "Why should I?"

"Because it would have saved a heck of a lot of time, don't you think?" I replied between gritted teeth. "Who knows what could be happening to Leah and Shelby."

Her smirk was starting to annoy me just as I realized why.

"You already know." It should have surprised me, but it didn't.

She studied the daggers on her draped hand. "I know enough."

"And yet, here we sit." Tamryn would have been hard-pressed to compete with the thickness of the sarcasm that I allowed to creep into my tone.

"I've got my eye on things."

I'll give her credit. If anything, she was confident and certainly undeterred, despite everything I had outlined that clearly, she'd already been aware of.

"And how's that working out for you?" My blood began a rapid boil as I thought of what I'd learned to date about the girls that had been transported and used as commodities and those that were about to encounter the same fate. I could not…would not…allow that to happen to my best friend.

"Hey! *You* contacted me. Let's not get snarky," Tamryn snapped.

Finally, I had gotten through that annoyingly cool indifference.

Still, she was correct. I had gotten her here. My hang-ups with her constant shifts in attitude would not help Leah or Shelby.

I raised my hands in a mea culpa gesture. "Sorry, it's been a rough few days."

Tamryn surprised me by nodding. "So I've gathered." She chewed her lip. "Listen, we didn't get off on the best foot. I'm not trying to antagonize you, either—chalk it up to a gnarly hangover. Can we start over?"

I narrowed my eyes at her. Was she for real? Because she certainly didn't sound like the Tamryn I'd initially met. Perhaps she was playing nicey-nice so that she could get intel and run back to her cronies at the operation. Where would that leave Leah and Shelby?

And it certainly wouldn't bring justice for Misty's sister, Jillian.

Tamryn studied me for a moment. "I get it. You're not sure you can trust me. I've been giving you mixed signals and probably mixed personas and until now, I've given you nothing more than a case of whiplash with a side of road rash."

"A succinct, if not accurate, summation," I murmured.

Abruptly, she stood. "I can see where I might come off that way at times."

Might? At times?

"You may find this hard to believe, but I honestly don't have many people in my friend circle—the real kind. I've always had a hard time knowing who to trust. And sometimes, it's easier to act like a royal brat so that everyone steers clear."

"Sounds lonely."

"It can be. But it's a monster of my own making."

That was probably the most honest thing she'd said. I'm sure it wasn't easy to admit.

"I can understand that, Tamryn."

She hacked out a chuckle. "Can you, *really*?"

I shrugged. "Yeah. Why not? I'm not saying that we've taken the same path. Sometimes things happen along our journey—some of them change us forever—that put us in a place where we feel like we need to self-isolate to keep ourselves safe. But at the same time, that means we miss letting the good stuff and good people in. Do you know what I mean?"

She tilted her head. "I do. A succinct, if not accurate, summation, AJ." She flashed me a wink.

I laughed. "Touché."

She nodded and chuckled before her tone went serious. "So, you got me here. And quite efficiently told me what you knew. I assume there is something…specific that you need from me."

"There is."

"And…"

"You may not like it."

"Perhaps you should let me be the judge of that."

"I need you to tell me everything you know." I checked to see if she was still with me. Despite the amused expression, she made no objection, so I blurted out, "And then I need you to get me inside."

Tamryn's brows hiked as she leaned further onto the bench and crossed her arms. "Wow, you don't expect much of a girl on a first date, do you?" I started to respond, but she held up a hand and laughed. "Relax, I was just joking. What do you want to know?"

I nodded. There was a lot I *wanted* to know, but not all of it fell under an immediate *need* to know. "Do you know where they are at this moment?"

Tamryn raised a brow. "Your friends? No."

"But you know them…both, don't you?"

Tamryn smirked. "When Leah showed at the club the first time, I knew something was up."

That got my attention. "You knew Leah…before?"

She laughed and waved a hand. "By reputation. I've seen some pieces she's written as an investigative journalist. Fierce, that one. Before that, our parents ran in a few of the same circles back in the day. Anyway, when I saw her, I knew she was hot on the trail of something."

I shrugged. "Well, she *does* like to dance."

She tilted her head back and laughed. "Yeah. And I like to knit. Seriously. Leah Campbell doesn't show up on the scene unless there *is* a scene."

"When was this?"

"The first time? Oh gosh, it's got to be more than a month now. Maybe more, maybe less. All the days start to run together. You know how it is." I didn't but gestured for her to continue. "Anyway, getting back to your question, yeah—I also knew Shelby but was not aware that there was a connection to Leah at the time. Shelby showed up long before Leah crossed my path, and by that time, Shelby was out of the picture."

There was so much to unpack there, but as she started to continue, I stopped her.

"Hold up—what do you mean by 'Shelby was out of the picture'?"

"She just stopped showing up. One day she was on like gangbusters—the next, she ghosted. Haven't heard a peep from her since."

That did *not* sound like the Shelby that Leah had gone on and on about. From what I had gathered, she was even more of a pit bull than my bestie and if something was to be unearthed, she'd bite down and continue putting pressure on it until she was satisfied there was nothing more to find. If she was anything like Leah, it also meant she often did so at her own peril.

"Sounds like she was around for a while before she…ghosted." Tamryn nodded but offered no more. "What was her role?"

Tamryn squinted. "A little bit of everything, I guess. She was a natural. Very business-minded but fun, and a good communicator. She could really work a room."

I chuckled. Leah had said as much and given she was precisely the same way, it was saying a lot. "Probably went with the territory."

Tamryn squinted. "I don't follow. How do you mean?"

"Before Leah went freelance full-time, she was Shelby's mentor."

Based on the way her mouth dropped open, I guessed she hadn't seen that one coming. "Shelby…was a journalist?"

"Yeah, investigative. Like Leah."

"Interesting." She chewed her lip before adding, "Perhaps that explains the sudden no-show. If she was sticking her nose in, as Leah was…" her voice trailed off as she shook her head and frowned.

"You really don't know?"

"I may be many things, but if this has anything to do with that girl's death—" she pressed her eyes shut and swung her head from side to side. She was either telling the truth. Or a really proficient actress.

And colder than a cryogenic chamber.

If that turned out to be the case, karma would be best served with a side of frostbite.

"So Shelby ghosts and Leah shows up shortly after, do I have that right?" She nodded. "And while you may not have drawn the connection between the two—someone did."

"That could very well be true."

"But, you don't know who." It wasn't a question, but she didn't seem to notice.

"It could have been anyone. And, even then, that person may have simply made an inadvertent comment to someone else…and on down the line it goes."

Something occurred to me.

"What about that night? The night that Misty mentioned seeing Leah? What was it you and Leah were talking about? After she left, Misty said you didn't seem pleased. What was that about?"

"I don't recall."

"You were worked up enough that you called another girl over after Leah left and appeared to have a very…animated discussion with her. Who was she?”

“Like I said, I don’t recall. I know a lot of people. And I’m sure to some, the conversation could have seemed animated, but it’s loud in that atmosphere…*everyone* ratchets it up a notch.” She waved a hand.

It was interesting to note that when I pushed her on a topic she claimed to know nothing about, she’d slide back into the less cooperative, more aloof persona.

“So you’re saying you don’t remember.” My tone was as flat as I worked to keep my mounting frustration under wraps.

“That’s what I’m saying.”

“Okay, moving on.” Again, I fought to remain calm, though I was anything but. “What about the girls? Were you aware of what they were doing with them once they were selected?”

Old Tamryn was in full form, picking at her nails as though I’d asked her about nothing more than her thoughts on oatmeal rather than the livelihood of an actual human being. One of which happened to be my best friend.

“It’s in my best interest *not* to know.”

The top of my kettle blew off with that one,

but as I opened my mouth, I caught a glimpse of a figure wearing the same oddly off-season calf-length coat and gloves emerge from the pathway just as a familiar hack of laughter filled the air.

"That's not true, Tami, and you and I both know it," the figure said before she turned to me. "And you, Arianna, *really* need a better plan."

CHAPTER TWENTY-SIX

"I see your theatrics haven't ceased."

"No more so than your dramatic entrances." Tamryn barely glanced at Dina, her focus more intent on studying a chipped nail than the fact our conversation had not only been overheard but interrupted. Not the reaction one would expect when encountering a complete stranger. Or so I thought. "Besides, that line is getting old, even for you, Auntie."

Auntie?

My head swiveled between the two. Why had Tamryn accused me of being in cahoots with the woman at the diner when she already knew who she was—and was, in fact, related to her?

Had it been one of her little tests? Had she been buying time? Or just stringing me along?

I surveyed her and after a moment, she finally grew tired of scrutinizing her manicure and raised her head to meet the older woman's icy glare as they sized one another up before each cracked a grin and broke into laughter. Tamryn jumped off the bench and threw her arms around Dina, and the two embraced. My bewildered expression must have been amusing because after one look at me, the chortles turned riotous, scaring a few birds into flight.

"AJ, I see you've already met this old bat. Dina is my aunt on my mom's side. If you want the inside track on this stuff, she's your gal. Aren't you, Auntie?" Tamryn winked at Dina, who had resumed to her former, less jovial demeanor as she smoothed invisible wrinkles from her coat, ignoring her niece's banter. "You might be interested to know that this ol' gal goes by the nickname, "The Curator." Why don't you tell her why that is?"

"That's enough, dear. Your roots are showing," Dina replied, but there was a curve at the corner of her mouth as she said it.

And here I'd thought I was going to pit the

two of them against each other? I sighed, realizing the likelihood that my plan had tanked and probably why Dina had said as much. Of course, part of it was no thanks to her, as she had made no previous mention of her direct connection to Tamryn—and in fact, had done quite the bang-up job of portraying the opposite. Martin and Ramirez would love this once they caught wind, especially considering I had no other backup plan.

Dina cleared her throat. Apparently, I'd mumbled a bit of that last portion out loud. "What my niece is trying to say is that I was *formerly* in a position where I could acquire certain things for people based on their needs. You might say I had particular…knack for pairing one vice with another."

"One-stop shopping," Tamryn added, slumping back onto the bench next to me.

Dina wrinkled her nose. "A crass way of putting it but—"

I wasn't sure what compelled me to interrupt, but this whole scenario, coupled with the family reunion, had set me on edge. "Trafficking *is* crass."

"Touché. Judgment does not become you, Arianna Jackson." Dina clucked her tongue.

"Neither does kidnapping, assault or murder, *Dina*," I replied through gritted teeth. "And don't tell me it's not personal. Because it is. Very personal."

Dina raised a hand. "I realize that. I won't insult you by making excuses for who I was or what I did in the past. All I can do is show you, through my actions, that I am on your side and will help you any way I can."

I nodded. I appreciated her honesty, but something didn't sit right.

"Why the change of heart? I'm sure that being in a position like that had its benefits."

"Nothing as noble as a change of heart, I'm afraid. I was forced into early retirement when someone spilled details to the wrong people and made sure it looked as though I had been the one who had been on the wrong side while getting paid well for my efforts.

"Unfortunately, there are no second chances in this business. If you don't disappear on your own, someone won't hesitate to help you on your way. I chose the prior, made an 'arrangement' and yet, have been looking over my shoulder ever since."

"Harsh. And the person who set you up?"

"I have my suspicions, and that's all I'm willing to say on the subject. Water under the bridge." The calmness in her tone didn't quite reach her eyes.

I nodded. "Alright. As long as it doesn't interfere with getting my best friend and Shelby back, I don't care."

Dina tilted her head back and laughed. "You let me worry about my issues. You've got bigger ones to contend with at the present, like that plan of yours."

"So you said. You also mentioned that your niece here was being less than truthful with me." I glanced at Tamryn, who had been surprisingly quiet during this entire exchange and found her checking text messages. I shot an exasperated glance at Dina.

"Tami! Ditch the phone. Tell Arianna what you know about the girl. Or I will. And you won't like my version."

"So much for family loyalty," Tamryn grumbled, palming the phone so that I couldn't see the screen. "And don't call me Tami."

I interjected before the two could divert the conversation with a squabble. "Spill it, Tamryn. Who is the girl you were talking to at the club? You know more than you're letting on. And don't tell me she's just someone you know from the bar scene. What role does she play in this?"

Tamryn glanced at her aunt, then at me, sniffing. "Fine. Claudia and I have known each other since diapers. Our moms were sorority sisters in college. Her mom introduced my dad and mom…she was dating his best friend. The two couples got married…made a bunch of money together…had some kids…happily ever after… the end."

Dina chuckled. "Nice embellishment on the fairytale ending."

I glanced between the two. "What?"

She picked up where Tamryn had left off. "A business deal fell through between the two men, which caused friction between the women and trickled down to the kids. Didn't Claudia have to drop out of that private school you were both attending as a result?"

Tamryn rolled her eyes. "She dropped out before that happened."

The history lesson was amusing but did little

to explain who Claudia was today and her involvement in the operation. Though I left the snark out, for brevity's sake, I said as much to Tamryn.

"Sometimes she's a hostess," she replied, shrugging. "Sometimes she claims she does… other things."

"What 'other things'?"

Tamryn scoffed. "Well, she's no curator, like Auntie here, but she's always had a knack for making a good amount of cash on the side doing sketchy crap."

"With a family like that, why would she be concerned with making cash on the side?" I asked.

"Claudia has been known to lead alternate lives. Ones that she doesn't want her parents finding out about."

I waved a hand. "Feel free to elaborate. Her parents aren't here."

"Fine," Tamryn huffed. "You could say she's has a few vices."

"Belgian chocolates? Jewels? Drugs?"

She tossed back her head, laughing. "All of the above. Sometimes all at once. But for our purposes, we're talking mostly vices of the flesh, stuff like that."

"What—as in she watches it?"

"No, more like she gets a kick out of *being* watched. She used to make these online videos, get friends to participate, that sort of thing. She still can't seem to help herself—it's just what she does—and it has been quite lucrative for her. Or so she claims." She rolled her eyes.

And while Tamryn was working hard to play it off as no big deal—it was just Claudia being Claudia—Dina's pursed lips confirmed otherwise.

"So she's always on the lookout for fresh talent," I pressed.

"Why, are you interested?" Tamryn teased until she caught a glimpse of my just-smelled-rotten-eggs expression. "Alright, all joking aside, yes. And, the riper off the tree, the better," she replied, scrunching her nose. When she noted my raised brow, she quickly added, "Hey, don't look at me—I'm with you, major on the 'eeew' scale. It's her customers who 'prefer' it that way."

"So she hasn't tried to recruit you?"

"No," Tamryn's response was terse and came

paired with a sizable frown. "And that's all I'm willing to say about it."

I guess that brought a conclusion to that story, but it made me curious why she was so touchy.

"Are you protecting Claudia?" I asked, hoping this didn't spur things into another sensitive arena, but Tamryn appeared thoughtful, as though it hadn't occurred to her.

"I wouldn't say I'm protective of her. In fact, I find her to be more annoying than anything. And, if I had the choice, I would rather not be associated with her."

"Choice?" I asked as Tamryn glanced at Dina, who gave her a "get-on-with-it gesture" with her gloved hand.

"She has some stuff on me that I'd rather not be made…public," she huffed after a moment.

Dina shook her head. "Come on, Tami, I think you may need to give her a bit more than that."

Tamryn graced her aunt with a dirty look before continuing. "Fine. In high school, we got involved in some activities that most parents would disapprove of. After one particularly… playful night, Claudia got busted, and that was the end of that. Her parents shipped her off to an all-girl boarding school as quick as you can say 'juvenile detention' to ride out her last couple of years. It was lame. Anyway, life went on and when she came back, she had a real chip on her shoulder."

"Well, that must be old news because she's back, and the two of you have crossed paths again. And for our purposes, that's fortuitous."

Tamryn squinted. "How do you figure?"

"Well, given her role, she was obviously familiar with both Shelby and Leah and may have some information that is pertinent to finding them—meaning she's the first person I want to talk to." Before Tamryn could protest, I turned to Dina. "At the onset, you mentioned needing a better plan—I assume you have one in mind."

Dina smiled, though it was cryptic. "Indeed, I do. Though you"—she glanced at her niece —"may not like it."

"What else is new?" Tamryn muttered.

Dina chuckled and clapped her gloves together, which made an odd "whumping" noise.

"Great. Now that we got that old business out of the way—shall we begin?"

CHAPTER TWENTY-SEVEN

"You're right. I hate it."

Yeah, it didn't come as much of a surprise that Tamryn wasn't thrilled with Dina's plan. If we went with it, it meant she and I would stroll in the front door of the operation—so to speak—and that she would vouch for me, claiming that I was her old pal from college, was trustworthy, reliable and motivated, and would be a perfect fit to be worked into the mix.

Dina, of course, would have to school me on everything I needed to know, with Tamryn's help—basically an undergrad degree condensed from four years down to a few hours. If it got me what I wanted, including access to Claudia and whoever else was involved, I was game. However, it opened Tamryn up wide—leaving her vulnerable—which is why she was now standing toe-to-toe with her aunt, hands thrust on hips.

"I won't do it."

"Oh, think you will."

Kudos to Dina. Gal knew how to stand her ground without raising her voice or blinking an eye.

I'll admit the latter was a bit unsettling.

"Ha. Without me, it won't work," Tamryn sneered.

"True, and while you may not like it, you *will* do it."

"Nope."

"This ensures you will." Dina pulled her cellphone and though I could vaguely see a video clip playing from where I was standing, couldn't tell what it entailed or who. "Perhaps I should share it with Arianna, get her opinion?"

"Uh—" I wasn't about to get into a family battle, much less start a civil war.

"Blackmail, Auntie…really?" Tamryn scoffed.

"Blackmail is such a classless word, don't

you think?" She winked at me. "I prefer to think of it as leverage."

"Call it whatever you want. I don't think your plan will work, but if I've got no choice in the matter then there's no point arguing about it."

I cocked my head. Was Tamryn really giving in this easily? Whatever was on that video must have been worth its price in gold.

"I think, at a minimum, with a bit of coaching, it gets Arianna inside and will give her access to the people who know what happened to her friends. In and out, then we regroup and figure out our next step."

Tamryn opened her mouth to speak but stopped, frowning as she squinted over Dina's shoulder.

"I'm afraid Tamryn is right. The plan won't work," a familiar voice called out. A familiar *male* voice.

"What are *you* doing here?" Tamryn growled as Dina and I turned.

"I believe my previous statement made the 'what' clear," Martin replied, a bit winded as he wiped the sweat from his brow. "As to the 'why'—for brevity's sake, assuming you're going to run the gambit of usual who, what, why questions—because the game has changed."

He stopped to catch his breath but continued before Tamryn could retort. "You no longer have time for the meet and greet and for the casual pumping of information, assuming you were still proceeding with that part of Arianna's plan." I raised a brow—how could he have known that? —and started to speak when Tamryn beat me to it. Apparently, she'd just been waiting for an opportunity to pounce.

"You still haven't said anything that is all that interesting, or that *thoroughly* explains why you barged into our conversation, uninvited, old man. You are making a habit of it, you know." She clearly wasn't asking and the way she fisted her hands, I wondered if she was willing to sacrifice a nail smacking Martin, despite the fact he had been in support of her opinion of Dina's plan.

Martin ignored her and focused his attention on me and then on Dina, his brow hiking as though he'd just noticed her standing there. The expression she returned—down-turned mouth, her own brows furrowing—suggested that she was not keen about the interruption either. Or perhaps, she was just not all that impressed by the sweaty older knight swooping in to save the day.

"What I was *about* to say was that I just received intel from a reliable source that there is going to be a shipment of cargo heading out of state tonight. We believe they're heading toward California under the guise of hauling oversized furniture, with the intention of putting the cargo on a boat and getting it into international waters as quickly as possible."

"By cargo, I assume you mean human," Dina clarified.

Martin nodded. "And, if Arianna's friend has been collected, there's a good chance she'll be in that shipment."

"Shelby, too?" I asked.

Martin shook his head. "To be honest, we have no idea who or how many they have, just that they are moving a live shipment tonight."

"If you don't know who they have, then how do you know Leah will be part of this 'live shipment'?" I clamped my mouth shut as soon as I said it.

By framing it in that way, Martin had eliminated the alternative as an option. An alternative reality that was unfathomable. Unthinkable.

Unforgivable.

As Dina and Tamryn watched us, I gave him a single head nod, letting him know that I'd gotten his meaning and perhaps, was thankful for it.

We were all well aware of the stakes by now.

"They wouldn't risk another body dump locally," Tamryn offered after a moment.

Neither Martin nor Dina responded, but thinking of Jillian—how she had died and then been positioned outside the last place she had been seen, hours later—I had to question that. If the operation was trying to *avoid* attention, why would someone among the ranks have so blatantly gone to the trouble of pointing a big red arrow at one of their prime locations?

They wouldn't.

Was someone trying to get back at them for something, or was Jillian collateral damage? There was, of course, the possibility that her death had nothing to do with any of this, but there were just too many coincidences that said otherwise.

Still, I wondered—what had made them

choose Jillian? Why had they needed to kill her? Or had something gone wrong?

"So this is our only shot," I murmured, turning back to Martin.

He nodded, his lips pressed firmly.

"Then, I'd say we have nothing to lose by going all in." I looked at Dina, received a head nod before turning to Tamryn.

She chewed her lip before responding, "If we're going to do it, let's blow this sucker up."

It wasn't quite the way I hoped it would go down, but I took her response for what it was—an acknowledgment and added my own thumbs-up to the mix.

"Okay, we've got a lot to do and not a lot of time to do it. Let's meet back and my house and get to work. Dina—you cool to follow Martin?"

The older woman nodded, so I turned to Tamryn. "I'll grab a ride with you. Martin, will you take Nicoh?" He, too, agreed.

I assumed he'd driven, which left the minor detail of how he'd found me. I had my suspicions as I called Nicoh over—he'd been not so quietly chasing birds all this time—and dug into the fur surrounding his thick neck and felt along his collar. When my fingers hit something small clamped to the underside, I leaned in for close inspection, noting Martin's feet shuffling in my peripheral view as I did.

Interesting what you can find when you know what to look for, especially when you know the habits of the company you keep. The object pulled away easily and I displayed it for all to see.

"A tracker, Martin? Really?" At least he had the good sense to look remorseful, his entire face reddening as he worked his mouth. "Was this your idea, or Ramirez's?"

He blew out a breath. "It was mine, though I ran it by him and he agreed."

"And he didn't mention that it might piss me off." Not a question.

"He did. But he said you'd get over it. Eventually."

"Yeah, well, you may want to ask how that's been working out for him the next time you two Chatty Cathy's meet up."

"I think I can surmise," Martin murmured.

"Whatever. I assume you drove. Take Nicoh and meet us at the house. And Martin? No more buffoonery."

Sufficiently chastised, he grabbed Nicoh's lead and retreated in the direction he'd come.

I glanced at Tamryn and Dina, who'd been wise not to intervene. Tamryn looked amused, if not a bit impressed by my dressing-down of Martin. Dina, well, it was hard to say.

And perhaps Tamryn was taking a page from my book when she turned to her aunt.

"That little bit of 'insurance' you're hanging onto? I want it back when we're done. Let's go, AJ." She waved for me to follow, but she wasn't done yet as she spun on her heel and yelled, "And *Auntie*? I hate to have to continually remind that moldy old Swiss cheese brain of yours, but don't call me Tami."

CHAPTER TWENTY-EIGHT

It took everything in me to refrain from hawk-eyeing Martin's retreat, though I wasn't sure why.

Then again, yes, I did.

While his plan to keep tabs on my whereabouts had been exposed, I guess somewhere in the back of my mind I wondered about the other schemes he had up his sleeve.

With Martin, you could always be sure there *were* others. The man liked his contingency plans.

"So you and Dina are close?" I asked Tamryn as we hustled out of the park to her vehicle.

Tamryn threw her head back and released a cackle so shrill that it raised the hairs on the back of my neck. "We're not the huggy-feely type—meaning we don't 'do' close in my family." She made air quotes with her index fingers. "I mean, even my parents weren't really all that into the child-raising and bonding crap—they have always been pretty hands-off—and don't really care what I do, as long as it doesn't interfere with their precious business dealings." She rolled her eyes, her lips curling.

"You've seen my track record, so you're well aware of how all of that turned out. But whatever—the alternative would have been far worse. They're the same way with one another —I'm not sure I can recall the last time I saw them in the same room, much less showing the other any form of affection.

"Same goes for extended family. My mom barely talks to my aunt, and I don't think they've had an actual conversation in the last ten years or so that didn't end in a cellphone getting obliterated." Tamryn chuckled when she caught my open-mouthed expression, but it lacked its previous luster.

"It is what it is. And, right now, it works for

me. I don't want them in my business any more than they want me in theirs." She was quiet for a moment. "But getting back to your original question—of all of them, Dina would be the person I connect with the most, though it isn't like we have Thanksgiving dinner together or share secrets. We just don't roll that way, if you know what I mean."

"That must have been rough."

Tamryn squinted and seemed to contemplate that. "Maybe when I was younger—yeah, it was hard figuring the world out on my own—but as I got older, I used it to my advantage. And before you ask, no, I don't feel bad about it where my parents are concerned. I earned my keep since the day I was spawned into their circus—I've served as nothing more than a check box on a list of acquisitions one must have to appear successful in society and among one's peers. I'm surprised my parents didn't just buy a kid and be done with it—seems like it would have been the easiest alternative, all things considered."

"I didn't mean to drum anything—"

"Like I said, it is what it is." When I raised a brow, she waved a hand. "Seriously, I'm cool with it. I've just never really thought about it, I guess. So score one for you—you caught me off-guard. That isn't easy to do.

"Anyway, now that I've gotten you away from the senior citizens, I think you should probably know that I've made a little adjustment to their plans and fabricated one of my own." She wiggled her brows conspiratorially and tugged me along with her, our destination unknown.

"This just came to you?"

"Pfft. I was born with a backup plan. And a backup for the backup. I never intended to go along with Auntie's plan—or Mr. Stiff Upper Lip's—for that matter. What a crock!" She laughed.

"Care to enlighten me?"

"Soon. Let's get in the car and make sure we've ditched them, shall we?"

"You don't seem all that surprised that either he or Dina showed up."

"I knew you'd have something up your sleeve. The fact that it was Dina was a nice touch if it hadn't backfired. But, then again, you couldn't have known she was family."

"I guess not. And Martin?"

"That dude is predictable. It's in his nature to interfere. Sure, he thinks he's 'helping,' but he's not the only one with people. His 'network'?" She hacked out a laugh. "Give me a break. Wouldn't be surprised if they got their messages through a tin can. Or some sort of smoke signal."

"Well, there *is* a burn ban in effect right now, due to all the smoke in the air," I replied, which amused her to no end.

"Clever."

"So, what do you propose we do once we've 'ditched' Dina and Martin?"

She gave me a wry quirk of her lip as she propelled me toward what I figured was the location of her getaway car.

"We head straight to the horse and drag the bit from her mouth, of course."

"We've gone from easing our way into a conversation with Claudia to implementing interrogation tactics?" I stuttered while stumbling over a crack in the pavement.

Never a good omen.

"It's not like we're going to tear her extensions out." Tamryn laughed.

Considering that's not where my mind had taken me, I hesitated. There was a lot left up to interpretation between having a chat and torture, not to mention that it was a smidge unsettling to learn that Tamryn had apparently already given the option some consideration.

"Still, I'm not sure—" I was interrupted by my cell phone. "Oh crap, it's Ramirez." Had Martin already put him on our trail?

Tamryn rolled her eyes. "Whatever. Answer it."

I chickened out and waited until the call went to voicemail. Even though Tamryn's grasp was still firm, I managed to listen to it, noting Ramirez's message was short but not too sweet.

"AJ, I know you're avoiding me. Martin filled me in. If he doesn't listen to reason, I'm hoping you will—you need to stop before things get too far. You know deep down that you won't get Leah back this way. Think about it. You're going to end up putting her in greater danger. Can you live with that?"

There was some shuffling in the background and I thought perhaps he would disconnect, but he had one more zinger to toss out.

"I'm on my way to your house now. You can respond to my question when you're looking me in the eye."

And that's when he disconnected.

I ignored the lump in my throat and pulled free from Tamryn, whose head whipped around in surprise. "What?"

Without realizing it, Ramirez had made my decision an easy one.

"You're right. It's time to change up the plan."

Nodding, she gave me a wide grin. "Plans do change."

Shrugging, I gestured for her to continue leading the way. "Well, I guess that settles that—let's go find Claudia."

The ride to wherever Tamryn thought Claudia might be was a silent one. The last comment had come from me upon seeing yet another one of her vehicles in the parking lot—this one, a beat-up Ford Escort that had probably seen its last best days a decade earlier. Though I hadn't made any reference to its condition—I was more interested in the owner—Tamryn had defiantly jutted out her chin, looked me in the eye and stated, "A friend lent it to me for the day. Let's just leave it at that."

I'd put up my hands in surrender before swiping pop cans, empty potato chip bags and a variety of chocolate-encrusted candy wrappers onto the floor, careful not to step on the glob of gum that was nestled among the heap.

Whoever owned it was either a teenager or someone who did stakeouts for a living. Still, I wondered, with all of her supposed loyal friends, why she had elected to borrow *this* car? Then again, it was easy to ignore and in our current predicament, it wasn't necessarily the worst thing to be going in incognito.

I noticed we were heading east toward Old Town Scottsdale. Before long, we entered the parking structure for one of the new bank of condominiums that had recently been erected. Its primary color scheme was a sharp contrast to the desert setting, as was its imposing industrial-inspired architecture, which was likely the developer's intention as they sought to attract an up-and-coming crowd that flocked to the area.

I noted it wasn't far from the club scene—including the establishment where Misty's sister had been last seen and then found—and wondered if the location was more than one of convenience for Claudia, who, according to Tamryn, dabbled in a bit of everything.

"Let me do the talking," Tamryn said after pulling into a numbered spot.

She glanced around the structure, frowning when her eyes caught a sleek midnight blue vehicle parked in the spot designated with a "P," which I assumed was the penthouse.

"Isn't that a Bugatti Chiron?" I only recognized it because I had recently caught Martin streaming some car show and it had been among the vehicles featured. It was way out of my price range, and I assume Martin's as well, and I'd backed out of the room quietly to let him ogle.

"Indeed, it is," she replied, a hint of disgust entering her voice and she hopped out of our rust-bucket and slammed the door.

I kept the side-commentary to myself, hustling after her as she marched toward the elevators. Once inside, she punched an intercom button next to the floor designated as "P" and tapped her foot. After a couple of seconds had passed with no response, she punched it again. And again.

Finally, a sleepy but annoyed female voice crackled through the speaker, "What the heck, Tam?"

Tamryn glanced up toward the conspicuous eyeball in the corner and frowned. "You gonna let me come up, or what?"

We were met with silence and just as Tamryn was readying her finger to stab the button again, the voice returned, "Now is not a good time."

"Make it a good time," Tamryn growled. "Or I'll use the override code."

"The place is a mess. Can I meet you at the juice bar in an hour?"

Tamryn glared at the eyeball before snapping, "Make it ten minutes, or I'm coming up, 'mess' or not." She stabbed both fingers in the air to ensure the air quotes translated.

I swore I heard a squeak from the intercom before it went silent.

"Um. Juice bar?" I needed to get Tamryn out of this mood before we met with Claudia.

"On the main floor," was the grumbled response.

"Oh…here?"

"Full amenities."

"Wow. She must make a pretty good salary." I couldn't afford the payments for such a lavish living arrangement, much less the penthouse suite. And not to mention the car.

"You don't know the half of it." There was no jealously in her tone, though I detected something else. Disgust?

She punched "M" and the doors snapped shut. After a short ride—I doubt it was more than one floor, based on where we'd parked in the structure—they opened with the same quiet efficiency.

We were presented with a foyer that matched the exterior in color and included modular furnishings with various pop-culture-themed tapestries that hung from the vaulted ceiling, alongside the exposed pipes and structural components. For something so stripped down, it looked hideously complex. It was all I could do to prevent my mouth from gaping open as I digested it all.

"Grotesque, isn't it?"

I glanced at Tamryn and noted her smirk.

"It's…something, all right."

She laughed. "It's okay to say you hate it."

"Okay, I hate it."

This made her laugh harder. "Nice. Next time I see my mother, I'll be sure to let her know."

Inwardly, I groaned. I'd effectively opened mouth and inserted foot.

Once I got that piece of shoe leather down my gullet, I squawked, "Your mother?"

"Designed it. Well, her team designed it under her overbearing direction. She just forked out the cash to have it built."

"I had no idea."

"No reason you should. Most people think my dad is the one with all the cash. But he made his. My mother was born with it. Her family is loaded. And stingy. Well, except for Auntie D., and she doesn't really count."

"Oh? Why is that?"

"Mostly because she doesn't roll that way. She's pretty self-sufficient and thinks that anyone who values money and possessions above all else should be exiled to the pit of the earth."

It was perhaps a harsh view of people and the world. It made me wonder if it were true, why had she gotten involved in an operation that thrived on both, much less stayed in it long enough that she was deemed a curator of it? Wouldn't she, in fact, be just as guilty as the people she judged?

I was pulled out of my musing as Tamryn prattled on. "Auntie was cast out of the family once they figured out she had a mind of her own anyway. One of the many reasons she and my mother don't get along. That and my mother is a spiteful hag with a personality that grates on everyone's nerves."

She hacked out a laugh that was more sinister than filled with humor before adding, "Case in point: she buys stuff up just so that she can tear it down and build crap like this, *solely* because it amuses her to piss other people off. For whatever reason, people keep flocking to her monstrosities, which puffs up her already over-inflated ego. She continues raking in cash, buying up old neighborhoods so that she can 're-vitalize' them."

"Your mother sounds…interesting," I uttered. If even a quarter of what Tamryn said was true, she was someone I'd prefer to steer clear of.

"Yup, she's a piece of work, alright. So, here's BTB—uh, the juice bar—where the heck is Claudia?"

I'd been so wrapped up in our conversation that I'd failed to notice that she had indeed steered us to what was a surprisingly normal-looking juice bar. Unlike the rest of the areas on the floor, BTB, as the neon signed indicated, was more like what you'd expect—a simple service area where drinks were ordered, prepared and picked up, combined with a spacious seating area that housed comfortable chairs and tables where patrons could enjoy their purchases and co-mingle.

"You like it?"

I nodded. "It's different from the rest of the space. More…cozy."

Tamryn bobbed her head, smiling as she plopped down in an oversized chair after giving the tanned platinum blond behind the counter a head-nod. "Thank you for saying that."

"You did all of this?" I quirked a brow as I sat in my own chair, which I probably could have copped a nap in had time permitted.

"Twisted the old lady's arm. She finally gave in so that she could shut me up." She chuckled, but the gleam of pride in her eyes spoke volumes.

"Well, you certainly have a knack for it."

She started to say something when the blond popped over and placed two fluorescent green smoothies in front of each of us. Her hair cascaded over her shoulders in beachy waves before she subconsciously pushed it back and smiled at us shyly. "Hey, Tam. Figured you and your friend would like the usual."

"Thanks, Bev. This is AJ. AJ, meet Bev."

We gave each other respective "hi's" and smiles before Bev turned to Tamryn. "What brings you by?" I noted a southern lilt to her words, giving them a smooth, song-like quality.

"Meeting Claudia in a few. Said her place was a mess and couldn't let us up."

Bev's smile evaporated as she sighed. "Oh, *that* one. She's never changed, has she?"

"Not one bit," Tamryn replied, her words clipped as she glanced at me before changing the subject. "Bev and I went to college together, though she was already leaps and bounds ahead of the rest of us and quickly headed off to grad school." Bev blushed deeply and absently tucked her hair behind her ear.

"Oh, do you live here, too?" I asked.

"My goodness, aren't you sweet?" Bev laughed and patted my shoulder, shaking her head. "I'm just the hired help."

To this, Tamryn clucked her tongue. "Bev's being modest. She rents this space—BTB is her gig."

"Wow. Congratulations! I was just telling

Tamryn that it's a refreshing change from the rest of the floor."

Bev blushed. "Well, Tam helped me figure out a lot along the way, including the design and decor."

Tamryn responded by wiggling. "Meh. Don't let her fool you. Bev's got a stellar mind for business and the dedication and tenacity to pull it off, even in this froufrou environment. All I did was offer some encouragement along the way."

"Yeah, right," Bev replied, rolling her eyes. I could tell she was about to add more when her attention strayed to something behind me. "Well, look what the dog dug up."

I didn't have the heart to tell her the actual saying, but when I glanced over my shoulder, decided that perhaps her assessment was more on par.

A twenty-something sashayed casually towards us wearing a powder blue jogging suit and pink flip-flops that exposed neon green toenails. Oversized cat-eye sunglasses covered the majority of her face and her multi-colored locks, which looked as though a three-year-old had eaten a box of crayons and barfed on, were corralled into a messy top-knot, revealing an indigo dragonfly tattoo behind her left ear.

"Nice that you could grace us with your presence, Claudia." Tamryn raised a brow as the girl plopped into an empty chair.

"Elevator was busy—stupid snowbirds. Had to hoof it down." Her nose scrunched as she pulled out a tube of lip gloss and applied a thick layer of a ruby shade which made the paleness of her skin more pronounced.

Claudia was not unattractive, but she was, aside from all the colorful additions, rather plain. Smacking her lips before tucking the lip gloss away, she toyed with her top-knot.

Tamryn waited for her to finish grooming before replying, her tone droll and her expression unamused. "One sympathizes."

No matter how self-absorbed Claudia was, there was no masking the thickness of the sarcasm in Tamryn's delivery, though she did her best to appear unruffled, her mouth pulled tight.

Even Bev raised a brow.

"And that's my cue to get back to work." She made no effort to hide her smirk as she glanced in Claudia's direction before turning to me and offering a genuine smile. "Nice meeting you, AJ. Good seeing you, Tam. We'll catch up later—for now, beverages are on the house."

"Where's mine?" Claudia whined, but Bev pretended not to hear her as she turned on her heel, flipped her hair over her shoulder and returned to the bar. "Witch," she growled at Bev's back.

"Careful, Claudia, those stiletto claws of yours are exposed." Tamryn enjoyed the girl's fuming way too much, her smile broad and mischievous and not unlike the Cheshire Cat.

"Well, just because she's got 'it' doesn't mean it needs to ooze it all over the place. Then again, what do you expect? Once trailer trash, always trailer trash," Claudia huffed.

"You utter those words one more time and you'll live to regret it." Tamryn's smile had morphed into something matching The Joker's, causing Claudia to squeak and slink further into her chair. "Bev has never done anything to you. And besides, whatever you've got going on up there in that shady little shanty of yours, she wants no part of."

"Says you," the other girl grumbled under her breath as she studied her inch-long blood-red daggers. Tamryn had been right. Her stilettos were out.

Tamryn leaned forward and gave Claudia's chin a brisk shake. "That's right, I *do* say, Claudia. Now, let it go." She released Claudia's chin and gave her face a swift pat.

"Whatever, Tamryn. You got me down here. What do you want?" Claudia sputtered out.

"What I want, Claudia, is a bit of respect. For myself and my guest. You haven't even acknowledged that you and I aren't alone."

"I saw her. Figured you had her on a short leash, too, considering she hasn't acknowledged my presence either."

"Nobody has me on any leash," I snapped, tired of Claudia's childish behavior, which was getting us nowhere.

She gave me a cursory once-over, scoffing when she was done. "Do we know each other?"

I leaned in fast enough to force Claudia to jump. "No, but you know my friend. Which is why we're here. She's missing."

"I told you I would handle this." Tamryn glared at me.

"Fine, get to it then. I'm getting tired of this high school reunion crap," I replied through gritted teeth, leveling a glare right back at her.

Oblivious to the sudden tension, Claudia surprised us both by spurting, "You hear what happened to that girl Jilli behind the club?" Breaking away from our stare-down, we nodded that we had. "Gawd, Rob was a mess."

Tamryn glanced at me and noted my raised brows. "Rob is the staff member who found her. And Claudia's boy toy of the week."

"Duh. That was *last* week." Claudia frowned, plucking at the hair that had escaped the top-knot.

"Ah, so that explains the shuffle maneuver," Tamryn surveyed the girl, whose cheeks had developed a splotchy pink cast under the weight of the attention. "Who is it?"

"None of your business." Claudia cinched her hoodie around her frame as though trying to disappear. "You're not their type."

"Sweetheart, sooner or later, I'm everyone's type." Tamryn chuckled, winking at me.

Claudia bristled and made a clipped squawking sound before responding in a petulant child-like tone. "Yeah, well, you're too old for their taste."

Tamryn rolled her eyes. "Honey, don't forget —your birthday is something like thirty-seven days behind mine, so it's not like your all that 'fresh' yourself." Claudia frowned at the use of finger quotes, causing Tamryn to hack out a couple of harsh laughs.

I had to remind myself that these were a couple of twenty-somethings, not two-year-olds. But, before it could continue, or Claudia ended up aggravating Tamryn to the point she did more than leave finger marks on her face, I had to rein it in.

"Anyway, Tamryn, you want to tell—"

"*Who* are you, anyway?" Claudia interrupted as she sized me up again, and for a minute, I thought I was living my own *Groundhog Day*.

Thankfully, Tamryn stepped in. "This is AJ. She's a friend of Leah's. Turns out, Leah's gone missing—as she alluded to earlier," she shot me a look to remind me she was handling this. "Funny how Shelby ghosted first and now Leah, such a short time later, don't you think?"

"Huh. I hadn't heard." Claudia avoided Tamryn's gaze and turned her pinched expression toward me. "Though, now that I think about it, that friend of yours had of a way of putting herself into places where she had no business going. Told her to cool it, but she was like a freaking pit bull—once she got her mind set on something, she just grabbed hold and wouldn't let go until she was satisfied, no matter the cost."

I bristled at the mention of Leah in the past tense and gritted my teeth as I pressed her. "How do you mean?"

Tamryn shot me a warning look that said she intended to control the convo for a bit. I pursed my lips but took a mental step back. I understood where she was coming from, but then again, she was also the one who'd indicated there wasn't time. Speaking of which, I was sure Dina and Martin had both noticed our absence by now.

Regardless, it didn't matter. Time was not our friend. Not to mention Tamryn was in charge of what little we had.

Claudia was unaware of the silent dialogue that passed between us, as she gave me a coy look, still choosing to avoid Tamryn. "She's *your* friend. I'm sure you know what she's like."

"I'm sure she does." Tamryn shot me a sharp look to ensure I was going to hold my tongue. Once satisfied with whatever she saw, she continued. "What AJ is trying to get at is—what was it, specifically, that Leah was after?"

Claudia pursed her lips. "The better question would be—what *wasn't* she after? Basically, she wanted the 'operational playbook'—her words —and demanded to know how everything worked. I mean, who the heck did she think she was? Overly curious, if you ask me."

Apparently, unlike Tamryn, she was unaware of Leah's previous career and her tenacity for ferreting out the facts. She was notorious for it and while it made her extraordinarily adept at her work, it also had a knack for putting her in precarious and often dangerous situations.

This was one of those times.

"And what did you tell her?" Tamryn prompted before I could interject.

"I warned her that asking too many questions would only get her into trouble, but she wouldn't listen."

"But you told her, anyway," Tamryn replied, posing no question, as she had likely already drawn the same conclusion I had. Claudia liked to talk because it made her feel important.

"What was I supposed to do?" Claudia's voice hiked to the point I was worried the shatter-proof storm-resistant windows would crack and rain down on us.

Tamryn put a hand up to silence her, causing the girl's mouth to form an unflattering pout. "Go on—what did you tell her?"

"She asked about that Shelby girl, straight off the bat. I had barely had a chance to make the rounds. I do have responsibilities, you know." Claudia frowned and her top-knot bobbed as she looked from Tamryn to me and back, perhaps hoping to garner some sympathy for her inconvenience.

I know I wasn't speaking solely for myself when I say it was in short supply.

"And?" Tamryn prompted, her tone impatient, bordering on hostile.

I couldn't say I blamed her. I had only known Claudia a matter of minutes and she was already wearing on my every last nerve. I couldn't imagine having to deal with this for years. I wondered why Tamryn bothered. It certainly didn't seem to be her usual M.O.

I silently studied her. Something told me she was doing this more for my benefit—she already knew the score—what was it that she wanted to draw out of Claudia?

Or perhaps, hoping that she wouldn't reveal.

Claudia huffed but complied. "I told her that everything about Shelby was off from the start—not that she was much better. But Shelby's appearance on the scene was...odd. First, she got fast-tracked. How the heck did that happen?" She looked at Tamryn, who shrugged. "I had to jump through a gazillion hoops. And that's saying something. I mean, she wasn't even that cute. Plus, she was old…like you." She glanced at me.

I bit my lip, tempted to school her. Not that it mattered, but she was sorely mistaken—I was not that much older than she was. She just wasn't used to dealing with people who had more maturity in their pinkie toe than she had amassed in her twenty-something years. Even Tamryn looked disgusted, shaking her head as she gave Claudia a healthy frown.

Claudia, however, was too in love with the sound of her own voice to notice. Or care. The spotlight was hers and she was going to leverage it for all it was worth.

"Anyway, once she wormed her way in, everybody *loved* her. It was all 'Shelby, this.' and 'Shelby, that.' It got pretty annoying. I mean, come on!" Claudia flapped her hands in a manner that made her look more like a land-locked bird than an exasperated drama queen.

"It wasn't like she was doing anything all *that* special but the minute she had their attention, she dropped the nice girl act and was ruthless when it came to pushing her own agenda. Seriously, asking all those questions like she was?" She clucked her tongue, looking from Tamryn to me for affirmation.

We were fresh out, but she didn't seem deterred as she prattled on. "I didn't trust her and I said as much to whoever would listen. For all we know, she could have been working for the competition. On the other hand, maybe she'd gotten all she needed and bailed. Either way, I'm glad she's gone. Not like she ever did anything for me, though now that she's out of the picture, my life has gotten a lot easier."

I chewed the inside of my cheek to prevent myself from letting her know my thoughts on the subject. Shelby wasn't stealing insider secrets—even if she'd gotten them, it had been for a greater purpose—and for her efforts, she'd gotten herself into a situation so dire, my best friend had followed her in.

"Anyway, your friend Leah came in here asking questions from the get-go about Shelby and didn't even attempt to hide it. I'm sure she probably cheesed more than a few people off, just by bringing Shelby's name up. Though she wasn't as much of an annoying kiss-up as Shelby, it's no surprise what happened to either of them."

I raised a brow at Tamryn, who frowned as she turned to Claudia.

"What happened to them?" We said in unison.

"Nobody knows. Which is my point." She scrunched her nose and shot us each disgusted looks that suggested we were complete morons. "Here one day—then poof." Her fingernails made an annoying clicking sound as she attempted to snap her fingers.

"Considering your position within the organization, it seems odd that you wouldn't be kept in the loop about what's going on, especially if it impacts your…responsibilities." It was hard toning my commentary down when all I wanted to do was share my opinion of her position and the associated 'responsibilities.'

I slid a glance at Tamryn, hoping that she

wouldn't box me for overstepping, but she was focused on Claudia, her lip curling as the girl unabashedly engaged in a series of self-grooming behaviors—including another fluff of the already weary top-knot—before indulging us her presence by way of a casual wave of a hand. At least she hadn't asked us to kiss it—it wouldn't have surprised me in the least, but it would have gotten her a quick trip to the floor.

"Above my pay grade. Don't get paid to know. I just filter them as they come."

"Filter?" Tamryn shot me a look that probably should have singed my eyebrows but I couldn't help it—Claudia had piqued my interest.

"You know, weed all the disgusting losers out."

I leaned toward Claudia, so close that she likely could feel my hot breath on her neck, ignoring Tamryn's shaking head and searing gaze. Good luck stopping me, I thought.

I hoped sidetracking me hadn't been part of her plan all along but quickly shook off that idea. She could have just as easily bailed on us at the park but had chosen not to. Something told me she needed to see this through to the end, perhaps not for the same reason but that she, too, sought closure.

"And, just how do you decide who makes the cut?" I asked, my tone sounding far calmer to my ear despite the blood boiling in my veins.

Claudia rolled her eyes, not even bothering to look at me. She may not have thought I was worth her time, but I was sure as heck gonna make sure she paid attention from this point forward.

I smacked the foot she'd draped over the chair, knocking it back to the floor and causing her eyes to widen as she said upright. Placing my hands on either side of her chair, I drug it until we were inches apart and I was sure she could see my pearly whites as I gritted them at her.

"Claudia, this is *your* area of expertise—the place that you shine. Enlighten me." I glanced at Tamryn to see whether she would intervene, but she settled back into her seat.

"Fine," Claudia huffed. "Dudes with no class, no cash, no car and no game are out. There's a sliding scale on each, if you know what I mean."

I didn't, but I shrugged. "Determined by you, I assume."

"Who else? If I didn't do it, no one would."

"I'm sure," I replied in a droll tone. "And the girls?"

"That one's a bit more challenging. You can clean a girl up, but you can't permanently remove her from the pigpen, as the saying goes." That was not how the saying went, but I prompted her to continue.

"She doesn't have to be a rocket surgeon, but she can't be a mouth-breather, either. If she looks decent and at least attempts a bit of self-care—nails, hair, skin, teeth, body—I can work with the rest. Oh, and she can't be too curious or nosy." In thinking about Leah and Shelby, this made no sense. She'd already alluded to the fact that they'd broken these rules. "I just added that one."

"Riiight," I clucked my tongue. "Okay, what happens to the parties once they are 'filtered'? And, just for clarification, I mean both those you can 'work with' *and* those you pass on."

Claudia released an exaggerated sigh. Apparently, having to explain her process wasn't high on her list, even though it gleaned her the attention she seemed to demand.

"Not sure why you care about the rejects, but after we get their digits, they are dropped back at their respective vehicles via our friendly drivers and they go about their lame-o lives.

"If they are so lame, why do you collect their info?"

"Duhhhh. So they don't make a repeat appearance. It's not like I can be at all the parties to ensure certain types aren't slipping through the crack." She sniffed. "It's been known to happen when I'm not there to oversee every detail. We don't need to start getting that kind of rep after all the effort I've put in."

"No, of course not," I clucked my tongue, feigning sympathy. "So when someone acts out, there must be some sort of chain of command when it comes to penalizing the offenders?"

"This isn't prison rules." Claudia snorted. "We just have no need for people like that and certainly don't want to encourage their type of behavior. Our parties are very exclusive, after all, and we don't want the vibe their kind usually drags in."

"In a Temptation Island sort of way," I muttered, just loud enough to receive a cackle from Tamryn, while Claudia remained oblivious, though maybe it was by choice. Up to this point, she'd been disinterested in anything other than the sound of her own banal voice.

Having said that, what she had said was contrary to what Tamryn had previously told me about her first experience with the organization. If anything, her assessment suggested that "anything goes" at the parties hosted at the vacation properties, though perhaps what transpired before or afterward was an entirely different story. It seemed to be the case, especially where Shelby, Leah, and now Jillian were concerned.

Claudia had lapsed into her grooming, ignorant that our conversation was not finished until Tamryn snapped her fingers in front of the girl's face. Claudia's nose scrunched and her mouth turned down, but at least the nail-picking had ceased.

I cleared my throat. "Okay…moving on to the people you've selected. Is this where the cards come into play?"

"Yes, there are two sets of cards—the first of which are handed out at the club and the second are handed to select girls and prospects at the end of the night as a means of following up and continuing on with us." She jutted out her impish chin, her frame a little straighter. Her role with the organization was clearly important to her.

"What happens from there? How does one work her way up…quickly if she wanted to? And what does she get out of it?"

For all the pride she'd just displayed, something in my question had made her uncomfortable, given the way she'd slumped back into her chair and was visibly squirming like a small child.

"Tell her," Tamryn commanded, giving her a hard stare.

Claudia frowned. "Sounds like *someone's* already been telling her."

I gave her credit—the gal did an excellent pout.

"Claudia… Just do it." This time, Tamryn sounded more worn out than anything. I was in agreement. This girl was exhausting and I was looking forward to concluding this conversation. Soon.

I only hoped it would yield something more

valuable than we'd already gotten out of her up to this point.

"Fine," she huffed then spent several nauseating minutes reiterating what I already knew. Of course, the bulk of that time was spent adding in various self-serving Claudia-isms that made her look like some modern-day Cinderella, overworked, under-appreciated, and often ignored for the likes of evil stepsister-types like Shelby.

It took me a moment to realize she'd stopped talking. Either my mind had wandered off, placing her on "silent mode," or I was already familiar with enough of what she was relaying that I could basically fill in my own blanks without her useless added commentary.

There was one area, however, that I noted she had been careful to dodge. "And what about the 'special clients'?" I used finger quotes to ensure I had her attention.

Her mouth twisted ever so slightly before she responded. "I don't know anything about any special clients."

Tamryn and I glanced at onc another and she rolled her eyes, to which I smirked and turned my attention back toward Ms. Evasive. "Come on, Claudia. You and I both know you can do better than that." When she shot me a flat look, I sighed and painstakingly enunciated each of my words so that there was zero confusion. "What was it that Shelby and Leah were getting so curious about? You said it yourself; they asked too many questions. I'm going to go out on a limb and guess that you supplied them with that information because it was just so juicy you couldn't help yourself."

When she balked, I added, "Hey, no judgment. It must have been excruciating to have to sit on that knowledge, being in the position you were." Her shoulders relaxed a bit and she gave me a curt nod, though she refused to meet my eyes. "There were things you held back, weren't there? You didn't want them honing in and running with them, especially not after you'd worked so hard. And I'm guessing it was those bits they *didn't* have that caused them to get snatched up. Am I right?"

She shifted in her chair, frowning.

I knew I had her.

"I want you to give me a truncated version of what you withheld from them—beyond the basics of the who, what, when, where, why and how—because I'm guessing we all know how this plays out. What I want to know, specifically, is what happens once the girls move on—whether it's to these special clients—whatever. What becomes of them? Do you ever hear from or see them again?"

I'll give her credit. Claudia sat up straight for once and actually graced me with a real look. "I don't honestly know what 'becomes of them'. And no, I don't typically hear from them again, but why would I? They've moved on." She sniffed and slumped back into the chair as though the interaction had worn her down.

Welcome to my world, Buttercup, I thought to myself.

"On?" I gestured for her to continue.

"To bigger, better people and things," she sighed, puckering her mouth. "I heard one girl got this sweet gig in Abu Dhabi as a personal assistant for some oil tycoon. Another girl met the dude of her dreams and now travels the world in his private jet."

I doubted the stories had quite the fairy tale endings that Claudia depicted but kept my thoughts to myself and played along.

"Because of the parties?" I quirked a brow.

Claudia couldn't be so full of herself to think their good fortune had anything to do with her fraternity-style parties when it likely had more to do with everything that happened after the fact.

"Well, they couldn't have hurt."

No, they just served as a launching-off point for what happened next. Still, I fought to stay on track and instead said, "But once they'd moved on—it's a 'no' as to whether you'd seen them."

"Thought I made that clear."

I ignored her snark. "So Shelby's disappearance must have come as a surprise then?"

"I don't know what you mean."

I shot a look at Tamryn and released an audible sigh before turning back to Claudia.

"Before Shelby came on the scene, you told us that everything was all rainbows and ponies and that the girls who 'moved on' were living out their wildest dreams. Yet, when Shelby showed up and started asking questions, it threw a wrench into the blissful days and before long, she was just gone. I don't recall you sharing *her* happy ending."

"That's because I don't know what she ended up doing," Claudia snapped, her tone indignant. "She could have taken what she was given and ran off on her own, for all I know. I don't know why you assume something sketchy happened to her."

"But surely you suspected her snooping wasn't appreciated?"

"Well, of course, there were rumors."

"Because she'd asked too many questions about these girls who moved on—she didn't believe they'd met a happy ending. And she wanted to know what path they had taken after the parties to get that way."

"If you say so."

"I don't need to say anything, Claudia. Your face tells me everything I need to know."

At that, her head snapped toward me and after leveling a glare, she shifted to Tamryn, though the frostiness had melted.

"She's right. Your nose turns beet red when you're lying about something and you pucker your mouth." The corner of Tamryn's mouth curled up as she pretended to squint at Claudia. "I'd watch that if I were you. I think you're getting preemie wrinkles, babe."

"I am not!" Claudia screeched, shuffling in her bag for a compact.

I shook my head at Tamryn as Claudia surveyed her face in the tiny mirror.

"Getting back to Shelby…" I prompted.

Finally satisfied with what she saw, Claudia snapped her compact shut, tossed it back into the back and huffed. "Fine. Yes. There were…rumblings…shortly before she disappeared. And after."

I didn't risk a glance at Tamryn, though the relief I felt at those words made me want to pump my fist in the air and release a round of whoo-woos that would have made Nicoh tilt his head and join in.

After pulling several teeth and clumps of hair, we were hopefully about to get somewhere.

"What kind of rumblings?"

"Dunno." Claudia shrugged and leaned back into the chair, fully aware she had our attention and loving every last drop of it.

"You. Don't. Know."

Perhaps I had gotten my hopes up too soon. What if she was just stringing me along for her own purposes? I glanced at Tamryn, who was studying her. Claudia caught it and for a moment, I was sure I saw a glimpse of fear cross her face.

"Well, there was a rumor that some of the girls who were slated to move on were shacking up in one of the rental properties while they waited for their travel arrangements. I don't how they got found out but once someone who cared caught wind, other travel plans had to be made." She offered me a knowing look. "Getting the right stuff together to travel abroad can take a lot of time if you know what I mean." I didn't but nodded so that she would continue.

Now that she had a captive and agreeable audience, she seemed pleased to comply. Though I also noted she was careful to avoid Tamryn's melting glare.

"Anyway, I don't think things were set up on the other end for their arrival because some of the girls seemed kinda anxious about it. I mean, it wasn't like they were squatters or druggies or anything. If the house wasn't being used, what could it have hurt to have them stay there?" She scoffed and rolled her eyes.

Her rationale was missing a few key factors, but I didn't belabor the point, anxious to keep her moving forward.

"Did this shuffling tend to happen a lot?"

Claudia tapped her chin. "Mmm…maybe a bit. But not the same house."

"And this is what made Shelby curious." It was not a question, but she bobbed her head.

"Yeah, first it was the rental property stuff and the girls getting caught hanging out. But then, when I told her about all the drama, she got *really* interested and wanted to know what the rumor mill was saying about what happened to the girls as a result."

"What *did* happen to the girls?"

"Well, typically, they would have already been flown to their destinations. On private jets, I heard," she sniffed and frowned, perhaps a hint of jealously leeching out. "Buuuut…because these situations got held up and they were forced to take up residence in the after-party properties—and then had to vacate pronto—alternative plans had to be made that weren't so…cushy."

"Why did they get held up?" For as much of a well-oiled machine as Claudia claimed the operation was, an oversight of this nature seemed unlikely. Had Shelby's digging caused them unforeseen "delivery" challenges?

"I'm not sure." Claudia frowned and seemed to give this some consideration. "Probably something to do with getting the passports and stuff like that. Not everybody has one and sometimes that causes problems.

"Though I've also heard we have people who handle that administrative nonsense, and they're probably just as efficient as I am—you know, to be in a position to take care of something so important. So these girls must have had something weird going on to get it hung up that long. In fact, now that I think of it, it's kinda weird there were so many of them."

Not if they were doing so illegally, I thought to myself. Some may have been under-age. I was guessing these passports that were getting expedited and the documents needed to procure the documents were not as above-board as Claudia liked to believe. Much like the private jets she alluded to, which I doubted existed.

"What about these alternative plans you mentioned?" I glanced at Tamryn, who had been quietly taking it all in, and she shrugged.

"They got picked up and taken somewhere else," Claudia replied, her mouth twisting.

I didn't mention that they were lucky they hadn't been arrested for trespassing. But then again, perhaps they would have been safer than where they ended up.

"The way I heard it, someone worked a deal with the owners and they were collected and moved elsewhere." Well, there you had it.

"Moved?" Both Tamryn and I said in unison.

Claudia's head bounced. "Yeah, somewhere out of state was the rumor. But they had to be super sneaky about it and I guess a couple of the girls put up a fuss or something, which is why the rumors started making the rounds. Something about a storage facility and some sort of transport vehicle. Sounded weird to me and I figured someone got their facts wrong. But then there were more rumblings about it being out west, near the Interstate. From there, I think they went to California, but beyond that, I have no idea how they finally made their way to their dream jobs."

Probably because they never made it. Or their "dream jobs" were nothing but a nightmare in disguise.

"And you told this to Shelby, didn't you?"

"Yeah, something along those lines. She didn't seem all that shocked by it, almost like she already knew what was going down. Then again, she was kind of a know-it-all that way, so she was probably just acting like she knew what was up."

I doubted Shelby was trying to one-up Claudia, though I wouldn't have been surprised if it wasn't these special transports that had drawn her to the operation. Perhaps she learned about it from someone on the inside?

"And by the time Leah came around, you sent her down the same path, didn't you? Because it was a whole lot easier telling those secrets you weren't supposed to tell the second time around."

Claudia couldn't have tried disappearing into her chair any farther as she glanced at Tamryn, whose frosty glare only seemed to seal her fate. But there was something more? Guilt?

"Or did someone tell you to tell her?"

"It wasn't like that," Claudia's voice crackled and she tore her gaze from Tamryn and focused on her hands.

"So what else do you know about this place out west?"

At this, Claudia seemed to relax. "Like I said, it was just rumors, but I heard it was some massive location. A yard of some sort with lots of space to move big trucks in and out and where oversized cargo is stored until it is ready to transport."

"And?" It wasn't much to go on in a metro area this large.

She shrugged. "That's really all I heard. Plus, it was a rumor anyway."

Tamryn shook her head. "Not a rumor. At all. I know exactly where it is."

CHAPTER THIRTY

I hadn't seen that one coming. Especially not from Tamryn.

"How?" Though it wasn't the only question I had, it was the one that first popped out.

"My *father*—" She levelled a glare at Claudia, who resumed her Slinky-like pose, the chair suddenly part of her again. It wasn't nearly as awkward as it sounds unless you took the sputtering sounds that exited her mouth into consideration, and then it just became weird.

"My father owns such a facility." Tamryn's lip curled in disgust before she tore her eyes away from Claudia and looked at me. "And it happens to be out west. Originally, he purchased it to store the custom trailers he had built to haul his cars. Then, he started leasing out space to friends who wanted to do the same. Others ended up talking him into making it a storage facility of sorts for those oversized cargo holds for transport on trains and boats and stuff like that."

"Okay… That certainly sounds like the type of place Claudia was talking about, but do you realize you are suggesting your father—"

"Do you want to find your friends or not?" she snapped, rising out of her seat. She shot a dirty look at Claudia, then glanced at me before growling, "Well—*come on*. Both of you."

Claudia gasped and shook her head from side to side, causing Tamryn to hack out a harsh laugh. "What? Not up for a reality check, Claudia?"

Before I could ask her what that was about— something about it had Claudia shaking, literally —Tamryn gripped her by the arm and pulled her out of the chair.

Claudia made a whimpering sound, but Tamryn cut her a look so sharp that she piped down immediately as she was hauled toward the elevator. I hustled after them, casting a glance over my shoulder at Bev, who simply smiled and offered me a little finger wave.

"I warned you not to get involved. How did you hear about this, and I mean other than from the obvious source?" Tamryn had Claudia right where she wanted her.

"Ro… Roman knew," Claudia sputtered, tears streaming down her face from behind her sunglasses.

Tamryn stopped short, barely holding Claudia upright as she stumbled into the elevator. "*My* Roman?"

"Wait, Roman?" I hustled in just before my cheeks got pinched by the doors.

"Her henchman," Claudia sniffled. "He's a beast!"

At this, Tamryn snorted, still holding a firm grip on Claudia's arm. I'm sure she'd claim to have a massive bruise later and hoped I wouldn't be around her by that point. I couldn't possibly fathom having to witness another one of her D-level performances.

"Aw, he's not so bad, unless you're being an idiot." The condescension in Tamryn's tone was as thick as a garbage truck is wide. Even Claudia and her ego couldn't have shifted without smacking into it.

Tamryn turned to me. "Roman used to be on my dad's security team before he came to work for me. I not only compensate him more fairly, but the perks also are better and he's got more freedom." When I tilted my head, she added, "My father's a bit of a control freak. Likes to have his mitts on everything—and control of everyone—my mother's the same, which is why they butt heads and can barely stand to be around one another, much less be involved in any form of business deal together. The one thing my father and I actually agree on is this building of my mother's—it's as obnoxious as she is."

Interesting family dynamic but it was a digression, so I herded it back around to the topic of curiosity. "So how did Roman find out if he no longer works for your father? It must have come from someone else who works for or is close to him."

We exited the elevator. Claudia was still sniffling as she was propelled forward. Tamryn frowned as she squinted off to the right. I followed her glance, my brow raising at what she'd observed.

The parking space the Bugatti had occupied was vacant.

Tamryn mumbled something under her breath before responding. Honestly, I was surprised she'd even heard me, much less digested my question, given the darkness that had settled over her mood.

"'Works' would be a loose term," Tamryn growled, glazing Claudia with a murderous stare as she gave her another hard shove across the parking lot. "Anyway, didn't realize you and Roman had become so chummy. You aren't keeping tabs on me, are you? 'Cause, we both know how that will fare."

"Would one of you care to enlighten me?"

My inquiry was met with a squeal of indignation as Tamryn steered Claudia toward our vehicle.

"What is *that*? Does it even run?" I gritted my teeth at Claudia's pitch. My eardrums would never be the same. "I am not riding in the front seat of that!"

Tamryn smirked. "Good, because you'll be sitting in the backseat." She hacked out a laugh at Claudia's horrified expression. At least the squelching had stopped. "It's either that or the trunk."

I shuddered, causing Tamryn to give me a sympathetic shake of the head. "Sorry, too close to home?" I nodded, the pit in my stomach growing impatient.

Still, I gave her credit. It had shut Claudia up and given her nowhere to go with that one—she'd walked right into it. Besides, I wasn't giving up my passenger seat.

"You were about to tell me what the deal was—"

Out of the corner of my eye, a flash of color exploded, followed by the screeching of tires. Before I could register what was happening, Claudia screamed. Tamryn shoved me from behind, knocking the wind out of me as I connected with the pavement under the weight of her body, blocking my view of our impending doom.

I may have gotten discombobulated for a moment but thankfully hadn't smacked my head. Then again, it could have just been adrenaline mixed with shock as I tried to make sense of the scuffling and muffled squeals, followed by the sharp clanking of metal as multiple doors slammed shut. A vehicle peeled away, filling the air with fumes from the exhaust.

"You okay?" Tamryn panted out as she rolled off my back.

I mumbled that I was and thanked her before slowly working my way to my knees. "Claudia?" I huffed out, still a bit wobbly and disoriented as I squinted around.

Tamryn frowned and swung her head from side to side. "But I may know where they are taking her."

"What? How?"

Tamryn made an attempt at brushing her pants, but the damage was done. Grime from our pavement dive stained the parts that my body hadn't buffered. I didn't even bother checking as I staggered to my feet, grimacing. There would be bruises and probably more than a few scrapes to tend to, but they would have to wait.

"You sure you're okay?" I nodded and waved a hand—painfully—gesturing for her to continue.

We moved toward her vehicle and I grimaced as I eased into the passenger seat. This time, all the junk didn't even faze me. I was beyond caring.

Tamryn blew out a breath, frowning as she examined the smudges on her face in the mirror. "To answer your question—the Bugatti? It belongs to my father."

"Your father…is seeing Claudia?"

She gave me a tight nod. "Unfortunately, it appears to be the case. Honestly, I didn't think the man could stoop any lower. She's my age— my age!" She ground out as the car sputtered to life and she whipped through the parking structure. "Let's hope they didn't put a tracker on this sucker because we don't have time to get it checked."

"Plus the Roman thing." Being one of her security guys, I assumed he was one of the individuals she usually tasked with doing that sort of thing.

"Yes. There's *that*, too," she huffed. "Anyway, now you've got your connection to the cargo yard."

But did I?

"Maybe…. Claudia, whether she was seeing your father or not, seemed to be in the dark about anything pertinent."

"Mmm…true. Then again, that's just the way good old Dad rolls." She gripped the wheel and stomped on the accelerator, jutting us forward as she merged onto the freeway heading west. "It's no wonder I turned out as twisted in the head as I did," she muttered under her breath.

I pretended not to hear and shifted the conversation. "There was one thing that Claudia said that troubled me."

"Just one?" she raised a brow. "I'm impressed."

"Don't be. The girl *is* a bit much to take."

"Tell me about it," she grumbled. "You were saying?"

"She mentioned Misty's sister, Jilli."

"Yeah, I remember that. Thought you said her name was Jillian?"

"According to Misty, only immediate family and close friends call her Jilli."

"And Claudia falls in neither camp. So how did she know about the nickname?"

"Exactly. Either she knew her better than she led on, or she was around someone else who knew her and had mentioned it in passing."

"I'm betting on the latter, but I'm not overly thrilled about either of those options."

"I'm sorry."

Tamryn tilted her head toward me. "Sorry? For what?"

"I know I've been focused on finding Leah. This has taken a turn for you that can't be—"

She waved a hand. "Don't be sorry. I've come to terms with the fact that I made choices that put me in these situations. Can't take 'em back now. But I don't need to let them own me —which is why I'm gonna make sure I help you see this through. No matter what."

"Alrighty, then. Don't suppose you have some stellar backup plan?"

"Meh. Figured we'd just storm the castle, kick some butt and take no prisoners."

"Works for me."

As we sped in the direction of the westerly skies, I realized that while we had a plan of attack, we were also walking into it blind with no reinforcements and no alternatives.

Essentially, in pursuing this path, we'd sealed both our fates.

CHAPTER THIRTY-ONE

The "yard" wasn't what I expected, though I wasn't sure what I had envisioned—some chain-link fences with barbed wires and signs that warned potential trespassers to "Beware of Dog" or to "Smile—You're on Camera." Or maybe even something along the lines of the salvage yard where the forensic accountant had been hiding out, but certainly not an imposing concrete fortress that spanned as far as the eye could see. Merely looking at it made me shudder. It made some of the state penitentiaries look inviting.

I belatedly realized that I had been thinking

out loud. Ever since Leah had left, I had the tendency to do that.

"Actually, my dad won this property on a bet over some college football national championship game a bunch of years ago. The guy who built it based it on some creepy haunted Scottish castle he'd seen where some bad stuff went down in the dark ages or something. He thought it would not only keep the riffraff out, it'd bring him good luck."

"I see that turned out well for him."

"Yeah, my dad wasn't super excited about winning the bet at first—especially not after he found out what the dude did behind those walls. And before you ask, you don't want to know." She was right. I didn't. "Anyway, what was that about a dead accountant hiding out in an old salvage yard?"

I quickly explained what Martin and I had stumbled upon when attempting to meet with the man Shelby and Leah had been in contact with before they disappeared.

"And your pops—err, sorry, Martin…found a journal containing coded details of the operation that the dude had hidden in that dump?"

"Yeah. Martin was able to figure out a few of

the codes but hadn't gotten too far into it the last time we talked."

"And you think that maybe this place ties in somehow," she commented as she pulled into the lot adjacent to the property and parked between a large block wall and a rusted-out van. I guessed it was probably the least conspicuous place she could find, considering there were limited areas to hide the vehicle in a lot that was otherwise vacant.

I nodded slowly, giving that some consideration. Truthfully, I hadn't had time to give the contents of the journal much thought in relation to the formidable structure that dared us to invade its privacy, but she could have been onto something. Everything else up to this point had led us here.

"It certainly seems like it serves as a home base of sorts, maybe a place where all the girls in the area are collected before they are shipped out."

Tamryn squinted in that direction, her frown growing. "My father has done many things, but I had no idca he would do something that low."

I shook my head, cutting her off. "We don't know anything for sure. I was just thinking out loud. I'm sorry—it's a bad habit." I gave her an apologetic look, which she waved off. Her attention was elsewhere. I followed her gaze. "What's that?" I pointed to a small opening in the wall.

"I don't know, but I think it could be our best way in." She tore her eyes away from the structure and wiggled her brows. "Ready to embark on our mission?"

"With no backup? Sure. I'm always up for the impossible. I just wish I'd been having a better hair day."

She shot me a look, not able to contain a snicker. "You're not so bad, AJ."

"You should stick around for my regular routine. I'm hilarious."

"It may come in handy if we get in a pinch." I noted that her tone had turned somewhat serious as her focus returned to the opening.

"Just so you know, if it comes to the point we have to rely on wry humor, we're pretty much done for."

"Haven't you ever heard the saying 'kill 'em with humor'?"

"I have. But typically not with regards to my own demise."

She laughed before turning to face the opponent before us, any hint of humor evaporating as her tone became fierce. "Come on. Let's go before we both lose our nerve."

We'd probably end up losing a lot more than that if the security in the place was as inhospitable as the exterior, but I had come this far and if it got me closer to Leah, I wasn't turning back now.

We jogged as stealthily as two gals can do in a concrete jungle with nowhere to hide. We hadn't exactly come prepared, either, so if we ended up facing opposition, they'd likely dispatch us in seconds and dispose of us just as fast. And no one would be the wiser.

I gritted my teeth. Perhaps Martin and his GPS antics hadn't been such a bad thing, but we were beyond that now. A quick glance at my cell heightened my anxiety when I realized we were in an area that, for some reason, had no reception.

Glancing at the structure before me, it wasn't that big of a stretch to think that some wizard behind that ominous curtain wasn't doing something to block the signal.

We squeezed through the opening, which in hindsight, should have been suspect. A fortress locked down this much would not just let anyone trespass.

Like I said—hindsight.

"You've been here before?" I asked once we were inside the gate. Rows and rows of car trailers—all of them empty—spanned for as far as the eye could see. Lots of metal. Zero humans.

"Once or twice, but it's been a while. That's the main building." She pointed to a massive structure that could have served as an airplane hangar.

"It's big," I murmured.

She nodded. "Previous owner stored all kinds of crap in there."

"And as you said earlier, I don't want to know." She gave me a tight nod as we crept in that direction, despite the fact we were out in the open, with no cover in sight. "Eerily quiet, too."

"Yeah, it's kind of the off-season, as far as places like this go. My father only staffs up when his buddies are here for the car auctions and need a place to store stuff before or after the auctions. At least that's what he *used* to use this place for." Her jaw set as she squinted at our surroundings which, truth be told, didn't look like anything that warranted much in the way of the security that the exterior exuded.

"I guess that makes sense. What are these, spares?" I nodded at the empty trailers.

Tamryn's lip curled. "Those are my father's —see the 'M'? That's his company logo. The cars themselves are at his various homes in their equally sizable garages. He's a bit extreme where his hobbies are concerned."

It was his current hobby that concerned me.

"What's in there?" I nodded at the oversized building.

"It's just one massive open space. I think the previous owner did some sort of betting or gambling or something like that."

My mind went to all sorts of places, and I wondered if her father had taken up the slack when the previous owner vacated. "Enough room to keep a handful of girls."

She nodded, even though I had not posed a question. "Plenty. Come on, let's see if we can find a window or some way of getting inside."

"Um. Maybe we could just try the door first?" I asked, noting the lowest window was over twenty feet off the ground, so even if one of us hiked the other on her shoulders and then vaulted ourselves inside, it would be an Olympic feat.

She glanced at the strangely unobtrusive-looking door—steel with a lever-style handle. No keypad in sight and weirdly, no visible camera overhead. But that didn't mean there weren't eyes on us…lurking somewhere. "Well, yeah. But I doubt—" her eyes widened as the handle on the door easily pressed down. "Huh. What do ya know?"

"This can't be good." I shook my head. "Someone's gotta be in there."

"Well, then they already know we're here." She shrugged, thrusting the door open. "Might as well announce ourselves."

She was right. They'd already seen us a mile away. If they wanted to eliminate us, they could have done so already.

Then again, we were making their job easy for them just walking into it.

We both peered inside. Tamryn glanced at me, her brow arched. I shrugged and we both stepped across the threshold.

What I had envisioned, I wasn't sure. And while it looked like the interior of a hangar, the overhead lighting cast eerie shadows across the space, as the windows we'd spotted from the exterior were masked in an opaque tint that prevented any natural light. The air was thick and musty, with a lingering scent of something mechanical. The space, for all intents and purposes, was otherwise immaculate. And empty.

"Is it usually this—"

"Vacant?" Tamryn finished. "Not that I remembered. There was usually *something* parked in here."

"What do you suppose that is?"

She squinted to where I was pointing—a sizable dark patch on an otherwise pristine concrete floor. "Looks like some sort of fluid."

I bent down and drug my index finger through it and sniffed the brownish-black substance that was slick to the touch.

"Oil. And it's warm."

"Well, this *is* the desert. Everything is warm." Tamryn waved a hand.

"No, as in whatever was here was moved recently," I replied, gaging the spot to be about three feet in diameter, give or take. "And either it was in really bad shape. Or it was big."

"Huh. Seems like they could pull big trucks in here if they needed to." She nodded at the roll-up doors on the far side of the structure. "I remember my dad mentioning having to move the cargo holds around so that they could keep certain cars under cover for as long as possible before shipment. Maybe they moved some in here before they transported them?"

"The cargo holds. Does he store those on the property, too?"

"Yeah, I think they're directly on the other side of those roll-up, so that would be convenient. Then again, it's off-season, and I'm not sure he'd have anything that would warrant the use of that kind of storage." Her voice caught as her eyes widened. "Oh, gawd. You don't think?"

"Well, I doubt they'd be transporting them in tour buses, Tamryn."

The color drained out of her face. I'd only known her a short while, but this was the first time I'd seen her truly shaken. Even though she and her family had strained relations, I'm sure it was hard to fathom that your own father would be capable of something so heinous and cruel.

"I guess I'd hoped they'd at least treat them better than cattle," she murmured.

I shook my head. Wishful thinking perhaps, though I doubt either of us was naïve enough to believe that was the reality we were dealing with. This sort of thing had been all over the news lately.

Humans, like cattle, were a commodity and if the goods got a little bruised, damaged or dead, it was all part of doing business. Any added effort on the seller's end only got subtracted from the bottom line. With the risks these business people were taking, sacrificing a few of the goods along the way was worth the price.

"Since there's nothing here, we should probably move onto the cargo holds. We're already tempting fate in just the short time we've been here."

I was surprised we hadn't tripped some alarm, causing a caravan of thugs dudded up in camo and Kevlar to surround us, then zip-tie and haul us off to who knows where.

At a minimum, I had already half-expected a rabid beast, snarling and slinging drool from its gnashing jaws—and ravished by malnutrition and abuse—to have made a snack of us and left nothing to suggest that we'd ever been present. Better than the vat of lye or barrel of crude oil that always terrorized me in my dreams.

Maybe a tad, anyway.

Tamryn nodded absently, though I doubt her thoughts had taken her to the same place mine had. Same dark realm, perhaps, but likely an alternative level. "Probably should head out the way we came rather than causing a commotion by rolling up the doors."

"Um, yeah. I'm sure someone is already aware that we're here. No sense drawing any more attention to ourselves."

I received a half-grunt in response and after a final glance around the disappointingly empty space, we made a hasty retreat the way we had entered. Dusk had fallen on the Valley of the Sun, casting a haze over the yard that made the fortress look even more foreboding.

I had to chuckle when Tamryn wiped the door handle clean with the cuff of her sleeve.

"You never know," she begrudgingly mumbled as we jogged the length of the front of the building, down the side and rounded the corner to find—nothing.

As in, we had a fabulous view of the backside of the property and its imposing wall, and nothing else.

"What the heck is going on here?"

That's what I'd like to know, too.

Only the question hadn't come from Tamryn, who was staring over my shoulder, wide-eyed and open-mouthed.

I swiveled on my heel to find an aging Ken doll advancing on us at warp speed, his pearly whites clenched as the veins in his forehead, biceps and neck bulged as he glared at her. "And what in the hell are *you* doing here?"

"Dad?"

CHAPTER THIRTY-TWO

Upon closer inspection, I realized the new addition to our little not-so-fun party was indeed none other than Craig Mayer. Truth be told, he looked a lot younger in person. Or perhaps he'd just had a refresher since the last time I'd seen him in the news.

"Good gawd, where are my cargo holds?" He waved an arm, oblivious that he'd nearly whacked me in the face with his flailing tree trunk. "And, who the hell are you?" He sized me up, his tone filled with no less disgust.

"Uh, this is my friend, AJ." I could only stare at Tamryn. She'd called us friends?

"Whatever." I ducked, narrowly escaping another close call with the wave of his limb. "You still haven't told me why you are here. I got an urgent message, saying that all hell had broken loose. I had to leave an important meeting because I couldn't find any of my guys, and I show up to find *this*?"

Tamryn's mood shifted at the mention of the "important meeting", and I shot her a sharp look—now was not the time to confront him about his extracurricular activities with Claudia.

She pursed her lips and returned an equally frosty glare but shifted it to her father. "We were checking something out. The place was obviously already cleaned out when we got here."

"'Checking something out'?" Mayer sneered. "Since when are you interested in anything that doesn't have to do with you and your online groupies?"

"Well, if you want to talk 'groupies'—"

"Tamryn!" I growled. "What she's trying to say, Mr. Mayer, is that we were alerted—by a mutual source—that something might be going down on your property, and rather than interrupt your…meeting, Tamryn thought we could swing by and give the place a gander and go from there.”

“Listen, I have no idea who *you* are, other than my daughter’s claim that you’re her ‘friend’, but if something was going on, typically one doesn’t just ‘swing by and give the place a gander’. You call the freaking police!”

Finished with his admonishment, he shifted his attention toward Tamryn. “A little common sense goes a long way. How many times do I have to tell you that before it sinks in?” Mayer released an exasperated sigh, followed by a dismissive wave, though he wasn’t finished jabbing his barbs. “Sometimes, I can’t believe you’re my child.”

Tamryn advanced on her father, stopping only when she was close enough that he could not only feel her breath on his face, she was in command of his attention.

“Common sense? That’s rich, coming from you.” She hacked out a sharp laugh as she thrust a hand on her hip and stabbed a finger at his chest.

“Don’t think that I—that we haven’t figured out what you’ve been up to. It’s a new low even for you, *Dad*." She released a growl and spun on her heel, casting him a seething, disgusted look over her shoulder. "It's *criminal*."

Mayer rolled his eyes, not fazed by the venom his daughter spewed at him.

"Always so dramatic. Too bad you couldn't put any of it toward a real career instead of all the childish buffoonery you've drummed up over the years—not to mention the messes you've made—that I've cleaned up. *That's* what's criminal." Mayer averted his gaze and began surveying the area where the cargo should have been.

Tamryn wasn't about to be sidestepped so easily. "Just mimicking my environment."

"Says the child of privilege."

I had enough of the family squabble, especially after dealing with Claudia, so I interjected before another snark could be launched.

"Mr. Mayer…who, exactly, called you here?"

"Already asked. And answered."

Yeah, absolutely zero sarcasm there.

I gritted my teeth. If anybody was going to ladle out the smart-aleck and dismissive retorts from this point on, it was going to be yours truly.

"Alright…*Craig*."

Dropping the formality got his attention.

"Actually, all you said was that you 'got a call'. Specifically, *who* called you?" I raised a finger as he opened his mouth and waved my cell phone with the other. "And before you ask me who I am again or retort with some snide comeback, understand that I have some friendly members of law enforcement on speed dial. So unless you want a bunch of uniforms breathing down your neck in, say…three minutes, give or take, I suggest you cut the crap and start leveling with us. We honestly don't have time for this. And by *we*—I mean all of us."

His eyes narrowed and I'm not sure what he saw when he surveyed me, but something spurred a response.

"My…assistant texted me."

Tamryn laughed. "Is that what you're calling her these days? Since when do you visit your 'assistant' at her condo?" She waved a hand. "Then again, I guess you can visit it whenever you want since you paid for it."

Mayer scoffed. "I have no idea what you're

talking about. And even if I did, I hardly think it is any of your business."

"I shouldn't have to tell *you* this, but when you do it in public, it becomes everyone's business. I mean—seriously? Even I have enough common sense to know that."

Mayer's brow creased and he shook his head. "What—"

"I saw your car. At her condo. But that's not the activity I'm talking about. What you do in your relationships—married to my mother or not —is between the two of you. And while disgusting, even for you, it's not criminal. I'm talking about your other ventures. The business-related ones that harm others so that you can line your already overstuffed pockets."

"It's getting dark. I have no time for this. I have cargo missing and need to find out what happened to my team." If he'd meant the prior as a dismissal, it missed its mark as Tamryn grabbed his arm when he started to walk away.

"Not so fast."

I stepped in. While I held Mayer in no esteem, if she aggravated him, we would get nothing. We needed to use this situation as an opportunity.

"Think about it. His *assistant* texted him." Tamryn's mouth formed an "o" and I gave her a single confirming nod. If she was right about Claudia, we'd have him soon enough, hook, line and sinker.

The fact of the matter was that if his assistant had actually texted him as he claimed, it had been *after* Claudia had been grabbed from the parking structure—meaning that either Mayer was making this up or was walking into a trap, along with the two of us.

Mayer glanced back and forth at the two of us. "What's really going on here?"

"She's talking about the girls, Mr. Mayer." He squinted as though confounded by my statement. I was more than happy to elaborate. "Girls, as in the ones picked up from the clubs, then chauffeured to vacation rental properties for what's being billed as innocent after-parties. You may even own some of these properties, or perhaps your companies do. Either way, it should be easy enough to check."

I let that sink in and while Mayer's expression was one of bland disinterest, Tamryn's could have melted a glacier.

"Anyway, we're not really concerned with

that at the moment. We want to know what happens farther down the lane in Candyland—at the point where you're procuring 'goodies' for your buddies overseas. I assume there's some sort of agreement made and that you receive compensation before you deliver these so-called goods to their final destination. Because it is final, for them, isn't it?"

I shot him a withering glance and still, there was little emotion in either his face or stance, which made me grit my teeth. "Everybody is happy at the end of the day—except for the girls."

I couldn't stand to look at him anymore. I shook my head and gazed toward the sky, which had darkened to a menacing shade befitting my mood.

After one last, sobering look, I blew out a long, exasperated breath and looked at Tamryn, whose fury was barely contained as she fisted her hands at her sides and glared at her father's profile. I couldn't say I blamed her and honestly, wasn't sure how she'd kept it together as long as she had.

Before the smokestack had a chance to blow, I pressed on. "How would you feel if that had been your daughter? If you never saw Tamryn again once she'd been hocked like livestock? Then again, the livestock probably meet a better fate—wouldn't you say, Tamryn? I mean, what's the going rate on fresh meat between friends these days?"

Still raking her father with that steely gaze, her jaw set firm—she responded with a single nod, causing her father to flinch, though he would not look at her. It had taken him so long to register a proper reaction I started to wonder just how cold one could be, even toward his own flesh and blood. Then again, in hindsight, all of those cosmetic injections could have been masking his expressions.

"It's time you tell us what's going on with these shipments, Dad. AJ's best friend got caught trying to help these poor girls, and now she's probably on her way to one of your friends."

Mayer barely raised his head.

"What's that? Suddenly nothing to bluster about?" Tamryn looked him up and down, sneering at the man before her.

"I honestly have no idea what you two are talking about."

Tamryn glanced at me, rolling her eyes as she tapped her foot. "As AJ already mentioned, we're talking about the girls you are priming and then plucking for your friends. The ones that never come home. And the ones, if they become troublesome, go missing. Or end up dead."

It was getting dark, but I could see his teeth fluorescing as he gritted them. I wasn't about to let him play innocent. It was time to put the pressure on. And there was no way I was going to let him walk away until we got answers. And he led us to Leah and the girls.

Based on what Tamryn had said and her reaction when she'd found out he was involved, he was well-versed in convincing people of all sorts of things.

"Come on, Mr. Mayer. It was your girlfriend who led us here. There was supposed to have been a shipment going out soon. It seems we were too late to intercept it here, but unless you want your operation to unravel before your eyes, you'd better tell us where it's headed so that we can hopefully catch up before it's too late."

"I really don't know what—" Mayer ran his hands through his hair, shaking his head as he started to pace. "I don't know what's going on. This…shouldn't be happening."

"You've gotta pick a side here. You either know what's going on, or you don't."

He stopped. "I don't know anything about these girls. The transactions, as you called them. I could never…" He shook his head. To his credit, Mayer looked…sick.

"But you are aware of shipments being made?" I prompted, waving a hand at the empty yard behind us.

"I've been allowing some…friends to store and facilitate shipments from here, but nothing like that was ever discussed."

"What *was* discussed?" I prodded.

"Cars. Boats. An occasional piece of artwork. But nothing…living."

Not human. Not girls. Living. I surveyed him. Could he really not attach a real name to what he had facilitated? Or was there some truth to his claims?

Tamryn must have seen something in my expression. "What is it, AJ?"

"Not sure. You'll have to tell me if I'm reading this right, but I actually believe him."

She raised a brow and gave me a look that

suggested I'd lost my marbles—and maybe I had —but then she looked at her father, who met her gaze and her frown deepened.

"I hate to admit it—for Leah's sake and for the sake of those girls—but I think you might just be right." She turned back to me. "But only because he lacks the stomach for it—not because he's such a pillar of humanity or anything like that. He certainly has friends who wouldn't think twice about selling anything to make a buck or to secure friends who could be useful down the road. Sounds familiar, doesn't it, Dad?"

When he didn't respond quickly enough, she tossed in a zinger. "You must have done something naughty to get your girlfriend wrangled into this. Time's ticking for her, too…so whatever you know, I suggest you spill it."

Mayer worked his jaw. "You mind if I make a phone call?"

We both shook our heads and when he started to move away, Tamryn grabbed his arm. "Right here will be far enough."

Mayer pursed his lips but complied and pulled his cell phone from his belt holder.

He stabbed at a contact and thrust the phone to his ear, immediately frowning.

"My assistant's cell went to voicemail. She always picks up when I call."

Tamryn withheld commentary. "What about your security guys? This place was a dead zone when we arrived."

"Like I said, that isn't that big of a stretch. We're off-season, meaning there normally wouldn't be anyone here."

"Okay… So who else has access?"

He glanced at me and sighed. "Unfortunately, a lot of people. Are you suggesting that…that some of them could be in danger?" Mayer's mouth twisted as he cut himself off and shifted gears when he started to utter a name, but not before Tamryn caught it.

"We're trying to figuring out what's going on, and you choose *now* to worry about your girlfriend?" she snapped. "Yes, she's in danger. Along with a whole bunch of other people. And if don't you want her to end up dead like that girl at the club in Old Town, then I suggest you start drumming up names, making calls or whatever you typically do *now*!"

"I will. But first, I need you to understand something."

"Dude! Seriously, I'm not twelve anymore. What is there to understand?"

"Your mother and I have an agreement."

"I don't give a crap about your stupid agreement! Okay?" This time, she threw her hands up. "For the record, I could care less who you see. Right now, we need to figure out *where* these girls are headed."

To his credit, Mayer nodded and punched another number on his phone. After a brief conversation with an unknown party, he shook his head and moved to the next. Terse words were exchanged, but little was actually said. Finally, he tucked his phone away and turned his attention toward us.

"I don't know what is going on, but someone authorized the removal of all the containers. Today."

"By 'someone', I assume you could not figure out who it was?" Tamryn asked, her brows raised.

He shook his head. "I've been playing telephone with a tin can, it seems. Everyone claims that someone else told them that a shipment was to be expedited to the coast. Yet, no one had the brains to actually confirm it with me," Mayer growled. "So, to answer your question, no, I was not able to figure out who it was. But when I do, they are going to wish they were as far away as that shipment is right now."

"And there's no way to stop it?" I asked.

"I'll need to head back to my office to deal with it directly. Another odd thing is that our typical carrier wasn't used and the destination we typically ship to out west has nothing on the docket coming in for us today or anytime soon."

"Seems someone has gone out of their way to sidestep you," I murmured.

"Yes, it appears to be the case."

"Well, let's get you to your office so that we can get this figured out." Tamryn gestured impatiently toward the gate. "Unless you want to linger here a bit longer and moan about your missing containers."

Mayer gave her a sharp look. "For once, I couldn't agree with you more. Let's go."

"We'll follow you there," I added, making it clear that he wasn't about to get rid of us so quickly.

"Wouldn't have it any other way," he replied through gritted teeth as he strode across the empty lot, stirring dust in his wake.

Mayer barely waited for us to exit before he punched a code into the keypad and the gate slid shut with an efficient clang.

Interestingly enough, the open space where we'd slipped in had been secured, though Mayer made no mention of it or bothered glancing in that direction, which made me wonder if he'd been the one to secure it. Or had it been done by the person who'd left it ajar, baiting us to enter and to ultimately be caught by Mayer?

He pulled keys from his pocket and disengaged the alarm for the sole vehicle on the street next to the compound. Surprisingly, it was a sizeable but unremarkable-looking work truck, which seemed more suitable for utility than comfort.

I glanced curiously at Mayer. I'd known that he'd built his fortune from the ground up and had started as a mechanic, working alongside his father in their small Midwest garage, until his father had gotten cancer and passed before he was the age Mayer was now.

Mayer had lost the garage to a large conglomerate, eager to buy property that stood in their way of a large shopping mall, and his father had been one of the last few hold-outs. Shady dealings with several of the city council members and government officials had made it difficult for Mayer to pay off his loan.

It was later discovered that essential paperwork had gotten lost along the way, thanks to those that were getting their palms greased to ensure the shopping mall came to fruition and that he'd actually done everything by the book.

By then, it was too late and the damage had been done. The garage had been leveled. Mayer had not only lost his father but his father's garage, as well as his family's home.

Broke, disenchanted and without family or home, he ventured west, landing in the southwest, vowing to never again let others control anything he'd worked for or to be at the behest of others where financial stability was concerned.

It was a common story and yet his path—which included a marriage of convenience to a wealthy socialite and a string of random business ventures—were often at odds of those of the simple, principled young man who'd come from humble beginnings.

Then again, maybe he just had a stellar public relations firm who'd curated a past that would make him more likable in the eyes of the people he needed to appease. If so, they were worth every penny he'd paid them.

Either way, all of it gave me pause when trying to figure Mayer out. Not that I knew the man personally, but from the limited amount I'd witnessed, his ego and attitude of indifference alone suggested that he wouldn't be above crossing into gray or even black areas if it was to his advantage, or ensuring he could control others in positions of power when it was warranted. Maybe he was also well-versed in the art of manipulation and was telling us precisely what we wanted to hear.

Tamryn should have been a pretty good judge, but even she seemed torn between what she hoped was true and the reality she knew from being his daughter.

I glanced in her direction and saw her frowning as she stared at the truck.

"I thought you were in the middle of a meeting when you got the call?"

Mayer halted mid-stride and studied his daughter. "I was."

"When did you have time to swap vehicles?"

He frowned. "Not sure what you mean."

"Your car, Dad. As I mentioned, we saw it in the Penthouse parking spot at your girlfriend's condo." Tamryn's tone was fierce, almost daring him to deny it.

He tilted his head. "That's not possible. My car's been in the shop all week. I've been driving the truck in the interim."

"If you haven't been driving your car, Mr. Mayer, who has? And why were they at your girlfriend's today?"

I glanced at Tamryn, the realization dawning that she'd been wrong about Claudia's guest.

Was someone playing us? Puppeting Claudia to make Mayer look guilty while drawing Tamryn into believing it was true?

"Who dropped your car off?" I asked.

"I did," he replied slowly, "but now that you ask, it doesn't mean much. I've had my guys drop it off and pick it up in the past, so…"

"So, one of them could have easily stopped by, picked it up, and you wouldn't have known."

He looked at me for a long moment. "I can't say I'm thrilled at the prospect, but you are right." He turned to Tamryn. "You shouldn't be too happy about it either. Roman's usually my guy."

Another mention of Roman. "You sure you can trust this guy, Tamryn?" I asked.

She frowned and mumbled, "I may need to rethink our working arrangement."

"Where is he now?"

"Let's find out, shall we?" Tamryn pulled out her cell and punched the screen, frowning a few seconds later. "Straight to voicemail. Definitely rethinking it." She turned to her father. "Let's get to your office, figure this out. The sooner, the better."

Mayer nodded, then scanned the area. "You…need a ride?"

"Nah, we're across the way. We'll follow. Need to get the loaner back soon anyway."

Mayer grunted something in the affirmative and waved a hand as we split off.

"You sure he'll wait for us?"

"He knows better than to cross me. Besides, in that monster truck, he shouldn't be hard to keep track of at this time of day."

We'd just reached Tamryn's loaner when a bout of expletives erupted from across the street.

"Dad?"

"Flat tire, if you can believe that," Mayer called out.

I looked at Tamryn and shook my head. I could believe it and I also didn't think it was a coincidence.

Someone had lured him here for the sole purpose of stranding him or making sure he was out of the way. They were either unaware we were here to bail him out or just didn't care. Then again, a skeptical person might also point out that Mayer himself could have done the deed to ensure he had eyes on us.

Though I typically would have agreed with the skeptic, there were easier ways to go about it than puncturing your own tire. Besides, Mayer was too clever for that.

"We've got room. You can schedule a service for that later," Tamryn yelled back.

Mayer jogged over as I cleared a space in the backseat for myself. If he was surprised by his daughter's choice of transportation, he said nothing as he squeezed into the passenger seat.

"I don't want to alarm you, but I think my tire was intentionally flattened."

"Alarm doesn't begin to cover the day we've had," I murmured, realizing that I'd said it a bit louder than intended when he swiveled in his seat and frowned from me to Tamryn and back. I sighed. "Sorry, we'd be more surprised if something hadn't happened. Not that I…we are happy it happened to you, of course."

I hadn't needed to add that, but given the shock that spanned his fact—which was saying a lot given all the injections he'd probably had—I didn't want to seem insensitive or cause him further distress.

In hindsight, perhaps I'd forgotten who I was dealing with.

"Of course not," he scoffed, then promptly turned back around and resorted to his demanding, condescending persona. "We've got a few minutes to spare. Why don't you two fill me in? Omit nothing." All I could do was shrug when Tamryn quirked a brow at me in the rear-view mirror.

He had a right to know what had happened. Besides, there was more of a threat just sitting in this deathtrap than there was from the man riding shotgun to his daughter. If all else failed, there was probably an ejector seat trigger in this contraption, probably hidden under a crushed can or disguised as an empty bag of pork rinds.

If I could only find it.

In the meantime, Tamryn and I took turns

elaborating on the events that had transpired throughout the day, as well as a few of the ones leading up to it.

"You mentioned a girl being found at a club in Old Town. What was her name?"

"Jillian. Jillian Rochester. I've been in contact with her sister, Misty, who was at the club the night her sister went missing," I replied.

"There are far too many coincidences. Certainly more than I can ignore."

Tamryn slid a look at her father. "What do you mean? Did you know her?"

Mayer nodded. "I hired her recently to do some work for me." He huffed when Tamryn rolled her eyes. "Work. Period. She didn't show up, and when my assistant called her, she never responded. We figured she was just a flake."

"How long had she worked for you?" I asked.

"Not long. A month. Two at most. It wasn't a forty-hour a week type job, just piece work, here and there," he replied.

"How did you find her?"

This time, when Mayer turned to look at me, his expression had darkened.

"Funny you should ask." He tilted his head

toward his daughter. "She came highly recommended."

"Well, we're not mind-readers, don't keep us hanging," Tamryn snapped. "Recommended by who?"

"Your boy toy, Roman," he growled in return. "Somehow, it always trickles back to Roman."

"Not *my* boy or my toy, Father," she spat. "He was just another one of the minions you tossed into the reject pile for whatever reason and I scooped up."

"Yes, so I guess we have you to thank for all of this?" Mayer waved a hand around.

"Enough!" Both stopped mid-insult as my wits snapped. "We don't have time for this! Yes, Roman seems to be at the center of this. Whatever *this* is. Yes, he is currently off the grid and yes, it sucks. But we have girls to find, regardless. Mr. Mayer, you have resources. Tamryn, you have connections, too. And I have a few of my own. Let's say we call a truce for the time being, put our differences—and our egos—aside and get to work."

I didn't ask for confirmation but got a tight-lipped head nod from Mayer and a foot to the pedal from Tamryn. Both were about as good as I could have hoped for under the circumstances.

If they wanted to continue their mud-slinging at the end of this, I wasn't going to stand in the way.

While both fumed in the front, I typed a quick text to Martin—a phone call would have been too awkward and strained in this environment—and explained things as best as I could in a few short sentences. I did the same with Ramirez, just for good measure. I didn't mention my current whereabouts or the destination but alerted both about the potential shipment heading west and let them know that I'd update them when I could.

It was Mayer who broke the silence.

"Something just occurred to me. I received another odd call today. It was from the management company overseeing a rental property I co-own that we rent out to CEOs and high-end business types. Typically, just for a week or two, depending on how long their business here lasts, whether they decide to take in the sights, catch up on their golf games and whatnot.

"Anyway, it's been slow the past couple of months, due to the weather, but there's a guy coming in from Tokyo next week—he's brokering a long-term deal for his boss with one of the IT firms here. When the management company dispatched the regular cleaning service to freshen up the place, they were surprised when another crew was already at the property and had just finished cleaning, so they left.

"As part of their protocol, the company called me to confirm that I had made alternative arrangements, to which I said no." He released an exasperated huff. "I seriously do not have time to manage that sort of thing—that's why I pay them. I told them as much. Of course, after a bit of investigation, they called to apologize and waved it off as an internal oversight on their part. But now—between the story you just told me and the flat tire—I'm not so sure it was an oversight after all."

"Where is this property?" I asked.

"Not far from Old Town but not close enough to be considered in Old Town, either. But if someone wanted to host a party there—"

"Or stash a few girls," Tamryn added, glancing at me.

"No one would be the wiser," I completed.

"I think we need to go there first, just to check, don't you think?" Tamryn glanced at me and then at her father.

We both nodded and Mayer rattled off the address to an upscale neighborhood northwest of Old Town.

"Do you think we should call the police?" he asked once Tamryn shifted directions. "Or notify someone, at the very least? Maybe even have them meet us there?"

"And tell them what, exactly?" Tamryn replied.

"Good point," Mayer drawled before clucking his tongue. "Would be a tough one to explain, especially if there was nothing to find."

If I'd known him better, I might have almost thought he sounded as though he'd be disappointed if that turned out to be the case.

Was he actually looking forward to the

prospect of catching something going on? Or *someone*?

"Park a bit away," Mayer commanded as we drew closer to our destination. "No sense announcing ourselves."

Tamryn rolled her eyes but said nothing as she shimmied the car to the curb half a block away. Unfortunately, the car would stick out like a sore thumb in a neighborhood like this and Mayer's comment about calling the police would probably end up being a moot point. I just hoped he could prove that he owned the property. Otherwise, we'd been in some deep dog crap.

From this vantage point, it appeared as though the property—a sprawling steel gray and white rancher that had recently been given a face-lift—was vacant. All was dark, aside from the decorative orbs that lined the pathway and the carriage light that graced the entrance leading to a bright red door with a festive chili wreath.

Tamryn turned to her father. "You never said who the co-owner of the property was."

"I'd rather not say."

Mayer scooted out of the vehicle, but

Tamryn growled after him. "Geez, Dad, why? Who are you protecting now?"

He squinted at her over his shoulder. "Protecting? No one. I just want to be sure I'm as far away from it as possible before everything goes south."

Tamryn muttered a few curses under her breath.

"What's that?" He frowned.

"Nothing," came the exasperated retort as Tamryn threw the car door open.

Frankly, his response hadn't surprised me in the least. Perhaps Tamryn had glommed on to a case of wishful thinking when he'd agreed to help. "Help" being a stretch where Craig Mayer was concerned. I was betting whatever hope she'd held out had just withered and died.

Still, there was strength in numbers. That was me hoping he'd at least *look* like he was taking a side—hopefully ours—if the situation warranted it.

The three of us were silent as we crept toward the house. Mayer nodded around the side of the house as we crossed onto the property, stopping at a small gate, where he punched in a code granting us entry to a long pathway that ran the length of the house. About halfway down, he stopped at another door with a keypad and repeated the process. Upon pushing the door open, we were hit by the overwhelming scent of bleach and lemons. Mayer blanched, scrunching his nose but still said nothing as he entered, his stance rigid as he fisted his free hand at his side and flipped on the light switch to the laundry room.

Nothing appeared out of place, though there was an abundance of cleaning products on the open shelves above the washer and dryer, which strangely did not include bleach.

Mayer moved quickly, opening the door that gave us entry to the main part of the house, throwing on the lights as he'd done before. Again, the scent was strong.

"My usual crew knows I hate any lingering scents of cleaning supplies," he growled.

Tamryn shrugged and closed the distance on her father as though to hurry him along. We peered around the open space—a large kitchen that could have made any number of caterers, chefs and home cooks swoon—with every appliance one could ever dream of. And spotless, with not a knife, cup, or spoon out of place.

Every room that followed was equally drool-worthy. And beyond immaculate. It was much like a model home used to reel one in, without the hominess. In fact, aside from the luxury appliances and furnishings, the home had absolutely no personality. It was almost too sterile, too antiseptic. I was pretty sure I'd been in emergency rooms with more personality. Then again, perhaps the copious amount of bleach had also wiped out my senses.

"Seems pretty empty to me," Tamryn murmured.

"Too empty," I replied.

"What do you mean?" Mayer craned his head in my direction and frowned.

I lifted my hands. "No offense. I was just hoping for a clue, some remnant that would help me find my friend. And those girls."

He gave me a long, hard look. "Yeah, well, the bleach should have been a dead giveaway that wasn't going to be the case."

"Can we please refrain from using the word 'dead' here?" Tamryn snapped. "We've had enough drama for one day without you throwing that notion into the works."

"Come on, Tamryn. It's not like you weren't hoping to find something."

"Something *alive*. Geez! Apparently, sensitivity isn't something that improves with age."

"*Apparently*, neither does respect for one's elders," Mayer sniped, squinting as he surveyed our surroundings.

After a moment of relished silence, Tamryn touched my arm. "You're awfully quiet, AJ."

I nodded and moved back toward the kitchen. It was hard not to be drawn there, even though food was the furthest thing from my mind.

"Perhaps I got my hopes up. There are never any shortcuts when it comes to things like this, I suppose." Something on the door of the fridge caught my eye.

"You make a habit of doing crap like this, do you?" Mayer retorted. "What did you say you did for a living?"

"She didn't. Probably because you never gave her the opportunity," Tamryn snorted and though she might have been goading him into another row, I had zeroed in on a note attached to the front of the fridge with a smiley face magnet. "Have an Absolutely Fantabulous Day!" it read.

To the casual observer, it was an exuberant and perhaps creatively phrased message, but I recognized that loopy handwriting style. Shaking, I grabbed it off the fridge, causing the magnet to slip and tumble to the ground.

It was a saying that Leah and I had made up over a massive pitcher of margaritas, which had been an attempt to cheer her up when she'd broken up with her last beau. We'd thought we were geniuses at the time, and though there were some cringe-worthy moments before we stumbled to the cab that took us home, both of us chuckled from that day on whenever the other belted the phrase out.

At the very least, it was sure to cheer the other person up when they were having a crappy day. I wish I could say that was the case now, though it did give me a small jolt of hope.

"What is it?" I hadn't heard Tamryn approach and my hand shook as she took the sheet. "Kind of silly, isn't it?"

"That's Leah for you." Turns out, my voice was just as shaky as my hand.

Tamryn's mouth opened in realization. "Wait —what? You mean?"

I nodded and sucked in a breath before responding. "She was here."

"Are you sure?" She held the paper up, studying it as though it was one of the Dead Sea Scrolls.

"What's going on?" Mayer leaned in, his breath hot and faintly tinted with spearmint.

Tamryn started to hand the note to her father when I snatched it, surprising them both. "Look at this!"

On the back were two sets of alphanumeric digits.

Both were in Leah's handwriting. And at least one number I recognized.

It was the license plate of the Bugatti we'd seen at Claudia's. The other had the correct number of digits for a plate, but it wasn't familiar.

Mayer's face, on the other hand, twisted as he looked between the two.

"You know this one, don't you?" I stabbed at the second number.

"Come on, Dad! We need to know so that we

can find it," Tamryn prodded. "What if it could lead us to the girls?"

I nodded. "Please. Before it's too late. We need to find that vehicle."

As Mayer pulled out his phone, a booming voice echoed behind us.

"If you want to find those girls alive, you won't make that call."

CHAPTER THIRTY-FOUR

A familiar figure emerged from the depths of the house. Where he'd been lurking was hard to say, though I doubt our party-crasher has been trying to disguise himself as a potted plant. Plus, the black combat-inspired ensemble did little to hide his hulking frame, as the light ricocheted off the gleam of his dome.

"Roman," Mayer seethed. "About time you showed up."

Tamryn and I frowned at each other, then watched the volley between the men. Roman kept his distance and his stance rigid. The bulge under his jacket suggested that he had no bones about changing that detail if the situation warranted it.

"What are you doing here?" The blackness of his eyes made it difficult to determine who he was directing the question toward, but it was Tamryn who responded.

"I should be asking you the same," she spat. "I've been trying to reach you all day and now you show up? Convenient, don't you think, AJ?"

"Indeed. Quite a coincidence, too."

Roman's head tilted at me, then at Tamryn, before training his gaze on Mayer. "Where is she?"

Mayer frowned. "I have no idea what you are talking about."

"I didn't ask you 'what.' I asked you 'who.'" Roman's tone was deep and even, yet there was an edge to it that made me shudder.

"I don't know *who* you are talking about." Mayer shrugged.

"What's going on here?" Tamryn demanded.

"Ask your father," Roman responded, his steely gaze never leaving Mayer as they embarked on a testosterone-infused stare-down.

"I told you. I. Don't. Know," Mayer replied

through gritted teeth. "By the way, I never figured you for a sellout, *Roman*, but first you dodge out on me, then my daughter. What's the going rate for a pound of flesh these days, anyway?"

"Love to hear *your* answer to that, *Mayer*." Roman's tone was as steely as all of his hard lines and angles. "All the dirty little threads lead back to you, one way or the other." He squinted as he studied the man. "Guess you figured you'd lined enough pockets along the way, but there were always traces of lint leading back to you. You should have been more careful."

"Perhaps I just should have hired better security." Mayer scoffed, tilting his chin up. "Looks like *you* were the greedy one in the end. "

Roman clucked his tongue, crossing his arms. "I'm not the one who pulled Jilli into your schemes, then got her killed."

"Jilli?" Mayer shook his head, his brow furrowing.

"He's referring to the girl you hired. Jillian Rochester."

I turned to Roman, hoping that I was correct in my assessment of Mayer. "He had nothing to do with her death." Roman's eyes shifted and for a moment, their scrutiny made me regret opening my mouth.

But then I reminded myself what was at stake and cleared my throat.

"It does make me curious, though. Only family and close friends knew about Jillian's nickname." I cocked my head, letting that fac-toid settle in as all eyes were now on Roman. "So, who told you?"

Roman's lips were pressed firmly together as the rest of us waited, his frosty gaze focused on Mayer.

Had I been wrong to back him up?

Finally, I could stand it no more. Time was wasting.

"Do I need to repeat the question?" I crossed my arms, mustered every last nerve and gave Roman my best stink-eye as I tapped my foot.

"She's just as rude as her snoop of a friend," came a disembodied voice as a screen I hadn't noticed illuminated on the wall, and the image of a *Real Housewives* wannabe wearing a shock-ingly tight patent leather cat suit came into view. Strobing lights pulsed to an amplified techno beat in the background. Her ebony tresses were wild as she flung them over her shoulder, exposing more than a hint of her ample cleavage.

"Either way, no need to answer that—especially now that we've finally gotten all the remaining…nuisances right where we want them. Isn't that right, darling?" Scarlet lips puckered, blowing an animated kiss with a gloved hand.

If the dramatics hadn't been so over-the-top, I might have been impressed with the woman's attempt at playing the femme fatale but as it was, I was embarrassed for her. Gaging from the mortified expressions in the room, I was not alone.

"Mother!" Tamryn's voice hissed. "What are you *wearing*? And, why are you…here?"

Perhaps an addendum to Tamryn's latter question was *how* was she here, much less know we were?

"This old thing?" she preened. "Just something I like to slip into when I'm feeling particularly feisty. Isn't that right, boys?" She giggled. Um…yuck. "As for *why* I'm here…someone's been very naughty. Several someones, actually. Which means I've gotta clean up the mess."

Tamryn certainly hadn't won any lottery where her parents were concerned, though it explained some things. That turned out to be an understatement when her mother surprised us by whipping out a freakishly large dagger.

"Just what do you plan on doing with that toy, Delia?" Mayer crossed his arms, his mouth forming an amused smirk.

"Keep it up, *Craig*, and you might just find out," she crooned. "And I assure you, this baby is quite real."

Mayer rolled his eyes. "Right. Well, if you're not going to use it, put it down, or you'll chip a nail."

"If you insist."

My heart thudded against my chest as the screen went dark. When it returned, the backdrop had transitioned from a dance club strobe vibe into a classic movie theater, complete with a silent black and white movie depicting a screaming damsel in distress tied to the railroad tracks, awaiting the arrival of her white-hatted savior atop his faithful stallion.

"Oooh, don't you just love the anticipation? I wonder who would be willing to save this poor girl from imminent death?" Delia's voice crooned as the camera angle shifted and was now trained on a small figure slumped into a theater-style seat, with wrists so tightly bound to the armrests the tender flesh had been rubbed raw.

Even before she grabbed the matted mop by the crown and yanked it back, I would have known that head anywhere.

"No! Why?" I fisted my hands and stormed toward the screen as Delia pushed the bloodied and battered face forward, exposing blackened eyes, blood-crusted lips and the pale, lifeless expression of my unconscious best friend.

"She's been a bad girl—snooped around like her little pet Shelby and caused me a world of trouble—*that's* what she's done." Delia leaned into the frame and sneered. "Question is —what are you willing to give me to spare her life?"

"You obviously already have something in mind. What is it?" I snapped, unable to tear my eyes from Leah.

Her tone turned serious. "Only Craigy-boy can answer that. And believe me, he won't give it up easily."

I was surprised to find Mayer at my side. I hadn't heard him move.

"What have you done, Delia?" The tan had drained from his face and his voice shook with each word. "What could I possibly have that you would want?"

"Everything, Craig. I want everything." She tapped her chin with her free hand. "But I'll take you for now. We'll work out the rest later."

"If I agree, will you release the girl? And tell us where the others are?"

"By 'others', you mean your twit of a girl-friend?" Mayer shrugged. Delia laughed, her tone haughty. "At least you aren't stupid enough to deny it. She was working for me, by the way."

"Seems like *a lot* of people I thought were loyal to me were actually working for you," he murmured.

"Better pay. Better benefits. How many times did I tell you that you can't be so cheap when it comes to people, especially if you want to inspire loyalty?"

"What would *you* know about loyalty?" Mayer scoffed, folding his arms.

"More than you, apparently," she sniffed. "Do we have a deal?"

"I don't find the arrangement equitable," he replied. "Besides, you haven't inspired any loyalty in me for a long time."

"Have it your way, Craig. Their blood is on you. All of it."

She backed up so that both she and Leah were in the frame. Leah's head lolled to the side. "Let's start with an easy one first, shall we? I'll assume you didn't sleep with her. She's got too much of a mind and a smart mouth for a sap like you."

I screamed as she positioned herself behind Leah and tilted her chin back with her gloved hand, exposing a pale neck beneath the mix of blood and grime.

"No! Do something!" Mayer's mouth opened in surprise as I pummeled my fists into his chest. He grabbed me by the wrists and hugged me awkwardly to protect himself from my assault as I struggled against him, tears stinging my cheeks.

"'*Do something!*'" Delia mimicked, laughing. "Honey, hate to have to tell you this, but my *husband* isn't a man of action. He pays people to do it for him. By the way, time's up, Craig."

"No! No! No!" I yelled, thrashing against

him, but was no match for his strength as he pulled me in tighter.

"Please, don't look," his voice was quiet and alarmingly earnest as he pleaded with me. "Just don't look."

Even as I screamed some choice words into his chest and probably even threatened his manhood in my tirade, Mayer stood his ground. It wasn't until I heard him gasp that he released me ever so slightly, but not so much so that I could move or see what had caught his attention.

"Wha—" I started when Tamryn interjected.

"M…Mother, *please*, you don't have to do this!" Her voice was shaking and sounded strangely distant.

Mayer loosened his grip a bit more, allowing me to lean back. His eyes were wide as he stared at the screen.

"Tamryn…no!"

He wasn't permitting me enough wiggle room to turn and see what he was looking at, so I craned my neck the best I could toward the place Tamryn had been standing. Consumed by my own frenzy, I hadn't noticed her reaction to her mother's declaration, much less that she was nowhere to be seen. My anxiety amplified when I realized that neither was Roman.

Finally, Mayer was so overwrought in his pleas that I was able to break free. I swiveled toward the screen, releasing my own gasp of horror as I took in the scene that was unfolding.

One that was utterly and impossibly out of my control.

Tamryn advanced on her mother, hands open in surrender, as Delia continued her knife play at my unconscious best friend's throat.

"Come on, Mother. I think I'm a fair trade. You know, keeping it in the family."

"Family?" Delia rolled her eyes. "It might have been an alternative worth considering if it were true. No, your father is the only one I'm willing to offer this deal to—it was created solely for him—a once in a life opportunity. His life for hers.

"Thankfully, just as your father has never been particularly discerning in his selection of female companions, he's also consistently predictable. So while he'd not give one iota's worth of thought to *this* one's livelihood, the next one will show us his true colors. I suspect he'll run a solid yellow." She snorted as she glanced at the screen, before feigning a pout. "It's sad, really. She made an excellent little spy, while it lasted. But just between…well, all of us, it's beyond me how he's been able to tolerate all that sniveling and whining for as long as he has."

"Yet *you* relied on her." Tamryn gritted her teeth.

"'Relied' is a bit of a stretch. She was a convenience I afforded to get the information I wanted when I wanted it. And it turned out she was quite motivated when she put her mind to it. Of course, it helped that she always thought she was in some sort of competition with you. She was all over my offer, practically drooling before I could get the words out. Pathetic, really." She chuckled. "No offense to you, my dear."

"None taken. What did you promise her?"

"I don't make promises—certainly not to individuals like that—I simply showed her the possibility of a future opportunity. In her case, opportunity equated to advancement." When Tamryn raised a brow, Delia added, "What? You seriously don't think she got as high in our little operation on her own merit, do you?"

"Probably not." Tamryn shrugged nonchalantly, though her voice shook. "By 'our', who do you mean?"

Delia smirked, then winked at her daughter. "Nice try, but I'm not biting. You haven't earned that response."

"Fine, so back to Dad. To be honest, I thought *he* was the one spearheading this little business venture."

I glanced at Mayer, who frowned at his daughter's admission, which only deepened as his wife hacked out a laughed.

"If we're being totally honest, your father doesn't have the constitution for ventures of this magnitude." She glanced at the screen, her tone thick with sarcasm as she added, "Sorry, Craigy, just speaking my truth." Delia gave us her best duck-lip pout before turning back to Tamryn.

"As for your other question—well, once we've dispatched this one," she tapped Leah under the chin with the flat side of the blade, "I think he'll be more amenable to a trade once he comes to terms with what—and who—is at stake."

Tamryn's eyes flitted from her mother to Leah and back. "And if he's not?"

"Let's just assume that he'll be highly motivated, one way or the other."

"Meaning?"

"Oh, you'll find out soon enough." Delia glanced at her watch—perhaps waiting on something? Or someone?

As she did, Tamryn glanced at the screen and gave us a tiny nod, shifting her eyes from one side to the next without moving her head. I knew she was doing her best to buy us time, but it was running out. We had to do something to help her.

I slid off to the side of the screen, tapping Mayer on the arm as I did. Tamryn caught my move and engaged her mother again. Before Delia could get Mayer any more worked up about whoever she was going on about, I needed his full attention. And his assistance.

Thankfully, he caught on and as Tamryn continued to engage her mother, I ushered him beyond the camera's view and out of the kitchen.

It wasn't until we were outside that I spoke. "Listen, Mr. Mayer. You don't know me any more than I know you, but we are going to need to work together here." His face was grim, but he nodded and gestured for me to continue.

"It hasn't been more than a couple of minutes since Tamryn snuck out and ended up with her mother—so she couldn't have gotten far, especially considering the car is still here." I pointed toward the loaner down the street. "Tamryn has obviously been there before or recognized it for some reason. Was there anything about the location that seemed familiar…something that rang a bell?"

Mayer blew out a breath as he scruffed his hair. "You mean aside from the media room that was modeled after a classic movie theater, which clashed with Delia's embarrassing get-up?" I nodded. "No, I can't say that anything about it resonated. I was so focused on Delia and that grating voice of hers—listening to that woman for any amount of time is like torture—she always manages to take years off my life."

I wasn't interested in contributing to his wife-bashing and instead quickly surveyed the surrounding houses. There were none on the other side of the street and the two to the right were double-gated. So unless Tamryn had skills she hadn't utilized at her father's storage yard, I doubted either was the house we were looking for. Mayer came to the same conclusion and pointed at a residence three houses down on the left. It was unremarkable from the outside as the neighborhood went, but it did make for a location that could easily pass one's notice.

"That's the only one within a short walking distance that doesn't have a gate around it." He reached for his phone. "I'll see if some of my guys are available—"

I gripped his arm and shook my head. "We can't trust them. Not after Roman showed up, only to disappear again. I think we need to call the police." I bit my lip, struggling to properly phrase what I was about to say.

Mayer was a quick study. "Okay, it sounds like there's a 'but' coming."

"But I don't think there's time to wait—we need to go in."

"Ah, 'we' again."

I placed a hand on his arm. "Listen. I can't do this without you. Tamryn can only distract your wife for so long. Delia's going to have a conniption when she notices we're gone—so the sooner we locate them, the sooner we can resolve this."

He tilted his head. "You think I should make the trade."

"I think you need to give Delia the illusion that you are willing to do so to buy us some time until help arrives and can take over."

"What about Roman?"

"We can't worry about him. He obviously has his own agenda." I just hoped that whatever it was, wasn't going down now. Tamryn already had enough on her plate.

Mayer nodded and as he dialed 9-1-1, I texted our location to both Ramirez and Martin. We hustled toward the house while trying to remain inconspicuous, though to onlookers we probably seemed quite the mismatched pair. It almost made me snicker. Focusing on the mission was the only thing that kept that sinking feeling in my core from rising, allowing the fear and dread of what could have transpired in our absence. That, and the likelihood that Delia owned this property and was paranoid enough to have cameras installed here, too.

Once again, we had to rely on Tamryn and hope that whatever form of distraction she was employing would be enough.

We reached the house and found a side-entry,

which was suspiciously unlocked. I glanced at Mayer and found him sweating heavily as he eased the door open and we crept inside.

Every light in the house appeared to be on, illuminating an interior in sharp contrast to its outer facade. Every surface was immaculate, every appliance and furnishing top-of-the-line, every accent or piece of artwork museum-worthy. And yet, for all of its lavishness, it lacked human touches. It was too pristine, too sterile. Much like the house we had just left.

And too quiet.

Still, we forged on, searching for the room that mirrored an old theater. Finally, when we reached the master, Mayer moved to the walk-in closet and squinted at the walls. Though empty, it could have fit the contents of my closet, as well as Leah's, ten times over.

I started to say something but he put a finger to his lips, then lifted it to his ear.

The sounds of muffled screams emitted from beyond the walls of the closet. Not of torture—but of anger and extreme frustration. Delia's.

What had Tamryn done to infuriate her mother to that level? Or, what hadn't she done?

Mayer and I looked for a point of entry and

quickly located the seam of a narrow door behind a section of decorative trim. I took a deep breath and after getting a nod from Mayer, inched it open.

I spotted Tamryn's bloodied face first.

She panted as she leaned against the far wall of the media room and from her vantage point, easily spotted us but made no motion with her eyes as we ducked behind a row of theater seats. Delia had her back to us and was hurling obscenities at her daughter, her arms flailing wildly with each insult.

I peered around the side and noticed that Leah was still unconscious. Thankfully, no additional injuries appeared to have been inflicted.

"Where's the knife?" I whispered to Mayer before popping down to my belly and scanning the area in front of us.

Whatever Tamryn had done, the knife had been liberated and was now beneath the seats. Unfortunately, it was also two rows in front of us. And directly behind Delia.

Holding my breath, I slipped out of the hiding spot before tucking into the next row, where I could reach it. All we needed was a bit of luck and the element of surprise.

Just as I'd crawled around the end of one row, down the next and then shimmied my way under the seat far enough to reach the knife, a human tank loomed over me, his soulless eyes piercing mine. He succinctly put an end to my laborious but measly efforts as he pulled me up in one fluid movement by my elbow, then freed the knife from my hand.

Mayer had also been exposed and was now squatting, the top of his head visible as he glared at us.

"Isn't there some saying about bringing a knife to a gunfight?" The captor whispered in my ear.

I just loved funny entrance lines.

Delia swiveled on her heel. "Roman, dahh-ling! About time you showed up." The words flowed out in a velvety purr as she batted her lashes at him, causing my stomach to churn. Then again, maybe she was having a false eye-lash malfunction, but I doubted it.

"Been hearing that a lot today," he replied, his voice as rough as the grip on my arm. "You should mind your surroundings, Delia. These two nearly got the drop on you."

"Well, thankfully, you were here to thwart

their efforts, just like I paid you to do." She zeroed in on Mayer and raised a brow as she took him in, still partially hidden as he gripped the back of the seats, his eyes hard as he stared his wife down.

"I knew it!" Tamryn screamed hoarsely, jamming her finger in Roman's direction. "First my dad, then me. He asked you earlier how much it took to sell out. So, how much was it, you bloody traitor!"

"It's not like that," Roman started, but Delia cut him off.

"You don't need to justify yourself to her, darling. In fact, contain her. Dispose of her. I don't care. Just make sure it's cleaner than the job your thugs did on Jilli and that pest of an accountant. If it wasn't for their sloppiness, I wouldn't even be here."

Roman released me but didn't move, though Tamryn hurled a few choice comments at her mother.

Delia raised a brow and glanced in our direction. "Your spawn has a nasty mouth, Craig. She must have gotten that from your derelict gene pool."

"Well, I'll take that any day over whatever

circus you've got running here," Mayer huffed. "But let's not dilly dally. You've got me here, woman. What do you want?"

"As I said before. Everything." Delia's tone was haughty as she gave her husband a disgusted grazing, but Mayer simply rolled his eyes.

"As ambiguous as usual."

"Then let me expound for your feeble mind," she snapped. "I want everything you stole from me. Freedom. Time. Youth. You are woefully unable, however, because you have nothing more to offer than that carcass you heave around while siphoning air that you have no right to breathe."

"And this—" he nodded at Leah, still unconscious and bound to the chair, "is your *right*? Your path to restored freedom, youth, time?" He shook his head, disgusted. "I may be no saint, but you, my dear, are no martyr."

"*Martyr*?" Delia threw her head back and roared with laughter. "God, Craig, only you would get philosophical at a time like this. This has nothing to do with martyrdom or something as banal as that. This is about capitalism. Pure and simple."

She tilted her head as she studied him. "What? Does that surprise you?" When he didn't respond, she snorted. "Figures. Anyway, we're behind schedule, Roman. Now that you're here, we can finish this and be on our way. Things to do. People to see. Money to make."

"Not so fast, Delia," Roman enunciated every syllable so crisply, her gaze shot toward him, eyes widened.

"What seems to be the problem, *Ro-man*? Are your pantyhose on backward or what?" Her lip curled as they stared each other down while the rest of us remained frozen, watching whatever "it" was play out. Hopefully they would turn on each other rather than continue their game. "Don't tell me you've gone and gotten yourself a crisis of conscience?"

He shook his head. Once. "Just. Don't."

"Or what?" She thrust a hand on her hip.

"Or you take your chances while I launch this into your chest." He brandished the knife—her knife—before reaching into his jacket with his free hand and extracting a gun with a silencer. "Or, if you prefer, while I put a round through your eye." He shrugged as he looked, quite pointedly and leisurely, from one to the other. "Either option works for me."

Delia said nothing, though she stepped toward Leah, whether to take her hostage or use her as a human shield, I wasn't sure, but Roman stopped her in her tracks.

"Your movement only makes the decision easier."

"That doesn't work for me, loverboy," she demurred, giving him her best pouty-lip. "I thought we were on the same side? Besides, you were supposed to bring me a surprise, yet I don't see it."

"There's been a change of plan."

She hiked a brow and crossed her arms. "Do tell."

"You've done a pretty bang-up job up to this point of convincing everyone of things that are not quite what they seem."

"Such as?"

Roman nodded at me, then at Tamryn. "You not only had these two believing that your husband was up to his neck in this operation, but that he had also been hot and heavy with Claudia for a while now and was paying for that swanky penthouse of hers. In reality, he had little to no interaction with her up until recently, when you sent her in to seduce him. It was all part of your plan to set him up."

Delia shrugged while Mayer stewed, though Tamryn still shot him a dirty look. My head snapped back toward Roman when he released a throaty chuckle.

"Well, hate to tell you, Delia, but Claudia happens to be my little snitch, too."

"You haven't said anything that's been even remotely remarkable." She rolled her eyes, though a hint of something flashed in them as she absorbed this revelation.

"Try this on for size, then. Considering I know *all* of your dirty little secrets, have absconded with your snitch, taken control of your thugs and for all intents and purposes, am currently holding all the weapons, I want a bigger cut."

Delia pressed her lips together as she gave his hands a cursory glance before casting her eyes back toward him. "Just how big?"

"All of it." If she was shocked by his demand, she showed no outward signs. Then he added a bombshell. "And your resignation from the organization. You will, of course, have a recommendation for your replacement."

At that condition, her brows raised. "That replacement being you, naturally."

"Naturally."

"See," Delia addressed the rest of us, "I told you it all comes down to capitalism."

Mayer grunted while Tamryn glared at all three of them, her mouth turned down. Frankly, the lot of them disgusted me, too, but my concern for my best friend heightened as she still had not regained consciousness, her limp and battered figure pale and lifeless.

"Not quite. It also has to do with control. And power," Roman replied, as Delia smirked.

"And you think once you have those things, you can accomplish all that I have?"

He shrugged. "They certainly won't hurt."

"Don't forget. *I* was in on this from the ground floor. *I* was the one who put the systems through their paces and nurtured and grew it into the international jewel it is today. You've only had but a mere snapshot of what it takes to run an operation of this magnitude, all while peering from behind my coat-tails. Someone with your limited…experience is no substitute for the caliber of expertise required at this level."

Roman gave her a tight-lipped smile. "I see holes where you have blinders on, Delia. You may be the old guard, but you are also long mired in old ways that no longer serve a changing environment. I hate to say it, Delia, but you're a lone dinosaur who refuses to concede that its entire species has long been extinct."

Frankly, I was glad he was the one holding the weapons because the frost she glazed him with could have stopped one's heart.

"Tell me, Roman. Let's say I agree to this… ultimatum. Do I get to lumber off and die an overdue but natural life? Or do you put me out of my misery to ensure you'll never have to be looking over my shoulder?"

"That's up to you, I suppose." He may have played a mean poker face, but I was betting he leaned toward the latter.

Delia's mouth twitched. "A condition of my own then, if you please?"

"I'll consider it." Yeah, probably about as much as he'd consider a suggestion to swap out his all-black closet for a more 1980s *Miami Vice* pastel vibe.

"I want to make a trade."

"You have nothing I want."

Delia wiggled a gloved finger. "Don't be too sure, Roman. I've been doing some of my own intel and have learned that there is something you want, possibly more than what you wish to extort from me."

"Extort is a bit terse, but I'll bite."

"Oh, I'm banking on it," she purred, laughing before she pointed at Mayer. "I still want him, safe passage and a handshake guarantee you won't come after me."

"I may be a bit wet behind the ears but I'm not that damp, Delia. That's pretty one-sided, not to mention it exceeds your one condition limit."

"Think of it as a package deal." She waved a hand, to which Roman grunted. "But you'll consider it?"

"If the other side of the coin suits."

"Oh, it does." Delia laughed, perhaps a bit too pleased with herself, given Roman's non-verbal jaw-grinding response, coupled with a "get on with it" gesture from his gun-wielding hand. Delia sighed. "Fine. One word—Shelby."

"Where is she?" Roman replied after regarding her for a long moment.

Delia pretended to examine her nails. Rather difficult, I would think, considering she was wearing gloves. I gave her props. The woman knew how to work the dramatics. "Oh, I'm guessing somewhere around Joshua Tree or Coachella by now."

"Joshua Tree alone spans a large area," Tamryn replied, receiving a chuckle and a wave of the hand from her mother.

"Oh, not to worry. Roman here is quite resourceful when he wants to be, I assure you." Delia tilted her head, regarding him. "Isn't that right? Or haven't I given you the right incentive?"

"If I were to agree, I'd want proof of life."

"Aww…that's sweet. Unfortunately, it's just not possible. Not only is it difficult to get reception in those areas, the storage containers can be quite…cumbersome to access once they're loaded on the trailer. The cargo also tends to shift during transit, so there's no telling what shape it will be in once it reaches its final destination. So I'll have to pass on the proof of life request. Sorry." Her smirk said otherwise.

"So you're just expecting me to take your word that she's okay," Roman replied, his tone flat.

"I think I've already answered that, darling. But I'll warn you, my internal GPS guesstimator could be off. And once that container hits the port and is in open water…well, all bets are off.

"I still have you."

"Sure you do, *but* you won't have all of those other things you wanted. And you definitely will never have Shelby. You pass on this once-in-a-lifetime opportunity, you lose. She loses. My way, we all win. But time is ticking." She tapped her head. "By the way, I *know* you'll say yes."

Roman grazed her with a look of amusement. "Don't be so sure. I think you've overestimated a few things. Such as my allegiance toward Shelby."

"I know Shelby was another one of your snitches—one with benefits, from what I'm told."

"Bad intel."

Delia raised a brow. "Oh? So I was wrong to inform my people to treat her with kid gloves? I should warn you, they despise snitches. Without my intervention, they tend to get a bit…physical. The ones with known personal attachments to their handlers get special treatment. If you know what I mean."

Roman remained silent, his expression and his body language unmoving. Perhaps Delia had played the wrong card?

Of course, as soon as the notion entered my brain, the other shoe dropped.

"Could become troublesome for that handler, especially when he's been keeping a secret of his own," Delia replied, giving Roman a pointed stare.

"Come on, *everyone* has secrets, Delia," Mayer snapped.

She released a handful of her own. "Oh, but *this* is a juicy one."

"Just spit it out, woman," her husband growled.

"Pooh. The lot of you is no fun." She thrust out her bottom lip. "Regardless, I doubt Roman wants the cat out of the bag, but he's not quite who he claims to be. Are you, darling?"

"No idea what you're blustering about, Delia. As Craig said, about time you spit it out," Roman replied dryly.

"Fine. I'll 'spit it out'. You're undercover law enforcement," she responded, grinning. "And don't bother denying it."

"I won't." Roman shrugged. "How long have you known?"

Like I said, other shoe. Ice must have run through his veins because there was no hint of emotion even remotely emanating from him.

"Long enough," Delia replied, looking more than a bit self-satisfied, if not triumphant.

"What the—" Tamryn looked from her mother to Roman to me. "Did we just enter the *Twilight Zone*?"

Roman ignored her, his eyes trained on Delia. "Then you also know I can't accept your trade."

"Well, it's not like it falls under the category of 'we don't negotiate with terrorists'," she chuckled.

"What you're doing is far worse in my book. It's a crime against the very nature of humanity." It was the first time I'd seen the big guy's armor come a little unhinged. And I have to say, his delivery was chilling. "You're a mother, for God's sake."

"Barely," Mayer muttered.

Great. Like we really needed commentary from the peanut gallery at this juncture.

Thankfully, everyone else had either not heard his retort or was ignoring him.

"Can you honestly say that *everything* you've done was by the book, in the eyes of the law?" Delia sneered.

"I don't have to justify myself to you."

"We aren't all that different, you know."

"Don't even go there, Delia."

"Troubling, when you really have to think about it, isn't it, Roman?"

"I don't lose sleep over it, if that's what you're getting at."

"Oh, my. So when Jilli showed up dead, it didn't matter? Better yet, when Shelby ends up…who knows where…you won't care?"

"As long as I can cut you off at the knees and stop you from shipping any more of those girls, I think that's a better day than most."

"But what about the others? The ones who slipped under the radar on your watch? Can you live with their lives on your conscience?"

"I'm done having this conversation with you. And just so you know, I've got a few more aces up my sleeve." Roman did play a good hand.

"Including that shipment you were going on about." He paused for effect, though he never glanced at Delia, whose smirk faltered.

Well played, Roman.

And, he wasn't quite done with her.

"It never made it beyond the Maricopa County border. Our fine Department of Public Safety pulled them over. The truck had a taillight out. Can you believe that? Anyway, the driver complied and was so freaked out that he confessed he was concerned about the contents of the cargo containers, effectively giving DPS the go-ahead to search the trailer."

This time, he looked directly at her. While he suppressed any form of amusement, Delia's confident sheen had worn off, exposing an open mouth worthy of netting more than a few juicy insects. Roman seized the opportunity to drive the point home.

"That's right. We cracked the container open and removed the cargo. So no, Delia, your condition will *not* be granted. Of course, I figured you would call my bluff, so I've decided to offer you the proof you would not. Come on, gang, Delia's ready for you."

On that note, the narrow door opened behind

us. Two females, flanked by another female and male, entered the media room—a fitting environment given the mixed reception from the rest of us.

Despite her disheveled appearance—likely from being tossed about in a dank storage container—I immediately recognized the first female who entered. Though she'd lost a considerable amount of weight, still present were those bright and inquisitive lapis-colored eyes as they scanned the room and landed on me.

Shelby offered me a tight smile, which faded quickly when her attention turned toward Leah's unmoving form, still tied to the chair. Her hand flew to her mouth as she released a small gasp. She started to move in Leah's direction, but Roman shot her a look and she immediately stopped.

The second to enter was barely recognizable without her multi-colored locks, penthouse Barbie attire and gum-smacking demeanor. Now clad in a fitted black ensemble that mirrored Roman's, coupled with an efficiently slicked-back ponytail, Claudia not only looked like a pro, her rigid form and stern expression gave one the immediate impression she could kick some serious butt.

Mayer's eyes widened in surprise but she simply gave him an expressionless head nod before her eyes flicked to me, then to Tamryn as she moved to Roman's side.

He didn't glance at her, but a slight smirk crossed his lips as he uttered, "I am sure most of you recognize Claudia. Also known as my partner, Detective Claudia Fielding."

Partner? Wait—*Detective*?

I shot a look at Tamryn. It was clear her old classmate had pulled one over on her, too. Now was not the time for explanations, but I assumed the two would catch up later and the truth about Claudia would be forthcoming.

Then again, I hadn't known about Leah's plans and she had been my best friend.

Delia garnered them with a look that suggested they'd both just been axed from her Christmas list—the nice one—and opened her mouth to elaborate on something along those lines when Roman cut her off.

"Before you say any more, you may want to remain silent from this point forward." He tilted his head at Claudia. "Detective, would you like to do the honors?"

She nodded, offering a wry smile as she strode toward Delia, the two other officers flanking her as one whipped a pair of handcuffs from his belt.

"I would be *more* than delighted. Delia Persephone Beatrice Mayer, you have the right —" Delia pretty much whelped like a stuck pig at this point, whether at being read her rights, having her middle name exposed or just being called out on the failed plan, I wasn't sure, but she did not go quietly.

Roman waved me on when he caught me gazing at Leah and I rushed to her, squatting on the floor as I worked to unbind her hands. Finally, the male officer came to my aid and swiftly cut away the bindings. I pushed her matted hair away from her face, frightened by how much paler she looked up close. She was, to my relief, warm to the touch and breathing shallowly.

"Leah, honey?" I whispered but received no response.

I jumped to my feet when an emergency medical technician gently patted my arm. "Miss?

We need you to back up so that we can check your friend out. We've been told she was given a heavy sedative"—I glanced at Roman, who nodded—"which she will come out of just fine, but we want to check her vitals, as well as her injuries."

"You did this?" My eyes snapped toward him.

Roman shook his head, his lips pulled tight before he responded, "Delia's thugs did before I illuminated them to the ways of the world. She was conscious then."

"*This* was part of your plan?" I growled, casting a hand at Leah's limp form.

"We needed to act quickly, and it was the only way the plan would work," he replied. "Besides, it was *her* idea."

How many times had I heard that line? I shook my head. That sounded like Leah. I could hardly fault Roman—she was hard to say no to once she had her mind set on something.

"We're going to need to talk—once all of this—is wrapped up." I waved a hand at the buzzing of medical pros and the officers, who were now strong-arming a vomit-mouthed Delia through the door.

"There will be a debriefing later and I will tell you what I can."

"Oh, you most definitely will," I growled, hawk-eying the techs as they eased Leah onto a gurney.

Just once, I wished these adventures wouldn't land one of us in the hospital. The tech stopped and stared and I realized I'd uttered that bit out loud. Shaking my head, he frowned but asked if I wanted to ride along.

I glanced at Roman, then at Claudia, who replied, "She can go. We know where we can find her for a statement."

I rolled my eyes, then glanced at Tamryn, who was still sitting on the floor with her arms wrapped around her legs, silently watching everything unfold as her father animatedly re-layed his version of the events to one of the officers.

"You okay?"

She sighed, looking as haggard as I felt. "I will be. You go on. I think the detective will want to hear my take on things once my father finishes his rant. It's the least I can do, you know, to give some accuracy to the situation."

"You may want to cut him some slack." I

tilted my head in Mayer's direction, hoping that she would notice he was visibly shaking. "He may not be the father you wanted, but he's the one you landed and I think you both could use someone to lean on right about now."

Tamryn nodded but said nothing, though her father glanced at her and their eyes connected. Something passed between them. I looked away, leaving them to their moment, and hopefully, to their first step in healing their relationship.

It would be a long road, but I'd seen worse paths with a lot more mileage and lost baggage scattered along the way. If anyone could patch that bumpy road, it was Tamryn.

I hadn't been so sure in the beginning, but little glimpses along the way had shown me who she really was. All that other "stuff" she carried around had been a façade—a mask she wore to protect herself from a harsh world. I couldn't fault her for that.

We all wore masks, whether we wanted to admit it or not.

And some of us just shed one, only to reveal another.

My guess was that her life had been filled with people like that. And that it hadn't been until this moment she realized that the only way she would ever know who to trust was by removing her own. To do so, she needed to be able to trust herself.

First.

In the end, don't we all?

CHAPTER THIRTY-SIX

A few days later…

I finally got my briefing with Roman. It was briefer than I would have liked.

It came as no surprise to anyone when Delia clammed up and refused to say a word about the role she'd played in the operation or her level of involvement, though according to whoever was keeping up her social media account on her behalf, she had a lot to say about the conditions in jail.

Rumor had it she didn't wear orange well.

Delia's henchmen, on the other hand, sang like canaries and ratted her out to save their own hides.

All claimed that she had been the one to administer the opioids to Jilli after knocking her out with a brick. Her thugs also admitted to stashing her body in the trunk of Leah's car until they realized, upon returning to the airport parking structure, that far worse damage had been done. The autopsy revealed that after Delia struck her, she never regained consciousness.

It was little comfort to her family, who had lost a sister, a daughter, and a friend—one who had just been trying to do the right thing. Unfortunately, for the sake of those still trying to track down and eliminate operations like the one in South Scottsdale, they wouldn't know that had been the case. At least not until a time came when it was safe to bring out the real story and the details of how she had helped bring down Delia and those in her employ. For now, she would sadly be added to the stats of individuals dying under suspicious circumstances at the hands of an unknown assailant.

Tamryn went quiet for a bit. Her world had been turned on its head, though she was the first to admit that it had been heading down the wrong path for some time—one that would have hit a brick wall sooner or later, if not ended badly. She also admitted she had been in denial for far too long about the fact that she was ultimately in charge of her own destiny and that her life was not defined by her parent's actions. Nor was she destined to follow the same paths they had chosen for themselves.

She permanently cut ties with her mother after the arrest but when her father, Craig, reached out and apologized for his indiscretions —several of which had been with Tamryn's friends—the two agreed to attempt a fresh start. And though it would be slow-going, both were willing to put in the hard work, patience, open-mindedness and, of course, time necessary to forge a new path. One that led toward healing.

It's a good reminder for all of us—the past is the past—and there's nothing we can do to change it. Rather than rehashing old ground or living with regrets, choose to be present, live in the moment and embrace what we have. Now.

Speaking of those living in and for every moment…

Claudia changed her ways when she was shipped off to boarding school, gotten interested in criminal justice and even interned in both high school and college for various law enforcement agencies. She excelled in her courses and was highly sought after by several upon graduating early from her university. Upon quietly graduating from the police academy shortly after —something that was known only by those closest to her, as she was being groomed for undercover assignments because of her youthful appearance—she exceeded the expectations of her commanding officers. It was clear she would be an asset to any agency, which was later proven when she became the youngest person assigned to the sex crimes unit.

So when Roman was tasked with forming a team created to monitor, infiltrate and eliminate human trafficking rings that were slithering into the Phoenix metro area under the guise of afterhours party destinations, Claudia was among the first officers he recruited and brought on board.

Though small, the team was tantamount in quickly identifying operations that primarily targeted properties of owners who lived out of state. Several owners had elected not to employ management companies to oversee those sites and monitor who was doing the renting. Sadly, even those who did learned that the companies often only did any managing when major events in the area warranted it, such as baseball season training or for premier golf tournaments or major car auctions, which typically occurred in early spring.

The criminals swooped in and took advantage of the less touristy seasons when the extreme heat made the valley a less than desirable vacation destination. Fortunately for these operations, this off-season could start as early as late March and continue all the way through October, making for an ideal time to target unsuspecting party-goers, entice them with the promise of opportunity and whisk them into the underbelly of a criminal world, often never to be seen or heard from again.

And while the task force was fairly new, with the help of the cities, the homeowners and management companies, along with people like Shelby, Leah and Jilli, they were able to start putting a smack-down on the operations, sending a clear message: the metro-Phoenix area—and Old Town Scottsdale in particular—wasn't going to allow operations of this nature to wreak havoc in their cities any longer.

Of immense help was a journal that mysteriously appeared one day, addressed to the team.

Between you and me, I think the only reason Roman mentioned it was because he believed I had been the one to deliver it. Claudia did nothing to dissuade him, though I think she suspected otherwise.

I had not been the mystery deliverer, but there was no convincing Roman of that fact, and while I knew who had, I never got a chance to confirm it with that particular source.

More on that in a bit.

With regards to that journal—it was the one that had belonged to Nick Oliveri, the former forensic accountant who had "retired" and was the owner of a salvage yard in Phoenix until his untimely death, which was still being investigated.

Though I suspected law enforcement knew who was ultimately responsible for his murder, they just lacked the evidence necessary to prove it.

Oliveri's body had not provided the evidence needed to close his murder investigation, though as William R. Maples, Ph.D., aptly suggested with his book, *Dead Men Do Tell Tales*, Oliveri's journal spoke volumes, piecing together links in the operation's chain that had been invisible to others.

Even in death, Oliveri helped the task force in ways no living person had to date.

The only way they could repay him was to honor his memory by bringing the efforts of his labor to fruition.

And despite having not much more than a snapshot's worth of insights regarding the journal myself, I was still convinced the techies on the team would have a field day scouring its contents and that they would be able to extract times, dates, shipping routes and beginning and ending destinations for scheduled shipments.

When I asked about names, however, Roman became vague and changed the subject. I knew that there were several codes within the journal that had been carefully secured, not behind a firewall or locked within a digital vault, but within a series of puzzles, created with Oliveri's own mind. In them were the girls' names, the locations and means with which they had been acquired, their destinations and the amounts paid. In addition, there were details pointing to various documents—emails, physical sources, etc.—that incriminated state, county and local officials, club owners and management companies nationwide, among others who had received incentives to aid the operation within the various jurisdictions.

Roman said he found it curious that the names associated with several of the individuals implicated had been redacted or were missing altogether. He stared at me, pointedly, ensuring he held my gaze when he said it, though I'd shrugged and suggested that having all the other pertinent details should make it an easy puzzle for his crack team to piece together.

Still, I had to wonder whether those particular nuggets of data had been purposely scrubbed before being handed over. If so, the mystery deliverer had given the team just enough juicy bits—knowing they would quickly unravel the clues—while giving himself enough of a head start for whatever plans he had in mind.

With Roman hawk-eying me, waiting to catch some facial tick or unintended reveal through my body language, I was careful about uttering that last mental meandering out loud. I knew he wouldn't be satisfied with my response for long and may have already realized that while I wasn't the actual source, he wasn't far off the beaten path.

I had my own theories, which wouldn't be confirmed until I heard it from the source's mouth.

Having said that, Roman himself was a bit of an enigma. He believed in his team's mission and knew the road ahead would be a long one and that there would continue to be losses and tragedies along the way. Yet he questioned whether he was the right person to lead them. In his book, too many girls had been lost on his watch, and his hands were tied when it came to going after them once they left his jurisdiction.

Despite his misgivings, Roman encouraged his team, keeping them focused on revisiting each incident, revamping and learning from the post-mortem and proceeding down the path with a new perspective.

Still, there was a darkness that filled him—it was clear to see when he mentioned in private that he had nightmares about what he'd seen, convinced he would forever be haunted by the lives of those he had not saved. Perhaps that's what drove him, though I wondered if his efforts ever kept the ghosts, or the demons, at bay.

I didn't pretend to understand what it must be like to live in that world but needed to start focusing on what I *could* control, in this moment.

And right now, what was most important to me, above all else, was attempting to rebuild the relationships with the people I cared about most.

Perhaps that was the biggest—if not the most important—challenge in life any of us could face.

Leah was unnecessarily apologetic about how everything had gone down. She had no idea things would go south as quickly as they did once she decided to go looking for Shelby.

She certainly wouldn't have concocted the story or gone to the lengths she had to keep me out of harm's way as she instigated her own investigation. Yet, she knew if she had mentioned it to me, I would have insisted on getting involved. Just as I knew she would have done precisely the same if the situation had been reversed. She had me there.

"I just wish you would have told me," I said

as I sat by her bedside in the hospital and held her pale, trembling hand.

The drugs Roman had given her to knock her out had worn off and were not life-threatening, but she had sustained other injuries at the hands of Delia's thugs. The external cuts and bruises would heal, and under careful monitoring, the internal injuries would too, though I worried about the emotional and mental damage that had been inflicted.

She would not talk about it and knowing Leah as I did made me realize that what she had endured had been far worse than she was letting on.

It had been torture.

"I thought I had it figured out. I knew Shelby wouldn't have gotten herself in over her head just because of some random after-parties, but I had no idea of the extent…the level of complicity…" her voice trailed off, wincing as she shook her head.

"I hadn't completely thought through the implications of what she'd gotten herself into. I know I still would have followed—stupidly, as I typically do—but I had no idea what was going on in our own backyards." Her voice was hoarse and I released her hand to feed her a few ice chips.

After a moment, she pressed her eyes shut and gripped my hand as best as she could. I knew she was in pain and tried to interject, but she squeezed my hand harder.

"Let me get this out." I nodded. "I knew that human trafficking was on the rise and that these…animals were getting more creative about it. But luring girls through the club scene, with the promise of an after-party at someone's house —how many times did you and I make those same decisions at that age? It could just as easily have been either you or me!" A monitor beeped. I glanced up and noted some of her vitals were escalating.

"Shhh… Leah, you need to calm down. You couldn't have known. This isn't your fault." I wiped the tears from her face. "Do you under-stand me? It's not your fault." Though she was clearly in pain, she sobbed and her breathing be-came erratic.

"I'm so sorry!"

"Leah, please…"

"No…no…no…those girls…I *promised* them…and Shelby…"

"Shelby's okay, honey." I pushed her hair back from her forehead, which was glazed with a sheen of sweat under her unhealthy white pallor.

"All those girls," she whimpered. Her voice was a mere whisper, but the intensity behind it was clear as another audible beep sounded. I dared not look, as my friend's eyes implored me to hold her gaze. To understand. And as fragile as her clasp on me was, I returned a squeeze.

"Shhh…it's okay. I *do* understand," I whispered, just as one nurse entered, followed by another. Both looked equally willing to do battle to ensure their patient was not subjected to further injury on their watch.

I squeezed Leah's hand a final time and leaned close, still holding her gaze. "I love you and I'll be here, no matter what." Gently releasing her hand, I stood and turned toward the nurses. "Probably time for me to leave."

Neither said anything but offered me cold, efficient nods before tending to their patient.

I didn't look back as I left the room, but my

heart was on the outside as I released an audible sob, covering my mouth.

"Your friend's goin' to be okay," the portly duty nurse I recognized replied, her tone filled with confidence as she appeared out of nowhere.

"Physically."

She nodded, glancing through the window as her team tended to the person who meant most to me in this world. "Physically."

"And what about the rest of her?"

She owed me no answer, yet graced me with a response.

"Being as tough as she is, she's gonna work through those demons when she's good and ready, I reckon," she stopped, then turned to me, "and not because she *thinks* she needs to deal with them any sooner." Her pointed stare spoke volumes.

I nodded but said nothing and she offered one in return as she returned to her station, satisfied that her message had been received.

Let my friend heal, but be there for her on the other side.

She'd done the same for me on more occasions than I could count.

So yeah, that I could do.

Because when it came to Leah, I would do anything to ensure she was whole again.

I stepped away from the window, walked a few paces and quietly took a seat in the waiting room.

Cause that's what family does.

I knew something was up the minute Ramirez walked into my house unannounced.

His usual confident stride and easy smile were replaced with hesitant steps and a pained expression, as though every move cost him something.

Perhaps it did.

"Busy days…" he said after surveying the room, focusing on nothing in particular.

He'd been here too many times to avert his gaze simply to absorb the surroundings. He was intent on looking anywhere.

Anywhere but *at* yours truly.

Mind you, it wasn't an awkward I-used-to-be-in-relationship-with-this-person type of thing. It was just…a thing.

So, I gave him a pass and nodded. The days behind us had indeed been busy. And not soon forgotten.

"Leah doing okay?" he asked after a moment, still not looking at me nor relaxing against the counter as was customary. Instead, he seemed oddly ill-at-ease as he shifted from one foot to the other.

"Leah is…doing." There was no reason to make the situation out to be any better than it was. Especially not with Ramirez. "I'm just happy she's still with us." He nodded, saying nothing but tucking his hands into his back pocket. I tilted my head. "You should stop by and say hello if you have time. I know she'd like seeing a familiar face."

"I'll make time," he replied, lifting his head to meet my eyes for the first time. His tone was earnest, but there was a sadness to it, though he joked, "Of course, fair warning, I may beat your record in setting off hospital alarms."

I chuckled. "You heard."

"Duty nurse is a friend."

"Of course she is," I laughed. "Can't get away with anything, can I?"

"Apparently not even if you tried." His chuckle was genuine, as was the small smile that played on his lip. "I will…stop by, though."

"I'd appreciate it," I replied, and silence once again filled the air. My curiosity about the true nature of this visit finally got the better of me. "So, what's up? Haven't seen a face that long or a man so…conflicted in a while. Then again, we are in the kitchen and you have tasted my cooking."

Again, he chuckled, but it was of the distracted variety and was not accompanied by a smile. "You caught me."

I shrugged and put my hands up in the air. "Hard not to. So…now that you're caught, might as well come clean."

"It's about Martin." I rolled my eyes. Of course it was.

"He's not here. Haven't seen him since… well…since Tamryn and I ditched him…and Dina, Tamryn's aunt. Sent him a couple of texts while everything was going down, but when I finally got home, he had cleared out."

Ramirez raised a brow. "Not even a note?"

"Not even a note. Though he left a doggie bag for Nicoh in the fridge, so I guess that was his form of acknowledgment for my not-so-hospitality."

"Are you sure it was for Nicoh? Maybe he thought you would need something to eat upon your return." I tilted my head, wondering where he was going with that. "I've seen the contents of your fridge."

"Whatever, Ramirez." I was not amused. "Believe me, it was for Nicoh." And while my Alaskan Malamute had engulfed every last one of the half-raw steak bites, still oozing with bloody juices, just getting it out of the bag to cut it up for him had caused me to wretch, especially after the days I had. And it wasn't from hunger.

"Huh. Still seems very un-Martin-like." When I shrugged, he added, "You heard a journal turned up at the task force's office." It was not a question.

Ah, he was fishing, was he? "I did. And I told Roman, Claudia, and every other member of the team, I was not responsible for that delivery, nor can I confirm who was." I gave him a pointed stare—it was, after all, the truth.

End of conversation.

Or not.

Ramirez surveyed me, perhaps hoping to glean something that the task force had not. "I received a special delivery of my own." He stared out the window, and once again, his demeanor shifted to one of unease.

"Go on."

Reaching into his back pocket, he pulled out a plain white envelope. Unfolding it, he handed it to me.

"It's from Martin."

The firm set of his jaw made me hesitant to reach for it, but I did. Noting the flap had been torn open, I glanced up.

"You read it." It was not an accusation, more a reaction of curiosity, and Ramirez took it as such.

"There was an outer envelope, addressed to me with a note, telling me to open and read the contents of the inner envelope."

"And?" I prompted.

Ramirez blew out a breath. "And to deliver it to you whenever I thought it best."

I raised a brow. Since when did Martin need an intermediary? And, why had he chosen

Ramirez? I quickly did mental calculations of how many hours it had been since I'd actually laid eyes on Martin.

"Okay. And when, exactly, did you 'receive' this letter?" Ramirez narrowed his eyes, not terribly pleased, I assumed, by my overly emphasized finger quotes.

"Yesterday," he replied. "Anyway, I felt as though now was the best time."

"Obviously. You're here," I snorted, none too kindly, still kind of annoyed by the fact that Martin had employed someone else to do whatever *this* was.

"Arianna, *please*."

My eyes snapped to his. I did not like what I saw.

"How bad is it?"

He shook his head, pressing his lips together, though he did not break away from my gaze.

I nodded. "He's not coming back, is he?"

"Just read the letter." He went to the fridge, grabbed a beer and sauntered into the living room.

I heard him sink into the chair and murmur something to Nicoh, who had emerged from his slumber, just in time to receive scratches from his old pal. Perhaps just in time for Ramirez, who needed conciliation or affirmation of something more.

I steadied myself, ignoring what Ramirez had placed before me, intent on hearing this conversation between man and canine play out. I could have been wrong, but it sounded something along the lines of, "Buddy, you and I are going to make a pact." This was followed by the sound of dog snuffing and a sad chuckle. "Glad to hear we're on the same page. We just need to keep making sure that your mom is okay—got it?" More snuffing sounds ensued, followed by a murmured whoo-woo.

I shook my head as I removed the contents of the envelope. I took a deep breath and leaned into the counter before unfolding it.

The letter was written on a piece of monogrammed parchment that Leah had bought me for my birthday several years back. Both of us had chuckled about it at the time and had a spirited chat about the lost art of penmanship.

Martin's clear, crisp handwriting was void of any ornamental flourish, much like the man.

———

My Dearest Arianna,

If you're reading this, my daughter, then Detective Ramirez has done as I've asked. My apologies for its brevity, but perhaps it's for the best. I feared that if I shared my plans in person, that stubborn streak—that both confounds me at times and yet I adore—would erupt in its usual spectacular and glorious manner, and that you'd most certainly insist on embarking on this mission with me.

Please know that I did not prevent you from doing so out of fear for your safety—quite the opposite, actually. I made the decision because I feel your attention and therefore, your efforts are best suited where you are at this moment in your life, where you can focus on your current priority—your friend—rather than off chasing the evils of this world.

Besides, isn't it about time you permit others the opportunity to slay the dragons? (This and the emoji, I believe you called it, that follows are my feeble attempt at humor. :D)

I know these evils tend to find you regardless, and I apologize for the times I played a part in that. I wanted more for you and your sister. And while I may have failed Victoria, I can at least make an attempt at forging a different path with, and for, you.

Having said that, Dina, who you know as Tamryn's aunt, and I have formed an alliance, combining her inside knowledge of these operations and the resources of my network.

Our mission is to bring an end to this heinous operation that Dina's sister, Delia, had embroiled herself in, by going directly after the head of the snake.

Our goal is to put operations of this nature on notice—to send a message to the others who perpetrate these crimes.

Their actions will no longer be tolerated—consequences *will* be enforced. And while we may not succeed and likely will not return—our goal *is* rather lofty—we are in agreement that to sit idly by and do nothing would be the equivalent of giving these monsters carte blanche to do as they please. We owe it to future generations to stop evil like this in its tracks and impart an important lesson learned from the past.

And, most importantly, I owe it to you, Arianna —my lovely, independent daughter, who has always been wise beyond her years. I hope in time, you can understand and perhaps forgive me, if not for leaving then for the sins of my past.

Speaking of time, give Detective Ramirez a chance and he will do the same in return. The two of you are good for each other. I may not have thought much of him early on—chalk it up to my heightened sense of protectiveness. Nor did I relay any of these shifting sentiments as time went on, though I do now truly believe it to be the case, having seen the two of you together firsthand. And even through the jaded and often overly protective eyes of an old man, think with time, and a little give and take on both your parts, you will come to see that, too.

As for me, I find this partnership with Dina intriguing. I've not had a companion for some time but feel that we will work well together, though she is no replacement for my beloved Alison.

And there never will be.

To capture another one of your many amusing phrases, *"This ain't that kind of thang."* At most, my hope is that we become trusted allies as we join forces in an attempt to hunt down this evil and rip it from this world, piece by piece.

But one thing at a time.

There's so much I want to say to you, my dear—things that I should have said long before now—but couldn't, for my own fears prevented me from revealing my truth. All I can do is tell you now.

I've always been proud of you. You have added so much more to my life than you can ever know. You are the best parts of your mother—I knew it from the moment I first laid eyes on you and again when we were reunited years later.

Alison would have been proud of the person you've become and continue to be, despite everything you've endured in your short life.

Anyway, I know I've already dispelled more advice than one probably should in one pass, but if you would indulge me two more small requests:

Always be true to yourself, no matter what.
And, never, ever question my love for you.

That's all, for now…

Sincerely yours,
Martin Singer

————

I folded the letter, placed it back into the envelope and set it on the counter before turning off the kitchen light and heading into the living room to join Ramirez and Nicoh.

I couldn't be angry at Martin for leaving in this manner. If I'd learned anything about the man in the short time we'd come to know one another, it was simply his way.

And, as he'd asked me to do with Ramirez, I needed to accept Martin for who he was, as he'd accepted me.

He was—at the end of the day and above all else—my father.

— The End —

ABOUT HARLEY

Harley Christensen lives in Phoenix, Arizona with her significant other and their mischievous motley crew of rescue dogs (aka the "kids").

When not at her laptop, Christensen is an avid hockey fan and lover of all things margarita. It's also rumored she's never met a green chile or jalapeño she didn't like, regardless of whether it liked her back.

For more information on the author and her books, please visit her at www.mischievousmalamute.com.

Story Chracters

The main characters and a brief description of each:

Don: The mastermind behind the operation, Don is resourceful and has a knack for planning and executing complex missions. He is responsible for assembling the team and providing them with the necessary tools and resources.

Jimmy Ko: A young man held in a detention center, Jimmy is the initial focus of Don's rescue mission. His role in the team and his abilities are not entirely clear from the excerpts.

Oliver: Introduced as Jimmy Ko's father's lawyer, Oliver plays a crucial role in the breakout mission. His relationship with Don and the rest of the team is not fully explained in the excerpts.

Nick Conner (Justin): A new recruit to the team, Nick is trained in the art of illusion and con-jobs, as well as martial arts. He is expected to play a significant role in the team's operations.

Kimberly Burk: Kimberly is the team's driver and also works on cars. She is described as a redhead with green eyes and a captivating smile.

Alexander: Alexander is a member of the team who has had some interaction with Nick, specifically in teaching him proper etiquette.

John: John is a member of the team who undertakes reconnaissance missions. He uses advanced technology, including invisible drones, to gather information and evidence.

Linda: Linda assists John in his reconnaissance missions by providing him with necessary information. She seems to have a role in research and intelligence.

Robin: Robin appears to be a target of the team's operations. John specifically undertakes a mission to gather evidence against Robin.

Team Basilisk Ldt.

Raleigh Minard

Team Basilisk Ltd.
First edition, published 2023

By Raleigh Minard

Copyright © 2023, Raleigh Minard

Cover design by Reprospace.com

Paperback ISBN-13: 978-1-952685-72-9

Published by Kitsap Publishing
Poulsbo, WA 98370
www.KitsapPublishing.com

To my LORD who provide inspirations
and imagination.

Thank You!

Chapter 1

Don Travis is a multi-Billionaire. His great-great-grandfather was a car specialist named Samuel Travon; it's rumored that he was employed by a man known as The Magician. Samuel had built a special car for this man (the car had weapons, and could become invisible). Over time The Magician (Paladin) disappeared without a trace. So did the special car. One night there was a fire in Travon's workshop which burnt the whole building down and everything in it. The fire appeared mysterious, but the investigation claimed it was an accident. All of the plans, specifications, and drawings for the car were destroyed. This broke my great-great grandfather's spirit.

Frederick (Samel's son) had a diary that detailed his meeting with The Magician and the car his father built for the man. Fredrick never named the Magician in his diary for fear if it fell into the wrong hands, it would be dangerous for his family. Frederick followed in his father's footsteps. Frederick design and build specialty cars and motorcycles. Frederick was thinking about other designs for planes and boats, but never got around to working on them. Over the years Frederick had earned millions of dollars for his inventions and designs. Frederick then got married and had a son Jason Travon; he wasn't into engineering; he was more of a businessman. Jason liked dealing in the stock market.

Jason took the money he inherited from his father. Jason made wise investments, and parlayed his millions into billions. Jason soon learned he needed to hide his success, so he set up many offshore accounts and fake corporations. His finance showed he made a modest few million while keeping the billions a secret. Jason soon married, and they had a beautiful daughter called Dawn, who grew up and married an engineer. He loved to invent things. His name was Oliver Travis, my father. His inventions also brought in money, which Jason showed him how to invest and hide his money, so the taxes would not be a burden nor draw attention to him or his family.

Soon after I came along Donald Travis, I followed in my father's footsteps and went to ivy league schools and universities to learn engineering and Physics. I also learned computers and programming. I didn't have a tough time at college; I was brilliant. In one of our classes, we had to team up to build a robot. It turned out to be the best thing at the science competition fair. My team took the prize at the science fair for that year.

One time I met with my great-grandfather Jason; he cared a great deal about me. He gave me the diary of his grandfather Fredrick. I keep it with me everywhere I go. While I was off at college, my parents decided to go on a world tour. While traveling on a train in France, a terrorist group blew up the train killing my parents. That was the turning point in my life. I wanted revenge; I remembered reading something in Fredericks's diary that interest me. In the meantime, I went to live with my grandfather Jason. He showed me his hidden empire and how to hide my money. Not long after this time, my grandmother died of cancer, and my grandfather would not live much longer. He died of a broken heart (I miss them very much).

I took care of my grandfather until he died. Not long afterward, I discovered something; I had been missing in Fredericks's diary. The car that Samuel had built for Paladin. Also, there was a description of a battle suit that Paladin wore. Now I'm in my late twenties, and I have decided to use my considerable resources to take my revenge on the terrorist who killed my parents. I decided to create a hidden base here on my parent's property. I burned down my house; I made it look like an accident. There was no fraud involved. I'd removed the insurance and all the valuables from the house before setting it on fire. Then I would let it become overgrown with trees and brush. This took five years for the brush to take over the property.

The next step was to contact a contractor to build my underground bunker. That part was easy to do. The contractor believed I was some crazy paranoid black man and wanted to keep it secret from aliens. The contractor accepted my commission because the money was good and paid in advance. I had my bunker, a rather extensive one, built underground. The contractor supplied power, water, a sewage system, and ventilation. All the entrances were hidden and were well protected from bombs being dropped on them. It cost a billion dollars. I paid off the contractor, and he and his people went off thinking that they made a crazy paranoid person happy.

A year later, I set off an explosion near my hidden base, making it look like the whole place went up. The rubble and the caved-in look are just about right, using the foundation of the old house I had burnt down some years before. Anyone who sees the rubble thinks the base they worked on is now destroyed. Once the commotion settled down and the police investigators wrote it off as an accident, I could return to my project of building my base.

I set about building up the underground base, adding to the lower levels, and putting in work-shops and labs. My next Item on the list is to create a secret team to help me in my vendetta against people above the law. Using my father's firm, I had contacts with the underground and the CIA. Using some influence, I was able to acquire files on potential personnel for my team.

CHAPTER 2

The first people I'm going to search for are computer Geeks. Don has a few connections with Home Land Security and the FBI. Through these connections, he finds a couple of people on the list as noted as hackers, a girl, age 20, and a boy, age 15. The girl is in prison for hacking into NORAD's computers. She's listed as a terrorist and managed to get a 20-year sentence. The boy is in detention. He hacked Wall Street and caused a stock market crash. He also managed to pocket a million dollars in the process.

Don reads over the file for Linda Tungsten, finds a CIA document, and sees some cryptic code at the bottom. Don calls a friend he knows in the CIA and asks him about the code at the bottom of the form. Don reads the code number to his contact, and the connection tells Don that the person in question is to be terminated. "Why?" asks Don. The contact indicates that this person is rated too high as a National Security risk and must be terminated. "Do you know when that'll happen?" According to the code, in three days.

Don makes arrangements to meet with Linda Tungsten at the prison. The next day Don shows up at the women's prison with an appointment to see Linda tungsten. The guards bring Linda to the interrogation room. Don posing as a lawyer wants to go over her case to plea for an appeal. Linda doesn't believe it. The guards leave the room with a warning that they're being taped with visual and audio equipment. Don thanks the guards, and Linda watches Don and says nothing. Don pulls a file folder from his case and hands it to Linda. Linda sits, looking down at the file folder. Don explains that he has some new evidence that might set her free if she opens the file and reads it. Linda reluctantly opens the file and begins to read. Suddenly, the words on the page change, and it reads. HOW WOULD YOU LIKE TO GET OUT OF HERE? And then the words vanish and return to being normal typed written nonsense.

Linda looks up with a question on her face but says nothing, but she nods her head yes very slightly. Don smiles and hands her another file folder, explaining that this contains the new evidence that will set her free. Linda takes the file folder and opens it again. The paper flares, and she scans it. BE READY THREE DAYS FROM NOW. I WILL GET YOU OUT. "I'll have everything ready for your trial in three days," said Don. Then the letters fade away to become more legalese that says nothing. Linda nods yes ever so slightly. Don smiles.

Linda, thanks, Don. Don gets up and puts on a pair of gloves, then, as an afterthought, hands Linda another file folder; Linda takes it, opens it, and is expecting a flash message, but nothing happens. Linda looks up, and Don smiles. *(Lind doesn't realize that the folder was coated in a slow-acting poison, not enough to kill, but will, at the right time, simulate death.)* A day later, Linda starts getting sick and collapses to the floor. Don has returned to his base and waits for it all to unfold. In the meantime, Don steals a uniform from the local morgue, allowing him to pick up Linda›s dead body and remove her from prison. The prison where Linda resides calls Don, Linda's acting lawyer to tell him Linda is dying. The poison reacts a little faster than Don expected, so Don is forced to pick up Linda's body a day earlier. Don dresses up in his uniform and appears at the gate to pick up Linda's body in an ambulance. The guard looks over Don's paperwork, which seems to be in order.

The guards let Don into the infirmary, and he collects two bodies, Linda's and another woman's; it would've been suspicious if he didn't taken both of them. Don stashes both bodies in the back of his ambulance and drives off. The nice thing about being a black man is that they all appear to look alike to everyone else. Don takes the dead bodies to a morgue, where Don drops off the other woman's body, and he carts off with Linda's body to his base. Don gives Linda the antidote to the poison he had given her at the prison. Don, with some help, manages to get Linda into bed in a room that will belong to Linda if she decides to stay. Don makes plans to get the next team member Jimmy Ko. Jimmy hacked into Wall Street and made a sizable amount of money, a million dollars. Jimmy didn't know how to hide his hack and was caught, so he, too, is in detention, serving time. Don is considering using the same tactic of extracting Jimmy as he did Linda from detention. A problem with that is Jimmy didn't realize that the million dollars he stole belonged to a gangster, who now wants him dead. The gangster set into motion a plan to remove Jimmy Ko and execute him gangland style; the bullet to the head should discourage other would-be hackers.

Before Don can get Jimmy, he must ensure Linda will be ok here by herself. Linda comes to, and Don is by her bedside. Linda opens her eyes and sees Don standing over her, and she screams. She nearly scared Don out of a year's growth.

"What are you doing here?" screams Linda.

"Just checking on you. Are you ok?" asks Don.

Linda gets ready to pull back the covers and get up when Don suggests that she not do that. Linda peers under the covers and sees she's naked.

"You, pervert, what have you done to me?" said Linda with some heat.

"Other than killing you, nothing," said Don.

"I'm not dead!" said Linda.

"Not now, at least, but in a way, I did kill you. And the authorities now believe you are dead."

"Now! Explain to me how I'm here and undressed," demands Linda.

"Ok, let's start with what I know about you. You hacked your way into NORAD, and they caught you. Now you were sentenced to prison without parole for being a spy. Am I right so far?"

"Yes, go on," says Linda.

"For the moment, all you need to know is I'm building a team for Justice, not law, and I need someone like you to help."

"So, you want me to hack NORAD and do what?" demands Linda.

"I don't want you to hack just NORAD, but other institutions for information when needed."

"No! What I did was to prove that no computer is safe, I'll not betray my country, and you can kill me outright if you think…."

"Hold on, Linda; I'll not hurt this country, hopefully, save it. Let me put my proposal to you so you can think it over. If you choose not to want to help then so be it; I'll let you go."

"I'm listing."

"I told you I'm building a team; you're the first member outside of myself. I hope to take on the people who are bad and above the law. That means I must work outside the law and go for justice. I hope to accomplish much, but I need others like yourself to accomplish this task. Now if you don't want to join, I'll let you go, but you'll wind up back in prison."

"Why? Will you send me there?" asks Linda.

"No, but you are well known and the first camera that picks you up. Well, you figure it out."

"Ok, I'll stay for now, just because I don't want to return to prison."

"Good, I'll explain more when I return with the next person of our team. The caretaker that I have here will see to your needs until I return. Just so you know, the caretaker is a woman, and she undressed you, not me."

Don returns to his grandfather›s home to make arrangements. Don purchases two mustangs color green with big engines; one car has a remote control built into it, and the other vehicle has nitrous oxide added to it for a fast getaway. Don also rents a semi-truck and buys a trailer with a specially built remote console and tv screen. On the day of the breakout, Don parks the truck on a straight stretch of Highway 101 in California, where there's usually no traffic. Don places the remote-controlled Mustang in front of the truck and puts up caution signs to indicate the truck is broken down so no one will think much about it.

Chapter 3

Don then changes his clothes into a business suit, backs the other Mustang out of the trailer, and drives to the detention center where Jimmy Ko is being held. Don introduces himself as Jimmy Ko's father's lawyer at the detention center showing his credentials, then demands to see Jimmy Ko. Don and Jimmy are ushered into a room with a guard.

"Jimmy, my name is Oliver, and I'm here to get you released into my custody."

"Why? Do I know you?"

"No, Jimmy, you don't."

"Then who wants to spring me from here?"

"All will be explained when we meet the man who wants you out of here."

"What if I say no?"

"You could stay if you like, but you'll be killed in the next 24 hours by the gangster you stole the money from. He wants you dead. My employer wants you alive." said Don.

"How do I know if you're not the person who wants to kill me?' asks Ko.

"Right now, you don't, and I don't have time to prove it. If I'm going to save you, you must come with me now," said Don.

"I'll go with you only because another detainee has warned me that my life is in danger. When do we leave?"

"How about now?" asks Don.

"Yes! said Jimmy

"Guard, we'll be leaving now," said Don

With his gun raised, the guard moves toward them, and Don pulls a pen from his pocket and pushes on the clicker spraying the guard in the face with knockout gas, and causing him to black out onto the floor.

"Wow! That was so cool."

"We need to get moving; once we get out the front door, run to the green Mustang; that's our getaway car."

Don lifts the keys from the guard and opens the door to the room. Then, both make a beeline to the front door; Don using the guard's badge and keys, got them out of the building into the parking lot. Don points to the green Mustang, and they both run for it. They get there, and both get in, only to find the police are almost there. Don fires up the Mustang and peels out of the parking lot, making sure the police see them leave and would be on their tail. Don winds up the large engine of the Mustang and leaves the police behind; Don wants them to keep up with him until they reach the straight away. They come to the curve in the road, and Don pushes two buttons, one to open the truck ramp and the other to start the other Mustang parked in front of the truck. As they clear the curve and are on the straightaway, Don pulls on the nitrous oxide switch giving the car a tremendous boost. When Don can see the truck in the distance, Don slows the car, maneuvers into the trailer, and closes the ramp concealing his car. Grabbing the remote, Don peels the other Mustang out and heads on down the road, to be followed by the police. Don takes them on a merry chase, then at the right spot overlooking the ocean, Don launches the car over the side of the cliff and then pushes another button to set off a bomb that destroys the car, which does significant damage to the two dead bodies Don had placed there.

After the police pass, Don changes his clothes to a tee shirt and jeans; he tells Jimmy to stay put, but Jimmy, a typical teenager, wants to go up into the cab to watch. Don doesn't want to draw attention to the fact that the truck driver has a rider pulls out his pen, and before Jimmy can react, Don sprays it in Jimmy's face causing him to be knocked out. Don puts Jimmy back into the car, Don gets out of the trailer and looks at his tires as if making an inspection of them. Don picks up the warning signs and gets into the truck's driver seat. Don drives down the road, passing the police as they look out over the cliff at the wreck.

A policeman stops Don and looks into the cab. "Hello, officer; what's going on?"

"Some stupid fool thought he could outrun us and drove over the cliff, and it looks like he and his rider are now dead."

"I'm sorry to hear that. May I continue down the road? I have a delivery to make."

"Yea, sure, take it slow and get out of the way."

"Sure, thing, officer." Don drives the truck slowly around the police cars and heads down the road. Twenty miles later, Don pulls into a truck stop where he rented the truck and drops the trailer off. Don backs out the Mustang from inside the trailer and wakes up Jimmy.

"Wha... Where are we?" splutters Jimmy.

"We're on our way to the airport; now be quiet; I must concentrate," said Don.

Jimmy mumbled ok. Jimmy was afraid that Don would put him asleep again. Jimmy watches the road as they drive on.

Chapter 4

An hour later, Don pulls up to the airport and drives around to the back side up to a gate where Don checks in with the guard who passes him and his car through to the private hangers. At a hanger with wide open doors, Don drives into it and parks the mustang, then herds Jimmy onto a Lear jet ready for takeoff. Once Jimmy and Don are seated, Don tells the pilot they're prepared for departure.

Once they're in the air, Jimmy starts asking questions, which temps Don in ejecting him out the door of the plane. Grabbing onto his patients, Don chooses which questions to answer. For each answer, more questions seem to multiply. Don waves for the attendant to come to him, and he whispers to have a lunch prepared and to spike it with something to put Jimmy to sleep, even for a little while. The attendant serves up the repast, and Jimmy is so hungry that he quits talking to eat and drink his lunch. As it turns out, the milk is where the drug is, and Jimmy gulps it down in a couple of swallows. Shortly after, the attendant clears away the dishes, and Jimmy is sound asleep.

At last, some quiet sighs Don; they have six hours of flight time before they reach their destination in New England. Don pulls out the files to see who will be recruited onto the team next. Don reads over the material of the four folders he has collected. Justin Michaels looks to be the best choice for the team, so Don decides to follow up with him. Justin is the most perfect of the four options. Single, in great shape, knows martial arts, was in the black ops, and knows how to kill if necessary. *I will contact him next week,* muses Don.

It worked out rather well, Jimmy woke up as the plane was landing, and during that time, Don managed to get some sleep. The Lear jet lands and taxies into a private hangar, and Don ushers Jimmy off the plane and into a Rolls Royce; Don gives Kim (driver) the order to take them to the base. An hour later, Kim pulls up to a field void of any buildings, then, out of nowhere, a ramp points sharply downward and through an open-door way. Jimmy is going nuts with all the questions he wants to ask. Kim parks the car in what looks like a huge garage. Then Kim gets out and opens Don's door. Don steps out and motions Jimmy to follow.

Jimmy is in awe and says nothing as Don leads him through the base maze to the computer room. As luck would have it, Linda was looking over the computer stations.

"What do you think?" asks Don.

"These computers aren't on the market, and they're prototypes. How did you get them?" asks Linda.

"Well, Jimmy, do you have any questions now?" asks Don.

"Just one; which computer is mine?"

"Well, before anyone touches anything, these are the terms here. You both are dead to the world, so that'll be a clean slate for each of you. I'll pay you a good wage, and you can live as you will; keep away from the mainstream of places. Or you'll find out that your life will be in jeopardy. If you don't want to work for me, I'll probably relocate you to a different country. Now what's your decision?

Jimmy asks, "Do I get to use all this equipment?"

"Yes," said Don.

"Count me in," said Jimmy in an excited voice.

"What about you, Linda?" asked Don.

"Will we get to leave here, or will we be chained to this place."

"You'll be able to come and go as you like, even take vacations. I'd suggest that you not go to places where you lived before. Your life would be in grave danger, as will this base."

"We get to use this equipment?" Linda asked.

"Most assuredly, this is why I selected you. I need someone with hacking skills, not to breach state secrets, but to breach certain individuals' files so we can bring them to justice and from time-to-time help people who need it."

"We'll do nothing to hurt our country?" asks Linda.

"No. Now what do you say?" asks Don.

"Yes, I'll help. What do you want me to do?" asks Linda.

Chapter 5

Don hands both of them two folders. "I need to find all the information you can for these men."

File one, Justin Michaels. (Linda)

File two, Master Powers. (Linda)

File three, Blake Rogers. (Jimmy)

File four, Turk Evans. (Jimmy)

I need to know their status and everything you can find on them, good or bad, and I need this data as soon as you can provide it. These computers here can hack any system in the world now; you should be able to locate these men and give me a status."

Jimmy and Linda stand there looking at Don. "What are you waiting for? Get moving," says Don.

Linda and Jimmy take the black book Don handed them with the codes to log on to the computers, and they start their searches. Don leaves them to retire to his lab in one of the lower levels to work more on a lifelong project. Don has been working on an A.I. (Artificial Intelligent) computer the size of a baseball. Don calls the new creation PING, mainly because it makes that noise as it is activated.

Don built PING capable of scanning an area using various types of scans, X-rays, different light spectrums, and heat signatures, and PING can perform infrareds scans. PING can interface with any computer. Right now, Don is working on the possibility of anti-gravity so PING can travel under its power. It's been a bit sticky. Don has tried Magnetism, and it works if there is a magnet to repel back. But Don wants to make it so Ping can defy gravity any place. Don taps into one of his advanced companies, which he keeps secret. Don uses this place to develop technology for defense. His other projects include invisibility and force field battle suits which act like exoskeletons. Then Don hits on the idea for PING. Force fields can be generated around the sphere, and it can repel itself up or down, and if applied correctly, PING can propel itself forward or backward. (*I'll get right on it.*) Thinks, Don.

I'll have to try to keep PING about the size of a softball when I add all this stuff. Maybe I can get the components to be smaller; I'll check on one of my other companies. To see if I can get smaller components, I can maybe add more to PING as time goes on. Another possibility is that PING will also be able to make himself invisible. Don continues on his project until late in the night. Don puts his hand to his face and wipes it. *"I have to get some sleep he says to no one."*

Don walks over to the far side of his lab, lays on a couch, and falls asleep.

In the late morning, Don is awakened by a buzzer sounding off. Don sits up, rubs his face with both hands and yells, "What!"

"It's me, Alexander, sir. Do you want breakfast?"

"Sure, Alexander, I'll be up in a few minutes."

"Do you want your usual, sir?"

"That will be fine, Alexander; give me a few minutes; I need to clean up."

"Yes, sir, also Linda and Jimmy have their reports ready for you."

"Thank you." Don gets up, takes off his clothes, and then off to the shower; after the shower and some clean clothes, Don feels like he can face the world again. Don climbs the stairs up four flights to the cafeteria, where he sits with Linda and Jimmy at a table.

"Alexander told me you have the reports for me," mentions Don.

Linda speaks up, "Justin Michaels is in prison for life for killing the people that he was guarding as a security guard. McMaster Powers has disappeared over the Amazon; he has been missing for the past six months. No one seems to know where or how he disappeared; they're searching for him in secret."

"What do you have, Jimmy?"

"Blake Rogers has been murdered; they found her body or what was left of it in the Nile River. Turk Evans is now the head director of a C.I.A. branch."

"I see. said Don. Linda see what more you can dig up on Michaels, and please be quick about it. The life expectancy in federal prison can be short. Also, I need to know why he killed his charges. There may be more to this than what we're seeing."

"Sure, Don, I'm on it. Give me a few hours. The equipment you have here is fantastic. They nearly hack the security of a secure computer almost by themselves. Oh, another thing, I saw a secret memo that Michaels must die for some national security reason. I'll be back shortly," says Linda.

Linda picks up Michael's folder and heads back to her computer station. Jimmy seeing Don's breakfast, realizes how hungry he is.

"Who do I ask to get a breakfast like yours, Don."

"Ask Alexander here; I'm sure he'd make you breakfast."

"Alexander, would you make me a breakfast like Don's"

"Young man, is that how you ask someone to do something for you?"

"Usually," said Jimmy.

"That will not do at all, young man."

"Ah, my name is Jimmy."

"Master Ko, you will address all your requests with "PLEASE, or a THANK YOU! Is that understood, or you'll be making your own meals."

Taken aback, Jimmy straightens up and makes his request again to Alexander, using a, please. Alexander looks at Jimmy, then turns away to go back to the kitchen to make Jimmy his breakfast. A short time later, Alexander returns and, with a flourish and places Jimmy's dish before him. Jimmy grabs a fork to start eating when Alexander takes the plate away.

"Master Ko, it's customary to say THANK YOU! Now after me repeat please, and thank you."

"Jimmy does as he's asked. Thank you, Alexander."

Alexander replaces the plate of food, and Jimmy starts to attack it with gusto. Alexander brings Jimmy up short again.

"Master Ko, don't eat with your mouth open, and keep your elbows off the table."

"Alexander, you sound like my mother."

"I see she failed to teach you manners. Sir, you will learn them, or you'll go hungry. From now on, you'll dress for meals; failing to do so will make you go hungry. Do I make myself clear, Master Ko?"

"Yes, sir! Alexander."

During the exchange, Don just sat there trying to keep from laughing out loud; Don hadn't had as much amusement in a long while.

"Jimmy, what do you think of my master chief and bottle washer?"

Jimmy is too stunned to say much of anything.

"Is Alexander always like that? asks Jimmy.

"Pretty much. When I was a child, I got the same treatment. Learn what he teaches you. You never know when you might need it," states Don.

At the end of the meal, Linda returns with concern written all over her face.

"Don, they're going to kill Michaels in prison."

"What did you find out about why they put him there?"

"The records say he killed his charges, a father and son. Michaels claims he didn't do it. They found Michaels knocked out with the murder weapon in his hand, and the two people lay dead in the next room. It's suggested that Michaels tripped and hit his head during his escape."

"Can you find more information? Also, look up who Michael's handler was, and the ones they was found dead; something is starting to get suspicious. I may need to get to Michaels as soon as possible."

"I'm on it." Linda turns away and heads to the computer room.

Chapter 6

A few months ago, Justin Michaels was sent to Syria as a bodyguard for a visiting prince and his son. They were there to make a deal for the sale of Oil to the country of Japan. Justin was to see to it that the prince was protected. Over the few days taking care of his charges, he became friends with them; the boy was full of questions about America, especially the cowboys, and Indians. Justin answered the boy's questions, knowing ten more would pop out. Justin didn't mind; he was thinking of when he was young and all the questions he had asked his grandfather.

The prince saw Justin's plight and told his son to give Justin some space. Justin smiled and said it was ok; I remember being a child. The prince looked at Justin and smiled a thank you. All the last four days went much the same. On the last day, while alone with his charges, a man in black kicked in the door and shot Justin with a sleeping dart. Putting Justin in a drugged sleep before he passed out, Justin said, "Run!" He was too late. The intruder pulls Justin's gun, kills the prince and his son, and then places the weapon in Justin's hand. Justin wakes with an angry security chief leaning over him.

"Why did you kill the prince?"

"I didn't," crooks Justin.

"The facts don't bear you out. They point to you as the killer. From what we can deduce, it's your gun that killed the prince and his son in the other room, in your hurry to escape, you ran into the table and hit your head. Hence we find you here."

"That's not what happened. I was shot and rendered unconscious. I yelled at the prince and his son to run, and that's all I remember," stated Justin.

"We don't believe you. You'll be deported back to the States and tried for this crime. Take him away."

Shackled and under heavy guard, Justin is taken to the nearest military base and shipped home. The military court condemned Justin to life in a federal prison. For the last six months, Justin clings to not killing the prince and his son. In prison, Justin soon realizes that he won't live long enough to serve his life sentence; the rumor is that whoever kills Justin will receive a pardon.

Justin is on constant alert. He has had to either kill or maim his attackers. It got to the point that the prisoners avoided Justin. Then one day, Justin is assigned to laundry detail in the dungeon, which is down in the bowels of the prison. As he arrives, Justin starts working and is beset on all sides by the other convicts. They manage to subdue him and hold him down while the biggest man, Truck, kicks Justin, breaking Ribs and smashing Justin's head, nose, and pretty much his face. With his jaw broken, Justin scums to unconscious the cons leave Justin to die.

Hours later, a guard, checking the dungeon, finds what's left of Justin and calls the medics to come and collect him. They transport Justin to the prison hospital and manage to stabilize him. Don, through the help of Linda, finds out the current status of Justin Michaels and that he may die. Don contacts his doctor, who happens to be his friend, and asks him if he would look over a patient and determine some things for Don. Will the patient live, and can they use any drug to kill him without killing him? The Doctor said he'd be willing to help Don. Doctor Phillips has been let in on Don's plans and has been helping him all along.

Don pulls a few strings with a Senator who owes him favors and gets permission to inspect the Federal prison's medical facilities.

Doctor Phillips enters the jail as the inspecting physician and Don as his secretary to write the final report about how well it's being run. Don and Phillips are met at the main gate, then escorted to the medical center.

"I hear you have a patient; I wish to see him and the attending physician," commands Doctor Phillips.

The orderly disappears down the hall to get the attending Doctor. In the meantime, Doctor Phillips looks over Justin as he lies in his hospital bed. He was reading his chart and the monitor equipment. Phillips is looking over the medical file and notes on Justin's injuries. He has broken ribs, a broken jawbone, and his face is bandaged but badly damaged. Doctor Phillips is amazed that Justin is still alive due to all the damage done to him. Phillips is surprised that Justin can breathe. The attending Doctor shows up, and Phillips asks all the questions about what has been done for Justin.

"Dr. Phillips, we're doing all we can in this facility to keep him alive. But I don't know why. No one in his condition would want to live; he needs to be rebuilt from the inside out. We don't have the funds to do that. From his chart, we're doing all we can. I don't expect him to live more than a few more days."

"I see, doctor; after looking over your patient and looking around here at your clinic, I see you're doing the best you can; I'll make a full report to Congress to see if we can get a few more improvements and updates to your facility," states Phillips.

"Thank you, doctor Phillips; any improvement would be appreciated. Is there anything else we can do for you?"

"No, I have what I want. I'll return in a few days to see how the patient is doing. Will that be alright with you?" asks Phillips.

"Sure, anything."

"Then we'll be back tomorrow. Then I'll inform the warden of the visit," said Phillips.

Don and Phillips are escorted out to the main gate. In the car. "Well, Phillips, can we safely kill him?"

"No, Don, if we do, we could kill him for real."

"Could we fool the equipment and simulate his death?" queries Don.

"How?"

"Just suppose I have one of my gadgets that could disrupt the equipment and make the attending Doctor believe Justin died. I have Kimberly, my driver, and Alexander show up and pick up the body and spirit it to your hospital where you can take over keeping him alive until I can get a specialist here to do the reconstruction," says Don.

"Ok, Don. You only have until tomorrow to produce this so-called gadget, and I wonder if it'll work. Let alone get it through the gate."

"I'll see you in the morning, Phillips."

They return to New York State, where Doctor Phillips leaves to go home. Don races to his lab to bring Ping out of his box. Don explains to Ping what he wants Ping to do tomorrow and that Ping has to stay invisible the whole time and remain silent.

Ping gets excited when he gets out in the world and pulls in some direct input.

The following day, Don tells Ping to go invisible *(The invisibility comes from a series of micro-cameras and L.E.D. screens surrounding Ping›s casing, what is on one side of Ping will reflect on Ping›s screen side, causing him to vanish.)* Don puts Ping into a bag; then, Don walks out of the base to pick up Doctor Phillips. They return to the prison to look over the progress of Justin Michaels. Just before the prison gate, Don releases Ping. Doctor Phillips looks at Don, «What did you just do? What›s all this waving at empty air?»

"Later, Phillips, right now, we need to get into Justin's medical room."

Both men show their I.D.s at the gate and are admitted; then, they are escorted to the medical bay and turned over to the staff there.

"Doctor Phillips, you're back."

"Yes, I said I would be."

The medical aide escorts the Doctor and Don to Justin›s bed.

"What's his condition today?" asks Doctor Phillips.

"Not very good; I suspect he'll die in a matter of days." answered the orderly.

Standing by Justin's bed, Don turns his back to the Doctor and the orderly and makes a sign to Ping, who happens to be floating near the ceiling. Moment's pass, the medical equipment flat lines and the bells and buzzers go off, bringing the medical staff to Justin's bed. Doctor Phillips starts to resuscitate Justin when the prison doctor stops him.

"You can't push on his chest. The broken ribs will puncture his organs. All we can do is hope."

The orderly checked Justin's pulse. And Justin's other vitals. Ping interferes, and soon Justin appears to be dead.

"Doctor Justin is dead time 12:23 PM." states the orderly.

Doctor Phillips turns to the prison doctor and asks.

"Doctor, I'm experimenting on organs and wonder if I can get this body moved to my clinic where I can experiment on them; the sooner, the better."

"Which organs, Dr. Phillips?"

"All of them, and I need them to be as fresh as possible."

"It goes against protocol, but your reputation precedes you. I'll give you the body at no cost to my department. And the paperwork will also be less. Thank you."

"Thank you, doctor; let me place a call." Doctor Phillips makes a call to a cell phone to Kimberly and Alexander, who are waiting with an ambulance to pick up the body. While waiting for the ambulance, the prison doctor works on the paperwork, and Doctor Phillips signs everything necessary. The ambulance arrives to pick up Justin's body at the finish of the paperwork. In the meantime, Ping is acting like a life support system for Justin, keeping him alive and still.

Kimberly and Alexander arrive with the gurney and are directed to the room where the body is. They start to move Justin and Don stops them. Don remains in the room with Justin and tells Ping to elevate the body using force fields.

"Ping, move Justin's body to the gurney," commands Don.

Kimberly and Alexander watch in amazement as the body elevates from the bed and moves over to the gurney; at the same time, Don has Alexander open the body bag and hold it open so Ping can slip Justin into it. Don takes a bottle of oxygen and puts it into the body bag attached to the tubes in Justin's mouth and nose holes. Ping, still invisible to the eye, slips into the bag with Justin to act as a life support system for Justin for the trip back to base. As Kimberly zips up the body bag, the prison medical staff and Doctor Phillips return to where the body is. Armed with the forms and signed paperwork, all four head out the prison's main gate.

Chapter 7

The four are stopped at the gate by the guards.

"We'll inspect your body bag to make sure no one is trying to escape." barks the guard.

Alexander opens the bag, and the guard peers in to see Justin's lack of a face, and nearly throws up. "Get out of here. The Doctor already cleared you. That's disgusting; it looks like his face was pushed into a meat grinder. The guard turns and runs to the nearest bathroom.

Kimberly drives the ambulance back to the base with Alexander and Doctor Phillips. Don drives his car and follows them. Back at base, Kim drives the ambulance into the garage and parks; Alexander and Doctor Phillips pull the gurney out, rush Justin to the medical center, and hook him up to life support. Don instructs Ping to remain invisible and return to the lab. Doctor Phillips has the nurse at the center take vital signs and blood for tests. Don and Alexander bring in the X-Ray equipment to X-Ray Justin. An hour later, Doctor Phillips looks at the X-Rays.

"My God! How is it this man is alive?" exclaims Dr. Phillips. "His ribs are all crushed, his face and skull have been cracked and broken, and he has no face to speak of. Most men would have died under these circumstances. He still might."

"Dr. Phillips, can you repair him?" asks Don.

"Not sure; I don't have any way to rebuild his ribs or his face. All you have, Don, is a soon-to-be corpse."

"Dr. Phillips, let's assume we could fix Justin. What do you need?" queries Don.

"A new set of ribs, sternum, and skull. Suppose If had them to hand. How would I go about to perform surgery to put all that into place. Then not kill him," said Dr. Phillips in a matter-of-fact voice.

"let's assume I can supply you with the ribs and sternum. Could you perform the surgery?" pleads Don.

"Ok, if I had a new rib cage and could graph it to his spinal column, I might be able to."

"Good; what kind of material should it be made from?" asks Don.

"A titanium alloy, that each rib would be hollow so I can fill it with the bone marrow from Justin's ribs; otherwise, let him die. The marrow is what will be needed to make new red blood cells. Without being able to replace his old blood cells with new blood cells, he will die anyway."

"Dr., how much time do I have to get you a new rib cage?" asks Don.

"A few days at best. I will have to open him up, remove all the shattered bones, and preserve them so I can extract the marrow. I will need to get the marrow into the new sternum. The new serum recently developed for cancer patients will help the bone marrow grow and start producing. There may be a chance. When can you get me that rib cage?"

"Dr., I will have that cage in two days; Now, I need to get moving. Dr. Phillips, get what staff you need, and Kimberly will pick them up and deliver them here."

"Ok, Don, let us both get cracking," stated Dr. Phillips.

Don contacts one of his companies, gives them the weight and size of Justin, and tells them to use a 3D printer to make a titanium alloy rib cage, and it's to be done around the clock to save a man's life. All production stops, and the printer is re-programmed to comply with Don's demand. In two days, the hollow titanium rib cage is complete. It's then rushed to the airport, where Don waits to receive it.

In the same two days, Dr. Phillips brought his best people to the base in a covered limo, so they can't see where they are. Dr. Phillips proceeds to open up Justin to remove all the broken bones in the chest cavity and to clean up some of the punctured organs, then cleans out the chest cavity to keep it free of infection. As the Dr. finishes, Don informs him that the new rib cage is here. Then asks the Dr. what he should do with the rib cage.

Dr. Phillips leaves his staff with Justin so he can examine the construct. Don brings the cage to the clean room and suits up before getting it to where Dr. Phillips is. Dr, Phillips is elated about the new ribcage; now, if the bone marrow takes, this young man may survive this first stage of surgery. In the next 12 hours, the Doctor and his staff transferred all the bone marrow they could into the new rib cage, then they placed the new rib cage into Justin's chest and managed with some difficulty to hook it up to the backbone. Dr. Phillips and his team manage to close up Justin, and now they wait. They inject the serum into Justin, hoping his body will accept his new rib cage and start growing new blood cells. All anyone can do now is watch and wait. Alexander is kept busy feeding the staff of Dr. Phillips. Undaunted, Alexander whips up a steak dinner for all and serves them as if everyone was at a 5-star eating place. After the repast, Don shows them some apartments where they can shower and get some sleep. Dr. Phillips sleeps in a room next to Justin and has his nurses keep an eye on Justin just in case.

Justin survives the surgery, and the cancer serum is working fine; his lungs are working on their own, and the subsequent surgery will be Justin's face and skull.

"Don, I don't have the skill to do the surgery for Justin's face and skull; someone more capable will have to do it."

"Dr., I've contacted just such a person, and he'll be here late this evening. I was wondering if I could keep some of your staff on hand to assist the Doctor coming from France?"

"Is this person who I think is Don?"

"Yes, Durant is going to fix the face and skull of Justin."

"I will lend my staff and be on hand as well. I want to meet Durant; he's world-renowned for his work. Have you given any thought to a brain surgeon?"

"No, I haven't. Do you have anyone you'd recommend?" queries Don.

"I may know of a couple of people; let me check up with them," said Dr. Phillips.

"I'll leave it in your hands, my friend," says Don.

Justin, in his current state, is having a reoccurring dream. He sees the prince and his son being gunned down by a dark figure as he falls to the floor. Justin considers the dark figure but can't make him out. It's as if he should know who it is. Then Justin falls into a pit of darkness.

Doctor Durant shows up the next day after a long flight across the Atlantic and is greeted by both Don and Dr. Phillips.

"Dr. Durant, it's nice to meet you at last," said Dr. Phillips.

"Why thank you, and you are?" asks Durant.

"Quite so; I'm Doctor Phillips from N.Y."

"I've heard of you; it's nice to make your acquaintance," said Durant shaking Dr. Phillips's hand.

"Don, my friend, it's been too long since I saw you last. How have you been?" asks Dr. Durant.

"I'm fine, Dr. Durant; it has been a few years. After you see the patient and make an assessment, we can get together and catch up."

"Lead the way, Don."

Don leads Dr. Durant to see Justin. On arriving at Justin's room, Dr. Durant removes the bandages from Justin's head.

"Oh my, this poor fellow is in bad shape. He'll need an extensive jaw work to rebuild. Then a full face rebuild, that will take large skin graphs from his back. His skull may be cracked. He'll need some work to fix or replace parts of it. What happened to this man?" queries Dr. Durant.

"A mob of men beat him up," said Don.

"That would explain all the damage; I'll start work tomorrow morning. Do you have any medical staff to assist me?" queries Dr. Durant.

"Yes, Dr. Phillips here will lend you a hand and his staff. Will you need anything else?" asks Don.

"That'll be enough for now. Do you have a composite picture of what the patient needs to look like?"

Don produces a laptop and calls up a 3D picture of the face Don wants to make Justin look like. It has a hawk-like appearance with a small scar on the left side of his face.

"This looks good to work with; why the scar?" asks Durant.

"It adds character to his face and makes it more rugged. Is this a problem?" asks Don.

"Not at all; usually, most people want a perfect face, no marks," said Durant.

"Can you work with this, Dr. Durant?" asks Don.

"Not a problem; who will make the prosthetics when we need them?" queries Durant.

"As you give me what you need in measurements and shape, I'll have it printed up. Is there a particular material you would like it constructed of?" asks Don.

"The type of plastic used in most prosthetics these days; it's non-toxic. I'd be interested in this 3D printer of yours that I heard about; that may be my payment for this job. It would speed up my future surgeries," comments Dr. Durant.

"Durant consider it a gift. I'll even have one of your techs trained in how to program it, and I'll see to it that you have a lifetime supply of the plastic and a printer," said Don.

"Enough talk; let's get started." Durant and the nursing staff set up to begin the operation, which will take many days. Skin grafts, and plastic parts all come together and Justin's new face is rebuilt, and each day for several weeks the bandages had to be removed, and his wounds cleansed and re-bandaged. Durant had to return to France, so Dr. Phillips and his staff continued a round-the-clock check on Justin.

"Don, I've contacted a brain surgeon to look at Justin's injuries to see what can be done," said Dr. Phillips.

"Thanks; when will he be here?" queries Don.

"He's on his way now and should be here tomorrow. I'll be at the airport to pick him up, then I'll bring him here to look at Justin."

"Thank you, Dr. Phillips," said Don.

Dr. Phillips leaves with some of his staff in the back of the van, so they don't know where they are and are returned to the city. Don sits by Justin's bed and talks to him.

"My friend, I hope you are dreaming well; the road I have planned for you will be dangerous. I've created some special tools for you to use in our quest for justice. I hope they'll be enough to keep you safe." As Don takes Justin's hand.

CHAPTER 8

Late the following day, Dr. Phillips and Dr. Stanton arrive via the van to look at Dr. Stanton's new patient to see if he can help bring him back to normal after meeting Don and reviewing the file and tests for Justin. Stanton makes his prognoses.

"He appears to be young enough to recover; he has sustained some brain damage; his long-term memory will be fine, but his short term is severely damaged. If you gave him instructions, he could understand and even accomplish them, but ask him an hour from now what he did, and he couldn't tell you," said Dr. Stanton.

"Dr. Stanton could we plant a microchip in place of the damaged area of his brain with sufficient storage to compensate for his loss?" asks Don.

"I guess it's possible; my collages have debated this as a possible way to cure mental Illness. To date, it hasn't been successful. Not to mention the Technology is not available to do this. This becomes a moot point for our patient."

"Dr., let's assume for a moment that the Technology is available. Could you implant it?" asks Don.

"I've done it to mice, never humans; I know the procedure. But as I said, without the Technology…" said Dr. Stanton.

"Dr. Stanton, I may solve your Technology problem; can you stay here for a week?" asks Don.

"A week? I'm not sure I should stay unless I have a patient," states Dr. Stanton.

"Please give me until tomorrow Doctor. And I'll give you access to the Technology you are unaware of," said Don.

"Ok, I'll be here tomorrow, Don; you have me curious about this unknown technology," mused Dr. Stanton.

"Good, let me show you to your room, and I'll have Alexander whip you up something for lunch. Do you have a preference?" queries Don.

"I'll take what I can get; it's not like you could whip up a good plate of Escargot," said Dr. Stanton.

"You might be surprised, Doctor; Alexander is a great accomplished chef. Among other things," said Don.

The following day, Don brings in the special chip and microcomputer to be implanted in Justin's head. Dr. Stanton is impressed.

"Where did you get this Technology? This is the very thing we've been looking for," chimes in Dr Stanton.

"One of my companies has developed it; this'll be the first time it's used, but the tests show that it'll work," says Don.

"Well, let's get started. Do you have a staff of nurses to assist me?" asks Stanton.

"They're in Justin's room waiting for you." indicates Don.

Dr. Stanton is led to Justin's room, where everything is ready for him. Stanton lays open Justin's scalp the cuts away a small section of bone, opening up the area that has been damaged. Stanton removes the damaged section of the brain. He inserts the micro-computer into Justin's skull, ensuring he can secure the computer to the inside to keep it from moving around due to possible impact causing more damage.

"So, how do we connect the computer to his brain?" asks Stanton to Don.

"Let me show you," Don pulls up a viewing screen to show Justin's head where the computer was placed and turns it on. It shows the computer; then, Don injects Justin with a syringe full of dark fluid. Immediately on the screen, there is activity as the nanites do the rest of the work connecting the computer to the brain.

"My GOD, man, what is happening?" exclaims Dr. Stanton.

"I've injected nanites into the wound, and at a molecular level, the nanites are making all the connections between the brain and the computer," explains Don.

"This'll make brain surgery obsolete. Do you understand the ramifications of this?" Exclaims Dr. Stanton.

"I do, Dr. Stanton. It'll make people whole again in time when they are programmed properly. Currently, it's not ready for the world to use. It's too dangerous."

"But you used it on Justin," stated Dr Stanton.

"Yes. But in this case, I had no choice; I do, however, have a way to control the nanites that only Justin has, that no one else has. You see, Dr. Stanton, if the nanites don't dissipate and get removed into Justin's waste system, they can cause a new type of incurable cancer. I can control the nanites and prevent it from happening," declared Don.

"Then why not present this to the world?" asks Stanton.

"It's not ready; I'll keep you apprised of the Technology and when we can make it full proof. You can have it for free," said Don.

"Great, let me finish closing up the skull and scalp to let him heal," said Dr. Stanton.

"Thank you, Dr. Stanton," says Don.

Chapter 9

Justin is now in full recovery; Dr. Phillips has the nurses back off on the drugs they've been giving him. In a week, Justin is now free of the coma-inducing drugs. Don and Dr. Phillips monitor Justin to see how he is breathing and whether his body works independently without help. All of Justin's wounds are healed; now, for the hard part, will he wake up?

Dr. Phillips has started Justin on physical therapy to get his body back to some form of the condition. One evening while a male nurse was working Justin's arms and legs. Justin kicked out, then started moving his fingers and toes. The nurse calls for Dr. Phillips and Don to come to see that the patient is moving on his own.

"You say he was moving alone?" asks Dr. Phillips.

"Yes, Doctor. When I was moving his leg, he shoved me away on his own, then his fingers were moving, and his toes." stated the nurse.

"That's a good sign; he is coming around," said Dr. Phillips.

Don and Dr. Phillips check on Justin; seeing all his scars and wounds are healed by this time. At the same time, in one of Don's secret labs. Someone working on the nanites. Copies all the files and steals the nanite generator along with a sample of the nanites. Sebastian Cross (a scientist) disappears along with the information and equipment. Back at base.

"Justin, wake up! As Dr. Phillips shakes Justin, son wake up!"

Justin appears to be swimming up from the deep, and he opens his eyes ever so slightly. He sees a black man hovering over him. "Where, where am I?"' asks Justin.

"You're safe here, Justin," said Don.

"But where am I? I'm still a bit fuzzy."

"You're in my lab; you are no longer in prison," states Don.

Dr. Phillips is checking Justin's vitals, and he pokes and prods inspects his ears and looks into his eyes. "Say Aaah." Dr. Phillips checks Justin's mouth and throat.

"You look reasonably fit for a man severely beaten to death. Starting tomorrow, you will be getting more physical therapy. It'll take a few months for you to be up to par, and I want you to take it slowly, or you'll cause yourself harm." said Dr. Phillips.

"Whatever you say, Doctor." croaks Justin.

The following day, the nurses remove all the IVs and monitors so Justin can move about. The physical therapist comes in and starts to massage Justin, but to Justin, it feels like a heavy-weight wrestler is manhandling him as the therapist twists Justin's arms and legs. When the therapist is finished massaging Justin, he helps Justin out of bed to help him stand up. Justin tries to stand up erect. The therapist moves away to get a walker when he sees Justin collapse to the floor in a heap. The therapist picks up Justin and sits him on the edge of the bed.

"Sorry about that, Justin. Are you OK?"

"I'm fine, Tony; how long have I been here?" asks Justin.

"Seven months, twenty days, and a few hours give or take a day," said Don, who just walked through the door into the room.

"Who are you?" asks Justin.

Don turns to the therapist, "Please continue Justin's exercise. Don turns back to Justin. My name is Donald, but please call me Don."

During the conversation, the therapist manages to get Justin into a wheelchair, and they all walk down to a swimming pool, where the therapist dumps Justin into the pool.

"Hey! What are you doing?" splutters Justin.

"You can't walk yet. This'll help you regain your strength as you exercise in the pool. The water is shallow enough to use your legs to stand on, and the water will keep you buoyant. You'll stay here for an hour today and longer each day after. I'll place the wheelchair at the far end and help you out. Now walk! If you like, I'll leave you long enough to swim." said the therapist.

Don asks the therapist to leave the room and says that Don will watch over Justin for several minutes. Don wants to talk to Justin alone. The therapist leaves the room.

Don pulls up a small bench while Justin bounces up and down.

"Son, I need to talk to you," says Don.

"Don, we're the same age, are we not?"

"In years, but not experience. Let's talk, I have much to tell you, and you'll have to make some decisions."

"What decisions?" asks Justin.

"I'll get to that. Now here's a mirror to look at your face."

"What the hell happened? This isn't my face!" shouts Justin.

"When you settle down, I'll explain," says Don.

Justin just stared into Don's eyes, with piercing brown eyes; if looks could kill, Don would be dead.

Don launches into what happened to Justin, his frame-up, time in prison, and all the repair work that went into him. Justin feels like a fool for what he is thinking.

"Alright, Don, what must I do to save my life."

"That depends on you, my friend."

"Explain it to me. Nothing is ever free. There's always a price." states Justin.

"You are correct; there's a price. The only difference is that you get a choice."

"OK, what choice?" asks Justin.

"I'll explain all to you that I can. If you choose to join us, I'll explain more about this new organization I'm building. Is that fair enough?" queries Don.

"Alright, I'll listen," says Justin.

Don launches into his explanation. He expounds upon what this new organization will be doing and the possible role Justin will be playing.

"You want me to be an assassin and a policeman?" states Justin.

"Yes, and no! I would rather that we discredit a person than hand him over to authorities, but there're some people too powerful to take down short of killing them," explains Don.

"OK, who picks the target? I'm not going to be a human robot and just kill as ordered. I did that in the CIA; I'll not do it again." stated Justin with some heat.

"You'll have the greatest say in the target. I present the arguments for my choices and the need to expedite the action; then, you choose if you'll take the mark. But not to worry, you need a lot more training."

"What kind of training?" asks Justin.

"Some training may seem strange, but it'll be necessary. Before we start your training, you need to be able to walk and run. Then I have a new friend you need to become acquainted with."

"Who is this friend you speak of?" asks Justin.

"It's not time yet. You haven't agreed to work with us yet, so until you do, you concentrate on getting back in shape."

"OK, when do I have to decide?" questions Justin.

"As soon as you learn to walk, you'll need to decide."

"I'll consider it then," says Justin.

Don helps Justin out of the water and into his wheelchair. Don pushes Justin to the cafeteria. "Justin, your first set of lessons will begin here; Alexander has been instructed to teach you how to properly order and eat your food."

"What? I know how to order and eat my food," said Justin.

"Do you know how in the presents of the gentry?" asks Don.

"What?"

"You may be called upon to eat in formal dining; a slip could cost you a lot, maybe your life."

"I've watched formal dining for the last two years of my service.I think I can muddle through," said Justin.

"Alexander takes this seriously; see that young man over there; his name is Jimmy. Alexander has been teaching him how to properly dress, order, and eat his food. Jimmy complies with Alexanders' requests, or Jimmy doesn't get to eat."

"Why so picky?" asks Justin.

"Alexander takes food and dining seriously. He had served Kings and other dignitaries before he came to work for me. He'll teach you how to fit in at places you may attend."

"I have not accepted your proposal yet!" said Justin.

"Well, let's just say I have faith in you, Justin," comments Don.

Alexander approaches the table, "what may I prepare for you, gentlemen?"

"Hi Alexander, my friend Justin can't have solid food yet, so one of your soups for now. And I'll have my usual veal special," says Don.

"Will there be anything else?" asks Alexander.

"No, that'll do. Alexander, meet your new student, Justin, for as long as he's here."

"Very good! Sir," responds Alexander.

Alexander leaves, and 20 minutes later, he returns to serve their dinner. Alexander watches as Justin starts to eat his soup with a disapproving frown on his face.

"You, sir, eat like a barbarian. You would give yourself away and prove that you are uncouth. Here let me show you." Alexander takes a soup spoon from his pocket, passes the spoon over the surface of the soup, and then places it into his mouth as if he were performing in a dance; his movements are fluid and graceful.

"That master Justin is how to eat your soup properly."

Justin was flushed with embarrassment, and for some reason, he wanted to win over this man Alexander. Justin then mimics what Alexander just did. "Much better, Master Justin." Alexander smiles.

"Alexander, I thank you, and I'll endeavor to improve. I'll look forward to further instruction," states Justin.

Alexander bows to Justin and leaves.

Don watched the exchange between the two men and was almost smiling.

"You handle that very well, Justin. Whether you realize it or not, Alexander seems to like you."

"How can you tell?" asks Justin.

"You told him you would try to improve. Jimmy, there is improving, but he never complements Alexander. Jimmy needs to learn that he should. Hence his harsher treatment. I enjoy watching them; it's amusing," says Don.

"Tell me more about this organization as we eat," says Justin.

"No. You've not agreed to join us. I've told you all you need to know until you make a decision." said Don.

As they sat eating in the dining room, a leader was assassinated someplace in Europe, and there was no mark on the body. The leader was very healthy and could not have died of natural causes. Poison is suspected in the death, but an autopsy shows no poison was used, or at least not one they can detect. It drives headline news, but it goes unnoticed for the time being.

Chapter 10

Don brings in a man who is a master at martial arts, and Justin is being retaught how to fight again. Justin is slowly recovering; he's now up and walking, then soon, he's running and swimming laps in the pool. Now the day comes, and Don wants to see Justin in his office. Justin comes in knowing what the discussion will be about.

"Well, Justin, what's your decision?" asks Don.

"I get to call the shots for the target?" asks Justin.

"There'll be exceptions, but yes, you'll call the shots on the targets."

"Good, I want the man who framed me and killed my charges," states Justin.

"I knew you would; we're building the file as we speak. Does this mean you're accepting the job?" asks Don.

"Ok, I'll accept. When do we get started?"

"You already have. You need some more training, and I'll introduce you to the rest of your team."

Don leads Justin out of his office and takes Justin on a tour. They stop at the brains of the complex to meet Jimmy and Linda.

"Justin, this is where we'll get our intel. Jimmy here is the youngest of our group and can tap into most money institutions. Linda here is good at getting government information. They both have been busy setting you up with a new identity as Nick Conner."

"Who is Nick Conner?" asks Justin.

"From this moment forward, you are; Linda will bring you your history file; I want you to memorize it. You'll find it interesting. Then I still have some classes you'll need to attend." said Don.

"What classes?"

"I have set it up to teach you the art of illusion and con-jobs coupled with critical thinking. You already have been working on your martial arts training. Follow me; I have some others you need to meet. Kimberly Burk, my driver, and you already know Alexander."

"Yea, I know Alexander; he wrapped me across the knuckles with a spoon when I was using the utensil the wrong way to eat." snarled Nick (Justin).

"Nick, you and Alexander will have to work that out. Right, Jimmy?" said Don.

Jimmy grumbled but didn't say anything.

"Come along, Nick; we have more to see."

Don leads Nick away from the computer center to the garage, where they meet Kimberly working on a car.

"Kimberly, come meet Nick Conner."

Kimberly is a redhead with green eyes and a smile that lights up the room. She's dressed in overalls and holding a socket wrench in her hand with a dark smudge on her face. Kimberly extends a hand to Nick, and he takes it for a quick shake knowing his hand will be greasy when they finish.

"Kimberly, do you have a clean rag?" asks Nick.

"Yes, I'm sorry I should've wiped my hands before we shook," said Kimberly.

"It's quite Ok. I need the rag to do this." And Nick reached up and wiped the smudge off her face, then his hands.

Kimberly turned bright red, and Don laughed. "Come this way, Nick; I want to show you something," said Don.

"Are you going to show him the car Don?" asks Kim.

"Yes, Kimberly, do you want to come along?"

"Yes! I would."

Don leads Nick and Kim over to the far side of the garage and opens a hidden wall. Behind it sits a silvery car, like no other car in the United States or any other country.

"This Nick will be your car. You'll become familiar with how it works, and Kimberly will show you how it works. Kimberly will also maintain it. Any questions?"

"Yea. When do I get to drive it?" asks Nick.

"Not today; I have other gadgets to show you. Kimberly will provide you with the booklet on the car so you can see its capabilities," said Don.

"I will do that right away, Don. I'll see you later, Nick." Kim blushes as she turns away.

"It looks like you have made a conquest, Nick," said Don.

"I didn't do that intentionally; I was just being friendly," confirms Nick.

"Be sure you let her know that. Now follow me into my dungeon."

Don leads the way to a lower level of the complex to Don's workshop.

"Ping! Show yourself," commands Don.

From out of midair, a baseball-sized orb comes floating over to Don. Don holds out his hand, and Ping sits down on it. Don turns to Nick.

"Nick, this is a member of your team; his name is Ping. He's an AI (Artificial intelligence) and will always be with you. I have set it up so he can interact with the chip in your brain."

"You mean he can read my thoughts?"

"No. But Ping can help you. What languages can you speak?"

"English, and Arabic. Why?" says Nick.

"Ping knows every language on the planet; through him, you can translate what you hear; he can also read and translate."

"What else can he do?" asks Nick.

"Ping has various scan modes; he can track spoor (DNA) with infrared he can show what happened in a room if the heat signature is not too old or has been diluted by too many other bodies. Ping will also go out of his way to preserve your life."

"Nothing like having a bodyguard around. What am I going to be; a glorified detective with a side kick?" asks Nick.

"As a matter of fact, yes! Ping can also drive the car too."

"That could be handy," said Nick.

"Follow me, Nick; I have another item to show you."

Nick follows Don to another room off the lab. "Here is the last piece of equipment I want you to see for now." Don opens a case to show Nick his battle suit.

"What is this?" asks Nick.

"I call it a battle suit; as you can see, it is silvery as the car; it can make you disappear; it has force fields to repel bullets up to 30-caliber in size; beyond that, you'll die," said Don with finality.

"When can I get started," asked Nick.

"I have your first assignment, and we are still collecting as much intel as possible."

"I thought you said I get to pick and choose my targets," said Nick.

"You do; however, you may have to follow my suggestion this time and at others. Let me explain."

Don launches into his explanation about his companies where they are experimenting on nanites, how one of his senior scientists disappeared, along with a nanite generator and all the files on how to manufacture them as well as program.

"What has me concerned is that the scientist is using the nanites is causing all these unseemly related deaths. He has become an assassin for hire. What scares me is if that technology gets loose in the world, it can kill everyone much like a plague," said Don.

"You mean an extinction-level event?" asks Nick.

"Very much so, not only people but every living thing," states Don.

"I see why you want me to do this job first; where do we start?" asks Nick.

"Aren't you concerned about the threat to your life?" queries Don.

"Don, you should know better; I have put my life on the line countless times; I'm not going to back down now!"

"Well, as it stands, we are safer here than anywhere else. You especially; see Nick, your force fields in your battle suit, and Ping will keep you safe from the nanites. The force fields in your battle suit will keep them from getting to you."

"Only if your scientist friend doesn't know where we are located," said Nick.

"As far as I know, none of my companies know of this place, only the people here and a few certain friends."

"Right now, we need to track him down; I have Jimmy and Linda doing that now. We need to find out where he went so you can run him to ground."

"Fair enough, and yes, I would've picked this target," said Nick.

Chapter 11

"Let's return to the computer center to see if Linda or Jimmy have anything on our man Sebastian Cross."

Don leads the way up a few levels and arrives at the computer center.

"Linda, Jimmy have you found our man Sebastian Cross yet?" asks Don.

"On the night of the break-in, we have a video on Sebastian in the lab. We see him steal the generator and then leave the building. Later we catch snippets of him taking a train and, hours later, boarding a plane to Britain. We get a clear picture of Sebastian leaving the plane in Britain. Jimmy is trying to follow him right now after he disembarked from the plane." states Linda.

Nick walks up behind Jimmy. "Well, what have you found so far, Jimmy?" queries Nick.

"What are you watching, Jimmy?" asks Nick. "Right now, nothing. I have a couple of computers sorting through cameras and looking for anyone with Sebastian's size and features; I'll have some results in an hour."

"Until the computer completes its process, I can only wait. I'm a Harry Potter fan watching The Chamber of Secrets; why do you ask?"

"What is that, a dragon?" asks Nick.

"No, it's a Basilisk, a mythical creature."

"It looks rather scary, doesn't it?" said Nick.

"I guess so; why are you interested?" asks Jimmy.

"I will need a symbol to work under; why not a Basilisk? Besides, Batman has been taken already."

"A symbol?" asks both Don and Jimmy.

"Yea, when we start operating in the background when people hear whispers of The Basilisk, this will make them edgy, and in some cases, fear can do more than pain. Jimmy, send me what you can on this Basilisk. I want to learn more about it." said Nick.

"Is it alright to send it to your terminal?" asks Jimmy.

"That'll be fine, Jimmy."

"It looks like you'll need a crash course on your suit and the car Nick; you'd better come with me," said Don.

While they wait for Jimmy to locate Sebastian, Don takes Nick to the lower levels and helps Nick put on the suit. Ping is now visible and is floating just above Nick's head.

"Nick, I want you to repeat after me. Mary had a little lamb; its fleece is as black as night."

Nick repeats the words. "I thought it was as white as snow?"

"It was; now, the suit will respond to your voice. Ping can also control your suit, and you're now tied together. Ping will follow you were ever you go. Now say helmet!" said Don.

"Helmet!" and a helmet forms around Nick's head. "Wow! That's so cool; how do I take it off?"

"Retract!" said Don.

"Retract!" says Nick. The helmet folds back into the suit." Oh my! This is so cool; what else does it do?"

"Many things, and right now is not the time to go through it all. To turn on the force fields, say exoskeleton!" commands Don.

"Exoskeleton! Am I supposed to see anything?" asks Nick.

Don walks over to a drawer, pulls out a gun, and before Nick can react, Don shoots him with a 9-mm pistol, and the bullet bounces off.

"Are you trying to kill me?" shouts Nick.

"No, just demonstrating what it can do; in a while, you will experience a bruise where I shot you; your force field will stand up to a 30-caliber bullet, but you'll feel the effects of the impact. You'll survive, but it'll hurt. I cannot change the laws of physics, but Ping can help to deflect bullets. Now walk over to the bench over there."

Nick walks over to the bench. "Do you see that 400-pound weight? Pick it up."

"You're kidding, right?" said Nick.

"Pick up the weight," commands Don.

Nick reaches out and grabs a handle on the weight, lifts it off the bench, and almost tosses it over his shoulder. "This is incredible!" exclaims Nick.

"One last thing, Nick, stand over by the wall."

Nick complies with Don's request. "Now say invisible!"

"Invisible!" Nick disappears all except his head.

"Now Nick walk over to the far wall."

Nick stays invisible, but as he changes position with each step, he shimmers like heat from a very hot highway.

"Won't they see that if I move?" queries Nick.

"You must take care when you use that mode. Walk over to the mirror over there."

Nick walks to the mirror, and instantly, it's like looking into infinity.

"That's a good reason to stay away from mirrors when invisible; it provides a feedback loop. I'm working on both problems. As I correct the glitch, I'll upgrade the suit and car."

"What about guns?" asks Nick.

"What would you like to use?" asks Don.

"I'd like a pair of 45's. "

Don walks to the drawer and pulls out a pair of matching 45s. "Is this what you wanted?"

Nick takes the guns and feels the weight of them. Don shows Nick where the holsters are, and then Nick asks for some throwing knives. "Sometimes these babies make too much noise."

Don slides a panel to one side and shows Nick a fine selection of knives. Nick selects a couple of them and slips them into his boot tops.

"Nick, this is all the time we have to go over how the suit works; there are other features. Ping will use them if needed. Trust him!"

"If you say so, Don.

At that moment, Jimmy calls down to Don. "I believe I've found our man."

Don and Nick head for the computer center. Jimmy brings up what he found on the large screen as they enter.

"It appears that our man has landed in France. I tapped into the street cameras and tracked him to this address." Jimmy hands Don the address.

Chapter 12

"Let's get your gear together, Nick, and get to the airport; I'll have a cargo plane ready to go," said Don.

Nick returns to the lower lab and collects his suit. As Nick returns to the garage, Kimberly checks the car over.

"Nick, let Ping drive it until I can show you how to drive. He's programmed on how to use all the features, and he'll return it in one piece," explained Kim.

Nick smiles and speaks. "By your command Kim."

Kimberly turns red. "Where can I store this suit in the car?" asks Nick.

Kimberly gets in the car and pulls a handle, and the trunk in front of the car opens. Nick stores the suit and weapons in the same place. Don shows up and gets into the driver's seat.

"Get in, Nick; we have to go," said Don.

Don drives out of the garage and onto the road toward the airport.

"Car Corvette-red," commands Don. And the car changes its shape visually but not physically.

"Don, why the red Corvette?"

"It's what the cargo crew has seen and will expect."

"All I have to do is say a command, and it'll change?"

"Yes and no, go ahead and try it."

"Car, change color to blue," commands Nick.

Nothing happens. "Why didn't it change color?" asks Nick.

"In a sense, you haven't been introduced to the car. You haven't been added to its recognition codes, and your DNA hasn't been entered. It'll only respond to Ping and me. The car is built not to respond to anyone it doesn't know." explains Don.

"That could be good or bad, depending on the situation," states Nick.

They arrive at the airport and drive to the private hanger; as they approach the hanger, there's a cargo plane waiting with the tail open and ramp down. Don drives aboard, and the car gets tied down to the plane's cargo deck. Don and Nick strap themselves into the not-so-comfortable seats to wait for takeoff. Once in the air, Don takes Nick to the plane's cockpit to introduce Nick to the cargo crew. Nick returns to his seat; it's a 12-hour flight to France; just as well get some sleep. Nick straps himself in and goes to sleep.

Don comes down to the cargo area and finds Nick sound asleep. Don is tired, but he can't sleep on a plane for some reason. Don won't admit it, but he hates to fly. Don reviews Nick's file. He was a Navy Seal, and you learn to sleep in the CIA when you can. Don dozes off. The next thing, Nick is shaking him awake.

"We're here, Don. You'd better strap in."

"Oh. Thanks, Nick."

The plane has landed, and soon Don is driving them off the plane and into an obscure town.

"Do you know where to go, Don?" asks Nick.

"Actually, no, but Ping does, and he's now doing the driving."

"Ok, I just thought I'd ask; I'm sorry I did." Nick looks over to the front console where Ping sits. Then shudders in his seat.

Two hours later finds them at a farmhouse in the country. Don takes over the wheel and drives past it just out of sight.

"Nick, you best change into your battle suit."

"Why, your scientist seems harmless enough."

"It's not Sabastian I'm worried about. It's the nanites."

"Yes, you're right," said Nick.

Nick gets into his battle suit, and he turns it invisible. Ping follows suit and becomes invisible, and tags along with Nick. As they approach the house, Nick gets a bad feeling, like he did when he was on a mission in the Middle East. It's as if something wrong has or is going to happen. Nick pulls out his 45 pistols, and as quietly as possible, he creeps up to a window.

Nick sees nothing amiss, so he proceeds to the next window; nothing appears out of place again. Nick is at the door, and he opens it slowly and steps in. Nick proceeds to investigate the next room when he realizes Ping can do this much more quickly than he can.

Whispering, "Ping seek."

Ping takes off, and in moments, he signals Nick to the back bedroom. Nick moves off cautiously in that direction. Nick enters the bedroom and finds Sabastian lying on the floor, dying. Nick moves over to Sabastian and comforts his head.

"Make me visible." And the suit changes to look like a tee shirt and jeans.

"Who are you?" squeaks Sabastian.

"Someone who's looking for you. What happened to you?" asks Nick.

"The prince, Sabastian, coughs roughly. He was coughing badly. He took the nanites, he thinks it's some poison, and the prince will use it to kill off all the people above him so he can take over the throne. Whoever you are, you must stop him!"

Sabastian grasps Nick's suit. "He'll unwittingly release the nanites, and they'll kill everything. All life on this planet will die in a year if you don't stop him." Sabastian releases Nick and dies.

"Ping, scan the house, and I'll riffle through the house to see what we can find out about this prince."

Ping starts in the room, and he records everything using infrared and other scans. Nick looks through Sabastian's belongings and finds papers and documents. Ping locates a hidden place in a floor vent where additional documents are located. Nick collects the information and puts it with the other papers to be looked at later. Upon leaving, Nick has Ping call the French police to come and collect Sabastian's dead body. Nick returns to the car with the information, and Don drives off to a more secluded place of concealment.

Chapter 13

"What did you find, Nick?"

"I'm not sure, Don. Sabastian is dead; he said some prince killed him and that he has the nanites and the generator. The prince, whoever he is, doesn't know what he has or how dangerous it is; according to Sabastian, the prince thinks it's an untraceable poison."

"Did Sabastian say anything else?"

"Sabastian said that in a year, everything will be dead if we do not get the nanites back."

"Nick, scan all that paperwork into to scanner; the prince may be named. We have to get to him before he uses the nanites."

Don contacts Jimmy and Linda to check the satellites to see if the prince's car may have been caught and where it went. Nick scans the paperwork he found in the hidden place on the floor, then follows up with the other documents. Ping downloads the scans he took of the house. As they review them, they can see where the prince and a few of his henchmen entered the house and what paths they took based on the heat scans of Ping. Based on Ping's scan, they determined that the murder and theft took place 30 minutes before they got there.

An hour later, Jimmy calls back to say that that area is so remote it's not scanned by camera or satellite; he's now searching Sabastian's finance records. A company has made a few transactions into and out of Sabastian's account. "I'm working on it, Don, and will get back to you in a bit when I peel this onion."

"Thanks, Jimmy," said Don.

"Don, what do we do now?" asks Nick

"We drive to the airport to see if we can head off our prey."

"Should I get out of this suit?" asks Nick.

Don looks at him and speaks. "Suit command change to jeans and a tee shirt."

The suit obeys and projects what Don has commanded. Nick looks down and sees a colored tee and blue jeans that look worn.

"Nice threads, and the funny thing is it feels like what I see."

"It's one of the programs I programmed into the suit. Suit command change into a formal suit black."

"Wow, it feels as restricting as a suit," and looking it over. "Hey, nice suit. I could get used to wearing this all the time," said Nick.

"I'm glad to hear it; you may need to wear it for long periods."

"Suit command change to tee and jeans," said Nick.

The battle suit complies with the command.

"Nick, we'll be at the airport soon; any idea who we're looking for?"

"No, Don. There are so many princelings in the middle east it could be any of them. Let's hope Jimmy can identify the company that paid Sabastian for the first few attacks."

"Agreed. Jimmy, have you managed to track down our man yet?"

There was a pause for a few moments then Jimmy responded. "Not yet, Don, I'm still hacking at the company, and it seems to be a shell within a shell. Much like a Russian doll."

"I understand, Jimmy. Time is of the essence; please hurry!" said Don.

"I have all the computers working now, and Linda is also helping."

"Give me an update as soon as any information becomes available. Nick and I are arriving at the airport in less than an hour; we'll need to know who we're looking for."

"Ok, Don, we'll keep you appraised as soon as we find out."

The prince is only forty minutes ahead, and instead of going to the airport, they return to the penthouse to prepare to leave. The prince clutches the poison (nanites) vile and the small hand-held activator-generator.

"This'll make me king of our region once I remove all the brothers and cousins between me and the throne."

"Prince Abdula, will this not make you a target or create suspicion in others about you?" asks one of his men.

"I'm sure it will. Fortunately, I don't have to be present to kill them, and I intend to poison myself to throw off suspicion. A poison that is easy to cure. I'll have someone else add the poison to the others and activate them from a distance. Who'd suspect me then?"

"Not a bad plan, my prince. One worthy of a great king."

"We're here now, so get up to the penthouse and collect what we need and check out before the authorities can detain us for the good Doctor's death."

They enter the penthouse and see it has been trashed, as if someone was looking for something. The prince's two men and the prince himself pull guns as they search the rooms for the intruder. The prince hears a muffled sound, much like a gunshot. Then another.

"Guards, where are you!" The prince gets silence. "Guards!" still silence.

The prince dashes to the door; as his hand grabs the door knob, another muffled shot rings out dropping the prince on to the floor. The prince is lying there as his life drains away; he hears footsteps approaching him. Then he's rudely turned over onto his back, and he can see the man who shot him.

"Well, prince, you won't be king after all. Now where is this so-called poison and the activator?"

The prince says nothing. The killer riffles the prince's pockets and finds the vial of nanites, and in another pocket, the killer finds the activator.

"Thank you, prince; I'll put this to good use. You know, prince, I could get used to killing royalty. I shot a prince and his son about a year or so ago. This'll make it easier to do in the future."

CHAPTER 14

The killer tucks away the items into his pocket and leaves the apartment. The intruder exits the elevator at the hotel lobby and then enters the crowd. At the airport, Don and Nick wait for the prince to show up when Jimmy calls them and informs them that the prince is dead in his penthouse. Jimmy gives them the address. Don drives them close to the hotel, and Nick and Ping exit the car stealthily. Nick and Ping move into the lobby of the hotel. They locate the penthouse elevator and enter it, and Ping zaps the controls, which allows them to go to the penthouse floor. The door opens, and the police guarding the entrance has his gun leveled to shoot anyone who steps off the elevator. No one steps out, so the guard looks inside and sees no one. When the door opened, Nick and Ping moved out of the elevator to avoid the guard, and they moved on down the hallway to where all the activity was taking place. Nick had Ping go through all the rooms and scan for everything. An hour later, after dodging the police investigators, Ping returns to Nick, and they both leave, bumping into one of the men and knocking him down. Then Nick and Ping exit down the hall to the stairs. The inspector picks himself up. "What happened?" he looks around to see who knocked him over and finds no one near him. The inspector shrugs and goes about his business.

Nick and Ping run down a few flights of stairs and reenter a hallway where he can board an elevator. Two policemen pull Nick to one side to question him as he steps off the elevator. Nick had turned off the stealth mode and settled for the tee shirt and jeans look.

"What's wrong, officer?" asks Nick.

"We want to know how you got onto that elevator; now start talking."

"I was on the 6th floor and had finished visiting my friend; I was just leaving," said Nick.

"That's a lie; put your hands on your head and turn around."

Nick complies, and as he turns, he whispers stealth mode and disappears in front of the officers. With that moment's distraction, Nick ducks down and then moves away from the officers toward the door. Just as Nick steps outside, the police shut down the hotel. No one leaves or comes in. After bumping into people on the crowded sidewalk, Nick manages to travel down the street to where Don is waiting. Nick opens the car door, steps inside, and commands the suit to put him into a business suit.

"Oh! There you are. You stirred up a hornet's nest in the hotel." states Don.

"Sorry, I couldn't help it, I tried to leave like any tourist, and they caught me coming off an exclusive elevator. And I bumped into a police officer as I left the crime scene."

"Well, the two incidents caused the problem, you should've stayed in stealth mode, and you wouldn't have caused a scene."

"Alright, Don, I need to take the classes you suggested; your right about the illusions it would have helped here."

"Did you get the nanites and the generator?" asks Don.

"No, according to Ping, they weren't there, and the prince and his men were dead. Someone beat us to the draw."

Don contacts Linda and Jimmy and has them pull down all the camera data from the motel before the police confiscate it.

"Nick, we need to return home and see what Ping and the others manage to pick up."

"Don, why do we need to travel all the way home? Can't we process what we have here?"

"No, Nick, I have not built the car as a command center, and it is limited. I will, in the future, make that possible. I'm as frustrated as you are now. We need to get the nanites back now."

Don Takes them back to the airport, where they board the plane and take off to return to the States. For the twelve hours in the air, Nick looks over the file sent by Jimmy about the mythical Basilisk. Nick reads one of the files. The Basilisk is a mythical animal that ranges from a foot to one hundred feet long. The male has a red plume running along its head. It's very venomous. But the deadliest feature is its eyes; direct eye contact kills instantly, and a reflection of looking in its eye causes you to turn to stone. The creature was created by having a toad hatch a chicken egg. In medieval times this was a crime punished by death. Nick muses over this information on the flight back and decides to adopt it as his calling card. Nick decides to talk to Jimmy to see what they can come up with program-wise.

Chapter 15

After several hours of flying, Don and Nick return to their hidden headquarters. Nick leaves Don after changing out of his suit and heads to the computer complex to talk to Jimmy about the Basilisk idea.

"Jimmy, I like the idea of the Basilisk. Can we program my suit and Ping to project this mythical creature?" asks Nick.

"What suit and who is Ping?" asked Jimmy giving Nick a strange look.

"You know, the battle suit."

"Not a clue Nick."

At that moment, Don walks in and catches some of the conversation.

"Nick, Jimmy has never seen the battle suit nor seen Ping. Ping show yourself," commands Don.

Ping materializes, shocking both Jimmy and Linda.

"Wow, says Jimmy, can I touch it?"

"It's ok, Ping. Allow Jimmy to touch you," said Don.

Jimmy walks over to Ping as it floats in the air, and Jimmy reaches out and touches Ping. It's warm and feels like glass as Jimmy runs his hands over the surface.

"This is amazing! What type of programming Don?"

"It's a new language one of my companies invented, but I can give you access. What Nick has been chatting about makes some sense. I'm not sure the Basilisk is the right choice, but Batman has been taken." Jimmy, Linda, I'll have a computer sent here by tomorrow where you can program both Ping and the battle suit. I have some other things I need to look into so you guys can put your heads together to see what you come up with about Nick's idea," said Don.

Over the next several days, Don and Linda analyzed the camera data in and around the penthouse and its lobby, trying to see who passed through it and if they could track down the prince's killer. While Nick and Jimmy play with some programs to make Nicks's battle suit project a Basilisk. Ping became the Basilisk's eye. And the program could expand from human size to twice that with the help of Ping's Hollo projector. Using the 3D printer, Jimmy was able to make some coins the size of silver dollars for Nick to use as calling cards.

Jimmy made two kinds, one with a silver edge and one with a gold trim. The gold-edged coins were toxic. If you touched it with your bare hands, you'd become paralyzed due to the toxins that coated it. The coins must be handled with gloves.

Meanwhile, Don and Linda spot someone in the pictures that suggests this person is of interest. Don calls Nick to come to view this person on the camera.

"Do you recognize this man in the picture?" asks Don. Nick looks at the man in question, and after a moment, Nick realizes this is his handler from the CIA.

"I do recognize him. He was my handler when I was in the CIA. He pulled me from the field and made me the bodyguard for the prince and his son." exclaims Nick.

"The very same," said Don. "I've been suspicious of him for several years. Linda, I want you to find out all you can about Mr. Lynch. I suspect he has the nanites."

"It can't be; he was my friend," Nick exclaims.

"I'm afraid it may be Nick; I've followed him and his team. All of his people are now dead in the field. Kill by accident or in the line of duty. You see, Nick, I had picked four people for your position; you're the only one currently alive or available."

"What happened to McMaster Powers and Blake Rogers?" asks Nick.

"Turk is one of the head men at the CIA; McMasters has disappeared somewhere over the Amazon; he was never found. Blake Rogers was murdered. What's left of her body was found floating in the Nile River. I'm sorry, Nick," said Don.

Chapter 16

As Don and Nick search for Lynch and the nanites, we turn back to the late 1700s, when we run into a promising doctor of biology who had just graduated from his school of advanced learning in Germany. Exeter is looking for a place to set up his lab. He wants to explore a project which is frowned upon by his peers; it's even against the known laws of the time.

Exeter wants to see if he can save people from death when they die. His theory is plausible, as yet untried. Exeter intends to remove a person's head and keep it alive so we don't lose the information the mind has or can build on. His experiments on rats have proven successful. Then one day, on his way home, he watches a dog get run over by a carriage and is dying, so he collects the dog and performs his procedure, and the dog's head lives.

Exeter now feels he can do a human head next; his time comes unexpectedly. A boy was run over in the street by runaway horses pulling a carriage. The boy's body was severely crushed, so Exeter collected the body and removed the boy's head, and performed his procedure. The head lived. Exeter found two problems with his experiment. The first one is how to keep the special chemicals coursing through the head, and the head cannot communicate. It can hear, maybe see. For now, he had to settle with yes or no answers using eye blinks.

Exeter had another chance to collect another head. Jon was headstrong and dueled a lot. This time, he insulted a Duke's son, who took exception to the insult and fought in the early morning hours. His friend was mortally wounded. Exeter managed to get the body back to his lab in time to remove his friend's head and place it next to the boy's head alive. At this time Exeter is getting old; he must pass on his knowledge to a younger man.

Exeter follows the students at his old university until he locates a student with similar views, then recruits the young man. Shows him all he has done and some of the problems he has experienced. The young man is impressed. Kurt wants to learn from Exeter. Exeter teaches Kurt all he knows about the solution and how to do the surgery. Not long after the training, Exeter is dyeing, and Kurt uses his mentor as his first subject, removes his head, and sets it up.

Kurt is forced to move the lab to a different place; any day now, he may be discovered by the police and put in jail. This process gets passed down through the years from mentor to student. The first world war is just on the edge of happening. The current student packs up the lab, and with help from an assistant, they cart off the lab to an abandoned castle and locate the lab in the catacombs below the castle. Safe from the war, Hans (the current mentor in a long line of mentors) and his assistant start to modify the head's environment using new technologies. By the time World War two started, Hans set up a way for the heads to be able to speak using electricity and a speaker, so now the heads could communicate. What Hans didn't know was the heads could communicate with each other without the speakers. Mind to mind.

Hans was getting too old; he contacted the German high command to talk to a German officer. He got the general's Aide and explained that he had a literal think tank and would like to show him how it worked. The Aide was offered the incredible heads, giving him much to think about. The Aide kept the place secret, and he added several more heads to the collection. The think tank was then turning out plans for superweapons that Hitler demanded.

Hans died, and the Aide took over; this place was on a need to know only basis. According to Hitler, only the Aide and a few assistants need to know. World War II ended, and the Aide tried to get to Hitler to get his head but was too late, so he returned to the castle. By this time, they had collected nine heads, each prominent in their field. The other heads were abandoned and left to die.

With time came the computer, then the intranet, and the heads had access to the world, and over time, they generated billions in money buying and selling companies. The companies they preferred; were computers and robotics. Over time they invaded the Japanese markets for robotics and AI (Artificial intelligence). The goal was to build android bodies.

In the meantime, the Nine would settle for using holographic projections to communicate with the people in the current world. Raven (Boy Leader), Sparrow (finance genius), Dove (Inventor), Swallow (Doctor of Biology), Crow (Chemistry), Magpie (Mathematics) woman, Cuckoo (Mechanical Engineer), Vulture (Doctor Exeter), and Seagull (Electrical Engineer).

The Dove and Seagull devised an idea to build a nanite factory where the nanites would be used for creating micro gears and micro hydraulic components to make androids that would go undetected among humans. Soon they would have the nanites and the generator. Lynch would quickly deliver them to us in a matter of days. At which time Lynch would become a liability and would need to be eliminated. This technology was still just an idea, hence the reason for buying into robotics and AI research in Japan and China.

Two days later, Lynch (Rick Stubbins) delivered the nanites and the generator to the castle of the Nine. Lynch entered the room and sat down; the hologram called the Raven appeared. "Place the nanites on the table with the generator," said Raven. "No, said Lynch, I'll keep them until I get paid."

"Take out your phone and dial up your account; it will increase by two million as agreed."

Lynch does as he is requested. Sure enough, his account increased by two million dollars, and he puts the nanites and generator on the table. With the transaction completed, the door opened.

"Lynch, will you work with us in the future?" queries Raven.

"If the pay is right, now, if you will excuse me, Raven, I'll be on my way."

Lynch gets out of his chair, exits the door, and travels down the hallway. As Lynch passes the last door, it springs open a huge mechanical hand reaches out and grabs Lynch and crushes him, then carries the body into the room to be disposed of in a furnace.

"This is Raven cancel the two-million-dollar payment to Rick Stubbins. Send in Patrick to pick up the nanites and the generator."

CHAPTER 17

Linda tracks Lynch from the building and down the street to a car without license plates, and she tracks it for a few miles and loses it because they run out of cameras and satellites, but at least they get a direction. Linda tracks ahead to the main road leading to Germany. Linda picks up Lynch as he heads from a sideroad to the main road, where she tracks him to another sideroad and loses him. Linda shows Don and Nick what she has.

"We need to go to Germany, Nick, let's go pack, and I'll call the airport and have my cargo plane readied for takeoff."

"Alright, Don, but shouldn't we have a more mobile command station so we don't have to fly back and forth from here and to where ever?"

"You're right, Nick, I'll adapt Ping to connect to here and itself, and it can act as a command station, as you say. I'll work on it on the plane, and Ping should be ready by the time we get to our destination."

Once in the air, Don takes Ping to a workstation and programs Ping to directly interact with the base computers in the States so they don't have to fly back whenever they need computer help. Upon landing, Don has Nick take the car wheel, and with Ping's help, Nick learns all about the car's systems. Ping can directly access them from where ever they are. Ping can access weapons, stealth modes, communications, and the ability to drive the car and its power plant.

"Nick put the car on autopilot and study the information on your battle suit. I have a feeling you may need it."

"If you insist, Don. Don't forget I was in the special forces and can care for myself."

"Maybe so, Nick, but with the suit, you will have more strength and speed; you have not used the forcefields of the exoskeleton yet and the enhancements it provides."

"Like how much stronger will it make me, Don?"

"At least twice a normal person's strength, and will allow limited speed, and you can jump much higher. We need to work with these things once this is over so we can determine your limitations with the suit."

"Wow, I could become the next comic book hero with this suit. It's bulletproof and has strength too."

"Nick, don't let it go to your head; we are to remain secret."

"I know, Don; it was just a whimsical thought."

"Do your musings alone, Nick; I need you to prepare for what may happen. Neither one of us knows what we're about to face."

Nick thought better than arguing further and turned to the manual online and studied the Battle Suits functions. Nick studies the suits invisibility mode, which he has already experienced. The different force fields, exoskeleton, and nanites that keep the suit in constant repair. And in an emergency, the suit can become airtight and supply a limited amount of air for up to 15 minutes.

"Don, if I read this right. If I'm in this suit and was dropped into a vat of acid, I could survive?"

"Yes, until the power or the air ran out. The force fields would last longer than the air."

"Yea, let's don't test that aspect of the suit. I'll trust what you say. Don, why do you want me to learn about illusions?"

"Study of illusions can be a great help; it will teach you how to do sleight of hand; while you misdirect everyone with one hand, you pull the trick with the other hand. Nick, only some jobs will require blazing guns and bombs. Sometimes a simple trick will accomplish what is needed."

"Like what, Don, being a pickpocket?" mocks Nick.

"Exactly! Learning to plan and use your head to pull off jobs with finesse," said Don.

"I see. What do you think of calling the organization The Basilisk?" asks Nick.

"I'm not sure about that, Nick. I agree we need a name; I'm not sure it should be that. But you and Jimmy seem to like it.

The car reaches the turnoff that Lynch turned on from the main road. Nick takes control of the car and follows the small paved lane into the deep woods. After driving for an hour, they come to an abandoned castle. Lynches' car is still there. Nick and Ping leave the car, and Don stays behind to monitor the progress through Ping's camera.

CHAPTER 18

"Ping, start scanning," said Nick.

Using infrared and other scans, Ping shows where Lynch left the car and walked up to the abandoned castle's foundation, where the scans disappear into the wall. Nick and Ping check around the wall to see if there is a switch or latch to open the wall. Nick can see an outline of the door, but he cannot see any way to open it. Nick tried to apply some pushing and shoving on the door, and it wouldn't move. Nick returned to the car to check if any C-4 explosive was part of the inventory in the vehicle trunk. To Nick's disappointment, there are no explosive devices in the inventory. Don opens his car window.

"What are you looking for, Nick?" asks Don.

"Some explosive to open the door. Do we have anything that will work?"

"Use Ping; he has a laser," said Don.

"A laser?" questions Nick.

"Ping, use the laser to cut down the door," commands Don.

Ping starts pinging away as a thin beam of red light flashes out, strikes the wall, and slowly cuts away the door leading into the castle. Nick returns, astonished at his AI partner's ability. In thirty minutes, Ping has cut down the door. Nick waits a few more minutes before they enter the castle to give the sides of the door a chance to cool down.

Ping starts scanning for Lynch and picks up his trail down a hallway. Nick pulls out his Colt 45 handgun and follows on the heels of Ping. They reach a point where Lynch is snatched and pulled into a room. Nick reaches the new door and begins to instruct Ping to cut down the door when Ping using a forcefield, shoves Nick back down the hallway. The door snaps open, and a claw protrudes to grab Nick, who isn't in its range. It returns to the room, and the door snaps shut. Ping had flown into the room as the claw reached out, missed its target, then returned to its position.

Ping finds Lynch's body and does a series of scans; the nanites and the generator are missing. Ping using the laser, begins to cut a small opening in the wall when a hollo-projected image of Raven appears in the room. Ping scans the rest of the room and finds nothing except for cameras and projectors.

"What are you?" asks Raven.

Ping stops cutting, so he scans the hollo image while making his pinging noise.

"Aha, you can't speak. Too bad, I must destroy you; I can't let you escape. Too bad for that sense, you look interesting. Claw, destroy the floating ball!" then Raven disappears.

The claw starts trying to catch Ping, and Ping manages to dodge the claw several times; then, using the laser, Ping cuts the hydraulics to the claw disabling it. After a time, the claw is on the floor. Ping using what little energy he has left, manages to cut his way through the wall. Ping leaves the room through the opening he made. Nick was there banging on the door when Ping fell on the floor next to Nick. Nick reaches down and picks up Ping.

"Hey, what's a wrong little buddy?" asks Nick.

Ping manages to blink a small light, so concerned for Ping, Nick picks Ping up and runs down the hallway and out into the open, returning to the car.

"Don, Ping is in trouble; what do I do?"

Don takes Ping out of Nick's hands and places Ping in the cradle in the car's console.

"Don, what is wrong with Ping?"

"Ping is low on power; he must have used the laser far too long; he'll be alright after he charges up."

"Don, I'm going back in there to see what's behind that door."

Nick reaches the hidden entrance when a rumble from deep within the castle shakes the castle. Nick barely escapes from the falling debris of the castle walls. Nick turns and runs. He returns to the car in time to watch the castle implode on itself. As he and Don watch, a cloud of rock dust covers the car and Nick. Nick's battle suit causes a helmet to form around Nick's head to protect him from breathing in the dust, and the face screen allows Nick to see the immediate area around him. Nick moves around to the driver's side of the car and jumps in, slamming the door.

"Shall we get back on the road, Don?"

"No, Nick, we wouldn't get far with the engine chocked with this rock dust. We'll have to sit here until it settles. We can't get reception with our base; the cloud is blocking our signal."

"Ok, Don, how is Ping doing?"

"He'll be charged enough in an hour to look at his scans; then we'll see what went on in that room."

Nick hates having to sit still. Nick tries to fill up the time with talking when Don asks him to be quiet so he can think. Don hates wasted time in this time of forced inaction. Don is thinking of installing an electrical motor and battery system into the car. Then they could drive away without hurting the engine. Don grabs a tablet and starts making notes and calculations for when they return to base. In two hours, the cloud settles enough to see the area, and Don decides to chance driving away, knowing Kim must rebuild the engine after they return. They return to the airfield, where they load the car back onto the plane for a trip back to the States, Ping has recharged and is zipping around the aircraft's cargo area.

"Well, Ping, what happened to you?" asks Don.

Ping returns to the cradle in the car, and on the car's display screen, Ping shows the recording of Raven and what Raven said. Then the fight with the claw that was trying to destroy Ping. Ping shows the scans of Lynch's dead body. Ping's scans also show that the nanites and the generator are absent.

"Who or what is Raven?" asks Nick.

"That's what I'm wondering?" said Don.

Don gets on the car's computer and contacts Linda and Jimmy to have them do any searches for Raven.

"Linda, Jimmy, I want you to chase down anything on a company or person named Raven. Expand the search as wide as possible; we don't know what we're searching for. Also, see who owned the castle we were just at."

"Sure, thing, Don, Jimmy, and I will get right on it. Did you recover the nanites and the generator?" asks Linda.

"No, Linda, the lead we had is dead. This is a new one. Consider looking into any corporations who use or deal with advanced holograms."

"We'll see what we can turn up before you and Nick return Don," chimed in Jimmy.

"Nick and I should be back in twenty hours; see you then."

"Don, what made you suggest holograms in the search?" asks Nick.

"Let me show you, Nick; Ping bring up Raven and display all other data you collected on Raven."

Ping puts up a display of Raven and splits the screen. On the left side of the screen is Raven; on the right side, all the data scans.

"Look here, Nick, you see Raven, he almost looks solid and real. See the right side of the screen; it's not alive; all Ping is showing is that Raven is nothing more than light and energy. A hologram."

As Don and Nick discuss their next moves in this game of cat and mouse, Raven and his disembodied gang are traveling in an underground railway system that was constructed in World War two underneath the castle to a new building in Germany where they will be housed and protected until they can advance the technology for androids that they can inhabit.

"Raven, what was that AI machine you encountered? Is it a threat to us?" asks Swallow.

"For the moment, I don't perceive it a threat; the claw and the castle's destruction destroyed it."

"Are you sure the AI construct was destroyed?" asks Dove.

"You saw the footage from the room. Did you see something we did not?" asks Raven.

No one spoke up; the trip to the new lab that they owned was made in silence. At the destination, the train car was hoisted off the tracks and pulled into its waiting slot in the above building, where the brains could be cared for.

"Vulture, can you program the nanites to take care of our maintenance so that we may dispense with some of these slaves," commands Raven.

"I can, but I'll need Cuckoo (Mechanical Engineer), Dove (Inventor), and Sea Gull (Electrical Engineer) to help," said Vulture.

"Do what you must, Vulture; I'll direct some of the nanites to the Chinese company we own to be incorporated into the robot bodies we are making," says Raven.

"Raven, we need to be careful with the Chinese Government. They're planning to take over our company by force, if necessary," states Sparrow.

"I have studied them for years, Sparrow, and knew they would try to break our agreement. They don't know that I've moved the information and specifications to Japan. When the Government moves in, they'll get a surprise. The battle bots will fight them off, then set off a small nuclear bomb destroying a great deal of that city," says Raven.

"Very good!" commented Sparrow.

"Yes, with all the safeguards in place, we can continue with our plans to make artificial bodies for ourselves, then we can conquer the world using the nanites to control the leaders of the world to do our bidding," states Raven.

Chapter 19

Don and Nick travel from Europe to the States to return to the base and go to the computer center to see what Linda and Jimmy have turned up in their search.

"Well, guys, what have you found in your search for holographic projections?" asks Don.

"We found a company in Japan that makes the grade of holographic projection you suggest, and that company was bought out before it could market the product. I've managed to track it back through several shell companies, but the trail ends in Switzerland," said Jimmy.

"What about the shell companies? Anything on them?" queries Nick.

"All but two of the shell companies are new or more recent companies, two of the shell companies are very old; we are talking a few hundred years old. They are not active like the newer companies, but they are active in purchasing chemicals and materials. That's all I have found so far," states Jimmy.

"Keep searching," says Don.

Don walks off, motioning Nick to follow him; they head down into the bowels of the complex.

"We need to check into the car and see how Ping is doing; now that he has a full charge, he may give us more information about what happened in that room," suggested Don.

They enter the underground garage and head to the car; Ping greets them, floating over the vehicle and pinging away as Don and

Nick approach Ping flies over to the men and floats over Nick's left shoulder.

"Hi ping, are you up to showing us what happened in the room at the castle?" asks Don.

Ping spins around, and on a blank wall, Ping shows a projection of what happened. Ping pushes Nick away from the door and enters the room, barely avoiding the claw; then, using his laser, Ping disables the claw. Then the hologram appears then disappears. Ping used echolocation to find a weak spot on the wall and, using the last of his power, cut a hole big enough for him to escape; then, he loses all his energy and shuts down.

"Don, why did you watch this again? We already watched this information?"

"Not exactly, we didn't. For instance, I didn't know why Ping pushed you; now I do."

"Yea, Ping did push me; I didn't think that was important. Now you say it is?"

"Did you not see your ex-employer on the floor? His body was crushed; Ping saw this, pushed you out of the way, and entered the room to gather information. Ping saved your life."

"Wow, I don't know what to say; I guess I'm glad I managed to scoop the little guy up and save him and his data," said Nick.

"The nice thing about it is that the programming I developed worked; otherwise, you would have joined Lynch in that room dead," muses Don.

"What!?" exclaims Nick.

"Nick, you have to understand all this equipment is experimental; I can predict what will happen within certain limits. It's when we reach the extreme limits; I'm not sure about it. This is why we need to run tests; some will be in the field," explains Don.

Nick goes to all the classes Don insists that Nick should take; in time, the magic lessons teach Nick some things he wished he had known for some of his past jobs in the CIA. Besides the magic tricks, the man taught Nick about con jobs and how they worked. This, too, would have been useful and may be useful in the future.

With all the learning, Nick had just remembered about the nanites and the generator when he was called to the computer center, where he was supposed to meet with Don and the computer team, Jimmy and Linda.

"We came at your call, Linda; please tell us what you found," instructed Don.

Jimmy pipes up, "I have managed to crack a few of the shell companies, and I found some very old companies formed in Germany during World War I. They kept buying certain chemicals and plasma or whole blood. The company was called The Nine. I ran across other companies called the triple triad."

Linda said, "They seem to create companies that use nine in their name. So, I started searching for companies with that name, and we found nothing else."

Don put his hand to his chin as if in thought, "Search anything that infers the number nine. For instance, September and other such words."

"Oh! I get it, Don. I will expand my search engine to go further afield," Jimmy mentioned.

"Don, the castle was owned by the group called The Nine, and they hold property around the world, most of it in Germany," states Linda.

"Good start, you two. I need the list of chemicals so I can consult with Dr. Phillips; maybe he can give a reason for using the chemicals. Keep searching and see what you turn up, be careful. They may build search traps with malware." said Don.

Nick was out of his element in the computer room and just listened. Nick is a good mission planner, he needs intel now. So, Nick can plan his next steps. Nick is beginning to see how Linda and Jimmy will be a big part of his planning.

Don takes the chemical list Jimmy printed out and heads to the garage to have Kim drive him to New York City to visit Dr. Phillips. "Nick, you need to ready the car and your battle suit; also, put the pilots on alert. We may need to fly back to Europe."

"Sure, Don. Does Kim have the engine rebuilt yet?" asks Nick.

"Let's go see," said Don.

Nick and Don enter the garage, where Kim is dressed in coveralls, wiping off her tools and putting them away.

"Kim is Nick's car ready to go?" asks Don.

"It was ready yesterday; I also managed to install the electric motor; it has increased the car's weight considerably. It now weighs as much as a Sherman tank."

Kim enters the locker room, changes her clothes into her uniform, then drives Don into town to meet with Dr. Phillips. Before they leave Don turns to Nick and tells him to get the car ready for a trip and to include his battle suit and Ping. Nick heads off to get the car ready to take them to the airport.

At the clinic, Don meets his friend Dr. Phillips. "Well, Don, you can't be here for a checkup. You're not on the schedule, so I assume it's a social call?"

"Not exactly; however, how about lunch at the club? Then you can tell me what these chemicals might be used for," Don hands Dr. Phillips the list of chemicals that Jimmy printed out.

Dr. Phillips wrinkles his brow and taps his glasses against his pursed lips in deep thought. "Are you sure about these chemicals and the plasma or whole blood?"

"Why yes, we found them ordered against an old company for over the last hundred years. Is there a problem?"

"Maybe, these are the same chemicals used in an experiment to keep a human brain alive after a man died of cancer. It was just an experiment to see if it could be done. It failed," stated Dr. Phillips.

"Has this ever been done in the past?" queried Don.

"Have you ever read Frankenstein by Mary Shelley?" asked Dr. Phillips.

"Yes, I have," said Don. "Why?"

"It was once stated that there is nothing new under the sun. There is a university in Germany where I went as an exchange student; there was a rumor about a paper written by someone called Exeter about this very thing. It was stored in the restricted section of the main Library. I would suggest you read it there," challenged Dr. Phillips.

"Ok, I will do that," said Don.

Both men leave Dr. Phillips's office and take the elevator to the parking area, where Kim picks them up and takes them to the club. As they wait at their table for the waiter, Dr. Phillips asks Don how he plans to read the paper because it's in German.

"Do you remember my softball-sized friend Ping? He can read German and give me an English translation," comments Don.

"Before you head out, let me give you a letter of introduction to give to the people at the university, and they will let you into the restricted area of the library," said Dr. Phillips.

"That will be a big help. Thanks!" said Don.

Kim drives Don and Dr. Phillips back to his office, where the doctor provides Don with a letter of introduction. Kim drives Don to the airport, where Nick is waiting. Nick opens Don's door and welcomes him, and then Nick turns to Kim, gives her a big smile,

and pays her a compliment which causes her to blush. Don and Nick
board the plane.

Chapter 20

Kim feels confused whenever she is around Nick. Kim watches Nick until he is out of sight. Kim returns to the base to wait for their return. On the plane Don calls up to the pilots and tells them the destination. Don then settles down with the book Frankenstein by Mary Shelley (first published in 1818).

"Don, why are you reading that book?"

"At this time, you would not believe what I suspect. For now, its research, and I hope I'm wrong," comments Don.

The rest of the flight is quiet, and Nick finds a comfortable spot and manages to fall asleep. Don on the other hand finds it hard to sleep on a plane and so reads his book and makes some notes. His friend Dr. Phillips's comment, "Nothing new under the sun, "keeps turning over in his mind. Then Nick is shaking Don awake and telling him they are landing and he should put on his seat belt.

They land at the airport which is a two-hour trip to the library Nick backs the car out of the cargo plane with Don in the passenger seat who soon falls asleep. For what seems like minutes, Nick is shaking Don to wake up; they are at the university library. Don takes a few minutes to wake up then he with invisible Ping enter the building leaving Nick behind. Nick's metal body parts would set off the metal detectors and bring every security man in the area; it's best to stay outside with the car. It would save time from having to explain his condition.

Don is directed to the restricted part of the library, Don hands over Dr. Phillips's request, and then Don is directed to a table to sit, then the attendant brings the paper Exeter had written back in the mid-1700s about the possibilities of keeping a human brain alive. The detail of the procedure it seemed to be very exact, like he may have actually accomplished it. Exeter had to say it was speculation because it would've been a jail sentence and then hanged. It was against the law to experiment on people, alive or dead, during that time in history. It was tampering with God's work so to speak.

Ping recorded the paper and translated it for Don to read later. Don called the attendant back and he turned over the paper to him and Don followed by Ping left the library to find Nick talking to a group of German students in English. The students learned that Nick was American and wanted to practice their English. Nick apologizes to the students. He indicates that his employer is returning, and he must take him back to the airport.

"Nick, what was that all about?" asks Don.

"One of the girl students came up to me ask me a question, and I told her I didn't understand, then she switched to English; she wanted me to take her to lunch."

"That explains one student; what about the others?" asks Don.

"When they found out I was American they all wanted to talk to me and ask questions, do we still fight Indians or ride in wagons, the usual questions," chuckled Nick.

They drove back to the airport so they could return home. On the flight back, Don mulled over the information from Exeter's report. The pilot informed them they would have to wait until tomorrow to leave, they are on a schedule for being refueled and won't get fuel until early in the morning this will give them a night to get some sleep and a chance to preflight the plane. Nick drove the car on to the cargo deck and tied it down, then he strung up a couple of hammocks for him and Don to sleep in. In the morning, they take off and return home.

They land at the New York airport and Nick drives Don and himself back to base and on the way, Don tells Nick what he fears about the information that he has gathered over these last days.

"Don, you have been quieting the whole way back from Germany. What have you been thinking about?" asks Nick.

"Ok, you must realize that I have no real facts, so what I'm about to say may be all wrong, but let me tell you what I suspect. Exeter's paper was written in the late 1700s, let's say 1780 or there about. Exeter made a hypothesis of how to preserve a living brain, and somehow, he got an opportunity and made it work," mused Don.

"You mean that this Exeter may have preserved a living brain, and over this much time, it could be alive?" asked Nick.

"I don't know; it may be possible. We can't discount that possibility. Dr. Phillips said two things that still haunt me. The first thing was, and I quote, "There is nothing new under the sun." The second was "that most if not all stories have or contain some truth" Exeter's paper was written as if he accomplished what he wrote about even though he wrote it as hypothetical.

"You mean that we may have a monster on our hands?" a shocked Nick asks.

"I don't know, but we need to find and take back the nanite generator or, if necessary, destroy it," stated Don.

"Don! Until we locate them, we cannot do any more than what we already have," said Nick.

"This is true, Nick, but this information from Exeter may give us a few leads to run down."

They check in at the base to see if Jimmy or Linda has turned up any possible leads for them to run down. Don and Nick enter the computer room to enquire if any leads have popped up. Don talks to the computer team and then asks them how far back in history they can probe. Jimmy says, " The records only go back to the first world war."

"No further?" queries Don.

"Not really; the only way we could go back any further is if someone has input the data into the computer archives," states Linda.

"However, the chemicals and blood records go back to the beginning of the seventeen hundred at the companies where they purchased the items," confirmed Jimmy.

"We did find three companies they purchased within the last ten years. The first one was a company that specialized in holograms in Japan, the next company was purchased in China it is a robotics company, and the last one was purchased in Japan another robotics/android company," commented Linda.

"Where in China?" asked Nick.

"We are not sure, but I can find out in a few days," boasted Jimmy.

"Ok, I will need that information to plan my infiltration," stated Nick.

CHAPTER 21

In Germany, the Nine make up a ghostly meeting of holographic people, with Raven leading the discussion.

"Fellow members, we now have the component we need to advance to the next phase of our existence; we have the nanites and the generator; I will send this to our Japanese plant and have the engineers working with Cuckoo (Mechanical engineer) and Seagull (our Electrical engineer) to create our new bodies,"

"What about our Chinese plant?" queries Sparrow.

"Dove has made up a mock generator, and I will include some of the nanites, to make the delivery appear to be authentic. Then the Chinese government will move in to take over. They want the war-bots we have created, but they want the nanites and the generator the most so thanks to Crow the plant will be leveled with a special explosive," states Raven.

"Who will go with the nanites and the generator to Japan?" asks Swallow.

"Vulture (Exeter) will go. He will get the first body; then he can test its limits, then he will be able to help the rest of us to transition to the robot bodies. Then eventually to the android bodies," said Raven.

"Are you sure you want me to get the first body?" asks Vulture.

"Quite sure Vulture, you have the most knowledge of the human body and will be able to make any corrections to the robot body that will be necessary for our survival. Also, you are the one who made us, so you, most of all, know of our needs. Then again, you are the most expendable of all of us," points out Raven.

"I see; when will I be leaving Raven?"

"I have set up your travel and as soon as this meeting is over you will be flying to our Japanese plant, you will be allowed to fly over Russia then over northern China to Japan. Have a safe flight," commented Raven.

"Yes, Lord Raven," as Vulture leaves the meeting to continue his trip to Japan.

"Raven, when do you want me to destroy the Chinese plant?" asks Crow.

"Have you removed the specs of all our robots and of the few of the robots we have constructed?"

"Yes, Raven, they are safely under lock and key in Japan. The Chinese spy is still unaware that we moved them out a week ago during a fire that was set as a distraction," smirked Crow.

"Very good, when the Chinese Government thinks we have the nanites and the generator they will move in to take the plant, then you may blow it up as we planned," stated Raven.

"You do realize that blowing up the plant will set off an earthquake? Don't you, Raven?" said Crow.

"I know now, Crow. No matter, do it anyway!" states Raven.

After a few more discussions, the meeting is adjourned. Exeter was packed up and shipped to the Japanese plant to begin construction of the nanite factory which will build the robot bodies for the Nine. Vulture will be able to start testing the bodies for their limitations and how to adapt to them, so they can be used by the Nine. Crow sent a locked box with lead bars to China by special courier to be taken to the China plant, which would trigger the spy to call in the Chinese army.

Within the week, Crow's fake box reaches the plant, so Crow begins watching the cameras at the plant to see when the army will show up to claim the factory for the so-called People's Republic. By the end of that day, the army invaded as Crow knew they would. Crow set off the explosives, it was a terrible destruction the whole plant was vaporized setting off an earthquake it even cracked the earth's mantle creating a massive pool of lava to form at the surface.

"Raven, the robot plant in China no longer exists, matter of fact all that is left is a rather large pool of lava according to reports. It's thought a nuke was used in its destruction," chuckled Crow.

"Excellent, Crow, now we wait for Vulture to make progress, and soon we all will have bodies again instead of a holographic one," purrs Raven.

Exeter arrives in his jar and is put in a particular office; with Exeter is his attendant to keep Exeter clean and fed. Exeter uses his holoprojector to work with the Japanese engineers to set up, and program the robot factory using the nanites. It takes three months to build the first robot for Exeter. During the construction Exeter directs the attendant in how to place his brain into the robot and activate the nanites to make all the proper connections so he can function.

Then the long process begins in learning how to use his new robot body. It takes weeks to learn how to stand up, then walk, and then run. The autogiros had to be adjusted in order for Exeter to complete this part of his testing. The robot bodies will make up for a few of the human senses they lost when they were removed from their bodies. Senses like sight, tasting, smelling, touching, and hearing. The robot body will now give them a few of the senses back.

Exeter can now hear and see. Over time, he may be able to bring about some of the other senses they do not have. Exeter and the Japanese have made some enhancements to the robot's ability to see. They will be able to see with infrared and other spectrums as well as normal sight. They have also enhanced the robot's ability to hear sounds and to be able to speak. The voice sounds electronic as he speaks; Exeter wants to improve this to sound more human. Then they will be able to pass themselves off as human.

Exeter continues to prove the robot body; strength control is the most challenging part. Over time Exeter manages to control that problem. After crushing several hundred hens' eggs he was finally able to control his strength so he did not crush the egg when he picked them up.

During that time, Nick has been busy planning his first assault on the Nine. Nick with the help of Jimmy and Linda he has been able to pull to gather a means of entering the plant and reaching the lower levels to spy out and to see who the Nine are. Will Nick be fighting normal men or robots? Nick studies the 3D map of the Japanese plant on his computer console, to see which way he can use to enter and leave the plant complex, hopefully without being detected.

Nick was not happy with the 3D map on his computer and then he recalls that there is a room which uses holograms this would give him the ability to walk through the plant and see everything. On his way to the room, Nick stops by the computer center and grabs Jimmy so he can show him how to work the controls.

With Jimmy's help Nick was able to plan several ways in and out of the complex. For Nick, it's best to use the easiest way to enter and have several ways to get out. The 3D hologram also shows Nick the surrounding landscape. Nick wished he had this when he planned his missions while working in the CIA.

The easiest way out would be the ventilation shaft that led to the roof for his escape. To get in to the plant, he would walk in through the warehouse as if he owned the place.

CHAPTER 22

Nick sat down with Don to go over the mission in detail with the possible changes. Don approves of the mission, hoping to get back the nanite generator, also with a chance of getting more information on the Nine.

Exeter was completing his testing and setting up the protocols for the others of the Nine to adapt to their robot bodies. Exeter communicated to Raven to let him know to send the rest of the Nine to the plant, three Robots were ready, and three more were on the table under construction. Raven agreed they would be transported to the Japanese plant in a few days, and the three members of the Nine would be chosen when they arrived.

Nick left with Ping and the car and headed to the airport to catch Don›s cargo plane for the flight to Japan to Pick up a couple of tractors and some tractor parts. With the plane loaded, Nick and the aircrew take off and head to SeaTac in Washington state, then to Alaska, and down to Japan. Nick puts up a hammock, and once in the air, he falls asleep; when he is not sleeping, he goes over the mission, looking for flaws in his plan.

After a couple of days, they land at Tokyo International, and the pilot taxis the plane over to the far side of the field near the private hangers. Nick drives the car off the cargo plane in its invisible mode and heads to Kyoto to execute his mission to locate and retrieve the nanite generator and the nanites. Then Nick was to gather further information on the Nine.

Nick drives the car to a place where they admit delivery trucks at the airport, and he waits until a truck leaves and the guards open the gate. Nick follows the truck up close and right out the gate; a little further down the road, Nick causes the car to go from being invisible to being a white Corvette, then continues down the road to Kyoto and to the robot factory. When Nick was within a mile of the factory, Nick had the car go invisible so he could follow another truck into the Nine's factory truck loading and unloading parking area.

Nick parks the car on the far side, where no cars or trucks are parked, and he and Ping leave the car. With stealth, they enter the ground level of the factories warehouse, where Nick and Ping locate an elevator to the next level. This building was deliberately set up to create a passage of mazes for security reasons. Cloaked in invisibility, Nick and Ping pass guards and people as they threaded their way to the elevator to the next level.

After an hour, Nick comes to the lowest level of the factory; Nick and Ping rode the last elevator down with a technician who was wearing a jumpsuit, so Nick copied it into his battle suit memory so he could move about visibly if he needed to. Nick paused after getting off the elevator to get his bearings. Nick proceeds down the aisle in the direction he thought would contain the nanites. Ping directs Nick to the room containing the nanites an hour later.

Nick is shocked when he enters the room and sees three complete robots and three more under construction. Fascinated, Nick watches the robots under construction they appeared to grow before his eye. *(If he had a microscope, he would have seen the micromechanical components being constructed by the nanites)*. Nick tore his gaze away from the robots on the table to look around for the nanite generator. He didn't find the nanite generator right away when he opened the cupboard doors and other components. Nick was about to move on to the next room when Exeter entered the room.

Nick stood stark still in hopes the robot who entered would not detect him; alas, it was not to be. In close quarters Exeter was blinding fast. Exeter smashed down on Nick and fractured Nick's left arm. Ping dropped in front of the robot and overwhelmed it by using its laser directly into the robots eyes, causing the robot to flail about blindly, giving Nick time to roll away and dash out the room door. In the factory aisle, Nick increased the force field on his left arm to act as a cast to hold his broken arm in place.

Nick tries to move out of the area toward the proposed exit when Exeter, the robot, uses all the cameras in the building to locate the intruder. The robot burst forth to pursue Nick and Ping. The robot is relentless in its pursuit of Nick. As the robot closes the distance, Nick tries an old football maneuver and sidesteps the robot watching it slide by him. Nick then takes off running, using as many obstacles to dodge around as he can to slow the robot down. *(Nick and Ping are still invisible to the human eye but not to the robot.)* As they are running away, Ping detects an electromagnetic machine (MRI) in the room up ahead. Ping has Nick enter the room, knowing that they could be trapped. Ping instructs Nick to dive through the device as the robot enters the room. As the robot rushes into the room to catch his prey. Nick dives into the MRI machine with Ping turning it on. The machine's electromagnetic field destroys Nick's battle suit. Exeter bulling his way through the door is moving too fast to stop from entering the MRI machine, shutting down the nanites in his body and rendering him inert. Nick removes his suit and finds that his nanites are still intact because his battle suit protected him.

Nick and Ping steal away to the main ventilation ducts to ascend to ground level. Nick removes his backpack, pulls the rope out, and stuffs his battle suit into the backpack. Nick takes out the roll of duct tape and winds it around his broken arm to make himself a temporary cast until he can get back to base. In the meantime, Exeter contacts Raven as he is dying to tell him about the intruder to make him aware. Exeter dies shortly after the communication.

At the duct, Nick pries off the cover and has Ping take the grappling hook and travel up the duct and hook the hook to an anchor point. Nick could not climb the rope because of his broken arm, so he used a pulley system to haul himself up the rope to each level. Then Ping would take the grappling hook up to the next anchor point. This continued until they reached the roof. Nick looks down into the parking lot to see that the place looks like someone kicked the ant farm.

This is going to make getting to the car a bit tougher. Nick sends Ping to get the car and bring it up next to the building. While Ping retrieves the car, Nick sets up the rope so he can repel down the side of the building. Ping gets the car and drives it to the side of the building, and to give Nick a diversion, Ping fires a rocket into a truck parked at the far end of the building. While everyone is putting out the fire, Nick repels down from the roof, and Ping opens the door for Nick to dive into the passenger seat.

Ping drives the car to the fence, where it paralleled the main road. Ping uses the laser to cut a hole through the fence, then drives through it and then on down the road back to the airport. A few miles down the road, Ping makes the car visible so people won›t run into it. Nick passes out from the pain in his broken arm. Ping brings the vehicle back to the plane under invisibility and drives onto the plane. The Pilot and co-pilot bring on the tractors and the parts crates and ties them all down for the trip back home.

The customs agents come over to the plane to ensure that nothing gets smuggled out of the country, but they only find tractor parts and a couple of tractors. They did not see the car. It was invisible. The agents gave their ok, and the Pilot wasted no time leaving. Once in the air, the co-pilot checks on Nick only to find him out cold, and Ping showed a projection of Nick's broken arm and indicates that he needs some strong painkillers to keep him out. When the Pilot landed in Alaska, they took Nick to a hospital to be looked after. With a cast and pumped full of antibiotics and painkillers, Nick could continue to travel as long as he would see his doctor when he returned home.

Chapter 23

Ping drives the car from the airport back to base when they land at the airfield near New York. Ping brings the car down into the garage, where Don and a concerned Kim help Nick out of the car and take him to the medical bay, where Nick gets checked out. The fracture in his left arm has a cast on it, and the instructions Ping gives Don from the medical doctor from Alaska indicates several weeks of rest for the arm. Nick doesn't fuss about it in the least; he is under the influence of pain pills.

In the meantime, Raven and the rest of the Nine arrive at the factory in Japan and demand to know what happened to Vulture. The security chief could not answer the question, but he did find Vulture in the MRI room slumped over the MRI table with it still running, and he was unresponsive. Raven using the holoprojector to appear before the chief wanted all the videos from the security cameras sent to his computer center so he could evaluate how the intruder managed to enter without being detected.

Back in New York, Nick was going over the mission to see if what he did caused his failure in obtaining the nanite generator. Upon reflection, Nick realizes he cannot confront the Nine or what's left of it by himself. He needs backup. With that in mind, Nick goes to Don to tell him about his needs for the future confrontation with the Nine.

Don agrees with Nick, but where to find people who are already trained and who would work with you?

"I know of two people I might recruit," states Nick.

"Who would that be?" asks Don.

"McMaster Powers and Blake Rogers," said Nick.

"Scratch them from your list Nick; McMaster was lost flying over Columbia going on a mission for Mr. Lynch. As for Blake, she was killed and eaten by Nile crocodiles. I considered these people until I learned they were dead," stated Don.

Nick smiled. "Were any bodies recovered?" asked Nick.

"Blake's body was recovered, or at least part of her was," said Don.

"They aren't dead; neither one trusted Lynch, and if he sent them to an obscure place, they figured they were to be killed. I would lay odds they still live. I want to bring them into your organization," states Nick.

"If they still live, bring them in. How long do you need to find them?" queries Don.

"I should be able to locate each person in a month of days. If I don't find them, we must recruit from somewhere else. But I'm sure they live. You will need to change their faces as you did mine otherwise, or we'll have all the alpha bit agencies here looking for them as soon as they show their faces to any camera," said Nick.

"When do you plan to start, Nick?"

"In a way, right now, I still have a week before I get this cast off; I will collect some intel and my gear for the trip," sighed Nick.

"What intel would you be looking for?" asked Don.

"Something that would not show up on CNN, Jimmy can search the dark web, and I'll wager he can locate some disturbances in and around Columbia due to the destruction of drug cartel property," said Nick.

"What makes you so sure of that, Nick?"

"I know McMaster; he hates the drug cartels. In a way, they killed his little brother. McMaster wants revenge!"

Nick and Don walk down to the computer center to ask Jimmy to search the dark web. I am searching for any disturbance along the Columbia and Brazil border. Jimmy takes a look and sees there have been several skirmishes in that area.

"Thanks, Jimmy; I'll get my gear together. Don, I will need a disguise for McMaster, or I will have everybody breathing down our necks at the first camera," commented Nick.

"I have you covered, Nick; come to my workshop, and I'll give you a new invention that I have been playing with," said Don.

Nick followed Don into the lower basement below the garage where Don's work area resides. Don walks over to a locker and pulls out a face mask that is as shiny as his battle suit. "Nick put this on!" Nick pulls this over his head and turns to Don, "Ok, what now?"

"Look in the mirror and say Judy Garland," smiles Don.

Nick looks into the mirror, "Judy Garland" right before his eyes, the mask displayed Judy Garland's face over his own. "I hope there are other faces in this mask! Otherwise…"

Don chuckles, "There are several faces in the mask and a function that can build a composite from many faces. Mask use program one alpha."

The mask changes and shows the manly face of no one he knows. "Now that's more like it!" said Nick.

"Here is another mask to give to McMaster; it is set to work with his skin tone so that no one will see it as a mask," comments Don.

"Thanks, Don. I need to go back to the computer center to get Linda to punch up a satellite over that area to see if there is a hole in the forest canopy where I can get closer to the ground when I parachute in."

Nick assembles what equipment he feels he will need for the next few days. Nick gets the pictures and the locations of where

McMaster might be. Ping hovers around Nick like a puppy waiting to go for a walk.

Nick looks up and talks to Ping, "Not this time, little buddy! I cannot charge you up, so you must stay here."

Not that Ping has any way to display emotion, but he manages to sulk or give the appearance of sulking. As Ping drifts away, Nick smiles and whispers, "I sure will miss you, little buddy."

By the end of the week, Nick's cast comes off, and he is told to take care; it has been mended, but it can still break if he is not careful. Nick collects his things and heads to the airport. Kim drives Nick in the rolls, and she tries to have a conversation with him. But to her chagrin, Nick says nothing and seems lost in thought. Kim gets mad and shuts up, and drives to the plane. When they arrive, Kim opens his door to usher him out so she can leave.

Nick turns to Kim. He reaches up and brushes her red hair to one side. "Now that looks better. You are adorable for a mechanic; Nick kisses her cheek and wishes her well. Then, he grabs his gear and boards the plane, leaving Kim even more confused.

CHAPTER 24

Nick boards the plane to travel to Panama City, where they will remove the aircraft door for Nick's low-level jump. It takes a day to get to Panama, where they spend the night before they leave at dawn to make the drop. They leave Panama headed for Columbia the pilot signals Nick to get ready as they approach the jump-off point. Then fifteen minutes later, he tells Nick to jump.

Nick standing at the door with all his gear strapped to him Jumps. As soon as Nick clears the plane, he pulls the rip cord to open his chute. The wind buffets him about, and his chute opens, slowing him down and giving him time to pick his landing spot. Nick drifts closer to the jungle canopy, and there is no opening. Nick plunges into the tree canopy, crossing his legs, and tries to become as thin as possible as he falls through the tree canopy until the chute hangs up and stops him.

Nick is hanging suspended off the ground and realizes he is about a hundred feet off the ground. Nick unhooks the rope strapped to his chest and clips it to his chute harness. Nick presses the quick disconnects and comes free of the harness. His hold on the rope keeps him from falling to his death. Nick slides down the rope to the ground. Nick survived getting here now for the tuff one, convincing McMaster he's not from Lynch and that he is Justin Michaels.

Nick takes account of his gear and then heads off in the direction he believes where McMaster would go. Using his map and compass, Nick travels to where the last disturbance occurred in hopes he can pick up McMasters trail. Nick was cautious in arriving more to keep from spooking McMaster than anyone else. Nick finds the burned field, and burned-out sheds from across the river where Nick stood surveying McMaster's handy work. Then Nick ducked as several men emerged from the jungle carrying automatic weapons.

Nick watches the men as they search the area; they're all together in a group, one of the men must have tripped a wire leading to a claymore, killing three of the six men and wounding one other. *(That's McMasters work, alright; he loves using booby traps)* thinks Nick. From off to the left of Nick, he hears a single shot and watches a man fall dead with a bullet hole in his head. The last man, still on his feet, moves to run into the jungle when another shot rings out, and he drops dead in mid-stride.

Nick heads off toward the shots to see if he can pick up McMasters trail. From his hiding place, McMaster watches this intruder (Nick). McMaster can tell he is a professional and wonders if he should kill him. Something about the intruder›s moves seems familiar, at least enough to pique his curiosity. If necessary, McMaster could kill him later. Nick follows the trail up to the area where the shots came from. Nick stands there for an hour before McMaster appears from behind a tree. Sensing rather than seeing McMaster, Nick puts down his guns and raises his hands in surrender.

"Who are you?" demands McMasters.

"You know me as Justin Michaels," says Nick.

McMaster raises his gun and levels it at Nick's head. "Wrong answer, stranger. Justin died in prison."

"I can prove who I am. By telling you what only you and Justin know."

"Ok, spill it!" commands McMaster.

"I know you have a daughter living in Ventura, California; she bears your sister's married name for her protection."

"Only Justin knew that. You do not look like him. How come?" queries McMaster.

"That is a long story, and if you like, I can tell you on the way back to New York."

"That's not going to happen. The alphabet boys will be all over us as soon as my mug shows up on camera."

Nick reaches into his pocket and pulls out the two new masks that Don gave him. Nick puts on his mask and says program one, and it gives him a new face. "Now you put your mask on," urges Nick. Nick holds up a shiny sheet-metal mirror. "Say program two alpha."

McMaster repeats what Nick told him, and he looks into the mirror. "Wow, this is cool! With this, I can move around and not be detected."

«Good, now let›s get out of here before they send others to look for these men,» said Nick.

"They won't send anyone right away. That is my usual tactic; they initially used to fall for it. Now they will take their time to get here," mentioned McMaster.

"What is the best way to get out of here and get to an airport?"

"We go downstream," said McMaster.

"Won't they expect that?" asks Nick.

"No, I usually lead them upstream and ambush them; it should be safe enough going downstream," states McMaster.

Nick follows McMaster downstream, and before he realizes it, McMaster leads them to a poppy field. «What are you doing, McMaster?»

"My parting gift to the drug cartel, we set this on fire and go up over that hill and steal the plane on the grass airstrip. The fire will give us a diversion," chuckles McMaster.

"Ok, we'll play it your way," sighs Nick.

"Here, take these flares, and you start at this end, and I'll go to the other end and set them off. When everyone comes to extinguish the fire, we steal the plane and get out of here."

Nick takes the flares and moves off in the direction McMaster pointed out, then Nick sets off the flares and pitches them into the poppy field, then runs off to meet with McMaster at the base of the hill. The two men met up, and McMaster pulled them into the brush to sit and wait. Soon the field is in a full blaze, and from off to their left come a small army of men and equipment to extinguish the fire. McMaster led Nick around the hill in the opposite direction and onto the edge of the airfield where a Cessna was sitting. Both McMaster and Nick scanned the airfield, looking for anyone who would be watching the plane. Just as they were about to break cover and make their way across the field, a man stood up to watch the fire. Nick pulls McMaster down, and using hand signals, Nick tells of the man on the other side of the plane.

McMaster nods, and they split up, crawl out of their hiding place, and head toward the plane, with each of the two men taking turns covering the other. The guard approached the front of the aircraft, where McMaster placed a headshot on the man. Then McMaster waved Nick to hurry to the plane. McMaster climbs into the pilot seat, and Nick opens the passenger door and pitches his rifle into the back then climbs in.

McMaster fires up the plane, then taxis down the field and comes around to run down the runway for takeoff. As the plane gathers speed and some lift, a barrage of bullets comes. McMaster got the plane off the ground and into the air. Neither man was hit, but the aircraft was not so lucky. The fuel tanks were shot, and they were losing fuel.

"Well, good buddy, we were hit, and we are losing fuel; we will stay in the air for about an hour," laughed McMaster.

"What are our options?" asked Nick.

"We can crash in the jungle, or we can try to land on the Amazon River or tributary," said McMaster.

"Any way we can land near a town or village?" questions Nick.

"The nearest village is two hours away by plane; we will have to hoof it through the jungle after landing."

"Ok, you call it McMaster!"

McMaster turns the plane northward and does a shallow climb to get some altitude so that when the plane runs out of fuel, they may glide a distance and cut down the distance they will have to hike through the jungle. An hour later, the engine sputters to a stop, and down they go; McMaster says nothing, and Nick buckles up his seat belt and almost closes his eyes as McMaster glides down to the river below, trying to miss the overhanging trees.

McMaster brings the plane down just over the water and misses a huge tree. They crash into the water. Nick uses his knife to cut himself out of his seat belt. Then he turns to McMaster and sees that he is out cold with a cut on his forehead. Nick cuts McMasters belt and manages to force open a door and pull McMaster out of the plane. Out in the current, both men are swept downstream. Nick spent most of his energy keeping McMasters head above water and trying to guide them to the nearest bank.

At an up-and-coming bend in the river, an inside area has a stagnant place. Nick managed to guide them into the calm water. As they hit the bank, a six-foot Kamen raised up as if he had found a new food source, Nick managed to assure the Kamen that it might cost its life if he tries to make a meal of either man, so it left. Nick pulled McMaster up on the bank, then examined him and saw that he was just knocked out. Nick was exhausted and collapsed beside McMaster and fell asleep.

Chapter 25

Nick was brought awake instantly as someone touched his face. Nick grabbed the man and held a knife to the man's throat. The man immediately held up empty hands and was gibbering incoherently. Nick came to his senses and realized he had hold of an aboriginal, so he cautiously let him go. Then he turned to McMaster to see if he would wake up. All McMaster could do was groan (*so much for getting a translation from this jungle man.*) thought, Nick. The aboriginal looked at Nick, then at McMaster; before Nick could enlist the man's help, the man disappeared into the jungle.

"Oh, great! When We could have a guide, he's now gone," said Nick to himself.

Nick grabbed McMaster by his armored vest and dragged him away from the stream in case the Kamen returned. "McMaster, you got to lose some weight!" said Nick out loud as he pulled McMaster a little deeper into the jungle. Nick found a spot in a small clearing and built a lean-to and was building a campfire just as Nick was about to start a fire.

"Don't waste your time with your fire," said a voice from a nearby tree.

Causing Nick to jump, and he reached for a gun. "Don't be foolish; you'll become a pin cushion as soon as your gun clears the holster," said the voice.

"Come out here where I can see you!" said Nick.

From behind the tree steps out a small white man. "I'm a missionary to the nearby village; Tutu returned and told me about you. I see your friend is hurt; let me look him over."

"Are you a doctor?" asks Nick.

"No, not really, but I have had some training."

"Alright, look; I believe he has a concussion," said Nick.

The missionary looked into McMasters›s eyes and felt his pulse and temperature. «You are quite correct; we must move him to the village.»

"That is going to be a bit tough with just you and me," stated Nick.

Smiling, the missionary waved his hand, and from all around them, the men from the village all appeared. The missionary in Spanish told the men what to do, and they disappeared into the jungle to return fifteen minutes later with the items needed to build a litter so they could carry the injured man back to the village. The travel to the village took three hours to cover the one mile to the village. Soon McMaster was put down on a sleeping mat and cared for by the missionary.

"Your friend only needs more rest and will be quite fine. I wouldn't be surprised if he woke up in the morning. I'll have the women give him water and a broth to keep up his strength."

"Thank you! By the way, what is your name!?" asks Nick.

"James will do," said the missionary.

"James, what would be the best way to get to a town where we can get transportation to a city?" asks Nick.

"The nearest town is forty miles to the northeast and another town seventy miles downstream," said James.

"Looks like we will go northeast then," states Nick.

James chuckled, "I think you will want to go downstream. The northeast is all heavy jungle and hills. Traveling there will take you weeks; if you go downstream, you can cover the distance in a week. You only have two waterfalls to walk around, and it is all easy traveling from the last fall."

"You're the expert, James; we'll travel downstream; is there a boat we can use?"

"Not a boat, but a dugout. Can you handle one of those?"

"I have used a canoe before," mentioned Nick.

"It is not the same; at least it is something," commented James.

The following day McMaster wakes up and demands to know where he is, Nick assures him that all is well, and if not for James here, you might not be here. James has mentioned that you should be able to travel in a few days. Soon McMaster is up and about and anxious to get back to civilization. James gives them a dugout canoe and warns them about the waterfalls. By the end of the week of travel down river, Nick and McMaster have reached a town, where they get a change of clothes for McMaster, Nick changes the program of his battle suit, and he is wearing blue jeans and a tee shirt.

McMaster finds sweatpants and a tie-dye shirt; the next day, they charter a river boat to Panama City, hoping to get a plane back to the States. Nick contacts Don, and he sends his Lear jet to pick them up and bring them back to the States. The pilot will have a copy of McMaster›s passport. Only it will have the name of John Little. All goes well with the plan, and John and Nick return to base in New York State without incident.

Don meets Nick and McMaster in the garage; Nick makes the introductions.

"You were right, Nick; McMaster is still alive; I hope you are right about Blake; when will you recruit her?" asks Don.

"I need a week to prepare; it is going to be harder to get close to her and convince her of our intentions," states Nick.

Nick takes most of the week to put together his plan (s) with a few possibilities if things go sideways. Ping will be taken along, and he can get charged up where they are going. Nick calls in McMaster (John Little) to go over the details of the mission.

"We'll start in Cairo and follow the Nile until we find Blake," said Nick.

John turned to the map of Egypt, then points at Esna and said, "Blake will be here if anywhere."

"What makes you say that?" questions Nick.

"Blake doesn't like large towns or cities; she prefers smaller ones where she won't be seen and where she can keep track of new people moving in and out of the area," said John.

"You're right; good call. Let's start there," answers Nick.

Nick tells Don where they are going and when they›ll be leaving. Two days later, Nick and John take Don›s Lear Jet and gear to Cairo, where Kim has a rental Jeep for them stocked with camping equipment, water, and a little food.

CHAPTER 26

John takes the wheel and heads south along the Nile River, headed for Esna, where they hope to locate and recruit Blake onto the team. The dirt roads were pretty rough. They spent more time off the road than on it. Along the way, they gassed up the Land Rover at every town they encountered. They would spend their nights camping away from towns. They feared that the Land Rover would draw too many thieves. At night the men went off to sleep, leaving Ping on guard. As it so happens, two strangers tried to break into the car and woke up John and Nick; they exited the tent, and one of the men held an automatic weapon on them.

Standing there with their hands up Nick said in Arabic, "I would not do that if I were you."

The man with the rifle laughed; his partner opened the door then he was flung backward as Ping tasered him. The man with the gun turned toward his friend, pointed his gun at John, and was getting ready to pull the trigger when Ping tasered the gunman. Nick walked over to the gunman and took away his gun. "I tried to tell you, buddy!" laughed Nick.

They broke camp and left the two men lying where they dropped and continued into the nearest town; Nick stopped at the farmers market and picked up some fruit for breakfast and some warm goat's milk. They continued on their way to Esna. Late in the evening, they entered the town and found a place to spend the night, and they managed to find a place to lock up the car for the night. Before leaving, Nick plugged Ping into an electrical outlet to charge him and guard the car.

Now to find Blake. John and Nick located a canteen and got a room and food. Nick did all the talking since he knew the language. John did not fuss over the food that Nick ordered. Nick took the time to show John how to eat with his hands. On the floor across the room, a belly dancer was performing. "She is good!" said Nick. When the woman finished her dance, Nick waved her over to offer her a drink and show her a picture of Blake so he could ask her if she knew her.

The belly dancer entered their enclosure and turned to close the curtain; before Nick or John could move, the belly dancer had a knife at Nick's throat.

"Why are you here?" she asked.

Nick's eyes went wide. "Blake?"

Blake pressed the knife harder to Nick's neck, drawing blood. "Answer the question!"

"We are looking for you," stammered Nick.

"Why?" hissed Blake.

"To recruit you!" said John.

"Who are you? CIA," questions Blake.

"We're not the company; if you would let up on Nick's throat, he can explain," commented John.

Blake looked at Nick. "How do I trust you when I don't know you?"

"By telling you what only you and Justin know," said Nick.

"Ok, then tell me!" said Blake.

"On October tenth eight years ago, you and I became intimate while on assignment."

"That's enough!" said Blake, "you're Justin!"

"And now, who are you?" Blake looked at John.

"McMaster, we did not work closely with each other only in passing," said John.

"You don't look like him," states Blake.

"If you allow me to move my hands, I'll remove my mask."

John slowly moves his hands up to his face and says, "Program off," A silver mask covers his head; John pulls the mask off, revealing his face. Blake stares at him. "You're dead!" said Blake, "and as I recall, so is Justin! I suppose you have a mask too!" accuses Blake.

"No, this is my real face," says Nick.

"What happened to your face?" asks Blake.

"It is a long story, best saved for the long trip back to New York," states Nick.

Nick, John, and Blake leave to return to Cairo to catch the Lear Jet back to New York; along the way, Nick tells his story, and then John talks about how he came to be in South America. Then Blake tells of her situation. When they reach Cairo and load onto the Jet, Nick tells them why he needs them. Nick tells them about the Nine and the robot he fought. Nick also had the pleasure of introducing Ping, his AI buddy.

Now that the mission was over, Nick tried to converse with Kim, but Kim refused to talk to him. John pulled Nick aside. Nick introduced Blake to Kim, which made her even more upset. Nick was confused about what he had done to make her angry. Back at base, Blake was introduced around to the rest of the team.

"The red-headed girl won't talk to you because you ignored her all way to the airport when she was trying to have a conversation with you."

"I didn't hear her, or I would have spoken to her."

"You don't hear anything when you go into the groove on the mission. I've seen it before; you shut down and reviewed the mission.

Not even an atomic blast can rouse you when you do that," stated John.

"I did that?" questioned Nick.

"You sure did; if I were you, I would apologize and explain what you were doing," said John.

Chapter 27

At the time, Nick was looking for John. Raven (Leader) had moved all the brain jars to Japan to the robot factory. Three robot bodies were nearly finished in their construction. Raven would take one body, and Cuckoo and Seagull would have the other bodies. To be followed by the next three Sparrow (Finance), Dove (Inventor), and Magpie (Mathematics). The last of the team to get a body would be Crow (Chemistry) and then Swallow (Dr. of Biology).

Raven conversed with the whole team and explained why that order was for getting the bodies. Raven needed Cuckoo (Mechanical Engineer) and Seagull (Electrical Engineer) to help devise a security system and trap the intruder who killed Vulture (Dr. Exeter).

Thanks to Exeter, the rest of the team now had a program for learning to use the robot bodies, and they could cut some time off the learning curve. It was essential to get Cuckoo and Seagull moving with the Japanese engineers to build a security system so they could allow the intruder to return and capture him. Raven wanted him alive so he could question him. Raven wants to know who knows about them so he can either buy them off or destroy them.

Raven and his first team learn how to use the robot bodies as set down by Exeter. The next three are getting theirs, with the last two waiting to manufacture their bodies. Cuckoo and Seagull devise a way to detect the intruder, even if he is invisible. They would use a light-curtain technology to blanket the lower floor of the factory. The curtains would lay out like a grid throughout the factory floor. Where the curtain is broken, it'll locate where the intruder is situated on the bottom floor of the building.

"If the intruder is invisible, will he set off the curtain?" presses Raven.

"Light does not pass through solid objects, even if the object appears invisible," said Seagull.

"Well, send the data to our computer center where we can monitor it; I don't know when he may return, so let's be ready to receive him. As I said before, I want him alive. I want to question him," says Raven.

While the Nine waits for the intruder to return, three more robots (Sparrow, Magpie, and Dove) receive their brains and begin training on operating their new bodies. This will now increase the number of the Nine to six working robots leaving the final two (Swallow and Crow) waiting for the nanite factory to construct their bodies.

Once the factory›s security has been set up, it›s a trap waiting to be sprung. Raven now returns to the plan of taking over the world. The Nine has been slowly working toward that end. Using computers, they have built worms to extract data and accounts from high-level people worldwide. Blackmail is usually a suitable method or a well-planned assassin to remove a problem. In Raven›s mind, the need to remain unknown is primary to their success, and this intruder must become known and eliminated.

Raven reviews the tapes from the night Exeter was killed to see if he can see what Exeter saw. Raven almost gave up until he saw a shimmering that Exeter was following down the factory floor. There were two shimmering paths, one near the floor and the other just overhead. Raven followed the path of the shimmering right into the MRI room, where Exeter (Vulture) died in the MRI machine because the electromagnets stopped all the nanites in his body.

Then Raven caught sight of the intruder as he left the MRI room, followed by the shimmering above his head; at one camera, Raven got a profile of the intruder. *«Wait, that is the same man at the castle, and I›ll wager that the shimmering is the AI unit I talked to before we destroyed the castle. It appears they both got out alive and well,»* thinks Raven.

Raven then searches the other cameras to see the intruder escape onto the roof of the building, then down the side of the building, and then disappear. Again, the shimmering is only larger now as it heads out to the fence, then the hole in the fence appears, and the shimmering appears on the road leading to Tokyo. Raven patches into the road cams to see if he can find the shimmer as it travels.

Raven loses the shimmering and tries to find it by going back over the files; after a few hours of reviewing the camera files, he spots what he missed. The invisible car becomes visible as a silver Corvette as if from nowhere. Raven followed the Corvette to Tokyo using the street cams. It was easy. The car went invisible as it approached the airport and the cargo delivery side.

Through some hard searching, Raven found the shimmering again. It was not so pronounced this time as the car was moving slower than before. Raven followed the invisible car onto a cargo plane. Using the airport cameras, Raven managed to get the aircraft registration numbers so he could try to find out who owned the aircraft and who was on to them.

Chapter 28

Back in New York, Nick is planning his next raid on the Nine. Nick turns to Don to see what help Don can provide against the Nine's robot body. Nick defeated the robot he fought by pure accident. They cannot rely on that for this next attempt.

"Don, we need some serious firepower to stop these robots. Is there some weapon we can use against them?"

Don looks off into space. "Nick, we cannot use electromagnetics like you used on the first robot; the power source is too big. Let me ponder this over for a few days, and I will reply. In the meantime, plan your assault."

"Ok, Don, I will plan a way to get in and out, but it won't be worth much if we cannot defend ourselves."

Nick returns to the hollo room to see what ways will allow his team to re-enter the Japanese plant. Don decides to collect some nanites samples from his distant lab so he can experiment with ways to cause them to destroy themselves. Don has a destructive test lab for testing new alloys. They could help try ways to stop these nanites.

Don spends a month away from his base of operations at the materials destructive lab trying to destroy the nanites. Don already knew an electromagnetic blast would do the trick, but the power source was too bulky to carry. They can't, with practicality, use that to fight the robots. Some other method has to be discovered. Don was pondering what to do when one of the technicians proposed using sound waves.

"Sound waves?" questions Don.

"Sound waves are being used by this mining company rather than TNT or C-4 explosives; all it takes is to locate the frequency to shake the rock lose then clear it away. Might this method work on the nanites?" queries the tech.

Don ponders the question of sound affecting the nanites. "Why not! Let's set up a sample and start testing." It takes several days, and they hit on the right frequency, destroying the nanites. Now armed with the frequency, Don decides to travel to one of his weapons factories to see what they can come up with that his team can carry into battle with the robots.

At the factory, Don pulls the research and development team together to brainstorm some solutions for making the sound frequency into a hand-held weapon. The research team comes up with a possible idea; the problem is still in the power consumption and the size it needs to be to make it work. At this facility, a new female tech was told to be seen but not heard. During the discussion, she tried to speak up, and the head man gave her a frowning look to be quiet. Don had caught the look, and when they broke for a break, Don pulled the young tech aside.

"What were you going to contribute to the conversation?" asked Don.

"We have an experimental battery that has enough power to power the weapons but only briefly," said the tech.

"Do you have a working battery we can test?" asks Don.

"Yes, I have a couple, but you need to be aware of this; they become radioactive when expended," said the tech.

"How dangerous are they after they are expended?" asks Don.

"They need to be stored in a lead-lined pouch and returned here to be properly disposed of," said the tech.

Don calls the head man and asks why he suppressed the young tech. The headman said the batteries were toxic once they were used up. This should have been brought up at the meeting. After a sound dressing down, they built the pistol and the rifle around the battery. Don had more nanites brought in for testing. The pistol only manages to fire once before draining the battery. The rifle could handle two shots with the batteries set up in series. The nice thing was that they could eject the batteries and reload in seconds.

The arms should be stored in a lead-lined box until they are needed. And each person should carry a lead-pouch for the expended batteries. Don was getting ready to leave with three each rifle and four pistols. Another tech asked Don if he wanted a sonic grenade with the other arms.

"Do they work?" asked Don.

"Yes, I tested them on the last of the nanites, and they were wiped out, and the grenade does not explode, so no spreading the toxic battery parts," said the tech.

"Make nine of them and have them ready to go by tomorrow," commented Don.

The following day Don collects the sonic arms and left to return to New York to give the team a demonstration of the sonic weapons. This will give the team a chance to survive and stop the Nine. Hopefully, the team will be able to recover the nanite generator that was taken from Don's lab.

Back at base Don demos the sonic pistol. Then shows the rifle, and grenades. Don shows them how to change the battery and that they must collect it after it's spent. If at all possible. The expended battery will be toxic. But for this use against the Nine, they'll be necessary. Nick now feels better about the mission. It now has an even chance of success. Nick doubles down in coming up with a plan.

Nick spends the next week solidifying his plans to get into the factory. Nick figures a three-way attack. John will be using the ventilation shaft, and Veronica will use the utility tunnel, while

Nick will just walking in as he did before through the warehouse. The utility tunnel will be unexpected; the other two. Nick suspects they will be watched, maybe guarded against entry. This will allow Veronica (aka. Blake) to enter without detection, an ace in the hole, so to speak.

Nick runs the plan by Don, then the team. While Don was gone inventing the sonic weapons, Don had two more battle suits made up, one for John and one for Veronica. Nick takes the time to show them how to use the suits and then the car. In time Don would design cars and baseball-sized AI robots for the rest of the team. They had to share what they had, except for Ping. Ping solely belongs to Nick.

The way Nick has planned the attack, He and John will take the direct routes of where Nick entered the plant and left the plant while Veronica (Blake) uses the utility tunnel. Nick will enter the warehouse entrance, and John will come down the ventilator shaft. Nick, has it timed out to enter first, hoping it will draw all the attention so John can enter second and then Veronica, this Nick hopes will take them by surprise so the mission to take back the generator will go off smoothly. Hopefully no one on the team will be at any risk.

Nick debriefs his team and gets them prepared to leave for Japan. Nick plans to send Veronica by car to the beginning of the access tunnel, and he and John will parachute into the plant at night. John will land on the roof, and I will land in the truck parking lot at the far end and make my way to the loading dock entrance. I will flag John when I'm in the plant, and he can descend the shaft; then Veronica can get ready to use the utility tunnel to enter into the factory.

CHAPTER 29

Nick and the team all pile into the invisible car and drive to the airport. Nick was in what the team has come to call the groove. All Nick is doing is going over the mission over and over in his mind, looking for improvements and possible failures. Nick has warned the team of possible pitfalls but they have been on missions like this before, and realize they need to be flexible and react accordingly.

Before boarding the plane Nick and his team checked over the equipment to make sure it is all in good working order, and that it is all there. The cargo plane took off and the team made their individual preparations. When they left the last refueling station in Alaska Nick sat down with John and Veronica to go over the timing of their assault.

The cargo plane would land at Tokyo and off load the invisible car for Veronica so she can drive to the factory location, this would take a few hours. The cargo plane will then take off heading to the Philippines flying over the factory where John and Nick would jump out of the plane. The plane with the pilots help would act as if the engine has problems and needs to return to the airport at Tokyo for repairs.

While repairs were being done, the mission would take place and everyone would return via the invisible car to the plane and exit the country. Veronica signaled on her com she was in the tunnel heading down to the basement of the plants building. This triggered Nick and John to have the plane launch and fly toward the Philippines which would take them right over the factory where Nick and John would jump off the plane at ten thousand feet.

It was pitch black and no moon John and Nick would parachute into the factory. John would land on the roof and Nick would land on the back side of the parking lot for the trucks. John would set up his rope to allow him to drop down through the ventilation shaft to the basement. John would wait until Nick gave the go ahead.

Nick entered as he did before and proceeded through the warehouse, and down the elevators. Where Nick would signal the team to advance. Nick enters the first elevator located on the North side of the building and he just gets on with a technician. With the battle suit in invisible mode no one can see him. Nick just keeps out of the way and hopes no one bumps into him.

On the second floor Nick quickly heads to the East elevator for the next ride to the third floor. It works the same way for Nick as it did for the first elevator. No one sees or hears him. The South elevator turns out to be troublesome. No one is headed down to the fourth floor, so Nick pushes the button and he steps on to travel down to the last floor. The elevator opens and the guard is alerted. The guard steps up to see who is on the elevator.

It's as if the guard knew that Nick was there the guard pushed a button to keep the door open and hold the elevator in place then the guard started jabbing his rifle into empty space searching for something invisible. Just as the guard was about to find Nick, Ping fired a static charge nocking the guard out and Nick pulled the guard off the elevator and stashed him into a cubby hole. Taking the guards rifle Nick signals, he's on the floor and moving to the robot nanite factory. It is time for them to enter and converge at the rendezvous point.

Nick when he stepped on to the floor broke the light curtain giving away his position, and the direction he is traveling in. Raven sent Sparrow and Dove to intercept Nick at the robot factory. Moments later John drops down to the floor alerting Raven there is another intruder in the building. Raven dispatched two more of the

Nine to intercept the new target. Raven sent Magpie and Cuckoo to the new point of contact. They were not to kill, but capture the intruders so they can be questioned.

After dispatching two of the Nine to intercept the new intruder, Veronica emerges from the tunnel then Raven sends his last robot Sea-gull to capture the last intruder. Raven then decides that they only need one intruder alive so kill if it becomes necessary. Nick enters the robot factory and watch the two robots that were being fabricated by the nanites. To Nick's eyes it looks as if they were being grown as the nanites were constructing the components in the robot's body.

Nick searches the room until he finds the nanite generator. Nick stashed it his back pack. At that moment the two robots enter the room and confront Nick. Nick tries to avoid direct contact as the robots attack him. Nick has his sonic rifle pulled from his hands and he is flung against the racks across the room the second robot grabs Nick by his harness and is about to deliver a blow to his rib cage. Ping tries to distract the robot holding Nick when the other robot grabs Ping and is about to crush it. Nick pulls a sonic grenade and pulls the pin. In mid strike the robot holding Nick grabs the grenade and throws it out the door when it goes off.

At first the robot pitches the grenade out the open door then it drops Nick to the floor and the robot holding Ping lets Ping drop to the floor and collapses to the ground holding its torso as it falls. Both robots are dead. Nick picks up Ping and puts him in his backpack and heads toward Veronica's position. Before Nick kills off his robots Raven had sent Magpie and Cuckoo to where John touched down. John pulled his sonic rifle and steps back under the rack holding parts to conceal his presents. The two robots show up and they manage to detect John despite his being invisible.

One of the robots grabs John's harness and flings him across the aisle. As John bounces across the floor, he loses his rifle. And the other robot is about to play socker with John's head he grabs a grenade and pulls the pin and hold on to the grenade as it goes off. The robots come to a halt and grab at their torsos then drop to the floor. John collects himself and the sonic weapons then beats feet to the rendezvous with a great deal of haste.

Sea-gull corners Veronica and is taking his time to close with her and he receives a message from Raven to retreat. Sea-gull chooses to ignore the command. Sea-gull closes on the intruder and grabs her harness. Veronica kicks, chops and curses at the robot and realizes she has no effect on it. Veronica pulls her sonic pistol and fires it point blank at the robot's torso.

The robot drops Veronica and grabs his torso and dies. Veronica shakes herself; she has never been handled like a rag doll before, and she finds it disconcerting. Veronica pulls her hand gun then conceals herself to wait for the boys to show up. They arrive shortly on the run.

Raven knowing, he just lost five more members calls in the sentries to cutoff and kill the intruders. Veronica leads the way into the utility tunnel followed by Nick and John to bring up the rear. John replaces the cover over the tunnel and then he removes his battle suit and harness and gives them to Nick. The tunnel is so tight John needs all the smallness he can get to pass through to the end.

John rigged a grenade (not sonic) to go off if they pull up the cover to follow them. Hoping it would make them weary about following. Fifty yards down the tunnel they hear an explosion, so the team picks up the pace. They soon come to the end of the tunnel. Veronica runs to the car and opens the trunk and stashes her sonic weapons and pulls out her automatic rifle to stand guard waiting for John and Nick to catch up.

Nick is next to emerge and he pulls Ping out of the pack and places him into the cradle where he can recharge. Then Nick returns to the tunnel entrance and he hears John. Nick reaches in to give John a hand. With some struggle and a loss of some skin John manages to shimmy out of the utility tunnel. Nick hands John his battle suit so he can get dressed. Nick listens at the entrance and can hear people moving in their direction. Veronica pointed out that some people were coming down the hill from the factory.

John climbs into the back seat and veronica gets into the driver's seat with Nick taking the passenger seat. Ping made them invisible and drove the car down an access road headed back to the highway. Ping pulled the car off to one side and sat still as the small army of people ran down the access road looking for them. After the people passed by Ping drove back onto the road and headed for the highway. Ping drove the car all the way to the edge of town where the traffic was beginning to pick up so Ping turned off into an empty alley and programed the car to appear as a minivan and then proceeded to the airport.

On the far side of the airport Ping went invisible to make their way to the cargo gate. When the team had reached the outskirts of Tokyo, Nick called ahead to warn the pilot they would be there in an hour so to get the plane back to gather and get ready to leave. At the closed cargo gate Ping caused the gate to open. The guard didn't see any vehicle so he stepped out to see what was going on. Ping drove past the guard and up to the ramp of the waiting plane. The ramp closed and Nick and John piled out of the car and locked the car down while the plane was taxing to the runway for takeoff.

The pilot took flight and headed for Guam instead of the Philippines. The tower questioned them as they left Japanese air space. The pilot gave a lame excuse and the tower shrugged it off, and the plane continued back to the US then back to New York. Along the way Nick reported back to Don and told him all went according to plan and they did get the generator back.

Chapter 30

Raven tracks the intruders within the factory until they disappear, then Raven resorts to using the street cams to track them; it is easy to do. Raven was able to follow the shimmering as they drove to Tokyo, Raven discovered that they had changed to a minivan, and he followed it to the airport, where they entered the truck loading gate where he followed the shimmering onto a cargo plane where Raven was able to get a good picture of the registration number of the aircraft so he could trace it back to the owner. Raven traces the cargo plane to a company listed to Donald Travis as the CEO and owner. Raven starts digging, and after several days of searching, he realizes that Lynch accidentally led Donald to them by not covering up the theft of the nanites and the generator. Things have gone too far to stop now. Raven and the Nine are now known, and that will be the death of Donald and his people. For the Nine to take over the world, it has to be done quietly and behind the scenes.

Raven was now the only one of the Nine who had a robot body. Sparrow and Crow were still alive and would get a body in a few months. But the nanite generator was now gone. Thanks to the work of Seagull and Cuckoo, they had reversed-engineered the generator so Raven could have the Japanese engineers and craftsmen build a new one. Raven also asked the engineers if they could reduce it in size and place it into the robot bodies.

The new generator was built in a month, and the new robot bodies were under construction. Soon the last two brains, Sparrow and Crow, will have their bodies. Meantime the Japanese scientist came up with a life-like skin covering for the robots. It was as flexible as human skin and would hold the same temperature. The color of the skin could simulate any race, from Asian to African and in between. Raven decided to use Exeter's suggestion and go with the Japanese features then the robots could mingle with the current population.

Raven lets the Japanese scientist apply the skin and hair to his robot body (Raven Black). They gave him brown eyes. When they finished, he looked like any average Japanese person except for his height. Raven would be taller than the average Japanese, but not so tall that it would be remarkable. Raven could blend in a crowd and not receive any notice from anyone.

Raven communed with the other two of the Nine, Sparrow and Crow, who would receive their bodies in a few more weeks. Raven, he needed to remove the threat of this Donald person and his organization before they returned to kill us off as they have the others. Sparrow and Crow agreed with Raven. They also wanted to know what they used to kill off the others. Exeter was killed using electromagnetics, but what killed the other five?

Raven set out to execute his plan of kidnapping and torture to get Donald's team and the information they would need to stop them. There is a terrorist group on the border of Peru and Brazil where the Nazis of Germany went to avoid trial and execution. To this day, they still recruit young Germans and train them for future use of world domination. Raven would call on a team of them to kidnap Donald, to begin with.

With his new skin and suit of clothes, Raven sets out to travel to New York to set his plan into motion. His bully boys will be along in just a couple of days. Raven passed some fake information to the New York Times that Donald Travis had created weapons of mass destruction and unleashed it on a small village in Africa, killing everyone there.

The news reports were headline news. It went from the papers to the TV news, and Don started receiving Calls from all over. The worst calls came from the military, and they threatened to cancel all Government contracts. Don contacted the law firm he had on retainer and discussed this problem with them. If the News was invalid, the news should print a retraction or get sued. The Papers say they will publish the retraction on the front page if Don, publicly denounced the claim in person. The lawyers talk to the newspaper about the article; the story has no factual information. Like where this village is located and so on.

Don agrees and sets up a press conference at the Men's club.

"Don don't do this!" said Nick.

"Why?" queried Don.

"I don't like it. It feels wrong; I can feel it in my gut," pleads Nick.

"Listen to him, Don," says Veronica. "He's usually right about his feelings."

Don turns to Nick, "Ok, explain!"

"There are no facts in the article; that's the biggest flag. Someone wants you out in the open! To me, that means assassination or kidnapping," states Nick.

"I would listen to Nick," chimes in John.

"Alright, what should I do? If I back out now, it will make me look guilty! We need to go through with the press conference," said Don.

"Then we take precautions; John, Veronica, and I will be stationed around you to protect you from assassination and or kidnapping," said Nick.

"I'll place myself in your hands; what do we do next?" queries Don.

"What do we have that Ping can track that will not be easy to find?" asks Nick.

"I have my microchip as we all have," insisted Don.

"They will find that immediately and remove it; it needs something else," states Nick.

"I have a low-level radioactive pellet I could swallow; as long as it passes through my body in a few days, it will cause no harmful problems to me, and Ping will be able to track it unless they put me in a lead-lined box," says Don.

"Let's go with that; Veronica will stand by you in her battle suit and be invisible. John and I will be in the crowd watching. We also will be in our battle suits, but visible and in disguise," said Nick.

John says, "We should have the car close to hand, armed to the teeth, in case we need to fight!"

"Not a bad idea, John; Ping can be in it and ready to drive just in case," mentions Nick.

"I'll be station so I can watch the crowd for suspicious characters and stop them with my pistol," says Veronica.

"For the short time, I believe we have a workable plan to fall back on. Kim and Don will arrive by the rolls. John, Veronica, and myself will get there early and scope out the area. Don you and Kim show up late, say by thirty minutes? This will put everyone on edge; it may give us the edge to prevent whatever takes place," said Nick.

Chapter 31

At the club where the press conference is being held, Veronica, in her battle suit, navigates through the building crowd and locates an out-of-the-way location where she can watch for any assassins. Nick and John, also in battle suits and wearing face masks, pose as interested parties to what is happening, trying not to look like bodyguards.

Raven posing as a Japanese press agent, is at the club waiting with the rest of the press for Donald to arrive. Raven quickly picks out Nick and John as bodyguards; he will interfere with them when his men make their move to kidnap Donald. Raven looks around for a third person who may protect Donald but cannot locate him.

Kim driving the rolls, pulls up to the curb and lets Don out of the car. Don looks around, then enters the club to address the press. Earlier, Ping parked the invisible car in a dead-end alley and parked way back so no one would run into the vehicle. Then Ping waited for the signal to come out and pick up Nick and John. A white van backed into the same alley and stopped short of hitting the car. Ping runs the Van's plates and quickly discovers they are stolen. Ping leaves the car. Ping floats over to the Van to scan inside it, and discovers four armed men in the back and two other men up front. Ping hovers over the Van and plants a magnetic tracker on it then flies back to the invisible car to wait.

On stage, Don begins his speech about not building any weapons of mass destruction and that he never will. Four men enter the stage area wearing work coveralls, and they start firing into the crowd of reporters, killing a few of them and wounding several others. The gunmen take care not to hurt Don. John and Nick grab Don and try to get him out of the room and shield Don with their battle suits. Veronica manages to get off a shot hitting one man in the knee bring him down, and her second shot disarmed him.

The three other men rushed up to grab Don. John let go of Don to fight them off; the first man to reach them cast a hand full of dust into John's face, and he fell to the floor, knocked out. The second man did the same thing to Don and Nick; they, too, were knocked out by the powder. A few security men tried to help but were attacked from behind by Raven, claiming to have tripped and knocked them down, allowing the terrorists to get away with Don. The third man was going to shoot Nick in the head when Veronica, from concealment, shot the man.

Hearing the commotion inside, Kim runs up the steps; as she reaches the doors, they burst open, knocking her down the stairs. At the bottom, she tries to get up when one of the terrorist kicks Kim in the face breaking her nose and knocking her out, causing a concussion. Veronica reaches John and Nick to see if they are still alive. She sees they are just drugged. Veronica manages to wake Nick and then heads out the door to know where the terrorist went. When Veronica hits the street, she sees Kim lying on the ground and a few people trying to see if she is alive. Veronica takes charge and sees that Kim needs help right away. Veronica has the men nearby put Kim in the back of the rolls, and Veronica decides the boys can deal with Don's kidnapping and drives Kim to Dr. Phillips's clinic for treatment.

Raven watches from the top of the steps as Veronica drives off. Raven moves on down the street and steals an old beat-up Volkswagen. Then follows Veronica to the clinic. Nick splashes water onto his face and then dumps a pitcher of water on John's face to bring him around. They head out the door to the blind alley, where Ping brings up the car. The men get in, and Ping takes off tracking the Van he had tagged earlier. The police arrived at the club to find one dead terrorist and one badly wounded. The police bag up the dead one and turn their attention to the wounded one, and just as they approach the wounded one, he hits his jaw very hard, breaking it and causing him to go into spasms and die. Now they bag up both men and take them to the morgue.

Veronica gets Kim to the emergency entrance of the clinic, and Dr. Phillips and his staff are waiting for them, thanks to Veronica calling as she is driving. They take Kim out of the rolls, and put her on a gurney, and into the emergency room to treat her injuries. Raven parked his stolen car in the parking garage and entered the clinic to see where he might find the injured party. Raven hopes to locate one of the intruders to settle a score with them later. Raven finds a waiting room and settles down with a magazine to watch and listen.

An hour later, Veronica shows up in the waiting room and settles into a chair to wait for the Doctor to come and give her some status on Kim. Raven is unsure, but he suspects that Veronica was at his factory in Japan and killed one of his colleagues. She fits the size and weight. He'll listen and decide later. Dr. Phillips came out to the waiting room.

"The news is not good, I fixed her broken nose, but Kim has a concussion, and I have no idea if or when she will come out of it. All we can do now is pray she will wake up."

"May I see her?" asks Veronica.

"Not now. Kim must sleep off the drugs we gave her to keep her quiet. But you and Don or anyone else she has affection for should show up to sit with her, read to her, or talk to her. This will help with her healing."

"Thanks, Doctor Phillips; I'll let everyone know!" Veronica chokes up. Frustrated, Raven considers going to the safe house where Donald is being held captive. Veronica then leaves to head back to base. Raven gets up to follow, and when Veronica drives off, she manages to get into traffic and lose Raven in the rush-hour gridlock.

Raven suspects that the intruder he is after should be well on his way to tracking down his safe house and locating Donald. If Raven hurries, he thinks he can follow the intruder back to where they have a base of operations. Raven intends to take revenge on Donald and his entire team for killing six of his colleagues.

By this time, Ping is closing in on his homing signal. When he gets to within a mile of the abandoned farmhouse, Ping goes invisible and shuts down the gas engine in favor of the quiet electric motor; Ping brings the car past the first guard and into the barnyard.

Nick and John launch a drone to recon the area looking for where everybody is located, especially Don. According to Ping, four men were in the house, three in the barn, and one at the gate. John decides he will take out the men in the house, Nick will take out the men in the barn, and Ping can get the guard at the gate. John and Nick grabbed their guns and grenades.

They exited the invisible car, and, using their battle suits, they remained invisible. Splitting up, they each moved to their respective targets. Ping quickly took out the guard at the gate. Ping stunned the guard using a built-in taser. John using a few claymore mines, placed them around the house, and then he started firing into the house to get the terrorist attention.

Nick waited outside the barn for the men to rush out shooting. The first came rushing out, and Nick dropped him with a taser; the second was more cautious and climbed up into the hay loft to view below. All he saw was his partner on the ground, and no one else was around. The terrorist grabbed the rope and slid down the rope. Nick was waiting for him as he hit the ground. The struggle was short and sweet as Nick took out the second target. Now for the third one.

Nick opens the door slowly and peered in to see Don tied to an overhead beam, and he was severely beaten up. Nick released him, carried him to the car, and placed him in the back, then made sured he was not dying. Nick was going to help John when he remembered that John would get mad if he interfered with his fun. Nick waited, and thirty minutes later, John appeared with a smile.

"Oh, man! I needed that! It was a great fight. Did you find Don?" asked John.

"Yea, he is a bit banged up. We should get him to Dr. Phillips for a checkup," said Nick.

John rides shotgun, and Nick sits in the back with Don to see how hurt he is; besides a few cuts, abrasions, and maybe a few cracked ribs, Don will be sore but ok. Ping drives the car in invisible mode and will do so until they reach more traffic. Ping reaches the end of the dead-end road and is fixing to turn onto the paved road when he spots the beat-up Volkswagen, and something is standing beside it.

Ping tells Nick the so-called person is not human as they pass by. Nick watches the Asian-like person and realizes that he was at the press conference. Ping takes a picture of the person, and they quietly pass by and on down the road.

Raven sees the smoke from the farmhouse and is watching for the shimmering in the air, which will tell him that the intruder is present. Then Raven sees the shimmering and realizes he should act as if he has not seen them. Looking around, Raven watches the shimmering as it heads down the road away from him. Then Raven gets into his stolen car and follows them.

Nick sees the Volkswagen following them, so Nick has Ping use the first off-road turn out to pull off and stop. Ping does as instructed, then the car following them passes by and continues down the road. Nick has Ping generate a holograph of a semi-tractor and then has Ping continue down the road. Ping takes them back to the base, and Don is rushed to the medical bay, where the nurse treats him for his injuries.

Don soon recovers, and Nick assures him he is safe and fine. Right now, Kim needs to be looked after. Her concussion is dangerous, and she needs time and lots of visits to help her recover. Nick debriefs Don to see what the terrorist wanted. Don informed Nick that they beat him up but did not ask for information. All he could glean from their conversations was that the big man would be there to question him, and they were to just soften him up.

Chapter 32

"Then you and John showed up and saved me," said Don.

"Thanks to Ping, we now have a picture of a robot. "Don look at this" Nick held up a picture. It was that Asian-looking man by the Volkswagen we passed after saving you at the farmhouse."

"Hey, he was at the press conference and showed up at the clinic where I took Kim!" exclaimed Veronica.

"Then we need to get back to the clinic to protect her; we should take some of the sonic weapons," said Nick.

"Which ones?" queried John.

"Veronica and I will go to the clinic, John. You stay here to protect this compound. Veronica and I will take a Sonic pistol and a grenade and protect Kim," commanded Nick.

Nick, Veronica, and Ping head to the car and take off for the clinic. Nick lets Ping drive the car with his computer mind. Ping can optimize the car›s best speed to get to the clinic, hopefully before the robot arrives.

After losing the invisible car, Raven decides to return to the farmhouse to see if he has any loose ends. The terrorists are expendable, so if any are alive, they soon won›t be. As it happens, there is a deep well that will conceal the bodies very nicely. Then Raven will return to the clinic to wait for his intended targets. In a way, he has a hostage. According to the clinic›s records, the young girl›s name is Kim. They all will be killed for revenge. (*The girl, Kim, will be the key to drawing them out.*) Thinks, Raven.

Raven returns to the clinic and heads for the waiting room. When the nurse›s station is vacant, Raven enters Kim›s room to get a better look at her. Then Raven returns to the waiting room to wait for the intruder and his team to show up. Raven contacts Crow to get the list of the life sustaining chemicals so Raven can make them up himself. Being a robot, he does not need sleep, but he does need the chemicals to replenish brain solution and some fresh blood to oxygenate his brain. As to the blood, there is a blood bank a few blocks away, and he can break in and take what he needs.

Raven decides to keep an eye on Kim›s room from the waiting room, hoping to keep from being found out until he can strike. Veronica and Nick reach the clinic and head upstairs from the parking garage. When they reach the floor, Kim is on; Nick and Veronica head to Kim›s room; as they pass the waiting room, Nick and Veronica see the robot, but they do nothing; they head to Kim's room to see if she is alright.

Currently, Kim is alive but still in a comma. Nick is relieved she is still alive. Nick tells Veronica that he will leave and draw the robot into the parking garage, where he can confront it away from innocent people. Veronica pulls out her sonic pistol, and Nick puts the sonic grenade into his coat pocket. Ping also will be with him so that Nick will have some backup in combat with the robot.

Nick leaves, then heads past the waiting room. Nick heads to the elevator to take it down to the parking garage. Nick passes the waiting room only to notice that the robot is gone. Nick takes the elevator down to the parking garage with his hand in his coat pocket ready to pull out the sonic grenade if attacked. Ping warns Nick that the robot is not far from the elevator door and to be ready. Even when warned, Nick is surprised; the robot's speed is nearly blinding fast. Nick feels the robot's hand around his neck, and then he is picked up off the ground.

Nick grabs the robot›s hand to try to break its hold. This leaves Nick gasping for air. The robot rifles Nick›s pockets and finds the sonic grenade. "This is how you killed my people?" asks the robot. Nick can't answer because he's choking. The robot pulls Nick toward him, so they are face to face. "After I kill you, that girl upstairs will be next, then the rest of your team."

As the robot handles Nick like a rag doll, Ping hovers over the robot and lets off a sonic blast. The robot drops to its knees and drops Nick onto the floor, which leaves Nick trying to catch his breath and coughing. The robot dies, then Ping drops to the floor and becomes visible. Nick realizes he must get Ping back to the car and plug into the cradle so he can charge up; otherwise, Ping could lose his core memory.

With Ping getting recharged up, Nick walks back to the robot and discovers it›s dead; Nick picks up the sonic grenade and puts it back into his pocket. Nick calls John to get a truck with a lift to transport the now-dead robot to some lab for Don to check out. In Germany, Crow and Swallow realize Raven is now dead. The two leftovers of the Nine will need to lay low until they discover what killed the others.

Nick called the base and let them know that the robot was dead and that he needed transportation to move it to a lab. John said he'd be there in an hour with his new truck. Nick said to bring some kind of wench or crane to pick up this heavy robot. It is too heavy to pick up and put into the truck bed. Nick manages to use his car to tow the body to an empty stall and then covers the robot with a tarp.

Over an hour pass, and John shows up with his new truck. It is like Nick's car, except it's a truck. John pulls up to the place Nick shows him and backs up the truck to the robot. John lowers his truck tailgate to the ground on extending guides run by hydraulics. Once the tailgate is down, John and Nick slide the robot over and onto the tailgate. Then John raises the tailgate and causes it to fold up, causing the robot to slide into the truck bed. John and Nick use the tarp to cover the robot so John can take it to a lab for Don to study.

John drives the robot to Don's lab at the city's edge. It looks more like a warehouse than a lab. John drives his truck inside the building and parks under a chain hoist. One of the lab techs pushes a work table from a side room, and John uses the hoist to lift the robot. Then he pulls the truck ahead until the robot is clear of the bed, then the tech lowers the robot onto the workbench, then wheels it off to a side room. John gets back into his truck and drives back to the base.

After John leaves the clinic with the robot, Nick stands there, and it hits him like a ton of bricks. The robot threatened to kill the whole team, but the one that shook him up the most was what the robot said about killing Kim. The others, he realized, would be a loss, but Kim's death would leave him dead and empty inside. What does this mean? In my mind's eye, I kept seeing Kim on the first day when he first met her and wiped the dirt off her face. That moment is burnt into his memory.

Nick gets a hold of his emotions and returns to Kim›s bedside. He wants to soak up all that he can of Kim›s presents. Nick is starting to come to terms with his love for Kim. All Nick can think of is protecting this young woman. Nick enters the room where Kim is. Veronica looks up and smiles. Nick tells her of his battle with the robot and that Ping saved his life. Veronica looks at Nick.

"Ah, I see you figured out how you feel about Kim; I see that look in your eyes. How did that happen?" asks Veronica.

"The robot threatened to kill her; my heart was feeling a great dread and pain at the thought of her death. I wouldn't know what to do if she were not around."

"Alright, you big idiot, don't tell me how you feel. Tell Kim how you feel; give her a reason to escape the coma!" said Veronica.

Veronica turned and left the room. Nick turned to Kim, sat in a chair next to the bed, and reaches out to take Kim's hand.

"I'm not very good at this sort of thing, Kim, but I will do my best. Kim, I don't quite know when. Maybe it was the day I first saw you, and I wiped the dirt from your face. I have fallen under your spell. I love you. Please come back to me! I need you; you have become my reason for living." Nick sat there and just held her hand and prayed to GOD that he would send her back to him.

Everyone showed up to talk to Kim; even Alexander stopped by to spend time with Kim. Nick would return day after day; he bought a book of fiction, something Veronica suggested that Kim liked to read. It was a love story, and Nick was dubious of it, but he gave in and read it to Kim.

A month later, while Nick told her how much he missed her, he made a statement to her. Touching her face with his free hand,, "Please come back to me; I would like to ask you to be my wife." A tear rolled down his face and fell onto her hand. "I must go for now, Kim; I'll be back tomorrow." Nick placed her hand beside her and was getting up to go when Kim's hand grabbed him and held him tightly.

CHAPTER 33

Nick called out to the nurse who was passing. "Does this mean anything? She grabbed my hand?"

"Yes!" exclaims the nurse and races down the hall, and a few minutes later, Dr. Phillips returns with the nurse.

"You did say that Kim grabbed your hand?" asks the doctor.

"Yes, I asked her to return to me, and when I was getting up to leave, she grabbed my hand."

The doctor checked Kim's vitals, then checked her eyes and saw a normal response, smiling. Dr. Phillips said she is well on her way to recovery.

"When will she wake up, doctor?" asks Nick.

"Any time now. What did you say to Kim exactly?" asks the doctor.

"I said if she woke up, I would ask her to marry me; then I said I had to go. Then she grabbed my hand. Is that important?" queries Nick.

"I believe so; Kim shows an improvement after each of your visits, now this. I can't be certain, but I suspect Kim has great affection for you, Nick. Keep talking to her; you seem to be the best medicine for her."

Nick sits back in the chair, and the doctor and the nurse check her over and leave the room. Nick decides to try something to shock Kim back to wakefulness. Nick decides to plan the wedding, picking all the colors, flowers, and the Venu where they will go on the honeymoon.

Kim grabs Nick's hand, opens her eyes, and says, "That's terrible!"

Nick shouts out in happiness and gets the doctor and the nurse back. Then the doctor kicks Nick out of the room to check out his patient. While in the waiting room, Nick calls the base to let them know Kim is awake, and the doctor asks that we not all show up at once.

Over the next few days, everyone trouped in to visit with Kim; Nick was sure to be there every day to ensure she would be ok. The doctor gave Kim a clean bill of health and sent her home with orders she is to rest and not work. Kim is to return for a checkup in a week. Nick was always about making sure she was resting and getting the food she needed. Then John and Veronica put pressure on Nick to propose marriage to Kim.

Nick finally bought a ring, and over a candle-lit dinner set up by Alexander and the rest of the gang, Nick asked Kim if she would marry him. That was the hardest thing he ever did. At that moment, he would have rather been in a battle with one of the robots. Kim accepted his proposal, and Nick felt sick as the butterflies flew around his stomach. This gave Kim, Linda, and Veronica things to do and plan. They were leaving Nick to his own devices. Of course, John, who had been married before this, gave John a chance to scare Nick about his up-and-coming wedding and, most of all, the bachelor party. John did this all in good fun.

In Germany, the last two of the Nine plan their next move to take out Donald and his team. This is more in the way of revenge for killing off seven members of the Nine. Right now, they have the bodies of their fallen comrades except for Raven's. Crow and Swallow study the bodies, hoping they can figure out how they were killed. According to the tech, except for Exeter, they all died of the same thing. Exeter died from exposure to the electromagnetic field of the MRI machine. The other deaths were caused by something else.

Whatever killed the others has yet to be found, and the forensics of the bodies are the same. The nanites degraded to a point they could not function; hence they killed the host bodies. They reviewed the security footage and could see nothing. Then a Tech posed a question. "What kind of energy could be produced for a moment and then dissipate?"

The techs kicked the idea around when one of them suggested, "What about sound?"

"We did not hear anything on the audio of the security footage," commented the lead tech.

"What if it did pick it up, and we can't hear it," stated the tech.

"Ok, let's assume you're right; check the audio and see if we can detect the sound," commanded the lead.

The tech pulled up the footage, ran it through a computer program, and, in a few hours, located the sonic sound that killed the robots or the nanites. The tech made a full report and sent it to Germany to Crow and Swallow, with caution not to listen to the security footage in case it may cause their death due to the sonics recorded on the footage.

The sonics killed the nanites, which then destroyed the brain. Swallow noted this is why they were killed off without even knowing why they died. Swallow told Crow, and now they needed to rebuild or figure out a way to stop the sonics from penetrating their robotic shell. It could take a few years to fabricate whatever they come up with. The two robots stay in Germany and tell the Japanese workers to take every precaution to protect the plant; in the future, they will return to get upgrade with theskin, the nanite generator, and the sonic protection.

Back at base, Kim and the girls make wedding plans; Nick is getting cold feet as the day draws near. Fortunately, John has been married before, so he helps Nick get through it, and John gets in a lot of teasing. The day of the wedding arrives, and the groom and best man face where the bride will enter on Don's arm.

"Nick, take it easy," whispers John.

"I can't," gasps Nick. "I feel like I'm going to pass out."

"Believe me, Nick, the bride is as scared as you are and just as nervous."

"How can you tell she has not appeared yet," whispers Nick.

"Just wait until she gets here. When you take her hand, it will be all sweaty. You'll see," comforts John.

Nick settles down and waits; sure enough, as soon as he steps out to take Kim's hand, it's as sweaty as his. Then Nick becomes his assured self-full of confidence, and the wedding goes off without a hitch. The two love birds leave for an all-paid trip to Hawaii for their honeymoon. In the meantime, Don and one of his techs tear apart their robot at the lab to see what makes it tick.

Don and the lab tech find the brain in the torso of the robot, and it is pretty putrid; the brain fluid and the blood they found mixed in with the micro servos and other micro components; it is no wonder these robots are so heavy and strong. In the back of Don's mind, he realizes that the story of Frankenstein's monster does have a basis in fact. As Dr. Phillips said, there is nothing new under the sun. He may be right. Ponders Don.

Don sent a brain sample to Dr. Phillips for him to run some tests and see how old this brain might be. A few days later, Dr. Phillips shows up at the base to ask Don where he got this brain tissue. Don takes Dr. Phillips to his office, and they have a discussion.

"The brain tissue tests out to be from the seventeen hundreds, but it's not as corrupt as it should be. It looks like it just died, not that it has been dead that long," stated Dr. Phillips.

"Here, Look at these pictures, as Don brought them up on his computer. These were taken a few days ago when I dissected the robot that Ping brought down."

"Correction, Don cyborg!"

"It doesn't matter, my old friend, it's more robot than organic, but we don't need to quibble about it. You did say the brain was as old as the seventeen hundreds, did you not?" asked Don.

"I did; the process used to keep the brain alive was very effective; was the process a match to the paper I pointed you to in the university library in Germany?" queries Dr.Phillips.

"It was just as the paper laid out. I, for one, was surprised it worked. This Exeter student was very talented," commented Don.

"No matter how talented he was, it was wrong that he did this to humans. Thank you, Don, for what you showed me; let's hope they are all gone," Dr. Phillips indicated.

"I suspect they are not all gone; if I miss my guess, there are still two left out of the Nine. I may need to devise a different way to combat them," said Don.

"How did you stop them this time?" asked Dr. Phillips.

"We used sonics; I fear that they have six bodies to study, and they may have discovered how it destroyed them and may find a way to nullify the effects, so I best come up with a new way to stop them," stated Don.

Chapter 34

Nick and Kim are on their way to Hawaii to enjoy their honeymoon, and both seem very happy and content. The rest of the team decided to take a break as well. Jimmy got a face mask and caught a plane to Florida to attend a gaming convention and computer fair. Linda and Veronica teamed up and travel to the mountains to Veronica's father's cabin for some peace.

John went to Oxnard, California, where his teenage daughter lived with his sister. His daughter was brought up by his sister as her daughter. John's daughter Beverly never knew her father or her real mother. At the time of Beverly's birth and the death of her mother, John (McMaster) was off saving the world, if you will, and the only way John's sister would raise his daughter is if John gave up all rights to the daughter and he would never let her know he was her father. John agreed.

With his mask and battle suit, John changed his appearance, the mask changed his face, and the battle suit dressed him in a beach comer look. A Hawaiian shirt, short pants, and sandals. John found a stick on the beach among some driftwood and waited. A few days later, Beverly and some friends showed up at the beach, and he was able to observe her. John is like a hungry man who takes in all he can just by watching her. He was proud to see how well she turned out.

That same day John started a fire in one of the fire pits when a group of teenage boys approached him and tell him to leave. John play, acting like an older man, asks the boys to leave him alone and says that he was there first. The boys were heckling John, believing him to be an older man. The girls saw what was happening, and

Beverly yelled at the boys to leave the man alone. She also compared them to weaklings for picking on older men to show they were such little men.

This angered the lead teenage boy so that he threatened her and her friends, and to prove it, the boy shoved Beverly down and took unwarranted liberties with her. Then the boy felt a vise grip on his shoulder. John snapped the boy's collarbone, causing him great pain. The other boys either were nursing other hurts or just ran off after dealing with John. John picked up his daughter and the boy. John turned the boy so only he could see John's face, and john's face changed to reptile, complete with scales and fangs.

"If I ever see you again, no one will ever find you or what's left of you; now get out of here!" growls John.

The boy crying from the pain and fear, ran off. John changed his face back to the older man and apologized to his daughter. Then he turned and left. John decided that he should return to home base before things got out of hand. John caught the next flight out headed to New York. Veronica and Linda also head back to New York after a week. By this time, Linda is ready to climb the walls; she is not used to not having some electronic device she can use. At Veronica's cabin, you cannot use a cell phone. There is no Wi-Fi, nothing, not even a TV. All the girls did for one week was sleep, swim, and fish for dinner.

Veronica took Linda to local dive for drinks to break up some of the quiet. There they ran into some questionable characters, which Veronica discouraged. The vacation was restful, but to Linda, less fun. Jimmy had a great time at the weeklong computer fair. He got to try out some of the latest games and computer hardware. Jimmy decided that the computers Don provided were better than the hardware he saw at the fair. Jimmy wore a mask to keep his identity unknown. He met new friends that he intended to follow online. Jimmy then returned to New York.

They still had a few days before the honeymoon couple would return, so Lind and Veronica put their heads together, moved all of Kim's things into Nick's quarters, and dolled it up for Kim's sake. Don and John also pitched in, bought a queen-sized bed and coverings, and manhandled the twin bed into storage.

A few days later, Kim and Nick return to base, Nick is still in shock, and the women run off to get all the details from Kim. Kim was the center of attention for a few days, and Nick wondered what she was telling Veronica and Linda. They either gave him a sly look or laughed when Nick passed them. It's enough to make a man swear off marriage and stay a Batcheler. Nick settled down to domestic life. Nick, at this time, needed a job, so he went looking for Don to see the next target.

Don called Nick, Veronica, and John to his office. Don had three file folders in his hand. He put them down and separated them, and gave a brief synopsis of each one. One folder was for a senator, the state will remain unknown, who is being lobbied to vote for a bill that will help the lobbyist company but will be against the people. This Senator Williams will need to be shown the error of his ways. The following folder is a gangster in Florida who is running drugs and has killed several people (He also has a mansion in New York). He needs to be stopped. His name is Robin Roe. Last of all is a judge in Alabama who will defend a murder case, and he has ties to the killer. He needs to be convinced to judge the case according to the facts. His name is Judge Howard.

"Who wants to tackle which person?" asks Don.

John snatches the gangster file, "I'll take this one; I'm used to tangling with the real bad guys."

Veronica takes up the judge's file. "This ought to be fun!"

Nick picks up the senator's file and says nothing.

The three turn away and head for their rooms to study their files on the subjects they have taken on. As Nick reaches the door to leave. "Nick, is there a problem? asks Don.

"I don't know, why do you ask?" queries Nick.

"You seem quiet; you usually ask more questions," said Don.

"I'm confused; I did something for Kim, she started crying. I thought I was doing her a good turn," complained Nick.

Don laughed, "I recommend you talk to John; he was once married and may have an idea."

"Thanks, Don, I will," answered Nick.

"Otherwise, is everything all right?" asked Don.

"I believe so; I will need a place to go over this file; how up-to-date is the file?" queries Nick.

"Linda and Jimmy pulled all the data they can from the computing system; you may want to collect more data firsthand," suggested Don.

"I think I will; a little undercover snooping might suggest more than looking at the file. Thanks, Don, for the suggestion," as Nick gets up and wanders off to the hollo room to study what information he currently has.

Chapter 35

An hour later, Veronica and John show up at the hollo room to talk to Nick about the Basilisk program you and Jimmy cooked up. Veronica asked Nick.

Nick chuckles, "Yea, I was watching Jimmy watching a Harry Potter movie, and he was fighting a Basilisk, and it gave me the idea to program my suit and Ping to use this creature as a scare tactic. Here follow me to the basement where we keep our battle suits, and I will put on a demonstration."

Nick puts on his suit with Ping, and they turn invisible; then, all of a sudden, a lizard-like creature with fangs all poised right in front of them.

"Wow! That is so cool!" coos Veronica.

John is a bit more skeptical. "Really? This lizard thing, why not something else?"

"Like what, John? Batman? Sorry that one is taken; we need something to make people afraid. Besides, who will spread the word that a mythical monster is chasing them?" asks Nick.

"I see your point," says John.

John and Veronica put on their battle suits with their new AI bots. John and Veronica practice the Basilisk program until they have it down. Then they all go off to work on their plans so they can use the new program. Veronica decides to check up on her target Judge Howard, to see what more she can learn about her mark. Veronica also wants to take her new spy car. That Don just gave her out for a spin to check all the bells and whistles. The car is much like Nick's, only smaller, and instead of being a gas-powered car, it is powered by hydrogen. Veronica's car can go from New York to San Francisco and back on one tank of ionized water. Veronica's car does not have Nick's weapons, but she can use the Holo projectors and guns that it has.

Veronica drove to the courthouse and found an alley where she could park her invisible car so it would be out of the way. With her floating AI she calls Girl, Veronica walks to the courthouse. When Veronica enters, she was still invisible, Veronica realizes the detectors would go crazy if she tried to pass security. Veronica has Girl disable the sensors for five minutes so she can get by. With that done, Veronica glides down the hallway looking for Judge Howard's office. Veronica gets to the last office door to find the Judge's office. Veronica listens at the door and hears nothing on the other side. Veronica works the door open, then steps inside and shuts the door.

Veronica checks through the desk and the in-basket for information. Veronica was in the process of looking for a safe when she heard the door open. Veronica moves quietly to a far corner of the room so she can watch the Judge. Judge Howard enters the room and heads for his chair. The Judge opens one of the drawers to his desk, he pulls out a glass and a bottle of Bourbon, then pours a stiff drink. Howard settles back in his chair when another man enters the room.

"What are you doing here, Armond?" hisses the Judge.

"The boss sends his best and wants this dealt with quickly before the pigeon can sing to the jury," said Armond.

"Kill the stool pigeon then," said Howard.

"Boss said no assassinations! It has to be natural, or it would point at the boss too much. Which would bring on more investigations," stated Armond.

"A natural occurrence?" snickered Howard as he raised his glass and drained it.

"An accident could work; it could point away from the boss and achieve what he wants," comments Armond.

"You had better leave and let me figure out a way to have an accident for our pigeon," smirks Howard.

Armond leaves the room; Judge Howard finishes another glass of booze, then moves toward his bookcase where Veronica has been standing. As Howard moves towards her, she moves out of the way. Girl continues to record everything. Howard pulls down a set of books to reveal a safe. Girl zeros in on the dial to record the combination to open the safe. Howard punches in the combination then pulls the door open, then pulls out a small box, and a strange smoking pipe. Howard fiddles with it for a moment, then loads a dart into it. Howard knows, the poison is undetectable unless you look for it in the toxic screening. It just looks like a heart attack, and they die.

Veronica moves to the room's far corner from the judge and has Girl project a holographic projection of a lizard man in the center of the room. "SSS, an interesting plot worthy of watching SSS," hisses Veronica.

"Who's there!" cringes Judge Howard.

"SSS Basilisk, a mythic creature SSS," hisses Veronica.

"What do you want?" asks Howard. Howard pressed a hidden button to call security.

Howard kept the Basilisk talking while security burst through the door to capture whoever held the Judge against his will. With guns drawn, they enter the room and see the lizard projection. Girl turns the projection off. Then the room is searched by security. While invisible, Veronica and Girl slip out the open door. The security men are baffled. They saw the creature, and now it's gone. From that time forward, Judge Howard only went places with guards.

That night the Judge went home under guard. He had been requested to go to a safe house, but he had too much evidence to secure before he went to the safe house. In case the creature invaded his home to rifle his files. Like the other two teammates, Veronica learned the art of picking the door locks. Also, Girl could have opened the door too. Veronica was looking around and found some evidence she was looking for. Veronica was getting ready to leave when the Judge and his bodyguards arrived.

Veronica was going to leave when she thought better and decided to stay and watch the Judge some more. After he closed the door, the Judge turned on the lights and went to the pile on his desk, then to a safe to open it up and stash the files, he took from his desk. Again, Girl zoomed in on the dial and captured the combination to the safe. When he finished, the Judge went to the cabinet, took down some whisky and a large glass, and poured a tall stiff drink. Then he downed it in one gulp and then poured another one.

Veronica had Girl project the lizard person across the room from the Judge. The Judge cringed and dropped his drink onto the desk as he gaped at seeing the apparition.

"What do you want?" croaks the Judge.

"SSS, I'm not sure, maybe your life, or better yet, information about the man you are to kill SSS," hisses Veronica.

"I can't; they will kill me," squeaks the Judge.

"SSS, I can kill you right now if you don't tell me SSS," hisses Veronica.

The Judge falls back into his chair and pushes the silent alarm to summon the security guards to come and help him. Veronica waits by the door for the guards to rush in. With the door open, Veronica slips out into the hall, followed by Girl. Veronica shuts off the holoprojection and then tosses a coin onto the Judges desk. They exit the building, and Veronica, with Girl, walks back to the car. Veronica travels back to base and forwards the information she obtained to Jimmy and Linda to go over and do more research.

Veronica wants to know who the witness is that Judge Howard is supposed to kill and when the grand jury trial was. Linda responded and told Veronica that the trial was supposed to happen next Thursday, less than a week from now. Two days later, Veronica decides to invade Judge Howard's office at the courthouse. That night Veronica and Girl Break-in at the back of the courthouse, and they proceed to the Judge's office. After negotiating the halls and corridors, they arrive at the Judge's door and find it locked.

Girl using her force fields, manages to unlatch the door. Girl enters the office first and disables the alarms. Allowing Veronica to enter the office without incident. Veronica opens the safe and takes out the box containing the poison darts and takes out one and places it into a sample bottle, and puts it into her pocket. Veronica then riffles the papers in the safe to see what else she can find by way of evidence against the Judge, and his puppet master, whoever they are. Veronica is hoping to bring the whole gang down.

Veronica finds nothing in the Judge's safe that implicates his confederates or even names them. Veronica closes the safe and gets ready to leave. Before she does, she writes a note saying, "I'm watching you!" and then leaves an other coin with the Basilisks symbol. The following day the Judge enters his office and sees the note. The Judge turns pale, gibbering, and flounders around the room as if looking for something. A security guard hears the noise, opens the door, and sees the Judge acting like a madman.

"Judge, are you Ok?" asks the guard.

"Do you see it!" the Judge turns to the guard and grabs him, "do you not see it?"

The guard looks around the room, "See what, judge? There is nothing here."

"It's invisible; it's a basilisk in human form and able to be invisible; it revealed itself to me a day ago. You have to protect me!" gibbers the Judge.

The Judge turns away, heads for his desk, and hands the guard the coin and the note; then, the Judge reaches into his desk, takes out a bottle of whisky, and downs a few drinks to steady himself. The guard looks at the note and the coin and calls his superior. The superior arrives, and the guard explains everything he has witnessed and hands the note and coin to his boss.

The superior was puzzled; he took the coin and note and walked to the surveillance room to watch the security tapes. As he views the footage, the camera turns off for about an hour. Puzzled even more, he calls on the police to see if they can get more information on this Basilisk and see if the coin and note contain any DNA or other clues. The police find nothing on the letter or the coin except the coin was printed out on a 3D printer. It was a dead end.

The superior assigned the Judge extra guards to protect him. Veronica suspected this would happen and was ready to deal with it. Veronica went to a curiosity shop, and bought a small blow gun Veronica was prepared for the grand jury to convene to question the man the Judge was to kill. Veronica with Girl was in the courtroom to watch the proceedings so she and Girl might intervene to stop the killing. The man was brought in and placed on the stand, and Girl was commanded to hover over the man on the stand so she could project her force field to protect him. The Judge was there, holding his pipe gun in his mouth.

Just as the man was starting to give his evidence, the Judge pointed his pipe stem at the man as if to punctuate his question and fired the unseen dart. Girl deflected the dart, and Veronica, hidden off to one side, shot the Judge with his dart in the neck using the blow gun. The Judge grabbed his heart and collapse to the floor dead.

It was not how Veronica wanted to complete her assignment, but she did save the witness, and he spilled the beans on the gang, causing several arrests. Don thanked Veronica for her excellent job. The evidence convicted several bad people and put them away for many years.

Chapter 36

John sat in his room to study his file on his target, a godfather named Robin Roe, or the butcher as he became known in his earlier years. John reads over the history and sees Robin's fingers are into everything. Robin has killed or killed enough people in his time to populate a small country. Robin has been indicted many times, and the witnesses have died or disappeared, so he has never been convicted.

John also received a copy of Veronica's report on the judge and how she used the Holo projector to project the Basilisk as a distraction. John was contemplating his next steps when a knock at his door brought Don into his room.

"Hi John, how goes the homework?" queries Don.

"This assignment is going to be nasty. Robin is quite the killer. I will need to study this a lot more before I approach Robin. He'll be tough to scare; I may be forced to kill him," said John.

"I came to give you something to help you with your case and have a trial run of some new invention of mine," stated Don.

"What is that, Don?"

Don hands John two boxes the size of a large match box. One contains what looks like ants, and the other box looks like it has flies in it. "What is this an insect convention?" asks John.

"No, not really. Here are some surveillance drones. They look and act like the insect they look like. They have audio and visual capabilities; your AI unit can use them to record all they see and hear. Like your AI unit, they can map a building and spy on people," explains Don.

"You mean I can break into Robin's mansion and turn these loose, and they will spy on him," asks John.

"Yes!" answered Don.

"We both know that is against the law," states John.

"That's a grey area, John; we're not the law in a technical sense, so we can get away with it," comments Don.

"I won't argue the point if I can bring down this scum bag!" says John.

"I'll leave you to your assignment." Don gets up and exits John's room.

John looks into the boxes and decides that he'll use the drones to get the goods on Robin. John decides to do a recon around Robin's property to see where he might park his truck when it's invisible, hoping no one will run into it. John puts on his battle suit and head mask. John has the suit make him look like a gardener in coveralls, and has his truck project an old beat-up pickup truck. He would drive around the neighborhood looking at the terrain and see what security Robin had. The only security John would have a problem with are the guard dogs. No matter how invisible you are, they can still smell you.

John arrives in the area to start his recon mission. Out of sight of Robin's property, John launches a drone. It's invisible, but it still makes noise as it flies. John drives around the neighborhood looking for an out-of-the-way parking place as the drone flies around Robin's house, mapping out the sentries, cameras, and sensors. And to John's concerns, there are sentry dogs roving the property. He must figure out what to do with them when the time comes.

John gets an idea of how to hide the truck. Find a vacant house or at least where the occupants will be gone for a time. Then he could park his truck in a driveway, and no one would be the wiser. John contacts Linda and Jimmy to have them look into the surrounding mansions to see if anyone has left for a time. Linda finds an estate where the family is on a six-month journey overseas, it only has a caretaker looking after the property, and it should be safe enough for John to use.

Using his disguise as a gardener, John could stash some of his equipment near Robin's mansion without arousing anyone's suspicion. John decided to use tranquilizer darts to put the dogs asleep. It would be quiet, and it would not hurt the dogs. John's next step is to recon the inside of Robin's mansion and release the drones so John could collect evidence against Robin.

John had Linda find a vacant house where he could park his truck, and the people would not be home for a few weeks. The best they could come up with was a mansion a mile away where the family was over in France, making a tour of Europe. The caretaker lives in the back, and due to satellite surveillance, no one uses the driveway, so this would be a safe spot to park his truck, visible or otherwise. John decided to make a recon of Robin's house that night.

John proceeds to the house and enters through some French doors after Bev, his AI unit, indicates it's empty. John was armed with a dart gun beside his pistols and a couple of beef steaks with some sleeping pellets inserted into the meat. John scales a back brick wall and purchases on the wall top. No human could see him, but the guard dogs soon find him, and John pitches them the meat. The dogs gulp down the meat, and fifteen minutes later, they curl up and sleep.

John drops down and makes his way to the house. John enters the house through the empty room then moves into the hallway and sees no one around. He opens his box of fly drones and sets them loose for Bev to direct them into places of concealment. Then John does the same with the ant drones. Bev will have them circulate throughout the house, looking for good places to station themselves.

For now, Bev also scans the house as they move through it, creating a map with the help of drones. John also walks through the house without being seen in his invisible battle suit.

John locates the area where the help (butler, maids, and so on) stays. Then he discovers the place where the security guards congregate. The armory is in the next room close to them. John moves off and locates Robin's office. And another office just off Robin's where it looks like an accountant works. John directs Bev to plant a few drones in the office areas. John turns to leave when he almost bumps into the bookkeeper. Carefully John moves off to a corner to watch this man.

All hell breaks loose, and alarms go off everywhere. John figures the dogs were found asleep; the whole place erupts into confusion. The bookkeeper rushes over to a wall, moves a picture to one side, and then opens a safe to check its contents. If Bev had not been busy else, where's John could have gotten the combination? So much for that. John moves silently out the open door and back into the hallway. John returns to the empty bedroom, then out the French doors into the backyard. With Bev following, John hops over the wall and returns to his truck.

John calls up a computer screen in the truck's cockpit, then calls up the information coming in from the drone's mapping of Robin's house, and adds it to Bev's data. Then, John has Bev direct some drones into Robin's office and the bookkeeper's office so he can listen in on any conversations that may happen.

John returns to base to let the drones do their work while he plans out his next steps. John has Bev redirect a couple of the fly drones to go outside of the house and record the guards' movements along with the dogs. With the times they patrolled around the property. John has decided to contact Robin to start his dialog to convince him to turn himself in. That night Don pays a visit to John in his apartment to see how the new drones are working.

A knock at the door to John's room, "May I enter?" asks Don.

John looks up from his computer screen, "Please do; what can I do for you, Don?"

"I just wanted to know if the drones were any good; I'm rather anxious to see how they'll perform," asks Don.

"I'll know more tomorrow. When Bev and I reach our parking place, Bev can download the data the drones collected. Otherwise, they did spread out throughout the mansion according to Bev's mapping," comments John.

"Ok, I'll return tomorrow to see how everything worked out," as Don gets up to leave.

"I should know how your drones performed tomorrow, Don." said John.

"I'll look forward to hearing your report. Good night, and good hunting," as Don departs.

John turns over the information he has seen and some of the data Bev has gained with the recon trip into the house. The room John was most interested in was the office just off Robin's room. What's in the safe? Would it be worth looking into? Muses John.

John would explore that possibility come tomorrow evening. John also expects to encounter Robin and see how the Basilisk program will work to force Robin to do his bidding. "Robin, you are about to have the worse day of your life!" considers John as he turns in for a good night's sleep.

Chapter 37

Morning finds John in the garage putting his gear in his truck for his day's adventure. This morning John intends to beard the lion in his den. John is also interested in the safe in the accountant's office. A few hours later, John approaches the vacant house and parks his truck. John sets out for Robins's mansion by taking the tactical backpack with his equipment.

John soon reaches the back wall, where he'll not be noticed. John sets Bev lose to spy over the wall to see if the way is clear for him to climb over it. Once John climbs the wall and discovers the dogs are not around. John makes his way to the servant's area of the mansion, figuring he can enter the house much easier there than anywhere else.

The two drugged dogs found the other day caused some concern for the safety of Robin. Since his last visit, the security has doubled; that was to be expected. John watches from beside a back door waiting for it to open, and be left open so he can slip in undetected. That very same opportunity happens. With his hands full, one of the butlers opens the door and steps out to call the dogs so he can feed them. In his invisible battle suit, John and Bev enter through the open door and move down the hall toward the central part of the house.

Bev has connected with all the drones in the house and can see all the rooms. Bev guides them through the house, avoiding the guards right up to Robin's door to his office. Just as John is about to remove the guards, Bev shows John a secret passage into Robin's office. John decides to take the passage. On the far side of the room is a stairway into the basement; the other leads back up through a false wall. Bev scans the wall and locates the trip latch for the door. John reaches for the latch when Bev stops him. Bev throws a screenshot on his face screen showing a peephole.

John collapses his helmet and opens the peep to look into the room. At his desk, smoking a cigar and holding s snifter of brandy, Robin stares off into the distance as if remembering something. John puts his helmet back on and opens the hidden door. Robin reacts by drawing his gun from the desktop.

"Come in slowly," says Robin.

Bev, unseen, slips into the room, then projects a human-shaped lizard man, and it walks into the room. Its appearance catches Robin by surprise.

"What do you want?" asks Robin.

"SSS, I want you and your people in prison, SSS," hisses John using Bev to simulate the snake-like voice.

"Why? What have I ever done to you?" stammers Robin.

"SSS, you asked me what I wanted! Because you are an evil man SSS," said John.

Robin reacts and empties the gun into the hologram, which brings three other men into the room with their weapons drawn. "What's wrong, Boss!" one of the men asked.

Robin pointed at the Lizardman, and the men started shooting at the projection, and all it did was stand there as if nothing was happening. From the other side of the room, John fires his dart gun, putting down all three men.

"SSS was foolish, Robin. I could have killed them and you instead of putting them to sleep, SSS," stated John.

"I will kill you; you freak!" screams Robin.

"SSS, I'll give you twenty-four hours to turn yourself in to the law, or I will be forced to take your life, SSS," says John. The projection disappears, and the hidden door closes. John and Bev stay in the room in a far corner watching Robin.

Robin calls in more men to remove the men lying on the floor and to search the grounds and house for the intruder. Soon everyone leaves the room, including Robin. Bev jimmies the door into the accountant's office, and they enter the room. The bookkeeper is cowering in a far corner. John was hoping for this so he could enter the office of the bookkeeper; John wants to open the safe and get a look at what it contains.

"Who's there?" stammers the bookkeeper.

"SSS me, The Basilisk SSS" hisses John. Bev projects the holo creature near the door.

"What do you want? Go away!" cries the bookkeeper.

"SSS, Open the safe, and I won't Kill you! SSS," John says in a gravelly voice.

"No! Don't ask that! Robin would Kill me!" squeaks the bookkeeper.

"SSS, aren't you afraid of my killing you, little man? SSS," said John.

"Yes, but Robin scares me more!" stammers the bookkeeper.

John shoots the bookkeeper with his drat gun putting him asleep. Then John closes the door to the office so he can work on the safe. John swings the picture aside and then lets Bev scan it. And a few moments later, Bev directs John to the combination and says it will set off an alarm when he opens it. John bars the door to the office to give him a little more time. Then John opens the safe, and the alarm goes off. John opens his backpack and stuffs the contents of the safe into it, then closes it back up, and waits for the door to get kicked open.

John is waiting beside the door with Bev, and the door is nearly ripped off its hinges; a few men rush in, brandishing their guns, and find the bookkeeper unconscious on the floor with the safe wide open. when everyone is past the door, John and Bev slip out into Robin's office, then slip through the open door into the hallway. John makes his way out of the house into the backyard avoiding the dogs John climbs over the brick wall.

John returns to his truck, taking the ledger and other papers out of his backpack to look them over. *"Wow! This ledger will put away a lot of people in high places. Not to mention getting someone killed for revealing it,"* thought John. John returns to base to consider what he might do. John returns to his room with the information and calls Don to his apartment to discuss what bomb shell John has managed to capture.

After a lengthy discussion, Don leaves the choice up to John as to whether or not to disclose the information to the world. John, after a night of self-deliberation, decides to tell the world. But how to go about it? John takes the info to Linda and Jimmy to see what might be done.

After a debate, they decide to shoot all the newsrooms, papers, and any news outlet simultaneously, including the Military. They dump the information; in such a way it cannot be traced back to them. And at the top of the information, "Team Basilisk Ltd" was printed. At first, it was thought to be a hoax. Then many suicides and disappearances begin. Even some significant players in high places resign and leave the country. It doesn't take long; in some cases, the Military takes a hand and arrests some players as traitors.

A few days later, Robin is found dead in his house. The police ruled it a suicide even though the bullet was at the back of his head. A mass purging has happened, but the real big fish managed to escape for the time being to be hunted another day.

While all the upheaval was occurring, Nick's target, shall we say, committed an impossible suicide. The senator shot himself and still held the gun that killed him. The problem was no gunpowder on his head or hands, indicating someone else killed him from a distance.

Chapter 38

Nick hates murder even more, the Senator is dirty, and Nick is not sorry for the Senator's death. But Nick hates unsolved murders more. Nick has decided to chase down the killer and his master to bring them to justice. The only lead is the lobbyist. Nick walks into the computer center at the base to see what Jimmy or Linda can provide him on the man. It doesn't take long for the two to track down the data. Linda tracks down Nick to give him a file on the lobbyist. Nick studies the file in the Holographic room. His Wife Kim is busy looking for a home for them outside of the base.

Nick is not sure that's a good idea at least the base provides protection which a home outside wouldn't offer. However, Nick decides to go along with it. Time from the base is a good idea. Setting aside his thoughts, he delves into the file. Nick sees the address for the lobbyist is a state away. Nick decides to take a road trip to visit the lobbyist to squeeze some further information from him.

At that same time, one of the Nine visits the lobbyists. «What are we to do with the vote in Congress? Our final Senator that we needed has been killed,» complained the lobbyists.

"Don't worry about it! I'm the one who killed him," stated Crow of the Nine.

"You killed him? Why we needed his vote to sway Congress to approve the bill to allow your company to manufacture the drugs," cried the lobbyist.

"Don't worry; it will all work out in the end," said Crow.

"You are being a fool, Crow, for killing him!" said the lobbyist.

Angry Crow grabs the lobbyist, picks him up off the floor, and pulls him close so they are face to face. "I have allowed you to ridicule me, even correct me, but you have lost your usefulness to me," hisses Crow. He shoves his finger into the back of the lobbyist's head, killing him. "You will not ridicule me any longer!" as Crow pitches the dead man to the floor. Then stalks out of the room.

The next day Nick arrives at the lobbyist's house and uses Ping to open the door to let them in. Nick, with Ping, finds the dead body. Nick has ping scan the place to see how long ago he was killed. Ping does not pick up any infrared impressions except the lobbyists moving through the house and maybe having a conversation with someone who does not register, then the lobbyist is suspended in the air and tossed to the floor.

Perplexed, Nick searches the house for other clues. Ping locates a safe in a closet hidden behind the hanging clothes. Ping soon picks the lock to open the safe. Nick riffles the contents and runs into a document detailing the blackmail of several senators, including the one Nick had as a target. At the end of the document, there was no signature but a black picture of a crow. *(Nick or the team never knew of the bird names of the Nine.)*

Nick turned to the dead body to see how he was killed. Nick rolled the body over and saw a puncture wound to the back of the head. Not much help here, Ping. Nick took the paper of blackmail from the safe, and they left the house. Back at the car, Nick calls the police to inform them of the dead body. He doesn't leave his name with the police. Nick drives down the street, becomes invisible, and parks to see what happens.

The police soon arrive then all hell seems to break loose. And the house is full of people. Nick uses his battle suit, changes his clothes, and has a fake press pass; then, he goes to the scene to see if he can get more information than he already has. The police refuse to answer his questions, then they drive him off. Nick decides to leave;

he figures he can get more information from Jimmy or Linda once the reports are filed.

Before Nick leaves to return home to base, Nick opens the file and sees who the lobbyist works for. A visit to his boss may be necessary to continue this investigation. Nick returns to base late in the evening. Kim is waiting for him as he pulls into the lower garage. Nick gets out of the car, glad to see Kim, his Wife. Nick pulls her to him for a kiss and hug, and she pushes him away.

"What's wrong, Kim?"

"You know very well what's wrong!" as Kim stamps her foot.

"You want to move out of here and into a house," sighs Nick.

"Yes!" as Kim turns her back and storms off.

"OK! We'll get a house."

"Really! Good, I have a couple picked out. I'll show them to you after dinner; you must be starving," said Kim.

After dining in the cafeteria on an excellent dinner coming from Alexander's kitchen, Nick lets himself be dragged to the computer room, where Kim pulls up pictures of some homes she liked and shows them to Nick; after a short time, Nick's mind wonders back to his case, and the images became a blur before his eyes. When Kim finished, she turned to him and asked which one did he like. Confused, Nick said the first one.

Kim looks at Nick for a few minutes calculating the answer she received from Nick and realized he was off in LaLa land. Then she said, "Good, we'll go to that house in the morning and look it over."

"Fine, Dear, yes, sure, why not," mumbles Nick.

The following day Kim tells Don he›ll have to drive himself and that Nick and she are going house hunting.

"Don, why is Nick not interested in a home?" asked Kim.

"I think he is interested; he is just afraid," points out Don.

"What is he afraid of?" queries Kim.

"Maybe several things. Here you are safe when he is not around to protect you. Nick lost his parents early, so he has not learned about marriage or a family. It would be best to push this on him slowly. Let him get used to being married, then move into building a family."

"Maybe you are right. If we were to have a child, he might see a need to have a home," muses Kim.

Kim, with Nick in tow, visits the house she might like to have as a home. Ping came along and acting like a puppy in new surroundings getting into every nook and cranny to see what was there. Nick ventures in to all the rooms and then looks around outside. Nick even crawls under the house, followed by Ping to get a look at the foundation. Ping maps the whole house for later reference.

"Well, what do you think of the house? Asks Kim.

"It's very nice. The foundation is sound, with no leaks anywhere. According to Ping, the walls are solid, with no bugs or animal infestations."

"Is that all you see?!" asks Kim.

"What am I supposed to see?" asks Nick.

"Nothing!" says Kim as she storms off to the car.

"What's wrong? What did I do?" queries Nick.

Kim says nothing on the drive back to base. Leaving Nick to ponder what he was supposed to say or do. Nick decides to tell her she can buy the house. The house was sound and spacious.

"Kim, I like the house. Go ahead and purchase it," said Nick.

Kim says nothing and runs off to talk to Veronica. Leaving Nick to think about the day›s events so far. Nick decides to have a chat with John about being married. At the end of the conversation, Nick is even more confused. However, he did walk away with the notion that no man will ever fathom the depth of a woman›s mind or emotions. Nick returns to his room and finds Kim there.

Not knowing what frame of mind, she will be in, he tells her, "Kim, you can buy the house if you want; we can go back and see what you want me to see with you."

Kim looks at Nick, throws her arms around his neck, and kisses him. Nick is even now more confused. Kim agrees to return to the house and point out what she has in mind. The next day they return to the house; Nick pays close attention to all Kim says and asks a few questions to participate in the conversation. While looking around, Nick notes a room for an office, and in the garage, he can put in a false wall to hide his battle gear. It's big enough to hide his car. The nice thing is Kim can maintain the vehicle. It will be necessary to buy her a set of tools.

"Now, are you sure you want me to buy the house?" asks Kim.

"Yes, when we have a boy, I can put up a rope swing for him to play on in the backyard."

"Who said we'll have a boy; it's just possible it will be a girl!" said Kim.

"Whatever we have, a rope swing will be enjoyed by either one," laughs Nick.

Nick has many conversations with Kim and decides to give her free rein to put furniture in the house. Nick needed to return to find the murderer he was trying to track down. Jimmy gives Nick the information about who was using the lobbyist to blackmail the Senator. Nick decides to visit the CEO of a local drug pharmaceutical company. Jimmy and Linda discover something about the paper Nick took from the lobbyist.

"Linda, look at the pictogram at the bottom of the page of this document."

"What about it?" said Linda.

"I have seen it or something like it before," states Jimmy.

"So, what? It's just a pictograph," says Linda.

"Yea, but one we have seen, like this one. When we looked into the Nine, we found several documents that used bird pictographs as signatures. What if these were the names the Nine was using to Identify themselves to the companies they were dealing with," remarked Jimmy.

"If that's so, then looking at the dates on the other documents, we may see what other pictographs have been used. Then we can see how many of the Nine have turned up," stated Linda.

"We had better contact Don and let him know immediately!" said Jimmy.

"You found it; you tell him!" said Linda.

Jimmy calls Don and tells him what he found and that it leads to the Nine. Don was concerned and came to the computer center to confirm Jimmy›s and Linda›s information. Jimmy shows Don some of the old documents they found on the Nine, and he shows Don the pictographs and the nine-pointed star at the top of the pages. Then Jimmy shows the record Nick just brought in, and then Jimmy compares it to an old document with the same pictograph from over a hundred years ago. The pictograph matched precisely. Don rushes to the communication console to message Nick about the Nine being here.

At the moment that Don sent the message, Nick was in the office of the CEO of the pharmaceutical company watching him be killed in a way that shocked him. The person had picked up a two-hundred-pound man with one hand then Nick watched that same man drive his finger into the back of the CEO›s head, killing him. Then the man turned to face Nick.

"You're the one who killed my colleges!" states Crow.

Nick turns visible, "I take it you are of the Nine?"

"Why yes, then you have heard of us?" smirked Crow.

"Then you know I can kill you as I did them," answered Nick.

"You think so? Maybe not as easy as you think. I'm going to enjoy killing you, my adversary." Crow moves with incredible speed to pin Nick to the wall.

At first, Nick can't move, then Nick uses his force fields in his battle suit to push the robot away. Nick essentially becomes like the greased pig, and the robot cannot hold on to him, so Nick slips away from the robot. At that moment, Ping unleashes his sonic blast and then falls to the floor, having expended all his power. But nothing happens to the robot.

"You just tried the sonic pulse on me. How foolish, we discovered that problem after the warehouse fight. We used our technicians to discover what you used against us then we countered it. Now I will kill you, and in time the rest of your team and your loved ones," smirked Crow.

"I took out seven of you. What makes you think I won't kill you first!" said Nick.

"Now, now! Let's not be rude. Before I kill you, let me introduce myself; I'm called Crow of the Nine. May I have your name?"

"Nick of Team Basilisk."

Nick remembers that the robots cannot shift direction as quickly as he can. Crow suddenly moves towards Nick, and Nick doges away from Ping toward the only door. Crow anticipated the move and dodged toward the door to catch Nick. At the last instant, Nick changes direction to side step Crow and dashes to Ping to pick him up, then turns toward Crow only to watch him crash into the wall opening a way out.

Nick takes advantage of the few precious moments to leave the room. A crash behind him tells him that Crow has followed him onto the stairs that lead to the roof. The impact behind him tells him that Crow is right on his tail. Nick again makes a sudden side step allowing Crow to overshoot him, giving Nick time to take the stairs to the roof. Nick pushes through the door onto the roof, runs to the closest edge, and pears over the edge to get his bearings. Then Nick realizes that his car is below him.

Nick jumps up on the very edge of the roof parapet, and Crow stalks toward him.

"I'm going to miss you, Nick; this cat-and-mouse game has amused me, and now you have nowhere to go except down. Or I can kill you outright. When Crow reaches out to grab Nick.Nick jumps out into space and falls five stories to the ground. Nick brings up his force field to full, hoping it will absorb the impact; as Nick comes within a few feet of the hard pavement, Ping adds his force field to Nicks's at the last moment.

Nick hits the ground very hard and rolls to help dispel the force of impact, losing Ping out of his arms. Crow watches from the rooftop and sees Nick recover. In that instant, Crow dashes back to the door and stairway to race down to the parking lot. Nick grabs up Ping and scrambles to his car and jumps in, and instructs the car to drive to the base. Nick plugs Ping into the console, where Ping can charge up. Nick is satisfied that Ping is taken care of. Nick assesses his condition; other than some to be bruises, he is still sound.

Chapter 39

Nick glimpses Crow in the parking lot as he pulls away and heads down the road. At the second crossroad, Nick pulls off and parks to wait to see if Crow is following. Sure, enough, Crow speeds by, not seeing Nick's car since it was visible and in a different configuration like a beat-up truck. Nick calls back to the base to inform them of the involvement of the Nine. Don tells Nick that they just discovered that fact. Nick also informs Don that the sonics no longer work on the Nine robots; we'll have to come up with something else to combat them.

"I'll give you a complete report when I return to base; right now, I'm hiding from the one called Crow. He just about killed me a few minutes ago, and he's in a car searching for me. Don, he can see us even when invisible. See you all soon!" said Nick.

Nick projected a semi-tractor around his car and drove off down the road, headed back to the base. As he drove down the road, Nick passed up Crow, who had parked beside the road a few miles from where he drove past Nick, and he looked like he was pitching a fit at losing Nick. Nick smiled as he passed Crow and moved down the road undetected. Several hours later, Nick returned to base and was greeted by Kim, glad to see Nick Kim hugs him, only to hear Nick grow from the pain. Nick with Kim in tow reports to Don. Kim decides to return home and wait for Nick.

Nick reports what happened and how he was present when Crow killed the CEO and then tried to kill him. And how Ping tried to stop Crow with a sonic blast, using almost all his power. Nick was able to escape by jumping off a five-story building. Nick also noted to Don that this robot or cyborg was chattier than the other cyborgs he had dealt with.

"Don, they figured out a way to stop the sonics, so what can we fight with?" asked Nick.

"The only thing I can think of is a laser. It would take a huge power supply to use it; the only thing we have are the AI units; they only have one shot, which may not be enough and could cause them to shut down indefinitely," states Don.

"The next thing is, we have to find Crow and one other, then we can bring the fight to them before they find us," says Nick.

"How do we go about finding them?" asked Linda.

"We can start by using the cameras from the pharmaceutical company where Crow killed the CEO and get his face, then using the street cams to see if we can track him down," said Nick.

"I'll get right on it!" chimed in Jimmy.

"Nick, we'll let you know when we find something," exclaimed Linda.

Nick left the computer room to check on Ping to see how he is doing in his charging station. When Nick entered the charging station, Ping, pinged to let him know he would be fine.At home, Kim is waiting for Nick, she has some news for him, and she is on pins and needles trying to decide how to tell him he will soon be a father. Nick arrives home and enters through the door. Nick is glad to see Kim, and sweeps her into his arms, then plants a large kiss on her lips. Kim realizes this is not the time to reveal her condition to him.

Nick holds on to Kim as if he might lose her. Nick fears for her life tremendously until this war with the Nine is concluded.

"Kim, you must return to the base until the Nine have been taken care of. To stay here is a great danger to you," stated Nick.

From his voice, Kim realizes he means what he says. "I'll do as you ask," said Kim. At that moment, Kim realizes again this is not the time to tell Nick about the baby. Kim decides not to speak to him about Her condition. It might cause him to hesitate at the wrong moment. Besides, it would be nice to see everyone at the base. Kim misses seeing Veronica, Linda, and all the others.

After seeing Kim, Nick retires to his privet room to concentrate on thinking about the Nine. Kim won't disturb Nick unless it's life or death. When Nick retreats to this room, he'll come out when he is ready. The following day Nick leaves his room and prepares Kim to return to the base. Once there, Kim makes the rounds to see her friends and return to their old apartment.

Nick meets with Jimmy and Linda to see what they may have turned up. It appears that Crow and another have appeared at several businesses, all related to electronic components. They also turned up at a weapons factory. Then they left you a message, Nick. They want to meet away from the city to settle the score where no one else will be hurt. Or so the sign they showed at one of the cameras said.

When Don had Raven's body, he discovered what stresses the robot's body could withstand. Don calculated that a fifty-caliber weapon could shatter the body of the robot. John could use a chain gun to that effect. With the AI units Ping, Bev, and Girl equipped with lasers, they may stand a chance in this war. What the team does not realize is that the last two of the Nine have built a small platoon of robots that can shoot, called warbots. These are all based on the Japanese models.

Nick pulls up a map and studies it to find a battleground to his liking and away from people who may be hurt or killed during the battle. Nick finds a couple of suitable areas, and using a satellite, Nick determines which one will work and notes the coordinates. Nick makes up his own sign, giving the information the Nine wants, along with a date and time. Nick had taken a page out of the Nine's book and used a street camera to send a message to them.

Crow and Swallow make their plans for the up-and-coming battle. They loaded their robots into a semi-trailer and locate at the site Nick showed them on the street cam. In the back of the trailer, Crow and Swallow place five each dog robots mounted with thirty-caliber weapons and five humanoid robots with small-caliber weapons. If the field test works out against Nick and his team, the remnant of the Nine will use them to take over the world for them to rule.

That night Crow and Swallow head out to the location and stage the robots to ambush Nick and his team. The following day the Basilisk team shows up at the location that Nick had picked out. John sent a drone up to scout the area in case the Nine were going to ambush them, and the team wanted to avoid being caught unawares. While invisible, John dropped Veronica off further out from the meeting place so she could set up her sniper rifles (fifty calibers with armor-piercing bullets). Veronica carried her two riffles with her as she hiked up to higher ground.

John returned to the meadow where they were to meet the Nine for the final confrontation. Nick and John left the truck, pulled their guns out, and checked them. John with his chain gun. Nick with a grenade launcher and machine gun. When they reach the meadow's edge, John and Nick become visible. Crow and Swallow step out into the clearing and show themselves.

"Oh, you showed up to our war," chided Crow.

"Yes, we did, so who is your friend?" queried Nick.

"Yes, I'm being remiss in my manners. My compatriot is named Swallow," bowed Crow.

"My friend here is called John, my name, you know," said Nick.

"What is the name of the third party of your team?" asked Swallow.

"There is only the two of us," stated John.

"I see that man has not improved all these centuries; they still lie. I see your friend up on the hill. She will still be killed after we deal with you," stated Crow.

CHAPTER 40

Crow turns toward Swallow, "Shall we get started?"

"Yes, this is getting tedious," exclaims Swallow.

Crow faces Both men and commands the dog robots to attack. From around John and Nick, the robot dogs arise and start firing at the two men. The thirty caliber bullets do not penetrate the battle suits, but each bullet leaves bruises John and Nick fall to the ground under the pounding assault. Veronica, with her fifty-caliber sniper rifle, brings down three of the dog robots, and then John fires his chain gun, bringing down the next one, and Nick brings down the last dog robot with the grenade launcher.

"Excellent gentlemen, you survived our first assault, but how will you handle the next one?" asked Crow.

Nick nor John said anything; they just readied their weapons for the next assault. It came very fast around them; the humanoid robots rose and as they approach the two men firing small caliber bullets more to distract than cause harm. Veronica managed to remove two robots from the hill and was about to remove a third when Nick and John were impeding her shot. John finished up using his ammo on a robot. Leaving Nick to finish off one of the last two robots. The robot that was left managed to bring down Nick, then it fell upon John and beat him down. This gave Veronica the opening needed to bring down the last humanoid robot.

During the battle with the distractions, Crow and Swallow move into the conflict to finish off the two men. Nick looked up and saw both cyborgs Crow and Swallow close in on them. Nick called for Ping and the other AI units. Ping, Bev, and Girl were invisible, and they flew to the men just as Crow grabbed Nick by the throat, and Swallow did the same with John, and they held them up to prevent Veronica from shooting them. Ping dropped down and targeted Crow, and fired his laser, destroying Crow's brain, and he died, dropping Nick; Bev did the same thing to Swallow with the same effect. Leaving both men incapacitated, lying on the ground.

Veronica checked the men over and need to get them back to base. Veronica managed to get the men into the back of John's truck with Girl's help using her force fields to pick up the men. Ping and Bev had to be plugged back into the charging console before their batteries died. Veronica returned to the base to get John and Nick some support for their injuries. At the base, Veronica was met by several people. One of them was Kim, concerned that Nick was injured. Kim hovered over Nick like a concerned wife holding his hand and hugging him at every chance she got. The following day Nick and John came around but could barely move or talk.

They had been shot so many times that they looked bruised from head to toe. It would be several days until either one could get up and walk around. It would take several weeks for them to heal. Worst of all, Nick would need a blood transfusions because his titanium rib cage could not replace his red blood cells as fast as a regular rib cage. By this time, everyone knew Kim was pregnant except Nick. Kim came into the dispensary to see Nick, and he asked.

"Kim, are you putting on some weight?"

Kim smiled, "Yes, you silly man, we're have a baby!"

"What did you just say?" said Nick.

"We're having a baby!"

"When? How? A baby?" exclaimed Nick.

"I was going to tell you sooner, but I decided to wait until after your last mission. I didn't want to confound your mind at that time. I tried to tell you while you were in the hospital, but you were so drugged up you wouldn't have understood, so I waited until today," commented Kim.

"When will it get here?" asks Nick.

"It is not an it, it's going to be a girl, and she should arrive in five more months, and we are both healthy and strong according to the doctor," states Kim.

"I would get up and hug you, but all these IVs in me, I don't dare. I'm going to be a father!" smiles Nick.

Kim kisses Nick and tells him she has to leave because the doctor doesn't want her to be here long. Kim tells him to hurry and get well. We have a lot of work to do at home.

Nick lies in his bed, dreamy-eyed, "I'm going to be a father."

John is already up and around and plans to fly back to Oxnard, California, to see his daughter. She is about to graduate from high school, and he wants to be there to see it. Beverly is valedictorian and has the highest grades of any of her peers. She has applied for a scholarship to a couple of Ivy League colleges back east, only to find out she needs more money. John decides to take care of it. The next day, John dresses up like a lawyer, goes to his sister's house with his disguise on, and tells Beverly she has received a special grant to go to one of the schools she wants. Beverly must work for Donald Travis Industries for at least four years when she graduates. Will she agree to these terms?

Beverly is excited but asks for a few days to think about it. John gives her all the information about Don's labs. John gives Beverly a phone number of where he is staying and tells her he will be leaving on this date and will need to know her decision by then. At the end of that time, Beverly agrees to the conditions. John returns to give Beverly her first check with a caveat that she must maintain her high grades, or that'll be the last check. Beverly agrees. John returns to base and is excited that he'll be seeing his little Girl a lot more and that she'll be going to one of the colleges on the east coast.

Back at base, Nick recovers and returns to his house, where Kim and the girls from the base are working hard to paint and set up a nursery for the new Girl to enter Nick's life.

This is not the end of the new team of heroes called "Team Basilisk LTD."

Other books written by the Author:

Paladin the Modern Knight

Bill Webber and the Sky Pirates

Phoenix the King of the Chimerians

Phoenix Reborn